shadows WITHIN US

Book 4 Shadows of Synd Series

by E. Abraham

ISBN-13: 979-8-9857684-8-0

Dedication

To all the readers who love and hate when the end comes–this one's for you.

And the ones who always cry, even when things aren't even sad. (You know who you are.)

Trigger Warnings

Anxiety/Depression

Attempted Murder/Murder

Blood

Death

Criminal Activity

Violence (guns/knives)

PTSD induced panic attacks/hallucinations

Hostage/Kidnapping

Physical abuse/Torture (not by MC)

Starvation

Morbid humor (suicide-one scene)

Content Warnings:

Adult Language

Adult Sexual Scenes

Light BDSM-choking, spanking

Lack of safe word (discussions of stopping)

Prologue

I'm officially a stalker.

I didn't mean to. Honestly, I should have stopped a long time ago, but something keeps pushing me toward them. Maybe I'm not a full stalker, though. Are there half stalkers? Quasi-stalkers? I don't want to be labeled a Peeping Tom, but it might be more accurate. It's not like I've been watching them for years. It's only been a little while. I don't follow them around town. I don't send creepy gifts. I don't want to slaughter any of them in their sleep or kidnap them from their beds. I just want to feel like I'm one of them.

They're the elite of Synd—gods walking among mortals. They run the city in full view of the public eye as well as the underbelly. I guess that's what happens when your families built the city. Oh, and the fact they're criminals. It feels weird to call them that. Mafia leaders and motorcycle clubs and all the things that go with it seem bigger than being a mere criminal. Engaging in criminal activity seems more appropriate. They're still the rulers of our city—untouchable.

At least, that's what I thought.

The last year proves they aren't entirely invincible. Between human traffickers, rival MCs, actual stalkers, and dirty judges, they've been hit hard. With each catastrophe that befalls them, the more human they appear. Yet they're stronger for the bonds they formed through the trauma. I wish I knew what that felt like—to be so intertwined with someone they'd come when I called, they'd fight for me no matter the cost.

The longer this goes on, the more my heart aches, the more I know it's wrong—to pine for a life I'll never have. It's ridiculous. Yet here I am, sitting outside Mason Byrns's boundaries, tucked away in the trees and watching his silhouette in his office window.

It's late, the crisp fall wind rattling the last of the leaves on the trees creaking above me. I glance at them, wondering if one of them will fall on my head. It'd be my luck too. I'd probably be decapitated, but if I wasn't, then he'd find me passed out on his property with a head wound, wondering what the hell I was doing. Or someone would shoot me. More likely someone would put a bullet in my body, and I'd live and then…it wouldn't be good.

"I wonder what it's like to get shot," I mutter.

Shaking my head, I focus on the shadow Mason Byrns casts through the window. He keeps weird hours, like me. Ever since he came home from the hospital, he wanders the halls of his mansion. I used to watch the Kings making the rounds. None of them keep regular sleep schedules either. It's just another thing that feels familiar when it really isn't.

Watching the Kings hurt more, with their tight-knit family. Mason is different. It's not rational, but I feel a connection to Mason as he bumbles around in his house, wearing his loneliness on his face. I doubt anyone else notices. The whole thing makes me think we'd get along, though it's preposterous. We'll never meet. There's no connection. Nothing will change and we'll both live our solitary existences, wishing for something that doesn't exist for us. My heart aches at the thought.

I should go home, but it's peaceful here. Sometimes the silence at my house presses in on me, suffocating what little air is left in my lungs. I used to walk around the city, especially the outskirts of the Barrens, watching people go about their lives. I've found there's not a lot of difference between those at the top and those slumming it at the bottom. We're all just searching for our place.

I skip around a tree trunk, hiding in its shadow as a guard comes around the corner of the house. The last thing I need is to be caught lurking. I might wonder what it's like to be shot, but I don't actually want to know.

Of course, my phone buzzes at the exact moment he crests the small hill, and he whips around. I hold my breath, cursing silently. Usually, I'm better than this. I've been rundown lately, and the lack of sleep is getting to me. Yet I'm still skulking around the Byrns's estate.

The beefy guard keeps moving after a minute, hopefully chalking up the noise to an animal, and my breath leaves me in a whoosh. There's always the chance I could make a mistake, but I've been playing this game for years. I'm pretty confident in my skills.

A twig snaps to my right and I freeze, crouching as I peer into the dark. The moon sits low in the sky, so I don't have to compete with the light casting shadows between the trunks. I slowly pull the fabric from my neck up, covering my nose and mouth. I'd look even more sinister if someone caught me right now with a bandanna wrapped around my face. After five minutes, though, I'm pretty sure the noise was just an animal.

I glance back at the house, the ache in my chest shooting pain through me when the light winks out. I should stop this madness. Nothing good will ever come from it. I should resign myself to living out my life as my parents always said I would—alone. I was never enough for them, and they made it clear others would feel the same. Exhaustion settling into my bones. I promise myself I won't come back. I won't seek him out. I won't force myself into his world.

All the while knowing it's a lie.

One

Mason

The shadows deepen, casting the night into gloom. It's been raining for three weeks now, and it's starting to grate on my nerves. I pull my gaze away from the window and stare at the papers strewn across my desk. They're old, yellowed along the edges, and brittle to the touch. I swipe my palms against my suit pants before I touch them. I've been reading them for months now, but I still can't make heads or tails of the time line. A knock rings out, jolting me from my thoughts. I glance at the clock, seeing it's well past three in the morning. It's late, much later than I originally thought. I sigh before calling out for whoever it is to enter.

"Byrns, we got another problem coming in." TJ grunts, collapsing in the chair across from me.

"What is it this time?"

I don't know what the hell Victor, my uncle, was thinking when he was running things, but I've been unfucking things for almost a year now. I don't know whether to be grateful he took over instead of Colin or pissed Victor couldn't keep his shit together.

"Shipment is fucked. Half the guns are missing barrels. Don't know what's up with Rima, but better figure it out. Our contacts are getting antsy."

I study the older man. He's been running part of our territory further north for most of my life. He's in his fifties now, still trim, but gray peppers his beard. He's survived our world longer than most, through the attempted coup ten years ago all the way up to holding shit together when the Guild came through over a year ago, trying to take over Synd. Shit would have gone a lot smoother if TJ would have taken over. Instead, I have to deal with Victor's fuckups.

"Things are a little volatile over there right now."

It's the only thing I'm willing to say about it. I've heard rumors of the Guild stretching into a city four hours away, but without concrete evidence, I'm keeping my mouth shut. The last thing I need is someone else coming in and demanding I go gallivanting off to Rima to help them take down an organization I've never dealt with. I was in a coma when they tried to come in and take our people. I barely made it out alive. Shaking my head, I rid myself of the memories of the aftermath.

"Also, King is here," TJ says, pushing to his feet before making his way to the door. "I'll send him in."

The last thing I want to do is have a sit-down with Ren King at three in the morning, but he won't take no for an answer. He keeps wanting updates on what's going on with the sensors, the shipments, the regime changes. I don't have anything for him, mostly because of the paperwork on Synd's history still strewn across my desk in haphazard piles. I gather them up as quickly as I can without damaging them. I'm planted by the window by the time the knock sounds at the door, echoing in my empty chest.

I don't bother to turn around as I call, "Come in."

"Mason fucking Byrns. Glad to see you're not laid up in bed this time." Alex King's laughing voice booms across the space and I wince. I was prepared to deal with Ren's stoic attitude, but Alex's boisterousness this late is too much.

"Alex. It's late. What do you want?" I grumble, turning to him. My tone doesn't faze him. He's still grinning like a loon, tilting his head when he settles in the chair TJ vacated minutes before.

"Don't be like that, Byrnsie. Had a little thing on the east side and thought I'd drop by. See how you're doing." He crosses an ankle over his knee as if he's in a three-piece suit rather than jeans and a hoodie.

"I'm fine. Not all of us have time to gallivant around the city at all hours of the night like you. And don't fucking call me Byrnsie." I glare, but that doesn't do anything either.

"Did you know you're more likely to get a computer virus from visiting religious sites than porn sites?"

"Good thing I don't go on religious sites then, huh?"

I smirk, but it falls from my face when I catch a dark shadow moving through the trees across the lawn. I squint, trying to figure out if it's someone sneaking around or just the leaves blowing in the wind. Rain lashes against the window obscuring my view. Alex chuckles behind me and I swing around, dismissing the vision as a trick of the eye before sinking into my chair.

"How is it that there's a hurricane out there and yet you're dry as a bone?"

"Suspicious much? I dropped off your car—pulled it straight into the garage. I'll need a ride home, though."

"I'm not dropping you off like you were at a sleepover. Find your own way home," I grunt.

"Rude. Scared you'll run into Sam?"

I scowl, wondering if I can get away with punching him. Someone will be on my doorstep cussing me out then, so it's probably not worth it. I really don't want to have another altercation with Shane. Sam would shoot me a disappointed look. I don't have it in me to deal with her judgment.

My little sister, who isn't so little anymore, keeps sending me texts, trying to get me to go to lunch. I'm not ready to hang out as if nothing has changed, and she's determined to pretend that we're back to normal. Nothing is normal anymore.

Logically, I knew she wouldn't live in this house forever, but I didn't foresee her moving in with three men who are portrayed as our rivals by the media. Whenever it crosses my mind, I conveniently forget that I'm the one who sent her shit over there mere weeks after the Guild left town. It's where she belongs, but it was still hard.

Every meeting I attend with them, I'm reminded of how alone I am in my house. I don't care Sam is with them. They take care of her, and even if they don't say it, they love her. In fact, I couldn't ask for more for my sister. Doesn't make it any easier to deal with the loneliness seeping into my veins a little more every day.

"I'm not fucking scared of Sam. Why don't you stay out of it, and I won't mention the fact that you're fucking my sister?"

"Jealous? Would you rather *I* fuck you?" He waggles his eyebrows and I scowl again. "Might help if you went out and found a lady."

"And when the hell would I have time to do that? Was that all you needed?"

He sobers and I sit back. "You know we can help you, right?"

I stare at the enforcer, expecting him to back down, but he's in the same business as me. Shane may be the head of the King family, but Alex and Ren are his brothers. Their word holds just as much weight as Shane's.

Alex merely waits for me to confess my deepest, darkest secrets. No wonder Victor couldn't get him to break. Although, according to Alex, my uncle didn't try very hard. There was a lot of shit Victor didn't try very hard at while he was in charge. Yet here I am, still cleaning up his messes.

"I'm fine. Why don't you worry about your side of the river, and I'll take care of mine?"

He rolls his eyes. "Heard you and Helms have been meeting. Anything we need to know about?"

"No. Just the shit going on up north." I don't know why I'm keeping shit from him. He wouldn't care that I'm looking into our family's history, but Alex is asking questions I don't have answers for yet.

"Well, if something comes up…" He pushes to his feet. "Oh, Ren wanted to know if you fixed the flashy thing."

I raise an eyebrow. "Flashy thing? What the fuck are you talking about?"

"The thing"—he claps, a grin spreading on his face—"sensor. The sensors you had tripping."

"No, but it's been happening for months now. Plus, it's more the cameras than anything. I'm not concerned about it. Tell him to stop worrying about it."

He snorts. "You know that won't happen."

The door snaps shut behind him and I'm left alone again. He'll go home, hang out with his family, and live happily ever after. My stomach turns at the thought. I didn't realize how much I relied on Colin when he was around. Between my second and Sammy, I thought I was fine. Now she's off living with the Kings and Colin is six feet under.

I didn't float him, sending him down the river, though I probably should have. I still don't know how shit went sideways with him. We grew up together, brothers like the Kings are. At some point, he started thinking we didn't have enough, and then he brought the Guild in, foolishly believing he could control them. I could have dealt with them had I not been shot. I could have fixed shit. When he tried to kill Sammy, though…

I couldn't let that stand. A gunshot cracks through the air, but I know it's all in my head. I've gotten good at deciphering reality from flashbacks, but sometimes it catches me off guard. I lean against the window, trying to find the shadow I saw earlier.

There's nothing but the rain tracking paths across the glass. A crash echoes outside the door and I whip around.

Flinging the door open, I scan the hallway, but it's dark and quiet. Another thump from downstairs has me racing forward. No one else should be awake other than the guards. In fact, most of them are probably hiding under the awning wrapped around the house. Not many will venture out in this tempest, much less try to break into a mafia leader's house.

Victor steps out of the front room, the door clicking shut behind him. He locks it, slipping the key in his pocket. He's still dressed in a suit, though it's rumpled and loose, much like his sallow skin that's practically falling off his bones. I've never liked him, but I never had cause to get rid of him. Sam has been on me for years to just float him. She doesn't understand why I keep him around.

I never confessed to her how afraid I was after the attempted coup ten years ago. I hate to admit how much Victor helped me in those early years. I was too young, too naïve, too full of myself, to run shit on my own. He kept the older guys in line long enough for me to get my feet on solid ground. The older I get, the less useful he feels. He still hasn't told me his reasons for stepping in instead of Colin, my second. Not that I'm upset about it. If Colin had pushed, I'd probably be dead, along with Sam. The Guild would have taken over the city, selling our people and leaving destruction in their wake.

"Victor. You're up late," I say, stepping from the shadows.

He starts, whipping his head back and forth before his eyes settle on me. They're dull, muted, and watery—the blue washed out, with little spark behind them. His mouth flaps open as he scrambles for an answer, and I make a note to check the room he seems to be guarding. I didn't care when he took over the space, since there's so many empty ones in this place. Knowing my luck lately, he'll have constructed a murder wall. With the way Victor has been acting lately, I wouldn't be surprised.

"When you get to my age, Mason, sleep becomes a thing of the past." He laughs lightly, but it's shaky. I narrow my eyes, but it's too late to start shit.

"What do you do when you can't sleep?" I should just walk away and get back to the problems scattered around my office. Or I could go to bed, though I'd end up staring at the ceiling for the next few hours.

"Oh, just a little light reading. Any updates on Samantha?"

I turn on my heel and march back up the stairs. Every conversation we have lately eventually devolves into him bringing up my sister. For years we kept from him and everyone else what she does under the cover of darkness. People who deal with the underworld of Synd have heard of the Wraith. No one knows my younger sister—the darling of the upper crust and the deadly assassin—are one and the same. Ever since the Guild came and I was shot, all the rules were thrown out the window, and more people have discovered both sides of her. Victor's been trying to suss out her secrets lately, and he can't have a conversation without trying to force them from me. I refuse to put her in that kind of danger.

The work from my office beckons, but I swing to the right, heading for my bedroom instead. Once inside, I stop and flip on the light since there's no moon to guide me. I could find my way in the dark, but the shadows put me on edge these days. I suspect it's because I spent so long within their depths when I was in a coma.

My feet carry me forward and I check behind doors and inside the closet and sweep the bathroom. I'm not stupid enough to believe I don't have enemies. The figure I saw skulking through the trees might have been a figment of my imagination, but I won't take any chances. I don't have anyone to take over now unless Sam suddenly develops the urge to run a criminal empire. More likely, the Kings would swoop in and deal with things. That thought no longer frightens me as it once did.

After checking the windows, I strip my suit from my body, sloughing off the final vestiges of responsibility, and settle into bed. Ten minutes later, I'm still wide awake, staring at the ceiling. I sigh as I grab the tablet from my nightstand and start the tedious process of checking every camera lining the property.

A groan escapes me when I see another sensor has been tripped and the camera was off for almost fifteen minutes. Whatever glitch we have is an old annoyance by now. Ren is convinced it's someone doing it manually to fuck with us, since it happened to them, and now they've moved on to me. I may not agree, but I'm not about to stop him if he wants to keep digging into it, no matter what I told Alex. Apathy washes over me as I set the tablet down again.

I should go back to the office, but instead I pull my cock out, closing my eyes as I grip myself. The image of a woman swims inside my mind, vaguely familiar but just out of reach. I don't hesitate, stroking hard and fast. I know how this daydream ends, with her slipping from my grasp long before I'm ready to give her up. When my cum coats my hand, the snapshot of her floats away, the last wisps of whoever she was fading into darkness.

And still sleep doesn't come.

Two

T he coffee shop is packed with bougie women chattering away over their fancy coffees. I could go home and escape the hustle and bustle of the early morning rush. Instead, I'm tucked away in the corner, pretending to work. The site on my laptop is a news site. It's one that rarely reports the news and instead stalks the elite across the city. They're not very good at their jobs, since none of them report on the illicit activities those same people engage in. It took me all of five minutes to find the skeletons in everyone's closets.

Between Ryker Helms running a motorcycle club in the north of the city and the west side of the river being controlled by the Kings, there's not much for the rest to haggle over. Throw in Mason Byrns managing the east side of Synd, and the entire place is locked down. I wasn't particularly surprised when I discovered the Kings and the Byrns were a part of the mafia. There were too many red flags pointing to organized crime.

I have little room to talk since I'm no better than they are, skirting the wrong side of the law. In fact, their systematized approach to running things around here has worked for decades.

It isn't much of a stretch to assume their ancestors founded the city. Even if they didn't, they've being ruling Synd long enough no one knows anything different.

When I had nowhere else to turn, I found my calling, as if it dropped from the sky and into my lap. I barely stop myself from thinking the worst, that if I hadn't found this, I would be dead. It saved me in the same way Synd did. Before I came here, I was floundering.

Shutting my laptop with a sigh, I scan the area as I sip my coffee. I'm a hypocrite, calling these women bougie, since my own cup contains more syrups and sugar than a sane person should be able to handle, but I don't like the taste of coffee. I'm content masking the flavor like I do everything else in my life. At some point, I should go home and sleep, but I lean forward on my elbows and wait.

The bell above the door jingles over the dozens of conversations and in steps the belle of Synd, Samantha Byrns. I smirk behind my cup, recognizing the mask she wears in front of these people. A socialite by day, Miss Byrns has made quite a reputation for herself, especially lately. The article I was just reading speculated she's being blackmailed, which is why she's sequestered in the Kings' mansion. Being in my line of work gives me an inside look the others don't have. How anyone else hasn't spotted the love in her eyes whenever she's with Shane, Alex, or Ren King is beyond me. It's clear to me, but then again, I'm trained to see the subtlety.

She's alone today, phone pressed to her ear as people clear a path for her. She barely notices, settling at the back of the line instead of skipping to the front as they've planned. They mingle back together, shooting Sam furtive glances as they do.

I peek out the front windows lining the place, but none of her guys seem to be here. I'm surprised they didn't insist on coming. Most of the time, one of them is attached to her hip, doting on her until she shoots them a look and they back off. Jealousy turns in my gut, but I clamp down on it.

I think Sam and I would get along if we ever met in person. The thirty feet separating us right now might as well be thousands of miles, though. Saying we don't run in the same circles doesn't quite fit, since I don't technically have a circle, and no one knows who I am.

Hot coffee spills down my leg as a woman runs into me and I shoot up, biting back a curse. Snatching the napkins from the table, I blot at the stain on my thigh even as the skin underneath my jeans burns.

"Ow, ow, ow," I mutter, bouncing on my toes, and then I see the puddle swirling toward my laptop. I drop the napkins and grab my computer, hugging it close to my chest as my black hair forms a curtain in front of my eyes. Pushing it out of the way, I finally look up at the culprit who almost cost me three grand. A thin, haughty face greets me, the empty cup dangling from her fingers.

She smirks. "Oops."

I gape, not sure how to respond. I sift through the files in my mind, trying to identify her, but I'm coming up blank. I'm pretty sure I've never met this person before in my life.

"Excuse me?"

"I'm sure if you stopped taking up a whole table by yourself, this wouldn't have happened." Her arrogant voice rolls over me, causing rage to simmer in my gut.

I don't have a response. I rarely talk to anyone, and my confrontational skills have fled in the wake of her audacity. Huffing, I tuck the computer under my arm and scoop up the napkins again. There's no way to get my pants dry, and my face is flaming. I could blast her, but I duck my head to concentrate on cleaning up the mess. I'd rather not draw attention to myself. I especially don't want Samantha Byrns to come wandering over to see what the fuss is all about. Flying under their radar is easy when I never engage, no matter how much I want to.

"Maybe if you weren't such a bitch it wouldn't have either," a gruff voice behind me growls, and I freeze.

My body refuses to move, even when he brushes my arm, sending a shiver through my limbs. My chin is still tucked to my chest, and I watch as his feet settle next to mine. My brain, usually my most useful asset, is muddled. I can't even begin to decipher what's going on inside of me.

"What?" the woman shrieks, but when she sees who told her off, her face turns sultry. Or at least her version of it. "Oh, Mr. Byrns."

She leans forward, resting her hand on his arm. He glances down as her fingers curl into the dark fabric of his suit, then he steps out of my view. Patting at my jeans, I realize it's a lost cause. They're fully soaked now. I'm not helping the situation, but the last thing I'm going to do is face Mason fucking Byrns.

"Go," he growls, sending another shudder through me.

"Well, I…Okay," she stutters, flushing as she stumbles away.

"Are you okay?" His feet come back into view, stepping in front of me.

"I'm fine," I whisper, not meeting his eyes. My entire body vibrates, refusing to settle into its usual calm state. This is not how I wanted to meet him. In fact, I never thought I'd come face-to-face with him. I thought the closest I'd ever get was watching from afar, wondering what it would be like to be a part of their family.

"You're clearly not. You're crying."

Rolling my eyes, I wonder if I can get away without him seeing my face. I've been hiding behind my hair, so I might salvage this. The fact he thinks I was crying is ludicrous. As if I would allow a salty woman more concerned about an empty table than the person sitting at it to affect me so much it caused tears. I'm not about to admit how embarrassed I am that it was *him* who rescued me.

His hand brushes my arm, sending goosebumps scattering across my skin even under the jacket I'm wearing. This man is bad for my health if he can elicit such a reaction just through a simple touch.

Peeking at the masses through my hair, I find several women staring at us. No, not us—him. Of course they're fixated on Mason. They flock to him, salivating over him like he's a piece of meat. Even if we've never met, I still feel like I know him more than they do. I shiver, a bolt of heat shooting through my body. I'm pathetic—no better than those ogling him from afar.

"I wasn't crying. I'm pissed but thank you for your concern. If you'll excuse me," I wheeze, ducking past him when he lifts his hand.

I push past the crowd that's gathered, and Sam's voice rings through the coffee shop as she greets her brother. I chance one last glance as I shove my way out the door. Again, I'm frozen when our gazes collide. He blinks, breaking the spell, and I duck into the biting autumn wind.

Swiping my hand across my face, I dash across the street, losing myself in the crowd. I hide between two buildings, eye fixed on the coffee shop. A minute passes and the door pops open, revealing Mason Byrns. His head whips back and forth as he scans the street.

Is he looking for me?

There's no way. He's probably already forgotten the weird woman with strange hair, who wouldn't look him in the eye and ran away. Hopelessness crashes into me, followed closely by relief. Wondering what it's like to be a part of a family like they have is one thing. Actually inserting myself into their world is something completely different. They especially can't know who I really am. Keeping my identity hidden is number one on my list, and probably the only reason I need to stay far away from them as possible.

He looks around one last time before shaking his head and heading inside. A gust of wind carries my sigh away, banishing my regret into the ether.

I turn toward home, bed calling my name. The work I've been putting off is piling up, though. I should do something about it, but exhaustion settles in my bones. I won't get any work done, especially after this morning. The back of my neck itches and I glance behind, but no one is paying me any attention. I walk a little faster and take the long way home, but the feeling follows me all the way to my doorstep. As soon as the alarms are set, I lean against the door and the tension flows from my muscles.

As I slip between the cool sheets of my bed, my mind replays *the incident,* as I've dubbed my run-in with him. It certainly wasn't the meet-cute I thought it would be every time I've fantasized about in my mind. I rub my eyes, and my throat tightens as numbness steals through my body. I can only hope he didn't recognize me.

Ironically, this isn't the first time I've run into one of the crime leaders. This is certainly the most nerve-racking. I doubt it will be the last one I have, especially if I can't get my obsession under control. None of them have realized how many times we've crossed paths, probably dismissing me as soon as they're gone. This incident shouldn't be any different.

"It's fine. It's done. Now move the fuck on," I whisper into the darkened room.

Even saying it out loud doesn't work. I still swear to myself I'll stay away from the mafia elite of Synd—especially Mason Byrns.

Three

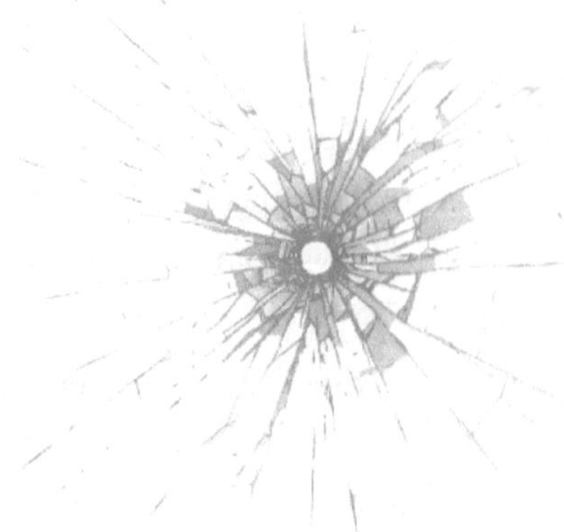

"Are you going to ignore me the entire time?" Sam's voice pulls me from my thoughts.

"I wasn't ignoring you, Sam. Are you expecting me to carry the entire conversation?"

I wrap my hands around the coffee she bought. We should have gotten them to go, walked around or something, but she insisted on taking a seat. We took the table the woman vacated, so at least it's tucked away in the back.

"Carrying the conversation would require you to actually say something," my sister grumbles.

Rolling my eyes, I swipe my hand across the wood. My fingers stick to the surface, and I grit my teeth. I wish I could have done more for the woman I saved. Hell, I wish I could have caught her before she dashed out the door.

I'm not used to women running away from me. Even the bitch who dumped coffee on her tried to slip me her number. I had to pry her off my arm three times before I called in a Byrns man to take her away after my mystery woman took off.

By the time I dealt with the situation, my damsel in distress had disappeared into the masses. Regret hits me in the chest, making it hard to breathe. It makes no sense, but it feels like I lost something I never had in the first place—as if fate dropped her right in my lap, then shoved her off without even thinking.

"Seriously? Mason, I've asked you the same question four times now. You're still thinking about that woman, aren't you?"

"What woman?"

She rolls her eyes, pulling her phone from her leather jacket. I sweep my gaze over the crowd, catching more than a couple people staring. There's always someone watching, which is exactly why I didn't want to meet in public.

"Why couldn't we meet at the house?" I ask, turning away from one woman's prying eyes.

"Because every time I show up there, you suddenly have some place to go or some meeting to be at. You're avoiding me and I'd like to know why." She folds her arms and glares.

"I'm not avoiding you," I mutter.

Narrowing her eyes, she leans in. "Cut the bullshit, Mason. It's been a year. I get you haven't had as much time to adjust to this, but I'm gonna need you to pull your head out of your ass."

"Did you ever think it has nothing to do with you, Samantha? Did it cross your mind for one fucking second that I'm not focused on how my life affects you because you have the Kings to take care of you now? No. You just want to bitch at me. You want to blame someone for your guilt at how everything went down with the Guild. Well, you're shit out of luck. I'm not going to exonerate you because it's not my fucking fault, and it's not yours either."

I push away from the table, glancing around to make sure no one overheard our spat. The last thing I need is someone spreading rumors about Sam and me fighting in public. The media will pick it up, and then the Kings and Byrns will be at war, according to them. I'll have to spend twice as long convincing everyone we're not about to level the city.

"Mason," she whispers, and I freeze.

I settle back in my chair, waiting for her to continue, but she merely stares at me, as if I'll have some grand insight to make this all better. I barely have enough for myself, let alone her. The amount of shit I'm dealing with pales in comparison to the rocky road our relationship has been since I woke up.

"I don't have anything for you, Sammy."

"I just don't want to keep doing this. I want us to be normal."

"We're not normal. We're the furthest thing from being normal. Seems fucking boring to me, though," I say, scanning the crowd before catching TJ's eye. He raises an eyebrow and I scowl.

"What the fuck is wrong now?" Sam hisses, glancing over her shoulder.

"TJ is stalking you. I think he misses you stopping by when you're gallivanting around the city. He thinks you're not friends anymore."

Rolling her eyes, she sighs. "I didn't want to step on your toes."

"Fuck that. Stop being so fucking timid. It doesn't suit you." I shove away from the table. "Tell Shane to stop being a little bitch and call me."

She snickers. "You know he wants to put a bullet in you. Thinks you're being stupid."

"Good thing the feeling is mutual. Doesn't mean we can ignore business."

Rounding her chair, I press a kiss to her head. "Next time just stop by, Sammy."

Crisp autumn air cuts through the alley, sending a shiver through me. I should make my rounds to the warehouses, but I turn toward home. TJ thinks he's being subtle as he tails me. I've seen him more in the last few months than I have in years. The excuses he comes up with for following me are becoming more outlandish by the day. Apparently, he thinks I need a bodyguard.

"You might as well walk with me, fucker," I call.

"Byrns. Fancy meeting you here," he huffs as he falls in next to me.

"Why are you following me today? Something going down in your area?" I ask.

TJ's section of the Byrns territory is the largest, sitting closer to the Reapers MC boundary line. I've been trying to get him to take over the Depot, our main warehouse, for years. Every time he complains, then flips me off, and I drop it. Shoving my hands into my overcoat, we weave our way through the streets.

"Just the shit we've been dealing with for months now. I'm handling it."

"You think about my offer?"

He grunts, and I already know the answer from that sound alone. "Byrns, I'm too fucking old to deal with that kind of shit. It was hard enough thirty years ago. You realize I'm pushing sixty, right?"

We come to a crossroad, waiting for traffic to subside, and I glance at the older man. He's been around my entire life, much like Victor. They couldn't be any more different, both in personality and looks. TJ's beard is more gray than black. Wrinkles that at some point were shadows are deep grooves now. When that happened, I have no idea.

"I didn't think you'd take it. Being a second isn't an easy job. You're one of the few people I trust, though."

Crossing the street, we duck between two apartment buildings. One is empty and the other is occupied by TJ and his group. Technically, they're a lower gang, but he's been working for the Byrns family for decades. He's more like family. He never wanted more, and I rarely press the issue.

The metal stairs rattle as we pound up them before slipping inside. One man sits in the makeshift living room, guarding the building. I nod to him before going to the back bedroom we've converted into an office.

"There a reason you're avoiding going home?" TJ asks, dropping into a chair.

"I planned on making the rounds today. Just starting with you."

"Bullshit."

"You realize I can still float your ass, right?" I ask, raising an eyebrow while the computer boots up.

He smirks. "You could fucking try. We both know you'd never shoot me."

"More than one way to kill a man, TJ. Thought you'd know that in your old age."

My emails are piling up and there's more than a few notifications on our encrypted app I've been ignoring. The missed calls on my phone are becoming unmanageable. All the while, my energy bleeds away a little more every day. Decisions need to be made and plans put in motion, but I can't find it in me to care.

Somewhere in the last year, I lost my will to lead. I can't afford to give up, though—too many people depend on me. I'd like one person to need me, not for what I can provide as a mafia leader, but as just Mason Byrns.

The image of the woman from the coffee shop flashes through my mind, but I push it away. She's long gone, mingling within the crowds of Synd. For some reason, she keeps popping up, as if she's a forgotten lyric in a song lost to time.

"What the hell is going on with you, boy?" TJ's voice invades my thoughts.

He's one of the few I'd allow to talk to me like that. He's also the only one I'd allow to turn down the position of my second. By all rights, I should deal with him the traditional way. Hell, I should have killed him a long time ago for the shit he pulls. I never will. He's one of the few constants in my ever-changing world. Life is hard enough without pushing away those I trust.

"You wanna be my therapist, TJ? Or you wanna run your area without being on my shit list?"

"You realize you don't scare me, right? I've watched you grow up. Not much I haven't seen you go through. So, why don't you get off your high horse and tell me what the fuck is happening to you?"

I push to my feet. "I'll tell you the same thing I told Sam. I'm fine. Leave it the fuck alone." I stomp out the door.

"Car's outside," he bellows and the kid on guard jumps.

Snickering, I bound down the stairs and straight into the backseat of a car. The driver is one of ours, thankfully. I won't have to make awkward conversation on the way home. My phone vibrates every ten seconds, and I turn it off after five minutes. I pass the miles scanning the houses streaming past as the noonday sun beats down. Crushing silence is waiting for me at home, but within the confines of this car, it's peaceful.

My mind wanders back to the woman in the café. Face hidden behind straight black hair streaked with muted green. She's a mystery. A puzzle I shouldn't gather the pieces to. I could find her. Gaining access to the cameras around Synd isn't that hard when we control them all. Hell, I could contact Ren's hacker and have her track the woman down. Synd is large, but not big enough to hide in usually. Not from someone like me.

"Sir? We're here," the driver says.

Pushing open the door, I almost get back in when I spot Shane King on my front steps. I scowl, resigning myself to another bullshit conversation. I've had enough of them today, and it's not even noon. The last thing I want to do is talk to my sister's boyfriend—*one* of her boyfriends—even if he does run the other half of Synd. I'm sure many are intimidated by him, with his tattoos and piercing blue eyes, towering over most other people. Good thing I'm not.

Tension rolls off him as he leans against my front door, tracking my way up the stairs, and I brace myself. My muscles bunch the closer I come, until we're eye-to-eye, staring each other down. We haven't been in the same room in weeks. I've also been avoiding his calls, but I doubt he's here for business. I'd rather avoid him lecturing me about not spending time with Sam.

"Byrns." He nods, stepping aside.

"King," I reply, sweeping inside.

Leading us to my office, we pass several guards who scatter as soon as they see us. One of them even trips over his feet in his haste, as if we'll put a bullet in his head otherwise. I'm starting to regret the decision to allow more people in my house. The day I shot Colin is seared into my brain, branding me forever. I couldn't handle losing myself, though I no longer knew who I actually was. I still don't.

Loneliness has seeped into the walls, staining the floors and covering the windows. I'm suffocating within the arms of isolation. The oppressiveness coats my tongue, choking me until I can't breathe.

"There a reason you're coming by unannounced, King?" I ask as I collapse in my chair.

He eyes me while he settles across from me. "Shit is going off the rails with shipments. None of the trucks in the last week made it through your territory. Someone needs to deal with the police chief. It's your turn to choose, though we've discussed changing the protocols on that. Not that you'd know, since you haven't been to the last several meetings. Helms is getting reports from Rima. He thinks the Guild moved in there. Wants to know what we're going to do about it."

"Why the fuck would we worry about Rima? We're not their keepers. It's hard enough to deal with our own city. I'm not gallivanting off to them because they can't keep their shit together," I say, starting my computer. If I pretend like I'm working, maybe he'll leave.

"Holy shit, she was right," he mutters.

"I don't have time for this, Shane. Is there anything urgent I need to take care of?"

"Did you not listen to a goddamn word I said? Synd is falling the fuck apart and you're holed up in this damn mansion pretending the rest of the world doesn't exist. How the hell do you think this is going to end?"

"Everything is fine. You're overreacting. Didn't realize you were such a little bitch. You worry about your side of the river, and I'll worry about mine. I'm sure you can find your way out, seeing as how our houses are identical," I sneer.

I won't get in a pissing match with him. Eventually, he'll run out of steam and wander off.

"What the fuck," he mumbles, shaking his head. "This is fucking bullshit, Mason. Either get your shit together or I'm taking over."

Rage flows through me, saturating my veins and sweeping through my body. It's been so long since I've felt anything close to this, and I don't recognize it at first. Once I acknowledge the flames licking inside me, tingles rush through my fingers and up my arms. I slowly stand, placing my fists on my desk and glaring.

"I'd like to see you fucking try, King. Keep bitching and pushing and see how far it gets you. I've taken enough shit from you over the past year. Don't think I haven't noticed you slowly eating away at my base. You can take my goddamn territory over my cold, dead body."

He doesn't move, sucking in a deep breath before he ducks his head. I expect him to blow up, maybe throw a punch, but he just sits there with his head bowed. I can't imagine what he's waiting for. I'm not about to back down, but we can't afford a territory war. The city wouldn't survive. I doubt either of us would risk it. The longer he sits there, the more I'm convinced he doesn't intend on taking my territory, no matter how deep into the hole of apathy I fall.

He pushes to his feet. "Good to see you still have some fucking life left in you. Now stop being an asshole to Sam. She's beating herself up over how you're treating her. For fuck's sake, she's talking about coming over here and staying until you pull your head out of your ass and neither of us wants that."

"Tell her no. She's not allowed in this house," I grumble.

"I'm not telling her shit. If you've got something to say to her, call her up yourself. I'm not a goddamn mediator. Pick the next police chief."

"What the hell's wrong with Grayson?"

"He thinks he can interfere in the Barrens, and we both know how that will go."

"I'll talk to him. He's got some sort of superiority shit going on. Thinks he can save the world, or at least the city," I say, collapsing in my seat again.

"Did no one tell him we're not worth saving?" Shane chuckles, taking his seat again.

"Apparently not." The tension eases from my shoulders. My mind is clearer than it has been in a long time.

"Mason, what the hell are you waiting for?"

Leaning back, I cross my arms over my chest and glance out the window. "I don't know, but I'll let you know when I find it."

The image of the woman from the coffee shop flashes across my vision, but I shake it away. Why she keeps popping up is beyond me. Even if she is what I'm looking for, she's long gone by now.

Four

Lacey

A chime infiltrates my dreams, pulling me from the depths of the nightmare I was embroiled in. Images of shadows and holes fade from my mind, no matter how I struggle to remember them. Opening my eyes, I'm met with the blurred image of my ceiling fan. I rarely sleep on my back, so the sight throws me for a loop until I roll over as my phone beeps again. Whoever is texting me better have a damn good reason for waking me up in the middle of the night.

Pressing the button on the side, the screen lights up in my hands, but there are no messages. Disorientation swirls through my head, but I chalk it up to my dream as I throw the device next to me and roll over.

I sigh as I close my eyes, but then the chime rings out again. Grumbling, I grab the device, but it's still dark. It takes me another minute before I realize I'm holding the wrong one. I swing to the other side and sure enough, my work cell is lit up like a spotlight.

Need help with the police chief. Whatever you can give me to get him to fall in line.

My heart skips a beat. Most of the mafia leaders think of me as a ghost, someone they call on and forget as soon as I turn the information over. They also probably think I have no clue who they are. They never reveal their identity, but it wasn't hard to figure out. Finding them is probably the easiest part of my job. The rest is easy too, because it's also all numbers. Code and digging and revealing secrets are my specialties. I fell into this, but I love it. I can't imagine doing anything else.

I don't bother responding to Mason. There's nothing to say until I have the information. Still, my thumb hovers over the screen, itching to say something. I sigh, falling back on the sheets as the phone tumbles from my hand.

I love the intrigue in this world, but the monotony is getting to me. The longer I spend behind a computer screen, the more I avoid people. Maybe it's not the tediousness, but the isolation of my job. There's no one left in my life I care about. I have no friends and that's no one's fault but my own. I wouldn't even know how to actually meet people. Snorting, I remember how ridiculously I acted with Mason yesterday. I'm sure I made a *great* impression on him and could totally call him up to see if he'd catch a movie with me.

The screen lights up and I grab it. My heart ticks in my chest, pounding by the time I'm done reading the message. My breath hitches as I read his words a second time. It's almost conversational.

Security cameras are shit.

Mason Byrns doesn't know I set up his security system. I sent someone else to install the actual cameras while I dealt with all the back-end things. He should assume Ren King is dealing with everything unless Ren informed him otherwise. Why is he suddenly texting me about it? I reread the message at least four times, trying to read between the lines, but it's useless.

I know you wont answer but I could really use some help.

I shouldn't respond, even now. I should turn it off and go back to sleep. Or I could get up and work, find the information he wants and send it off. Hell, I should have moved on from Synd a long time ago. I tell myself it's because the jobs are plentiful, but I'm comfortable here, which is dangerous. I came to this city seven years ago, hoping I'd be in this exact position—working with the men behind the scenes, but I never thought I'd still be in Synd. I thought I'd be here a couple years, then move on. Maybe retire or some shit. I snort again, knowing that wouldn't be any better than the monotony I'm currently stuck in.

I need to find someone. Black hair with green streaks in it. Average height. Was at Morning Brew yesterday around 8.

Shit. Fucking dammit. I could ignore him, but then I'll be in even worse shit than I was yesterday morning when I ran out on him. I wasn't supposed to leave an impression. I could tell him it's not enough to go on, but I've already shot myself in the foot there. I've found people on less for them. I fucked myself over when I allowed myself to be at their beck and call.

Inserting myself into their world more than I already have would be disastrous, no matter how much I've fantasized about being with Mason. There's something about him that keeps bringing me back and I'm drowning in the what–ifs I've created in my head.

My hand trembles as I type out a message, though I shouldn't.

Might take awhile.

I wait ten minutes for a reply, but then I throw my phone back on the nightstand. Still groggy after only four hours of sleep, I'll spend the next four staring at the ceiling waiting for the darkness to close over me again, and it'll never happen. I'm better off getting started on Mason's first request.

I pull on a pair of sweatpants and grab a hoodie. My house is small with only one bedroom, but I didn't get it for the spacious upper floor. I bought it for the basement. I took the money I earned from odd jobs, buried it in shell corporations, then bought this place.

Flicking on the light over the wooden stairs, I shuffle down them, avoiding the creaks. I keep the rest of the lights off, letting the glow of the computer screens illuminate the space. It's cooler down here, soundproof, and lined with electronics. I try to keep it organized, but I should go through it all. I'm sure there are things in here that are outdated.

The only thing I accomplish over the next hour is straining my eyes. The police chief's files are pushed off on another screen, forgotten in my quest to wipe all evidence of my existence within Synd. The cameras inside the coffee shop were easy. Searching the random ones lining the streets? Not so much. I blame Mason Byrns. He's the reason I was so frazzled and why I took such a winding route home. He's also the reason I'm up at four in the damn morning combing through a bazillion images to delete my face from them. The ridiculousness of the situation isn't lost on me.

My phone buzzes and I absentmindedly pick it up. It doesn't compute at first, and I have to read the text twice for it to fully sink in. The device clatters across the desk, but I snatch it up as soon as it settles, anticipation winding through my empty stomach.

"When the hell does this man sleep?" I whisper. His hours are as erratic as mine.

Can you find who dropped off the hippo in my driveway?

I throw it down again before deleting the last image of my face. Groaning, as I lean back and wonder how the hell I can get off Mason's radar. This will not end well. He'll either fixate on me, determined to figure out who I am, or he'll forget I exist by the time the sun comes up. I don't know which one would be worse. Fuck, I'm becoming morose. Too much whining and I might puke.

My chair twirls when I tuck my legs up, watching the shadows in the corner of the room spin by. My phone buzzes and I flip around. I'm developing an obsessive response whenever it lights up, hoping it's him. My stomach tightens, fingers tingle, and I can't pull in enough air. It's ridiculous and I need to stop.

Instead of Mason, Ren King's name flashes across the screen and my heart drops. He's called me every day for the past three weeks, but I never answer. He's the only one I've actually spoken to. The phone goes dark, and I wait for his inevitable text.

Stop ignoring me. I have a job for you.

I send him a question mark. Before long, my responses will only be emojis, but I'm not sure he'd understand what they mean. Sam could decipher them for him. Ren is the closest thing I have to a friend, and I'd rather not alienate him any further than I have. I've been trying to decrease my interactions, but Ren isn't making it easy. Rationally, I know he's not truly my friend. The only reason he'd notice if I disappeared off the face of the planet is because he'd no longer be able to hire me.

What is it?

His response comes immediately, asking about some random trucks coming in the south side. Every single time he has some asinine request he could do himself, but he foists off on me instead. I didn't care at first, since it was easy money. Now, it's just annoying. It's obviously a ploy to get me to do something he's not willing to ask. There's no reason for him to worry about me, because we're not friends. Reminding myself of that isn't as easy as it once was.

Its the same story as last time. I text, hoping he'll leave it be.

No way you could have looked into it that fast. Actually do what we are paying you for.

I scoff, glancing at the clock. I've been at this for over two hours. I'm actively ignoring the ache in my chest from both Mason's and Ren's texts. It's a reminder that I'm nothing more than an asset to them. One that's easily replaceable. I don't blame them. They don't know me from the man on the moon. I've kept my identity from them, hiding so much of myself, I'm not sure I know who I would be if I ever truly met them.

At some point, I need to accept that I'm meant to be alone. They're probably shitty people when they're behind closed doors, just like my parents. Wrinkling my nose, I know these guys aren't terrible humans hiding behind a mask of politeness like I've experienced most of my life. I'm jaded by the many charlatans I've met in my twenty-seven years.

The screen in front of me flashes as I pull up all the info Ren could have gotten himself.

Theyre being rerouted through Rima still.

I move on to the police chief, Jason Grayson, but the man is squeaky clean, other than the weird name. I dive as deep as I can, but nothing pops up other than an estranged aunt who seems to live off-grid in the mountains to the north. The chief has never had so much as a scrubbed speeding ticket. Grayson is probably the most boring person on the planet. He collects stamps, for fuck's sake. I contemplate sending all of it to Mason but think better of it.

Jason Grayson is clean

The hippo is easy to figure out. In fact, I don't have to check anything. I watched Hawk, the Reapers' MC's vice president, and his woman drop it off in Mason's driveway a few weeks ago. Watching Willow, who's all of five feet tall, attempt to push the statue in place was enough to send me into a fit of giggles. When they fell into each other and he spun her around before disappearing into the night, jealousy burned away any amusement I felt. Their love is something I always thought of as a far-off dream I'd never experience, even when I was young. Mason's face flashes through my mind, concern lining his eyes, just like in the Morning Brew. Shaking my head, I dismiss him. He's not the happily ever after I'm looking for, because it doesn't exist for me. I won't out Hawk and Willow to Mason.

Are you sure

It takes me a minute to remember what I sent him and then I roll my eyes, wondering if I can get away with cussing out a mafia leader. No one would be able to find me, but then he'll stop texting. Talking to him feels different than with Ren, though it shouldn't. Apathy runs through my veins, making my arms heavy and my lids droop.

Youre welcome to ask for a second opinion
I didnt mean it like that
Sure

Five minutes pass before he responds. I'm curled up in my chair, debating whether or not I could fall asleep again. I don't know if it's even worth it. It's too early to go anywhere, but too late to go back to bed. I'm in the weird in-between where the sun hasn't risen, but the hint of it is on the horizon, like the twilight of my life where most of the world disappears into long shadows, swallowing any hope of a new dawn.

Anything about the woman

I knew it was coming and yet I still jolt upright. Mason isn't the kind of guy to let things go easily. Lying would be the best thing for both of us. He'd never know either way. He'll lose interest before long, moving on to the next important thing.

You already know who left the hippo
The woman?

I stare at my phone, thumb hovering over the screen as my eyes go blurry. The knife in my chest twists a little bit more as I type out a reply.

Shes no one

Five

Mason

A week after my run-in with the mystery woman from the coffee shop, I'm stuffed in the back of a car with Ryker Helms following a trailer with a giant golden hippo statue strapped to the back. Since Nemesis wasn't any help with finding the culprit who decided I needed a new lawn ornament, I asked Helms for help. He feigned ignorance but showed up three hours later with a trailer and some bikers who loaded it.

Usually we wouldn't be able to get through the traffic surrounding club row, but they've been closed for hours. The Barrens are quiet as we cross the river, its black depths hiding secrets even we don't know about. I've been pretending to text back and forth for the last ten minutes so Helms won't talk to me, but there's only so many times I can message someone who never responds.

"Who the hell are you texting?" Helms grumbles as he stares at the buildings flying by.

"No one. Tell me again why you insisted on coming along?"

"Kenz is with Sam and Willow tonight," he says, as if that explains anything.

"Didn't mean you had to tag along with me. It's just a fucking hippo."

He snorts. "And give you the chance to drop it off in Reaper territory? Abso-fucking-lutely not. I housed that shit for way too long."

Shaking my head, I go back to my phone. Another fifteen emails have popped up during our short conversation. I don't bother with them, pulling up my messages again, sending yet another one that will sit on read.

You realize itd just be easier to answer right?

I sigh, slipping it back in my pocket. This excursion seemed like a good idea when I decided to do it, but now that I'm here, I want to go home. It doesn't matter that there's nothing waiting for me there. I can't decipher what's plaguing me. Things haven't been right since I woke up to my world burning around me, but something is missing. I can feel it in my bones. I lost a vital piece of myself when I was shot, and I've been searching for it ever since.

The only time I've felt close to normal was when I was at the Morning Brew. I thought it was because of Sam, but after I asked Nemesis to find the woman I helped, I realized it had nothing to do with my sister.

"You talk to the Kings lately?" Helms asks, pulling me from my thoughts.

"Talked to Shane a week ago. The police chief pissed him off. He asked me to replace Grayson, but he'll fall in line."

"You get dirt on him?"

"No. Apparently, he's squeaky clean. Which probably means he's buried his sins deeper than most."

"Tell me you didn't do that shit by yourself. You actually hired someone to fucking help you, right?"

"Ren's hacker, dickwad. You going to tell me she isn't qualified to dig into shit?"

He huffs out a laugh, shaking his head. My phone buzzes, making my chest tighten. I wipe my sweaty palms on my pants before I pull it out and check the messages.

you shouldnt be texting me.

I smirk at the screen before tucking it back in my pocket since we're almost to the Kings' estate. Plus, I have no idea how to respond.

"What the fuck are you grinning at?"

"Mind your own business, Helms. Don't you have enough to deal with?" I mutter.

The truck pulls to the curb half a block from the mansion while our driver continues on. I don't know how we're going to get past the guards. I didn't think this through. I should have sent someone else to deal with it.

Helms pushes from the car, then ducks back inside. "You coming or am I doing this shit myself?"

We spend the next hour wrestling the statue in front of the hideous mermaid fountain. The kid in the guard shack looked like he was going to shit himself when we showed up, but he hasn't called anyone yet. Hopefully Shane lets him off easy. I doubt I'd have the guts if I were in his shoes to stop a mafia leader and the president of a biker gang.

I'm sweating balls by the time we're done, but at least Helms hasn't had the chance to grill me again. Swiping my hand across my forehead, I try to catch my breath. My heart pounds, adrenaline rushing through my veins. I feel more alive than I have in a while. Leaning against the hippo, I pull out my phone. Nemesis' text greets me, and I grin.

Shouldnt doesnt mean I wont.

"You realize that's like three negatives practically in a row?" Helms chuckles.

I scowl, finding him peering over my shoulder. "When the fuck did you get so nosy, Helms? That Mac's doing?"

His face morphs, settling into a frown. "Don't, Byrns. We're not going back to the way shit was before. I realize you weren't around when everything went down with the Guild—"

"Wasn't around? Nice way of saying I got fucking shot in the goddamn head because of you."

"Me? I didn't shoot you in the fucking head. I also saved your sister's ass twice during that hit, so don't come at me like that whole bullshit wasn't hard on everyone," he says, a vein in his forehead popping out.

"Hard on everyone? I was in a goddamn coma for six fucking months! I came out of it to my entire territory gone to shit, Sam shacking up with three mafia shitbags, and I had to shoot my best fucking friend after he beat the shit out of her, so excuse me if I think the shit I went through was a little more jarring than dealing with a limp dick organization." I'm panting by the time I'm done. Helms has the same look he wore when Sam was in the hospital six months ago, after the Night Slayers came to town looking for Mac. "Don't fucking look at me like that."

A light flashes in one of the windows, and we bolt for the car. Diving inside, I barely get the door closed before it takes off, the truck and trailer left behind with Helms's men. At least Shane will think it was the Reapers and not me who dropped a fucking statue in front of his house.

I lean against the leather seats and close my eyes. I'm exhausted, both from the prank and the late night, not to mention the altercation with Helms. My dreams are filled with blood and gore these days. I avoid sleeping as much as I can, but the erratic nights are catching up with me. TJ keeps pointing out the dark rings under my eyes. As if I don't know I'm fucking shit up.

"Go straight to the Byrns estate," Helms says to the driver, then turns to me. "We going to talk about your little hissy fit back there?"

"Go to hell," I say, but there's no bite behind my words.

"So, I won't have to pull you back from the ledge again?"

I scowl. "What the fuck is that supposed to mean?"

He sighs, gazing out the window. Clouds scatter across the moon, making the night even darker and stretching the shadows into every corner. Autumn has finally settled on us, and I make a note to send supplies into the Barrens. The people who live along the river have their own laws and ways of taking care of themselves, but there's a few who will take the extra blankets and food. The wind off the river is enough to get them to accept our offerings.

"Mason, I get it. You got some shit you're working through, but we're out of time. The Kings and I can't keep picking up the slack," Ryker sighs.

"I don't know what you're talking about. Things are fine. If shit is going sideways, maybe you should look closer to home."

"Deals are falling apart. Shipments are going missing. The lower gangs are seeping into the Barrens. Sam's been getting calls from her contacts down there, asking what we're doing about it. Plus, the police chief with his new initiative to clean up the streets? You seriously don't see any of it? Where the fuck have you been?" Ryker pierces me with a thunderous look.

We pull into the driveway, and I push the door open, stepping out. Leaning back in, I scramble for something to say. I don't have an argument for his accusation. This isn't just Shane King being an asshole. Or Sam, searching for a way to assuage her guilt over Colin's death. Things are going off the rails, and I don't know if I care anymore. He may be right, but admitting it isn't something I'm prepared to do.

"You're overreacting. Leave it, Helms," I say.

"Get your head out of your ass, Byrns, or we'll have to take drastic measures."

"Is that a threat?"

He ducks his head. "Don't fuck this up, Mason. We've come too far to fall apart now."

I slam the door, watching the car's taillights fade into the night. My head of security materializes from the dark and waves me down. Scrubbing my hand down my face, I wait for him to reach me.

"What do you need, Moss?"

Exhaustion settles in my bones again, the last rush of adrenaline bleeding from me. I need a fucking vacation. This is the time having a second would be ideal. They could take some of the pressure off. Instead, my second is six feet under and the one person I trust enough to ask turned me down. I can't run my part of the city on my own on a good day. When I'm unfucking everything Victor did and rebuilding the family…I'm drowning.

"Sorry, boss, but the security cameras are off again on the west boundary."

Moss has been with me for years, using his size to intimidate people who think they can overrun us. We may be the same height, but his arms are twice the size of mine. If he ever turned on us, shit would go to hell pretty damn quickly. Thankfully, he's one of the few I trust, which is exactly why he's the head of my security.

"I'm on it," I say, turning away.

"That's not all," he says, waiting until I spin back. "We've got some issues in the south. Hitch came by earlier, gave a report."

"Well?" I say when he doesn't continue.

"Looks like a group might be moving in. Some of the lower gangs down there have been getting hit. No one got floated, but it's escalating. I also caught Victor skulking around. I don't know what he's doing. Doesn't look good, though."

"I'll deal with it."

I pivot, skirting around the house to check on the cameras. Pulling out my phone, I bring up the feeds, but nothing's been tripped on my end. Ren never found who was fucking with theirs, and after the Guild left, their problem went away. Soon after, it started happening to me. The Kings don't seem very concerned with that fact, except for Ren expecting me to magically fix what he couldn't.

Thick brush weaves between the trunks surrounding my property. The covered moon creates a shadowed existence—a world hidden behind a veil the people of Synd will never experience. Thunder rumbles in the distance and lightning flashes across the sky, illuminating the leaves shivering above my head. I glance behind, tracking a guard's progress across the lawn. The last thing I need is someone sneaking up on me.

A branch snaps deeper in the trees. I whip my head around, scanning the darkness. Another bolt of lightning streaks through the clouds, and I catch a glimpse of white between the trunks. I pull my phone from my pocket and a new text message snags my attention.

Your camera situation is taken care of

It was sent a couple minutes ago, which means Nemesis is finally getting around to dealing with something at least. I wonder if my random texts have anything to do with her sudden interest in actually doing what we're paying her for. I pivot, stomping my way through the brush. Whatever is in the forest will be there tomorrow.

Six

Lacey

"You've got to be fucking kidding me," I mutter as the skies open up, sending a deluge of water down on my head. It's bad enough I'm out in the middle of the night, but now I'm stuck in the rain. In the forest. With a fucking twisted ankle. I knew my luck would run out eventually, but I didn't think it would hit me like a ton of bricks, and certainly not all at once.

I breathe a sigh of relief when I remember how much worse this could've been. Mason was thirty feet from me when I sent the text. He spotted me, though at this point, I assume he had no idea what he was actually seeing. I wore all black tonight, going so far as to cover my face with my bandanna, but I forgot about the bottom of my shoes. The white is a beacon in the blackness, drawing all sorts of attention. If he would have caught me…

I shiver, both from the cold and the threat of almost being exposed for my nighttime wanderings. Foolishly, I don't have a lie readily available. I can't tell him I was checking the cameras. Even if he didn't recognize me, I can never reveal who I am. I don't know how any of them would react. And I'm not going to find out.

My ankle throbs as I probe the bone. I doubt it will hold my weight. I need to get the hell out of here any way I can. Rolling onto my hands and knees, I swallow a yelp. My hand slips and I crash to my elbow. A sob slips free as tears fill my eyes, mingling with the rain pelting my face. I'm pretty sure there's a scrape on my arm now, along with my bum ankle. The longer I spend out here, the more injured I become.

The burning in my arm is the final straw. I never should have come, but the pull toward Mason was too much. It overwhelmed my common sense, and I told myself these were innocent excursions. Jealousy ran rampant through my veins when I was watching the Kings. Longing filled me when I focused my attention on Mason. His loneliness called to my own, and I convinced myself we could save each other. How wrong I was.

A strong arm wraps around my waist, and the howling wind swallows my shriek. I'm yanked off the ground, my back hitting a hard chest, and I scream again. This has to be a guard out on patrol. His other arm locks around my body and my breath stalls in my lungs as he swings us around. The brush is heavy here, hindering his progress. I can barely make out the lights across the yard through the storm.

"Put me down," I screech, kicking my legs.

My foot catches on a branch, almost sending us crashing to the ground. Dizziness sweeps over me as my injured ankle screams in pain. He curses, arm flinging out. I kick harder to break free, but he's a lot stronger than I expected. My lungs seize, tears stream down my face, and I might drown in the downpour.

"Knock it off," he says gruffly in my ear.

"Fuck off!"

His arm encircles me again, and he continues his trek toward the light. The rush of adrenaline seeps from my body, and I sag in his grasp. We break free of the tree line, and I twist. Once I'm in the house, it'll be that much harder to escape the man's clutches. He'll bring me to Mason, and I'll be fucked.

The need to be a part of their world any way I could was overwhelming. I should have stopped before my luck ran out. Sucking in a deep breath, I buck and my heel hits his kneecap, forcing a grunt from him. I do it again and his leg crumples.

He twists, arms gripping me tightly, and I land on top of his body. The rain batters me, like icicles piercing my exposed skin, but at least he didn't fall on me. Rolling to the side, he tries to stand while still gripping me, but I flail. I should have taken classes on how to get the hell out of these situations, but I opted for subterfuge. I used to know how to use a dagger, but they're tucked away in a closet. Regret slams into me that I didn't bring them with, but I shove it deep as I finally slip from his grasp.

Limping across the lawn, I head for the trees. The adrenaline is the only thing keeping me upright at this point. I dropped my phone somewhere along the way, not that it would do me any good right now. I can't call the police, and I have no one else.

My vision blurs, the trees warping as he bellows behind me. I don't dare look back, since that's exactly how people die in horror movies. I don't think they'd shoot me, but I'm not willing to risk it. Zigzagging across the muddy grass, my shoes sink more with each step, and I almost crash to my knees.

"Fuck," he bellows over the thunder.

I'm dead if he attracts other guards. Someone around here probably has an itchy trigger finger. With the way my luck is going, they'd be the one to answer his call. I'm almost to the safety of the trees when my foot sinks into a mud hole and my injured ankle rolls. A wave of pain washes over me, and I crash to my hands and knees, retching. Stars dance behind my lids as another bout of wooziness hits me. No man is worth this.

"Shit." His low voice reaches me through the lull in the tempest swirling around us.

My body tilts of its own accord, but the man's hands grab me before I hit the ground. He scoops me up, cradling me in his arms, and I slam my eyes closed. The fight within me has fled in the wake of the pain swamping me. I don't have it in me anymore and can only hope I'll be able to talk my way out of this shitshow. Mason probably won't even appear. I'm sure they have protocols for dealing with errant people who wander onto their property.

The rain cuts off abruptly as he carries me inside, and I shiver. I peek at whoever is holding me, but I can't make out any features in the darkness. I concentrate on the squishing of his shoes instead of the pounding of my heart or the pain radiating up my leg. A wave of panic hits me when we step into another dark room. He grips me tighter when I attempt to roll from his arms.

"Would you knock it the fuck off?" he says, and I freeze.

I know that voice. This isn't some random guard. Nope, of course Mason Byrns fucking came back. Embarrassment swirls with panic and roaring fills my ears.

"So fucking stupid," I mutter under my breath, all while curling my body closer to his.

We're still in the dark, so he probably has no idea who I am. He wouldn't recognize me anyway, so I may still be able to get out of this. The throbbing echoing through my body isn't helping me come up with an excuse for why I was in the woods, but it'll come to me.

He sets me on a hard wooden chair, the back digging into my shoulder blades. The cut on my arm smarts, and a hiss leaks from my lips. Tears fill my eyes, mingling with the rain and streaking down my face before dripping off my chin. The droplets disappear into my soaked shirt as if they never existed.

Lights flash on and I duck my head, strings of wet hair sticking to my face. I can't get my breathing under control, and I'm pretty sure this is what a panic attack feels like. Or maybe it's just raw pain radiating through me.

"You," Mason says, accusation lacing his voice.

So much for him not recognizing me. I lift my eyes, taking in his clothes, just as soaked as mine, and plastered to his frame. At one point he was thin, emaciated from his time in the hospital, but muscles stacked on more muscles line his body now. My eyes catch on his coffee-colored ones, making my brain short-circuit. The magnetism of his presence is electrifying even with ten feet between us. He breaks the connection, glancing away as he runs a hand through his dark hair. It's usually lighter, but the rain makes it almost black in the shimmering lights.

"Who are you?" He fixes me with a stare, pinning me in place.

"Lacey," I whisper almost immediately.

There's no use in lying. He's the type of man who can probably taste them or some bullshit. Why I picked my actual name, the one I haven't used in years, makes no sense, but I'll blame my injuries. A shiver runs through me, and my teeth chatter as the cold seeps into my bones. Disappointment rolls through me as the last of my dreams drain away, starting with the one starring the man seething in front of me.

"Why are you hiding in the goddamn woods in the middle of the night during a fucking thunderstorm?"

"Uhh…"

"The truth. Now," he commands, crossing his arms.

"I got lost."

"Bullshit. We're not in the middle of bumfuck nowhere. This is the city. You can't get lost in the forest here."

I huff. "I didn't say I got lost in the woods. I said I *got lost*. As you so helpfully pointed out, it's the middle of the night and there's a storm. So, it stands to reason it was dark and I couldn't find my way. Then I twisted my ankle, and it started raining and I'd like to go home now. Please."

Crossing my arms, I wince. I glance down, finding blood seeping from the wound. My head swims, and another pulse runs through me. I thought I could talk my way out of this—maybe use enough snark and he'll let me go merely because I annoy him. The look on his face says otherwise.

"Stay," he grunts, pointing at me before he turns away to march out the door. It slams shut behind him and my stomach flips.

Glancing around the room, I finally take in my surroundings. The furniture leaves something to be desired, with a raggedy couch pushed against the wall next to me. Another door probably leads to a closet. All that's left is the chair I'm sitting in. The glass rattles behind me when another bout of thunder rolls through the night. I shiver, imagining slipping out the window and into the downpour, but I doubt the move would grant me freedom. Mason would probably follow, dragging me back into the room to interrogate me. I would break eventually and confess who I am, spilling all my secrets at his feet.

Gingerly, I stand, wavering on one foot. As soon as I put weight on my injured one, I crumple to the floor. Pain erupts from my ankle, sucking me into a pit of agony. My vision swims and I slam my eyes closed to stop myself from puking. Ears ringing, I bite back the moan in my throat. The last thing I need is him coming back and finding me on the floor. Who knows what he'd do then. Probably shoot me. The nausea subsides, but the dizziness remains as I curl on my side.

"For fuck's sake." Mason's voice cuts through the ringing in my ears.

Suddenly, I'm floating, but I can't feel his arms around me. The fabric from the couch is scratchy against my cheek, distracting me from the pain.

"She needs pain meds. Remove her shoe before we have to cut it off," a man says.

My arm stings as something cool brushes over my cut. Yanking my limb away does nothing but make him grip my wrist harder. I dry heave as Mason tugs on my shoe. I really don't want to die from choking on my own vomit, which is exactly what will happen if he keeps yanking on my leg.

"Careful," the man snaps. "We need to get her out of these wet clothes before hypothermia sets in. She's shivering and her lips are turning blue."

"No," I moan, twisting away from their hands.

"Stop fucking moving and let the doctor fix your shit. You're not going anywhere, anyway," Mason growls before going back to wrestling with my sneaker. My entire foot is probably swollen. Stars explode behind my lids and darkness sweeps in.

Warmth envelops me and I burrow closer. I must have passed out, but I don't know how long I've been under. Low voices swirl around me, and it takes me a minute to recognize the doctor's voice. My ankle is numb, relieving most of the pain, but the cut on my arm sends needles through me. Then we're moving, the shift sending nausea through my stomach. I should not throw up on Mason fucking Byrns.

"Do not throw up on me," he grunts, and I wonder if I said it out loud. "You did say it out loud. Now stop fucking talking."

My entire body trembles, even as the heat from his body seeps into mine. At least they didn't strip me while I was passed out.

"I'm not in the mood to defend myself after the shitshow tonight, but I'm not going to take advantage of you. If you can't take your clothes off yourself, though, I'm going to have to do it. You'll freeze to death otherwise, and then I won't get the answers you owe me."

"Just let me go," I groan, all while tucking my body closer to his.

Tears wet my face and I shudder. The coffee shop incident was bad enough. This is a whole other situation I've landed myself in. I'll just enjoy this moment I'm stuck in until I'm forced to move on. Darkness sweeps over me again, and I settle into its sweet release.

Seven

Mason

Bright sunlight shining through the window flashes across my face, jolting me from sleep. At first, I don't recognize where I am, but then I spot the woman fast asleep in the bed and it all comes racing back to me. A war rages inside me, a remnant of last night. Questions sat on my tongue long after I carried her to bed, each more urgent than the last. I have half a mind to wake her up right now and demand answers.

A text from Helms pops up on my phone, bitching at me to get my shit together. I scowl, throwing it on the end of the bed. I can't believe I've added another problem to the millions of others plaguing me these days. As if I don't have enough to deal with. With Helms on my ass, I doubt I'll be able to push off the things I need to handle anymore. The gangs in the south are getting unruly, the police chief is still pissing me off, deals are falling through the cracks every day, and now I've added the mystery woman lying in this bed.

Finding her in the forest by my house was a shock. I don't buy her excuse that she was lost. Now I'm stuck trying to figure out who the hell she is. Same black hair as the woman at the coffee shop, though it's a streaked with bright red instead of green. I didn't get a clear look at her face before, other than a flash of plump lips when she fled, but I'm convinced it's her.

I admit I wanted to find her, going so far as to ask Nemesis to look into it. When she fled from the coffee shop, it was as if she took a piece of me with her, which is ridiculous. We had a five-minute interaction where I didn't even see her face, but she felt familiar even then, as if we knew each other in another life. Shaking my head, I grimace. No reason to get philosophical over a random woman, no matter how beautiful she is.

Her lids flutter open, revealing green eyes that widen gradually the longer I stare. Scrambling up, she winces, collapsing on her back again. I take one step forward before I can stop myself. The urge to comfort her aches in my chest as her groan reverberates through the room. I'm moving again, unable to stand by while she's in pain. For some unknown reason, she doesn't feel like a threat.

"Arm," I grunt, holding out my hand. Untucking herself from the covers, she yelps before yanking them up to her chin again.

"Why do I not have clothes on?"

"Clearly you have clothes on. Now give me your arm."

She sputters, peeking under the comforter. "I do not have *my* clothes on. Whose shirt is this? Oh shitballs, who the fuck undressed me?"

Rolling my eyes, I grab her wrist and gently turn her arm over. Her eyes track my movements as I peel back the bandage.

The cut isn't deep, but it bled a lot during our struggle. Her ankle is another story.

I use her distraction to tug the sheets back, revealing her splinted leg. The doc didn't think it was broken, but the more it swelled, the more gruesome her skin became. I keep my gaze on her foot, instead of traveling up her bare leg like I want. The doc had to cut her pants off, which left her in only her wet shirt, which had to go too. Thankfully, my black shirt is long enough to cover her.

It's hard to make out the bruising between the swaths of bandages, but the swelling has gone down at least. I poke at the splint and prod at the exposed skin on her foot. She jerks her leg away, grumbling.

"The doctor said you should stay off of it for a week or two, which gives you plenty of time to answer my questions."

Lifting my eyes to hers, I track the emotions running across her face, namely guilt. It swims in her eyes as she purses her lips.

"Well? You gonna stare at me or ask me a question?" she sneers, false bravado tinging her tone. I raise an eyebrow and she scowls. "What do you want?"

"Your name, for starters."

"I told you my name last night," she says, and her eyes skip away.

"Tell me again."

"Lacey. Anything else, or can I go? And where the hell are my pants?" She gathers the sheets in her fist and yanks them to her chin.

"Seems like you're making yourself comfortable, not getting ready to leave."

She rolls her eyes, and a memory tickles the back of my brain, but I can't put my finger on it. It's more than running into her at the coffee shop. Synd isn't small, but the feeling of familiarity tinges the air again. I flip through memories, but I've been in a haze for the last year. She could have done a tap dance in front of me with a bowler hat on six months ago and I probably wouldn't have registered it.

"Have we met before?"

"Uh, what?" Her eyes dart away again, and she pulls her knees up, wincing as she does.

"Other than at the Morning Brew. Have we met?"

"No. Can I go?"

She's lying. In my line of work, paying attention to the tells of other people is crucial. Plus, she's not exactly an adept deceiver. We have met, but she doesn't want to say where. That's fine. I'll get it out of her eventually. The ultimate question is whether she's a threat to me. Only time will tell, even if my gut is telling me she's not. I can't let her pretty face distract me.

Flushing, I snatch up my phone and stuff it in my pocket. The last thing I need is her calling someone to save her from the scary mafia man. We may run the underbelly of the city, but I'd rather not off random people if I don't have to.

"You're going to stay in that bed. You're not going to sneak out the window. I advise you not to seek help from anyone here, as they'll merely direct you to me or shoot you, which would be a fucking shame. Until you're ready to tell me why you were skulking around my property and who you really are, you'll remain here." I stalk for the door, despite her squawking.

"Hey, asshole. I told you my name. And I told you I was fucking lost. You can't just keep me here," she shrieks, struggling to sit up.

I eye her flushed face and flaring nostrils.

"You'll find there's very little I can't do, Kitten."

"Oh, for fuck's sake," she mutters, rolling her eyes.

"We'll continue this later. Don't try escaping. You'll only hurt yourself more, and we wouldn't want that now, would we?"

Something thuds against the door as I tug it closed, probably a pillow. I grin as her muffled curses fade away while I make my way down the hall. I might not trust her, but having her around will be entertaining at the very least.

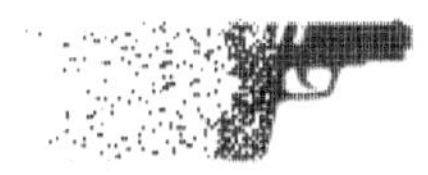

"Mason, there's an issue with the lower gangs on the south side." Victor's nasally voice interrupts my thoughts.

I spin in my office chair, sighing as I prop my elbows on the desk. "I'm well aware. I'm dealing with it."

"I only bring it up because it seems as if they're becoming unruly. We wouldn't want another repeat of the coup or, heaven forbid, an organization such as the Guild swooping back in." He settles in the chair across from me, unbuttoning his charcoal suit. It hangs from his frame, like it has for months, but at least it's pressed.

"As I said, Victor, I am taking care of it. Now, if you'll excuse me, I have business to attend to," I say, pushing to my feet.

"Oh, you're actually going to lead? A wonder what a little talk can do for someone, hmm?"

He sweeps from the room before I can respond. Collapsing in my chair, I set my elbows on the desk, dropping my head in my hands. The older I get, the less I'm convinced of his usefulness. I'll need to figure out what he's been doing in the front room before I can take any drastic measures, though. I'd love if he'd just disappear. Sam would do it, complete with a grin on her face. I'm sure he'd be one of the few people she'd reveal her identity as the Wraith to before she killed him. She'd revel in the idea of him dying in shock.

As if I manifested her, Sam sweeps through the door, kicking it shut behind her before she takes Victor's vacated seat. Crossing my arms, I lean back, waiting for her to start in on me. This is the first time she's been back since she left all those months ago to recover at the King's house. I fought to keep her here to heal, but after watching her fall apart, crying out in her sleep for the men across the river, I knew I wasn't what she needed anymore.

"Reason you're here, Sam?" I ask after several minutes of silence.

She tucks her foot under her leg, peeking up at me from under her hood before focusing on her phone again. I'm not surprised she's dressed all in black, like normal. Today is no exception, but I'm pretty sure her hoodie is one of the Kings'. My mind flashes to the image of her when I found her in the basement of this very house, but I push it aside. I focus on how she is now—dark brown hair falling in front of her face and hiding auburn eyes that match my own.

"Any day now, Sammy."

She sighs, tucking her phone away and pulling out a bag of cheese crackers we used to eat as kids. Her eyebrow tips up and I mimic her. Leaning forward, she shakes half the crackers onto my desk before sitting back.

"Alright, here's the deal. Something is going down on the south side. Shit is going sideways, and we're sick of tiptoeing around because they're on the east side. The police chief is off his rocker. Also, TJ called and said you're being an asshat about choosing a second. Oh, and I wanted to know if you wanted to go feed the ducks before they fly south."

"You want to feed the ducks?" It's the only thing I can focus on without blowing up at her.

"Yeah. We used to do it all the time and now we don't. They probably miss us."

"They're fucking ducks, Sam."

She stabs a finger in my direction, a stern look on her face. "Do not start. We're not going to utter the words 'ducks' and 'fuck' in the same sentence."

"What the hell are you talking about?"

"Every time I bring up the ducks Alex loses it, Ren smirks, and Shane scowls and no one will tell me what the hell their problem is with the ducks. No one wants to feed the ducks with me, and I thought you'd want to go since we used to, and now we don't," she grumbles, pushing to her feet. "Clearly, you've got beef with the ducks as well, so forget I mentioned it."

"Sit your ass down. I don't have beef with ducks. They're just ducks."

She sinks into the chair, scowling. "What about the other stuff?"

"I'm looking into the south side. They're not exactly being forthcoming with the shit going on. I'll probably have to drop in and have a chat. The police chief is a poser, but he's harmless. Let him tout all the community programs he wants. Nothing will come of it, and it'll make the suburbs feel like they're safe. If he starts going after the Barrens, I'll deal with it."

"You mean, *I'll* deal with it," she whines.

"I'm capable of killing someone, Samantha. I don't always need the Wraith to do my dirty work."

"Oh, please"—she rolls her eyes—"who is the last person you…?"

She sobers, ducking her head. Sighing, I glance out the window. This is the most normal we've been in months, but eventually the conversation always dissolves into awkwardness. We used to be close. I'd like to blame the Guild, but the last few years we've drifted apart, too busy with our own lives to notice. I wish we could go back to those days when it was the three of us. With my life in shambles and her thriving, there's an imbalance we can't seem to get past.

"Sammy, we need to stop doing this. Shit happened, we dealt with it, and it's time to move on."

"Are you actually moving on, Mason?" she whispers.

I don't like her like this—timid and hesitant. This isn't who she is. She's strong and confident and sure of herself. When she's around one of the Kings, she's her usual snarky self. This new version of my sister is solely for me. Quiet, jittery, tripping over her words—it sends a stab to my heart every time.

"Stop acting like a scared little doe, Samantha. It doesn't suit you."

Her head whips up, a snarl on her lips. "Don't tell me what to do. I can be whatever the hell I want to be. If I want to sob on the damn floor like a fucking baby, I will. Stop being an ass because I'm worried about you."

"Stop worrying about me. Focus on your own shit. I've got enough to do without you coming around trying to assess my mental state."

"Whatever. You doing anything today?" Hope swims in her eyes, all while the image of Lacey pops into my mind.

I wasn't lying when I said I have a lot to do. Shit is going sideways and all I've done is pile on more by bringing Lacey into my house. The sooner I find out her intentions, the sooner I can move on to the next task and start pulling myself out of this hole.

"I can't feed the ducks with you today." Her face falls. "But later this week I'm free."

Sam tugs the hood lower, ducking her head again, but not before I catch the small smile dancing on her lips. Pushing to her feet, she shuffles to the window and throws it open.

"Sam, please don't crawl out the damn window. You freak Moss out every time you do it. Use the tunnels like a regular fucking person." I point to the secret panel tucked behind the bookcase, and she skips over to it.

"You should come by and check out the Kings' tunnels. I swear the houses are the exact same. Oh, and the neighborhood. It's freaky," she says as she opens the panel, revealing stairs trailing off into darkness.

"I know. Pretty sure Shane isn't very happy with me right now, so that'll have to wait."

She rolls her eyes. "He's not mad at you. You two are grown-ass men in a pissing contest—"

"You ever think it has nothing to do with you?" I raise an eyebrow, tucking my hands behind my head, and her mouth drops open.

"You left the damn hippo in our driveway, didn't you? Oh, yeah. He's fucking pissed," she laughs.

"I don't know what you're talking about. Take care of your-self, Sammy."

She smirks before slipping through the opening. The panel cuts off my view a second later.

"Love you," I whisper into the empty room.

Eight

Lacey

I had every intention of breaking every one of Mason's directives, but instead I fell asleep.

Now, the sun is setting and I'm pretty sure my bladder is about to burst from lying in bed all day. My ankle is hot, throbbing with each heartbeat. My cut stings every time I twist my arm. Mud sloughs off my skin, grinding into the sheets, and I feel like I spent my night wrestling, which isn't far from the truth. This isn't exactly how I thought things would go if I ever met one of the shadowed leaders of Synd in an official capacity, random run-ins aside.

The room is massive compared to my house, with several doors leading off to fuck-knows-where. If I hadn't dropped my phone in the forest, I could probably find a way out of here. Swinging my legs over the side, I suck in a breath at the rolling waves of pain coursing through me. My head swims as I tuck it between my knees. Black spots dance in front of my eyes, and I slam them shut so I don't puke on my legs.

I never did get an answer to why I'm not wearing pants, which seems like an important issue that should be addressed. My shoes are missing too. And the shirt I'm wearing is definitely not mine. I'm not exactly swimming in it, but it's giving me a complex. The fabric is too much, too comfortable. I'm loath to admit how soft it is against my skin, even with the mud that's caked on my body.

When the nausea passes, I push to my feet and then immediately thump back on the bed. I'm swamped with pain, and I resign myself to either hopping or crawling to the bathroom, which is becoming an urgent mission. Hopping would probably end up with me down for the count, so crawling it is.

Sliding to the floor, I peek under the bed, just in case. Of course, there's nothing there, but the need to check is ever-present. Crawling isn't much better, but at least I'm moving. Of the three doors, I pick the center one, hoping it's the bathroom. Once I get there, though, I find a closet, full of absolutely nothing—just an empty space devoid of even shelves. Eyeing the door by the window, I contemplate rolling, but I'd probably end up breaking my other ankle or busting my head open.

I'm not particularly clumsy usually. Fate apparently needed to take me down a notch. As soon as I heal and find my way out of this damn house, I'll skip town. There's no way I can stay in Synd, regardless of whether I want to or not. I'd be risking my identity—my life—if I stayed. I won't have to worry about money. Between the Kings and the Byrns, I've amassed more than I could be able to spend in a lifetime.

No, the problem isn't money. It lies in the unknown. If I leave Synd, I'll have to find another way to live. I'll have to learn a new world I know nothing about. My stomach turns just thinking about navigating a new city. I hate not knowing where I'm going or how to get around new places. The familiarity of Synd eases the anxiety within me. Plus, other cities don't have Mason Byrns, as silly as that is. I've been infatuated with him for a while. I can't just turn those feelings off because I'm on his shit list now. This whole thing is only sucking me further into his orbit, which is terrifying, and sends a rush of hopelessness through me.

I could go to Rima, but four hours it doesn't feel like it's far enough away. Not only that, but Mac and Willow, women embedded within the Reapers, have ties in that city. With rumors of the Guild infiltrating Rima swirling through the shadows of the net, I especially want to stay as far away from there as possible.

I'm huffing by the time I reach the next door, but the knob won't turn. A sob slips out as I roll, leaning against the door. The pain is an echo compared to how much I have to pee. Imagining wetting myself all over the floor has horror running through me. There are very few things that would be more embarrassing. Maybe shitting my pants.

"What the fuck are you doing? I told you to stay in bed," Mason growls, his shadow falling over me.

"I have to pee, and I can't find the bathroom. And you're an asshole," I choke out through a sob, all my emotions swamping me at once. Covering my face in my hands, I can't stop the tears.

Everything crashes into me at this exact moment, and I'm just done.

"For fuck's sake," he murmurs before scooping me up.

My stomach protests, but I swallow hard, keeping my hands over my face. I might pass out before we get to the bathroom, and then I'll probably pee all over him. It would be the icing on the cake, really. Might as well piss all over his clothes and end it all right now.

"Don't fucking piss on me," he grumbles as the warmth from his body seeps into mine.

"I'm cold," I whimper. I didn't mean to say it out loud, but it came out anyway.

"Well, you don't have any pants on, so that's to be expected." He chuckles, as if there's any humor to be found in this situation.

I peek at our surroundings and find we're already in a bathroom. Clearly, the bedroom he shoved me into didn't have one and he brought me somewhere. I was too busy worrying I would pee my pants and relishing in being in his arms to pay attention where we were going.

Mason twists as he glances around the room, making my vision swim. After what seems like an eternity, he lowers me to my feet, keeping an arm around my waist to steady me. In any other circumstance, his actions would be endearing. I can't even enjoy it between the pain and him technically kidnapping me.

I've never been kidnapped before, but I didn't imagine it'd be like this. I thought it would be like the movies—bag shoved over my head, hands zip-tied together, and a lot more blood. At this point, I'm pretty sure if I tell Mason what a good little mafia leader he is, he'll let me go.

I'm next to the toilet, teetering on one leg. I hop once and he reaches out, keeping me upright.

"I'm fine," I snap, pushing his arm away.

"Fuck, you're fickle."

"What the hell does that mean?" I demand, even as I snatch at his arm when my center of gravity is thrown off.

"One minute whining about being cold and the next snarling like a kitten backed into a goddamn corner. If you're hoping I'll let you go based on your attitude, you're going to have to pick a lane and stick to it."

He steps back, eyeing me as if I'll keel over at his feet.

"Or you could let me go just because."

His face shutters, brows pulling low. "Not until I get my answers."

"I gave you answers. Just because you didn't like them doesn't mean they're not accurate. Now, can you get the hell out? Unless you're cool with me peeing on your floor," I say. He spins, crossing his arms, and then stands there. "You can't be fucking serious."

"I'll be right outside the door. Don't try to drown yourself in the toilet." He stomps back through the door, slamming it shut behind him.

"As if I'd use the toilet when there's a perfectly good bathtub right there," I mutter.

"I heard that."

Sitting on the toilet using only one foot is one of the hardest things I've done, but I make it. Getting off is another story. I almost cave and call out for Mason to help me, but my cheeks burn just imagining it. There's no way I'm washing my hands. I end up on the floor, the cool tiles sending a shiver through me. I sigh as I finally take in the space. It's ginormous, as big as my living room. I spot a towel hung on the back of the door and a toothbrush next to the sink. The walk-in shower, complete with not one, not two, but three fucking benches. One has bottles haphazardly scattered across it. Apparently, the shelf on one wall is too far away, or he's just too lazy to put them back. It finally hits me where I am, and I scowl.

"You've got to be fucking kidding me," I mutter.

"You fall in?" Mason's muffled voice calls.

I snort, tipping my head back and spot an honest-to-fuck chandelier hanging from the ceiling. The door creaks open, revealing Mason's head, hand covering his eyes.

"What are you doing?" I ask, realizing my voice echoes off the tiles.

"Are you done?"

"Yes. Did you find me pants?"

An auburn eye peeks out from between his fingers. He drops his hand before tossing me a pair of sweatpants, smacking me in the face before pooling in my lap. All my energy drains out onto the cold tiles, replaced with exhaustion and shame. I wonder if I could convince him to just smother me with a pillow instead. I've heard it's less painful than getting shot.

He never came across as the type of guy who would randomly kill someone, even if they did sneak onto his property in the middle of the night. Mason Byrns is dangerous, but not malicious. At least, from what I've seen while stalking him. I wonder if he'd kill me if I admitted I've been watching him and everyone else in his circle for over a year now. Probably. I can't bring myself to care.

"You gonna put them on or will them onto your body?" he asks, his shoes coming into view. Lost in my morose thoughts, I didn't hear him coming over.

"You should just get it over with."

"Get what over with?"

"We're in a catch-22 and eventually you'll get annoyed enough and do something drastic."

He crouches, tilting his head to catch my eye. "I'm not going to kill you. And the fact you think I would just for loitering on my property is a little insulting."

"What if I piss you off?"

The corner of his mouth tilts up, hinting at a smile. "You're still alive, aren't you?"

"What if it's *really* bad?"

He ducks his head, but not before I catch the full-blown grin on his face.

"Even if it's really bad." He tips his head up, sighing. "Who are you?"

"Lacey," I whisper, closing my eyes.

He snorts. "Why were you on my property?"

"I got lost."

"Bullshit. You're hiding something and I'm going to figure it out. You're better off telling me yourself before that happens, Lacey." His tone is laced with something I can't put my finger on, and my heart skips a beat anyway when he says my name.

I huff out a laugh. "What's the point? You won't believe me anyway. So, go ahead. Do whatever you're going to do and then whatever happens, happens."

Guiding my body down, I splay across the floor. The porcelain is freezing, but I can't keep myself upright anymore. Numb doesn't begin to describe my body right now. Cold has seeped into my bones, rendering me useless.

I couldn't escape even if I wanted to. Even after all I've said to him, I have to admit it's nice to be taken care of. I can't remember the last time someone cared enough to make sure I was safe. All my life I've looked after myself. The fact it's Mason Byrns who is coddling me is just icing on the cake. I should soak this up as long as I can. I'll probably never have the opportunity again.

"Is this shock?" I murmur. Another muttered curse falls from Mason. "You cuss a lot."

"You're one to talk," he mutters, and then I'm floating. "Don't pass out again."

"I already told you everything. Stop asking," I mumble. It occurs to me that my answer doesn't match his question. I'm fading in and out, his low voice rippling through my body, ebbing and flowing as it bumps into the emotions rolling inside me.

"If you die, then I'll never know the truth. I'll be left with unanswered questions. So, stay awake or we'll have problems."

His words filter through the fuzziness. "This is the weirdest kidnapping I've ever been to."

"I didn't kidnap you," he snarls, hands tightening on my body. "And even if I did, a kidnapping isn't something you attend. It's not a party you dress up for, for fuck's sake."

"Whatever. Still won't let me leave. Seems like a kidnapping to me. Are we going somewhere or just standing in the bathroom?"

He tenses and then moves. Neither of us talk the entire way back to my prison. It's not that bad. In fact, I don't even know if the doors are locked. Maybe he assumes I won't know where to go even if I do leave. Slight problem is, I know the general layout of this place, along with the secret tunnels. I could probably escape if I really set my mind to it. I won't be revealing how much I know to him.

Keeping my eyes closed until a door opens, I peek out from under my lashes as he starts lowering me on the bed. He yanks me back to his chest, and a shriek falls from my lips.

"What the hell?" I cry as we swing around, and I clutch at his shirt.

The chair he puts me in is terrible, but I clamp my mouth shut as he stalks back to the bed and rips the sheets off. Chunks of mud scatter across the hardwood floor and I cringe. My skin itches just watching him. Dirt coats my body with streaks running up my arms and flaking from my hair. I need a shower. Picking at my nails, I try to dig the mud caked under them.

The numbness fades from my limbs, letting the pain in my ankle seep back in. Pain meds are definitely needed, but that would require asking Mason, and I don't know if I want to. He's wrapping the sheets up and pulling out new ones.

"Are you actually making the bed?" I ask, immediately wanting to stuff the words back in.

He doesn't bother to look up as he pulls the sheets on. "I'm not going to call someone else in here to do it."

"Wait, doesn't anyone else know I'm here?"

"Other than the doctor, no. Don't think that means you can sneak out."

"Escape. The word you're looking for is escape."

He flips the comforter back in place before planting his fists on his hips and scowling at me. "I didn't kidnap you. You came onto my property and won't tell me why, so let's call you an unfortunate guest who's not allowed to leave until I figure out who the hell you are."

"This is ridiculous. I told you, I'm Lacey and I got lost. It was a dark and stormy night. I'm not from around here."

He eyes me when I suck in a breath. I shouldn't have said the last part. The more I lie, the more I'll have to keep track of later. A smirk forms on the corner of his mouth.

Pointing to the nightstand, he says, "Meds. Take them."

"Can't exactly reach them."

"Figure it out."

"Excuse me?"

"You want to be snarky? You want to insist I've kidnapped you? Fine. Figure it the fuck out," he snarls.

I swear he mutters "brat" as he walks out the door, the thunder of the lock echoing in the silence of his exit.

Nine

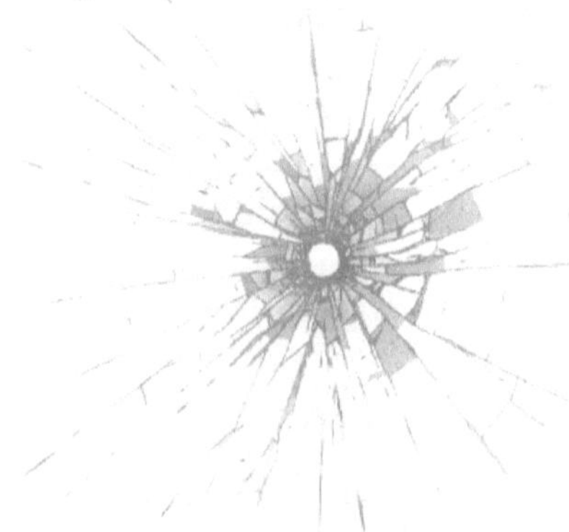

Mason

Slamming my fist into the bag for the three hundredth time isn't as satisfying as the first one. Yet I'm still hitting it again and again, waiting for the tension in my shoulders to melt away along with the pulsing pain in my chest. I need to get back into shape. I've been working my body harder every day, but it took a long time to get anywhere near where I was before. My time in the hospital took a toll on more than just my body, but focusing on anything else is too much. At least right now.

My mind isn't on my workout this afternoon. It's three floors up and one wing over, on the raven-haired woman who's probably crawling across the floor again. When I checked on her last night, I expected more lies and sarcasm.

Instead, I found her fast asleep, just as I have for the last five days. The covers were trapped underneath her, as if she got halfway through the act, then passed out. I felt bad for making her find her own way back to bed, but her constant refusal to tell me the truth annoyed me enough I didn't think too hard about it.

At some point, I have to figure out what to do with her. She doesn't seem like she'll be telling me what I want to know any time soon. I should just let her go, but with the reports coming from the south, I can't shake the feeling that something is coming. Whether she's involved in the shit piling up or not doesn't matter to anyone but me. I'm positive she's the one responsible for tripping the cameras. And if she's been fucking with mine, then it's safe to say she's been to the Kings' house as well. They were dealing with this for months before the problem came to my doorstep.

Bracing my wrapped hands against my knees, I struggle to catch my breath. This woman has infiltrated my brain, presenting a puzzle I need to solve. I have enough on my plate getting back to running my territory. I should just let her go and hope for the best. But the urge to keep her close is riding me hard. Under all her sarcasm lies a magnetism I can't ignore, no matter how much I try.

"Mason." TJ's voice echoes through the gym, and I hold up a hand until my breathing returns to normal.

"What is it, TJ?" I ask as I unwind the tape from my hands.

"There was a hit in the south. Rimmer's area. No one was killed, but the warehouse was demolished."

"Are you fucking kidding me?"

"You want to tell me where your head's at? Because shit's been falling apart for months and yet the last couple days you're missing in action."

"Do your fucking job, TJ. I don't need a keeper," I grumble as I push past him.

I should take a shower, but I need to get to the warehouse before the cops show up. Halfway to the bedroom Lacey's been staying in, I realize where my feet are taking me. I've kept her presence here from everyone else so far, but if she starts making a fuss, I won't be able to keep it quiet. I could start using the tunnels to reach her room from my own, but I'd rather she didn't know they're connected until my hand is forced.

Glancing down the hall, I unlock the door as quietly as I can. When I push it open, something flies past my head, slamming into the wood, followed by a shriek. Slamming it shut, I look down the hall again, praying no one is close by. I don't need Victor sneaking up behind me and discovering my stowaway. He'd probably shoot her in the head before asking any questions. Or he'll try to use her in some way. The thought sends a pang through me.

Slowly, I push the door open again, and another thud hits the wall. Peeking through the crack, I eye her sprawled on the bed, foot propped on a stack of pillows. Clearly, she's pissed at being left alone. Or maybe because I won't let her leave.

"You done throwing shit?" I ask, watching as she crosses her arms.

"Seeing as how I can't reach anything else, I guess so. You done holding me hostage?"

I push open the door, closing it quietly behind me. "Hostage implies I'll be asking for ransom. Since you won't give me your name, it would be hard to collect. Also, I'm hardly in need of more money."

"Can we not have this conversation again?"

Her ankle isn't as swollen today, but I still need to get the doctor back here. Even if she wanted to run, she wouldn't be getting very far.

"We can stop having it when you tell me why you've been sneaking around my property and fucking with my security system. Oh, and while you're at it, you can tell me what your friends are doing on my side of the river. Can you walk on this yet?" I ask, pointing to her foot.

"I don't have friends, so you're barking up the wrong tree. And no, I can't. Which is entirely your fault."

Scowling, I pick her up, ignoring her muttered curses. When I get to the door, muffled voices filter through and I do an about face. I didn't want her to know about the tunnels, but I'm apparently out of options.

"Close your eyes," I grunt.

"You've got to be kidding me. This is fucking ridiculous."

Despite her protests, she covers her eyes, and I press the knot hidden in the frame next to the false panel and step inside. It swings closed, plunging us into darkness. Usually, I can navigate these tunnels in the dark, but carrying someone else makes it difficult. I'm already tired from the two-hour workout earlier, and hauling another person up two flights in the dark isn't helping.

"If you drop me, I swear I'll…" she whispers harshly. I tighten my grip and a shiver runs through her.

She can pretend all she wants I don't have an effect on her, but we both know she'd be lying—again. I've focused on her injuries to keep my mind off the rest of her body, but I can't help how my own responds to her, especially when I'm carrying her so close every chance I get. Sure, I tell myself it's because she can't walk on her own, but having her in my arms is an added bonus I'm not examining too closely.

"You'll what? Tumble off into the dark? Because that's about all that'll happen."

Pushing open the panel to my room, I don't hesitate as I step inside. After Sam told me about Victor sneaking in while I was in a coma, I had a keypad installed, along with sensors on every possible exit. The room is three times the size of the one I had Lacey in. I doubt she noticed she was in my bathroom yesterday.

"Where the hell are we?" she snarls, practically spilling on the floor when she twists. "Put me down."

"Then how the hell would you get to the toilet? Fancy crawling there?"

"It's not that bad. I'm sure I'm fine now," she protests, but her arms cross, settling more into me as I step into the bathroom.

"Here's what's going to happen," I say, lowering her to her uninjured leg. "You're going to do your business. I'll bring you back to bed and get you something to eat…"

"I'm not hungry."

"Shut the fuck up and listen," I snap. "You'll stay here until I get back and then we'll deal with this shitshow you've created in my life."

I march from the bathroom, slamming the door behind me as she curses me out. I won't be able to keep her locked up forever. Especially when all the things I've been neglecting are coming to a head. I need this done with now. I wonder if anyone is missing her. Is her family frantically searching for her? Is there a boyfriend wondering why she hasn't called? When I checked, no one had filed a missing persons report, which makes me think she was telling the truth when she said she didn't have friends.

I pound on the door. "You done in there?"

"Go to hell!"

"Already there, Kitten," I mutter.

Snorting, I slip out my bedroom door, setting the code as I leave. She wouldn't get very far if she did make it to the door, but I still set the lock. No one will be able to go in or out. I thought Ren was taking it a bit far when he explained putting a lock on the inside, but now I'm wondering if there was a time he needed something like this. I push the thought from my mind. The last thing I want to do is mull over what happened before my sister fell into a relationship with the Kings.

The kitchen is deserted, thankfully. I should make soup or something, but I pull a sandwich from the fridge instead. A deli deep in my territory drops them off to the house several times a week, along with more at the Depot. Marie comes in on Mondays and cooks more food, but I rarely see her. She's been around for years but keeps to herself. Most of the time, I order food instead of heating up whatever she's made, much to her dismay. The rest of the guards, including Moss and TJ, take advantage of her cooking at least.

"Mason, I thought you already left. Perhaps I should go down to check on the warehouse instead?" Victor asks, and I close the door before spinning around.

"Not necessary. The warehouse will be just as fucked up whether I rush down there or not."

"Ahh, but the men might not be there, should you dally too long." He raises an eyebrow, straightening his cuff links as he does.

"Why don't you let me run things around here, and you can…do whatever it is that you're up to."

"I'd like to say I can trust you to do your job, Mason. The more time passes, however, the less I'm inclined to believe you're still capable." Tucking his hands in his pockets, he rocks back on his heels and my chest tightens, rage running through me.

"Is that a threat?"

A sly smirk graces his face, as if he doesn't realize the danger he's in. Victor has outlived his purpose, stirred my wrath, and finally put himself directly in the path of my rage. I'm done giving him a pass based on his previous usefulness. I've spent months fixing the shitty deals and dissent he sowed deep within the men under the umbrella of the Byrns name, even though he doesn't share it. He's forgotten his place, yet no matter how much I warn him, he always oversteps. His treatment of Sam alone should have had him floating long before now.

"Of course it's not. I merely wish you were as strong as you were before the Guild came through. If only Samantha could have lived up to her potential and done something useful for the family. Instead, you allowed her to flounce off with the Kings. You realize they'll take over before long. They'll couch it in concern and pity, but at its base, it will be a silent invasion—a systematic takeover of everything east of the river. You won't have to worry about them, though, as you'll be six feet under long before that happens," he sneers.

"Careful, Victor. Or I'll start to think you'll be the catalyst for such an event."

"Never fear, nephew. I have the Byrns family at the heart of all my plans," he murmurs before disappearing out the door.

Fuck. Whatever he's planning goes way beyond silly little deals with shitty contacts. I didn't take him seriously enough, assuming I could handle him later. Which is exactly what I've been doing with everything in my life. All the problems were put on the back burner, for no other reason other than I didn't want to put the energy into them. Now they're all coming to head at the same time, and I can no longer ignore them, or Victor's words will become reality. So why am I bothering with the woman in my room? I should let her go and worry about the rest of the problems in my life.

I jolt as my phone dings with a message from Rigger, asking where the fuck I am. Snatching up the food, I take the shortcut of the tunnels up to my room, coming out in the hall. It takes three times before my fingerprint registers, and I find my hands are trembling. The tension bleeds from my shoulders as I step inside, and I freeze.

Lacey is seated at my desk, foot propped on the wood, and scowling. At this point, I can't keep calling her *that woman.* Even if her name isn't Lacey, I'm going to use it anyway. Although, I'm pretty sure she's telling the truth. I should ask her what her last name is, but I doubt she'll give it to me, and I don't have the time to banter with her.

"Did you flush? Or am I going to have to do that for you, too?"

"Fuck off. This is the worst kidnapping ever. And I'm hungry. And my fucking ankle hurts. Instead of worrying about whether I trashed your ridiculously large bathroom, why don't you just call me a car or something? Actually, scratch that. Call a taxi. Less chance they'll be in your pocket and tell you where I live," she snarls, crossing her arms.

"If I let you go, who would feed you?" I ask, plopping the plate next to her foot. "This would go a lot smoother if you told me what the hell you were doing in the woods. And don't tell me you were lost. We both know that's bullshit. You could also tell me if you have ties to whoever is wreaking havoc down south. Or if you have ties to the police chief and whatever the fuck he's up to."

"You realize you're revealing a lot of shit without *actually* knowing who I am or what I'm capable of, right?" The disappointment on her face makes my stomach flip.

"You tripped in the woods in the middle of the night and haven't even tried to escape. You've passed out, multiple times in my arms. And you can't walk. So, excuse me if I don't think you're a threat," I scoff as I stalk into my closet.

I don't have time for a shower and I refuse to wear a suit to the warehouse. The last time I wore one to the Depot, the initiates thought it was hilarious. They weren't laughing when I sent their ass on the next gun run to Harris five hours away from Synd. None of them knew what the fuck they were doing, and the contact we have there wasn't very considerate of that. Good thing Young and I have known each other for years and he was willing to help get their asses in line.

"There's a gun in this desk. Did you know that?"

I freeze, deciphering her words before grabbing a black hoodie and slipping through the back of the closet and into the tunnels. It takes me a lot longer than it would to get to the other false panel in my room, but at least if she has a gun pointed at the closet, I'll have enough time to react. Her profile comes into view when I ease open the wall. I don't know what I expected, but it wasn't Lacey with her hands raised over her head as if she's being held at gunpoint. She turns to me, a terrified expression on her face.

"You wanna back away from the desk?"

"How the hell am I supposed to do that? I can't fucking walk," she snarls, but her voice is laced with fear.

"It's not going to jump up and bite you," I say, prowling forward and snatching the gun up.

"Don't wave it around. For fuck's sake."

"It's not loaded." Tucking the weapon in my hoodie pocket, I trudge back to the closet. "You've never handled a gun before?"

"Uh, no. I have other…well, I mean, I'm not exactly down with that stuff."

She could be acting, but the trembling in her hands and bone-deep fear in her eyes say otherwise. With each revelation, I'm more inclined to believe she isn't a threat to the Byrns clan.

Dropping the gun in a drawer filled with socks, I slam it shut. I'm not convinced she's here to bring us down, but she could be working with someone. There's an edge to her. Lacey clearly doesn't take shit from anyone, even when she has the disadvantage of being injured. She meets me at every turn, and I hate to admit it, but her attitude invigorates me like nothing else has in the past year.

A smile overtakes my face when I remember how much vitriol she threw at me. Hell, she chucked a pillow and a water bottle at my head. She clearly doesn't give two shits who I am. It's so rare to meet someone who doesn't cower, whether they know I'm in the mafia or just think I'm a wealthy businessman. I still need answers, but it's nice to have someone who talks to me like a person instead of a boss.

"Who do you live with?" I ask, leaning against the door frame.

"I'm pretty sure I shouldn't tell a kidnapper that."

"I didn't kidnap you. Who's going to make sure you don't fucking starve?"

She looks up from the sandwich she's been inspecting before jamming what seems like half of it in her mouth.

"I dunno."

I swallow hard, trying not to gag. "Slow the fuck down before you choke. Even if I let you leave, you have no way to get home, no way to feed yourself, and no way to make it to the bathroom. Who would take care of you? Partner? Family?"

"Is that your clever way of asking if I'm involved with someone? Or to figure out if someone will come for me should I mysteriously go missing?" She narrows her eyes before taking another bite.

"For fuck's sake. You realize an actual kidnapper wouldn't care if you could feed yourself, right? Most of them would starve you. Now, how do you plan on taking care of yourself?"

"I'll be fine. And I promise I won't tell anyone who you are or the fact you kept me locked up."

"This is hardly locked up. I had a doctor come and look at you. I've fed you. Hell, I even gave you a place to sleep. I changed the goddamn sheets. Do you know how long it's been since I've done that?"

"Have you ever done that?" she smirks, raising an eyebrow, and I scowl. "Why do you care so much?"

"About what?"

She rolls her eyes. "About whether I can feed myself."

"Doesn't really make sense to take you home for you to slowly starve to death." I rub the ache that's formed in my chest.

"Oh," she breathes, rubbing her arm as she stares off.

"Just eat your sandwich. I'll be back later. Don't try to leave. You'll only hurt yourself more," I say, pushing off the frame.

She mutters something I can't make out, but by the time I think to ask, the door is clicking shut behind me.

Ten

Lacey

Silence presses into my head and I'm pretty sure I'm slowly losing my mind. I'm used to the low hum of computers and whatever random playlist I've pulled up. Even when I sleep, I have a fan going. Now, there's nothing. No slamming doors or people shouting. I expected there to be something in a house this big, but I'm left whiling away the hours tracking the sunbeams across the hardwood floors. My stomach gurgles. My ankle throbs. My head pounds. And there's absolutely nothing I can do about any of it.

Groaning, I slither down until I'm staring at the ceiling. I'd never admit to Mason how comfortable his bed is. I could write poetry, expounding on all the amazing attributes this piece of furniture possesses, but right now I just want out. The last time I was in his bathroom, I spied the ginormous bathtub taking up an egregious amount of space, though I didn't know it was his personal one at the time. It looks like the tub has been severely neglected. Only problem is, I can't get there. I could crawl, but I doubt I'd be able to get inside, much less out again when I was naked and slippery. I'm still wearing Mason's shirt and it's a little worse for wear now. I swear my skin is flaking. I need to be clean.

"This fucking sucks!"

I'm no longer worried about someone hearing me. I already tried to open the bedroom door, which took more energy than I'm willing to admit. When I caught my breath, I shuffled over and pried at the panel in the wall, but I couldn't pull myself up to search for a hidden button somewhere. An hour was spent on the floor, wallowing in self-pity. At some point I was singing, but I couldn't remember the words and I eventually gave up.

"Lonely…so fucking lonely…" I belt out, slapping the comforter to a random beat.

"Those aren't the words," Mason calls, making me jump.

"You could have fucking knocked," I grumble, tracking him as he disappears into the closet.

"Are you always this irritable?"

I snort, staring at the ceiling again. Seventy-seven swirls. I've counted them so many times, I can pick out the ones that aren't centered with my eyes closed at this point. I track them again, if only to keep my mind off the fact that he's probably getting naked in his closet. A shiver rolls through me and I scowl.

He thinks I should be all sunshine and rainbows, which is ludicrous. Maybe he thinks I should be cowering, but honestly, I don't have it in me to care. I probably should tamp down on the sarcasm while I'm being held hostage. Although, the longer I stay here, the less I'm convinced he's holding me against my will. From the beginning, I didn't really think I was. I assumed it was my personal obsession with him skewing my view of things.

"Well?"

"Apparently being kidnapped and held against my will brings out the bitch in me," I say, tilting my head to the side.

"Those are the same things. And you're not a bitch," he murmurs.

Rolling my eyes to him, I'm met with his bare chest. There's blood streaked across his abs, mixing with the ink from his tattoos. I suck in a breath, and whatever saliva I had in my mouth is now caught in the back of my throat. I swear I'm dying. Mason's eyes widen and he rushes for me, pulling back at the last second as he spies the red splashed across his hands and deep under his fingernails.

I wheeze, finally able to swallow. "Are you okay?"

Glancing down, he examines his palms before looking back up. "Not mine."

"Gotcha, well, in that case, get the hell away from me. I don't want someone else's blood on me." I shudder.

A smirk appears and his eyebrow pops up. "But you'd be fine with mine?"

"I didn't…you know what? Just fucking feed me and get me some pills and then send me home. I'm not going to get caught up in whatever scheme you're running over here."

"Let's not pretend you don't know who I am or what I do, Lacey." He says it with such condescension I swear red flashes across my vision, and I black out. It's the only explanation why there's a pillow laying at his feet and he's gaping at me.

"Let's not pretend you're not an asshole, Mason."

I cross my arms with as much dignity as I can muster while stuck flat on my back. Putting on a show for him as I struggle to sit up is not on my agenda today. I can't figure out if he's the asshole I just accused him of being or some benevolent being who saved me from myself.

I wanted so badly to be in their circle. With every passing day, they become closer, more akin to a family, which is something I haven't had in a long time, if ever. I wanted to belong somewhere. Lying to myself was easy when there was a layer between us. I could convince myself that if I just had a chance, they'd see how I fit in.

Fantasizing about Mason being my person, the one who wouldn't care about the internal scars I carry, became my favorite pastime. Now, I know I'm not enough. I never was. I'm meant to live on the outskirts of everyone else's world, content to be on the sidelines. Especially with the way we met, I doubt Mason would see me as anything other than an annoyance—a blip on his radar that will fade from memory as soon as I'm gone. Trading thinly veiled insults isn't enough to build something on, even if he wanted to.

He throws his hands up and retreats to the bathroom, slamming the door behind him. I start singing again, as loudly and obnoxiously as possible, if only to hide the despair burrowing a hole in my chest. The shower starts up, so I really belt it out. I clamp my mouth shut when he rips the door open, a growl in his throat.

I shoot him a false smile that sits on the surface of my face and say, "Can I help you?"

"Would you knock it the fuck off? Someone is going to hear you, then we'll both be fucked," he snarls, going to close the door again.

"Wouldn't complain about that," I mutter, gasping when he's suddenly glaring down at me.

"You think this is some game? Do you suppose someone else would be as nice as I've been? Or do you suppose they would dismantle you, bit-by-bit—tearing apart every piece of your essence only to scatter them in the wind? You think I'm an asshole? I'm nothing compared to others, some of whom are in this very house. I may be keeping you here against your will, but it's as much for your safety as it is for my morbid curiosity as to what the fuck you're up to. Think about the torture you'd be subjected to at another's hands before you start spouting off stupid shit."

Tears spring to my eyes as he stalks away. Pushing away my response, I jump as he slams the door again. A flush spreads across my cheeks and I swipe at my eyes. The quiet permeating the house gave me a false sense of security, thinking no one would hear me even if I screamed at the top of my lungs.

I'm sure as hell not going to tell him I was talking about having sex. I can't even count how long it's been since I've gotten laid. Admitting that to Mason Byrns would be an embarrassment I don't know if I could recover from. With his abs stacked on top of muscles and lean forearms, I'm sure he has no problem pulling girls.

"Do people even call it that anymore?" I whisper, swiping away at the tears.

Rolling to the side, I slide off the bed to my knees, careful to not jostle my ankle. It's not nearly as swollen today, but the bruising covers my entire foot. It looks like my toes are about to fall off. I probably should be at a hospital, but Mason won't take me. Maybe if I fake my own death, he'll try to bury me in the woods, and I could finally get off this rollercoaster of emotions I've been riding since I got here. I sigh, resting my forehead against the mattress.

I don't want to leave. Even now, after the last two days embroiled in a shitshow, I still don't want to leave. Is it Stockholm syndrome if I was stalking him for months before I met him? At this point, I don't know who is more in the wrong. I was fucking with his cameras long before he realized. And he still doesn't know for certain that it was me. I can't even blame him for everything. He didn't mess up my ankle. He has actively tried to make it better, and all he asked was a couple questions.

The shower water cuts off and I groan, rubbing my face into the blankets, hoping to erase the tears from my cheeks. He might not care, but I will. Decisions swirl in my mind and the tension eases from me when I settle on the one thing I need to do. I won't tell him who I am or what I do, but I can twist it just enough that hopefully he'll let me go and I can disappear. I still don't know where I'll go, but that's the least of my worries right now.

"Why is it every time I come into the room, you're sprawled across the floor?"

"Are you dressed or am I going to be subjected to your naked body?" I mumble. My voice is muffled and I'm not sure if he's heard me, but he snorts.

"You wouldn't be in a position to do anything with my body regardless, so I fail to see why it matters." Footsteps echo across the floor and then back a few minutes later.

"Are you decent?" I ask, peeking out to watch him pull a white shirt over his head. "Gray sweatpants? Are you fucking kidding me?"

"They're pants. I wouldn't complain if I were you."

"Not complaining." My voice is quiet enough this time that he doesn't hear me. "I wasn't lost."

My stomach flips as I say the words I'm sure will be my damnation.

"I figured that out already. Tell me why you were there."

"I was just watching the house. Not in a bad way, just because."

"Just because." He says it more like a statement than a question.

I sit back, grunting when my knee pops and I catch his body swaying toward me.

"I mean, okay. I may have been wondering what it was like to live here. It's just very different from where I grew up. I promise I won't do it again. In fact, I'm going to leave Synd altogether. You'll never have to see me again."

The apology sticks in my throat. I can't actually say the words "I'm sorry". It feels too much like an admission of guilt. Technically, other than trespassing, I wasn't doing anything wrong. Spying on a mafia leader isn't exactly great, but it's not against the law. Unless they got me for being a Peeping Tom. But again, I wasn't peering through the windows, watching him undress or anything. A shiver rolls through me at the thought.

"Why?"

"Clearly, I shouldn't stay. I've been meaning to move on, anyway." I bury my flushed face in the comforter again.

"No, the better question is how."

"How?" I ask, scrunching my nose and finally meeting his brown eyes.

"How did you get around my cameras?"

Scrambling to come up with an answer he'll buy, I turn my head away. "Dumb luck, I guess. Seems stupid to assume there wasn't cameras. I thought you would have guys marching around outside to chase away any unwanted people instead of state-of-the-art security systems."

"I said cameras. I didn't say anything about security systems…" he murmurs.

"You have a keypad on your bedroom door. Stands to reason you'd have some security. I told you I'm not exactly that smart."

"I doubt that. Can you walk? Or am I going to have to carry you again?"

I huff. "Where are we going now?"

"You are going back to the other room. I have shit to do," he says, stopping next to my leg.

"Fine. But I need more pain meds. And food. Then can I go home?" I tip my head back and a pang shoots through my chest as our eyes meet.

Shaking his head, he scoops me up. I don't bother resisting. Maybe when my ankle is finally better, he'll let me go, then I can run far away from the what-ifs buried in my time in Synd.

Eleven

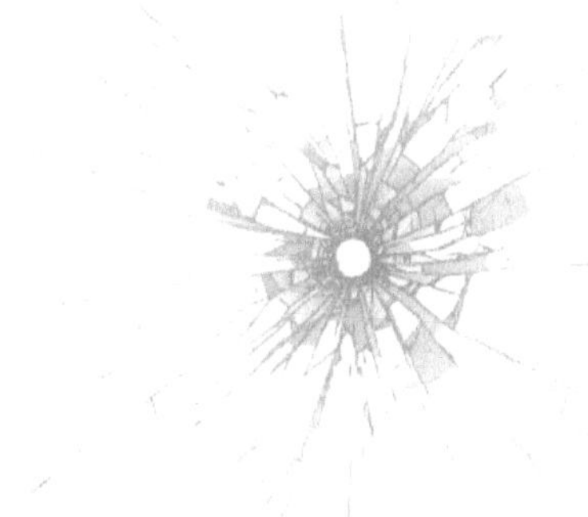

Mason

Ten days since I found Lacey in the woods, spitting mad and fighting like a rabid cat, and I'm once again watching her sleep. I moved her to Sam's old room three days ago. She's right down the hall from my own. The more time I spend with her, the less I'm convinced she has anything to do with the things happening anywhere else in Synd. If she wasn't injured, I would let her go. At least that's what I tell myself. There's still a lot of unanswered questions, though.

The research I was immersed in two weeks ago sits next to me, forgotten. My phone rests on top of the old newspaper articles and random accounts, reminding me every two minutes of the emails and texts I should respond to. Instead, I'm staring at Lacey, who's wincing in her sleep. She's been rustling around, rolling back and forth for the better part of an hour. I've been waiting for the doctor to appear, but he's taking too long.

Running my hands through my hair for the millionth time in the last hour, I glance at the screen again, but it's dark now. My palms tingle, begging me to do something, but there's nothing *to* do other than wait. I fucking hate waiting on others, especially for something like this.

Lacey has progressively gotten worse with every passing minute. Every time she winces, my chest tightens. Leaving her in pain is eating away at me. I'm not being rational. I should take her to the hospital and let them deal with her, but I can't let her go. She doesn't have anyone, and I can't exactly go waltzing through the halls to visit her without someone finding out.

The memory of visiting Sam in the hospital after her car accident six months ago floats to the forefront of my mind. My sister ended up with barely a scratch, but Alex didn't fare so well. I blamed Mac, and by extension, Helms, but it wasn't anyone's fault but the Night Slayers. Thankfully, the rival MC seems to have disbanded, their few remaining members fleeing. I remember the nurse who tried to record us, probably to sell to whatever media they could. Helms and Shane took care of it, but there's something sitting on the edge of my brain I can't recall.

She rustles again, yelping, and I'm out of my chair before I've fully registered the decision. Laying a hand on her forehead, I expect her to be hot, but she's freezing, even with the comforter tucked around her. Throwing another blanket over her body, I make my way to the bathroom to call the doctor. I keep the door cracked just in case Lacey wakes up.

"Where the fuck are you, Sanders?"

"I'm sorry, Mr. Byrns. Your sister called and requested my services with something more urgent."

"What the fuck is going on?" I growl, my stomach flipping.

Scenarios skip through my brain, each more disastrous than the last. We can't afford the shit we have going on. Any more and we'll fold. If Sam called him, then she's safe at least. Small miracles.

"I'm not—"

"Never mind. I'll call her. The one I've got here is cold. What do I do?"

"Excuse me? Mr. Byrns, did you call me because she's cold?"

"Watch it, Sanders. She's fucking freezing. I've got three blankets piled on her and she won't stop shivering," I hiss, rage burning away the anxiety of someone else being hurt.

"It's most likely from the weather you two were caught in. I'm surprised you're not sick. Get her in a warm bath—not hot. Body heat would help too."

I hang up, immediately dialing Sam's number. Muscles bunching with every ring, the line finally connects, but her frantic voice is too far away to understand.

"Byrns, what do you need?" Alex asks, voice laced with tension.

"What the fuck is going on?"

Shouting drowns out his response, followed by a pop of gunfire and my body seizes. I don't freeze up when I hear gunshots like I did after I got out of the hospital, but Sam is wherever they are on the other side of this call. She's clearly in some type of danger, and I'm not there to help.

"Alex!"

"Some fuckers thought it'd be funny to gallivant around the Barrens. Sorry we stole your doc. Ours was dealing with shit down south and yours was the first one to answer."

"Where in the Barrens?"

"Now, Mason, don't get your panties in a twist. We're dealing with shit. No need to come racing in to save the day."

I grind my teeth together, wishing I could reach through the phone and strangle him. "Put my goddamn sister on the phone. Now."

"She's a little busy at the moment keeping someone's intestines inside their body. But she can call you later if you want."

"Fuck," I yell, pacing across the room before I remember Lacey in the other room.

Peeking from the crack, she's still shivering, but her eyes are closed at least, and I start pacing again. Rational thought trickles back in as my bare feet slap across the tiles. Someone would have called me if it was serious. At least, I hope they would. Sam can take care of herself, and Alex wouldn't be so nonchalant if shit were truly going sideways.

I've been so far in my own shit the last couple months, I'm sure they think I'm teetering on the edge of sanity. I haven't given them much to think otherwise. The woman currently suffering in the next room is the only reason I've felt more grounded lately. Finding out who she is and why she's come into my life has consumed my every waking moment. Even when she's not in sight, I can't get her out of my head, wondering what she's doing and why I can't just let her go. I wonder how much other shit I've missed because I've been so wrapped up in my own head.

"You okay there, buddy?" Alex asked, laughter lacing his voice.

"Fuck off, Alex. Have Sam call me."

I wait, listening to Sam's shrill voice yelling in the background. I can't make out her words, and I run a trembling hand through my hair.

"Mason, she's fine," Alex murmurs. "It's not any of us. Just take care of whatever you're dealing with over there."

He hangs up, and I throw the phone across the bathroom. Unfortunately, it doesn't shatter. It bounces, the case protecting it from my wrath. My entire body vibrates as I struggle to pull enough air into my lungs. A thud from my bedroom makes my heart skip a beat.

Sprinting for the door, I see the glass I left on the nightstand tipped over, water spreading across the rug. Lacey's hand drapes over the side of the bed, barely peeking from under the blankets.

"Sorry," she whispers, and my gaze flies to her face.

Tears track down her flushed face and she sniffs, burrowing further under the covers. As I snatch up the glass, she flinches, and I slow, some of the tension bleeding from my body.

"Just water. How you feeling?" I ask, setting the glass on the table and crouching next to the bed.

"I'm fine. What are you—" She clears her throat. "Doing here?"

"You're sick," I murmur.

All the sass and snark from the last few days has fled, leaving misery in its place. Yesterday she was cursing me out for not feeding her. Overnight, all her energy seeped away. An ache has been sitting in my chest ever since. I already decided I wasn't going to stop her from leaving, but now I'm worried she'll die if I let her. I can only imagine what would have happened if she was like this and all alone.

She's still crying, body shaking uncontrollably. "I feel like shit. Make it stop."

"Fuck, you sound pathetic," I mutter, pressing a hand to her forehead to find her burning up now. "Shit."

Curling in on herself, her body shudders as she coughs.

"Let me die in peace. No one needs an audience while they wither away."

"Dramatic much."

Shaking my head, I flip the covers back. She moans, curling into a ball. The splint is still wrapped around her leg and foot, but at least she can stand now. In her current state, I doubt she'd be able to walk to the bathroom.

Gathering her in my arms, I realize how feverish she's become in the last fifteen minutes. Thankfully, Sam insisted on a shower with a huge-ass door, so I don't have to put her down to get into it. Stepping inside, fully clothed, I try not to smack her head against the wall and turn the knobs at the same time.

"Why? I just want to sleep," she whines.

Swinging her up so she's clinging to my shoulders, legs wrapped around my waist, I'm able to get the water going. When I step into the spray, she yelps, burying her face in my neck and a shiver runs through me. The last thing I should be concerned with is her body pressed to mine, but I can't help my reaction. I start listing every annoying thing I can think of about her, all while keeping the water away from her face.

"It's cold," she gasps.

If she had enough strength, she'd probably be crawling over me to get away. Instead, she just shivers. After adjusting the temp, I sway back and forth, waiting for her body to stop shaking.

Twenty minutes later, I'm pretty sure she's asleep, face still tucked into the crook of my neck, hands hanging limply over my shoulders. She's no longer shivering, but my arms are trembling from holding her up.

As I stumble over the threshold of the shower, her legs tighten around me. The list I made up is no longer working, but now I'm more concerned with her becoming cold again. The bath towel hanging on the bathroom door isn't enough to cover both of us, so I rip a blanket from the bed and wrap it around us as best as I can.

Peeling her from my body, I lay her down and run to the closet. I sent Sam's things to her when she moved in with the Kings, but she's been leaving random pieces of clothing behind. Half the time, the only reasons I know she's been here are the snack wrappers in the trash can and a random shirt thrown on the floor. When I moved Lacey into this room, I started stashing my own clothes here, just in case. The irony of the decision isn't lost on me, but I don't want to examine why I've been doing these things. Quickly, I shuck off my wet clothes, pull on sweatpants, and grab another shirt. She's still sprawling across the bed, black hair sticking to her face.

"Lacey," I murmur, cupping her face. "You need to change."

She groans, pressing into my palm. "My foot is wet."

"Put the shirt on and I'll deal with the rest."

Turning my back, I wait for the shuffle of fabric, but nothing comes. When I glance over my shoulder, I find her eyes closed, lips parted, and I sigh. I spend one minute debating whether I should close my eyes before I just do it, peeling the wet shirt from her body and yanking on the dry one. She barely twitches as I do it, rolling over as soon as I'm done. She rolls again when I tug on the blanket, leaving it in a wet pile on the floor. I'll have to deal with it later, but it's the least of my worries.

When I throw the covers back over her, I notice the blue tint to her lips, and a curse falls from my lips. Climbing in next to her, I wrap an arm around her waist, and she burrows into my body. I doubt I'll be able to fall asleep with her pressed against me and with how worried I am that she'll die if I close my eyes, but soon after darkness envelops me.

Twelve

Lacey

*L*acey

The shadows lift slowly, and I burrow further into the heat behind me. My mind skips around, deciphering reality from nightmares. I remember being so cold I thought I'd never be warm again. Once I got my wish, I was blazing hot, with no relief.

Memories come flooding back and my eyes fly open. Sunlight filters through the gap in the curtains. I don't know how long I was out, but it was obviously long enough for my body to fight some of the sickness that had me in its grasp.

Holy fuck, Mason Byrns had to take care of me.

He took a shower with me. Lifting the comforter, I see not only a new black shirt but also Mason's arm wrapped around my waist, keeping my back tucked against him. My skin heats and I shiver. The move makes my muscles cramp, and I'm reminded how much shit I've put my body through the last week. Actually, I don't know what day it is either.

I wiggle and his hand tightens, keeping me in place. I have no idea how he'll react if he wakes up next to me in bed. Honestly, it could go either way. I shimmy again, freezing when he sighs.

"If you keep doing that, we're going to have a whole other set of problems to deal with, Lacey," he murmurs, his breath ghosting across my hair and making me shiver.

I haven't heard my name since I left home, especially devoid of venom. My parents made it a curse, falling from their mouths with such disdain I washed my hands of it as soon as I could. There's something in the way it rolls off his tongue, though, that has heat pooling in my stomach. Maybe I won't hate my name so much if he's the one using it.

"I have to pee," I say, then wince.

I'm woman enough to admit I might have a tiny obsession when it comes to Mason Byrns. I've all but killed any chance I had of winning him over with my stunning personality, which was obviously very fucking slim. Doesn't mean I need to make a fool of myself as the opportunity to win him over dies a slow death in my heart. I've already decided that ship has sailed, no matter how much I wish otherwise.

Even if we had met under normal circumstances, he probably wouldn't have noticed me. The only reason he did at the coffee shop was because the other woman was louder than me.

He groans as he rolls on his back, flinging his arms over his head. As soon as I lift my injured foot, though, I wince again. The bandages are soggy and the splint is heavy. The moisture trapped inside makes me gag. I wish I could rip it off, but the doctor said I needed to keep it on for another couple days.

"What day is it?" I ask, glancing over my shoulder before whipping back around.

He's naked again, covers pulled low on his hips. The white sheets make the tattoos etched into his tanned skin stand out. I've kept my wandering eyes far away from his body the entire time I've been here. I'm proud of the restraint I've had. There were a couple times I thought about indulging in some self-care with him starring in my fantasies, but I've been in too much pain.

I slide to the edge of the bed, hoping I can finally take care of shit myself without his help. A white shirt hangs off the end of the footboard and I glance over my shoulder at him. Eyes still closed, he sucks in a deep breath.

"Saturday. Why?"

It takes a minute to remember what I ask and then process his words. "A week?" I yell.

My mind blanks and I jump to my feet. A sharp pain shoots through my leg, and I crumple to the floor. Mason rolls across the bed, sliding to my side while his hands hover over me as I clutch my foot, tears springing to my eyes.

"What the fuck, woman? He said you could take it off today, not try to run a damn marathon," he snarls.

"I forgot." I can't keep the whimper inside and he sighs.

His arm slides around my waist and he hoists me upright, pressing my back to his chest. It's awkward, hopping while he holds me. I swear I've lost what little strength I had while lying around in bed. Crawling across the floor apparently doesn't count as exercise.

"Would you knock it off? Just stand still." He grunts when I elbow him in the stomach. I didn't mean to, but I can feel his annoyed scowl.

"I don't want to fall," I grumble. "You realize you wouldn't have to deal with this if you would have taken me home, right?"

"Again, who would feed you if you weren't here? Would you even go to a doctor?"

My response is lost in a squeal when he swings me into his arms. I couldn't enjoy this the other times, since I was freaked out and in pain. After the initial shock wore off, I was too embarrassed to revel in the fact I was living in a fantasy, despite my despondency toward the whole thing. Now, I'm just annoyed I can't walk by myself. When he makes his way around the bed, he slips, practically taking both of us down. His arms tighten and my heart leaps into my throat.

The bathroom is just as big as his, and I'm convinced it's Sam's old room. I'm not about to ask him to confirm that, though. Revealing the shit I I know about the Byrns family isn't going to happen. I'm still holding out hope I can get out of this without him figuring out who I am.

"So, you finally believe me then? And once I can walk on my own, you'll send me on my way?" I ask when he sets me gently on my feet on the cool tile.

Another pang hits me at the thought of leaving. His hand lingers on my waist, and I lean into him before I realize what I'm doing. For all the words we've thrown at each other, he's taken care of me, kept me safe even if it was from myself.

"Still planning on skipping town?"

He leans against the sink. When he crosses his arms over his chest, the tattoos meld together, creating a tapestry of ink painted across his flesh. I force my eyes away before I start drooling.

"I don't see how that's any concern of yours." The words are ripped from my mouth and I do what I'm best at—I lash out. "Are you going to leave so I can do my business?"

I'm about two seconds from tipping over as I balance on one foot. I refuse to pee in front of him. In the best of circumstances, I doubt I would use a toilet in front of someone, especially him. He rolls his eyes and the move softens his face. Most of the time, he's scowling. An image flashes across my mind of his concerned face inches from mine, but I don't know if it's real.

"If you're staying in Synd, it's in my best interest to know." Walking toward the door, he stops at the threshold. "Don't fall off the toilet. You'll probably crack your head open or something and I'll have to deal with that, too."

It takes me an embarrassingly long time to do my business. Standing up after is harder than I thought, but my ankle doesn't give out on me when I hobble to the sink. Random toiletries are scattered across the counter.

Sighing, I limp to the door, peeking through the crack. Mason's on the phone, and I strain to hear his one-sided conversation.

"I can't right now. I'll deal with it tonight." He pauses, listen-ing to whoever is on the other end of the line. "You going to tell me what happened last night?"

My leg shakes with the effort of holding me up. Leaning against the wall, I slide to the floor to listen. It's only a matter of time before he reveals something I probably shouldn't hear, but in my line of work, I've become adept at gathering information. Usually it's behind a computer screen, but it's amazing what people will let slip when they forget I'm standing there.

"You can't just tell me not to worry about it, Sam." Another pause. "Well, that makes two of us."

I'm so out of the loop there's no way I can figure out what they're talking about. I wish I had my phone, but I'm pretty sure it's lying forgotten in the woods. I feel like I've lost a limb. Even if Mason went searching for it, he wouldn't be able to find anything damaging. He wouldn't even get it unlocked.

"I have shit I'm dealing with here. And no, you can't do anything to help." Pause. "Just tell Shane to call me. We need to set up a meeting." Pause. "I'm not going to go through all the shit over the phone with you just to turn around and repeat it to Shane. Then all your boyfriends will blow up my phone wanting the same fucking story. I'm not doing it. I have to go." Pause. "Because I actually have things to do, Sam. We'll feed the ducks next week." Pause. "Yeah. Me too."

I jolt when the thud of a fist against the wall echoes through the air. For as much as Mason acts like things are back to normal, they're clearly not. The longer I spend here, the more I realize he's all alone. Maybe the reason he's keeping me here is because he's lonely. I shake away the thought, scoffing to myself. Even if he is lonesome, I'd probably be the last person he'd choose to keep him company.

"Are you done?" Mason bellows, and I jump again.

"Are you going to keep being an ass?"

The door swings open, and I tip my foot just before the edge clips it. Reaching down, I pull at the straps keeping the splint in place. It's halfway off before Mason bats my hands away and finishes the job. The bandages are damp, making me cringe as he peels it away. My flesh is still covered in bruises, but it's not swollen anymore.

Mason starts barking out demands, telling me to turn my foot this way and that. I listen if only to get it over with. I'm hungry. I'm tired. I'm dirty. Not to mention, I really want to leave this room. Being close to him doesn't overwhelm my senses anymore, but when he's kneeling half naked in front of me, my lady business goes off the rails. I keep scolding her but she doesn't listen. She's been hibernating for fucking years, but perks right up around Mason Byrns.

Fingers brush along my arch, and I tamp down the shudder, but I can't help jerking my foot away. His other hand clamps on my leg, holding me still, then pokes and prods at the bruises.

"Do you even know what you're doing?"

Even I can hear the breathlessness in my voice. He freezes, staring at my foot for so long I'm pretty sure he's going to ignore my question. Abruptly, he releases me, pushing to his feet. He backs up so quickly he runs into the counter.

"Get up."

It's harder than I thought it would be, but I finally stumble to my feet. After the last week, I expect him to catch me, but he's a statue, staring at the floor. I want to snap back, but it's not worth it. I'm too out of breath to get into a verbal sparring match with him, anyway.

Leaning against the wall, I splay my hands and my stomach growls. I thump my head back, wishing the ground would swallow me whole. Honestly, it might have been better if he'd have shot me when he found me in the woods. Everything would have been a lot easier for both of us.

Clearly, between snuggling up to me in bed and now, he's come to his senses. My chest tightens as the last ember of hope that he cared winks out. Despite knowing it was a razor-thin chance, it was still there, resting right next to my heart, that I would be enough for him to choose. I should have done more to keep my distance.

"Now, get out," he growls, sending a flush to my cheeks.

Limping as fast as I can from the bathroom, I almost jump out of my skin when the door slams shut behind me. I could leave right now. I found the secret tunnel two days ago, but I wasn't in the position to crawl around in the dark trying to find a way out.

The blueprints I found for both estates didn't include the schematics for the pathways twisting inside the walls. Knowing my luck, I'd miss the exit and end up right back where I started. Or in someone else's room, like Victor Smith.

I've never had any interaction with him, but I watched the havoc he caused when the Guild swept through. After Mason came home from the hospital, Victor laid low, but before I was caught, small things started popping up. I'd put cash money on the fact he's up to something, and I doubt it's good for either mafia family in Synd. I'd already been organizing in my mind how to inform Ren of what I found.

The shower starts and I jolt, tearing myself back to reality. Staying here one more day won't hurt anything other than myself. All things considered, it's probably the wisest decision, even with the threat of Mason discovering my identity. For all my complaints of wanting to go home, I want to steal as much time here with him as possible. My wishy-washy attitude toward the whole situation is going to be my demise.

Collapsing on the bed, I resign myself to another day of staring at the same four walls, wishing we lived in a world where Mason and I could meet, fall in love, and live happily ever after like normal people.

I sigh, realizing that's a dream that will never come true.

Thirteen

Mason

"Let's get on with this. I need to get home," I grumble.

"Got a hot date, Byrnsie?" Alex asks, his laughing green eyes finding mine from across the conference table.

"Shut the fuck up, Alex. Not all of us can sit around all day schmoozing rich bitches at parties."

Shane clears his throat and I huff, tucking my chin to my chest. We've been stuffed in this room for almost three hours. We're not accomplishing anything important, but at least Sam isn't perched on someone's lap this time around. I just want to get shit over with so I can get home and deal with Lacey.

Her fever is gone and her ankle isn't swollen, so I can let her go whenever I feel like it. I was blinded by her injuries before—lulled into complacency. I thought I had her figured out, but with her no longer at death's door, I'm able to see things more clearly. I don't think she used her injuries to distract me from her real agenda, but she might have used it to her advantage.

Sleeping next to her last night was a mistake. I justified my actions because she was sick, but when it comes down to it, I wanted to. I've used her presence to combat my solitude. The gravity of what I've done didn't hit me until I had my hands on her under the guise of checking her ankle. Her reaction to my nearness finally cleared the fog from my mind.

The issues in the south are creeping further north. I thought they were isolated incidents, but I can't ignore what's going on anymore. Lacey could be the distraction while someone tries to dismantle the Byrns family bit by bit, but every time the thought crosses my mind, it doesn't sit right.

I wouldn't put it past someone to use a beautiful woman to further their own plot. Hell, most people would probably say I did the same to Sam whenever I paid her to be the Wraith for us. Shame seeps into me, realizing how blinded I was when it came to my sister. After a while, I stopped asking her if she would take a job and started expecting her to. I had a ready-made explanation that I was running half the city, but that's no excuse. Repeating my mistakes won't do any good. It's doubtful Lacey is in the same position. Either way, there's nothing to point to her being the mastermind behind all our problems.

"If you want to get this over with, perhaps you should actually pay attention, Mason." Ren's low voice rolls over the silence that's fallen, and I snap my gaze up, finding them all staring at me.

"We've been here for three hours. We're not accomplishing anything, anyway. I can't give you information I don't have. I want to know where the fuck your hacker fucked off to and what's going on with your shipments. And where the fuck is Helms?" I glance around the room, smashing my knee on the table, and I curse. "What the hell is this fucking table?"

Ducking underneath, I find extra planks, buttons, and random hinges. Alex's face appears as he leans under the table, his usual grin firmly in place, and he wiggles his eyebrows.

"Don't ask questions you don't want the answers to, Byrnsie," he chuckles, and a shudder runs through me. I don't even want to think about the meaning behind that warning or the purpose of this conference table.

"Nemesis is none of your concern. Our shipments are going missing again. Lots of empty trucks, bullet holes in the side, and no sign of product or men. It's starting to disrupt the chain. The Barrens are getting hit and no one can figure out where they're coming from. It's random and deadly. One of our lower gangs went missing..." Shane tips his head back, fingers digging into his hair.

I catch the concerned look Sam shoots Shane before she ducks her head, burying her face back in her phone. She's barely said two words during the meeting, opting to text most of the time. She's not even snacking, which is probably the most concerning part.

Our conversations lately have been easier, closer to what we had before, but they're still stilted. It took me too long to realize that we need to talk about what happened in the basement at home. The conversation is coming and it'll either repair our relationship or completely break us apart. She's tried a couple times to bring it up in a roundabout way, but neither of us were ready for it—not really. The last discussion we had she skirted around the topic, tripping over her words, then changed the subject. I wouldn't even know where to start bridging the gap anymore.

Jealousy curls in my gut, but I force my face into a blank mask. They all came together, bonded through tragedy, and built something without me. I don't need to be accepted by them to run my territory. Closing my eyes, I realize I want to be. The more time that passes, the more I know that's probably not going to happen.

Pulling myself from my thoughts and my eyes from my sister, I notice everyone else is staring at me again. My mind skips back to what Shane said, picking apart the various things I can actually deal with.

"Wait. What about the lower gangs?" I ask, straightening.

"One of them is missing. No one in the river. Just gone. We've got a couple guys looking, but it seems like they've defected," Shane says with a scowl.

"Defected? Not to me. Doubt they'd go to Helms. Hell, he'd probably float them just for asking," I say.

"They're not in Reaper territory," Sam chimes in, still buried in her phone.

She's probably texting MacKenzie, Helms's woman. Mac coming back to Synd after ten years shouldn't have affected us down here, but then another MC showed up, demanding her back as if she was their property. Their conflict bled over, making it all our problem to deal with. The ensuing shitshow demolished a lot of Reaper territory, but it helped bring us even closer together.

We didn't use to meet like this. Meetings were maybe once a year and fraught with tension. We may not have seen each other as rivals, but the media's portrayal of the relationship between our families tinged each gathering with stress, not to mention the way our fathers interacted with each other. Our families weren't always like that, but something happened a while before the attempted coup. I've been trying to dig up the why for the last month but found nothing so far.

"One of our warehouses got hit. No one killed. We've got shit going down, too. Any whispers of the Guild creeping back in?" I may not have been present when they swept through, but the Kings have told me enough to know this isn't their usual way of taking over a city.

"Probably terrorizing another city. Thought they were in Rima, but you know how quiet they are in the beginning. They've laid low since their failed attempt here. We need to wrap up our current problems, though. Higher ups are taking notice and starting to bitch," Shane says.

"Tell Grayson to suck my dick. He's pissing me off. You know he tried to get me to give a goddamn speech at the last charity thing? I had to fake explosive diarrhea to get him off my ass." Alex rolls his eyes.

"Sam?" Ren murmurs, face buried in his tablet and her head pops up. "Perhaps you would be best at dealing with him."

"He's harmless. I already had a little talk with him," she says, dismissing us again.

"When was this?" Shane growls.

I push to my feet. I won't get caught in the middle of the spat they're clearly about to have. Sam scrunches her nose, pulling a bag of candy from the front pocket of her hoodie.

"Sam, text me what Grayson had to say. I'll do some more digging, see if I come up with anything," I say.

Shane rounds the table, leaning into Sam's space, and they start a heated whispering match.

"Mason," Ren mutters, gesturing me out the door, leaving the other three to deal with whatever argument is about to ensue.

"I don't have anything more, Ren. I'm getting to it."

"Contrary to popular belief, I care about things other than business, Byrns," he says, stormy eyes finding mine as we make our way down the hall.

"I *didn't* think that, but go on."

He's quiet until we reach the front door, and I itch to sprint to my car parked in the driveway. I've been gone long enough, Lacey's probably bemoaning how her stomach is eating itself.

Shaking my head, I push her from my mind. There's no reason I should be rushing home to her. She's not mine. Lacey doesn't even belong in my world. I fucking kidnapped her, for fuck's sake. And besides, I've already settled on her being aligned with whoever is messing with us. Even in my own head, it's a hollow statement. It's like I'm trying to convince myself she's the villain in my story. It's not working.

"Victor has been quiet, but I believe he's biding his time. Also, I'm concerned about your security. I believe it might be time you removed Victor, at least from your household. If you'd like one of us to take care of it instead, let me know."

"I'm dealing with him," I mumble, knowing damn well I'm putting it off. Handing the task off to one of the Kings feels like a cop-out.

"Deal with it sooner rather than later, so we don't run into another situation," he warns. "You need to choose a second. We'd rather not have to step in if something happens to you."

"I'm working on it. Not many clamoring for the job."

He gives me a look, and I glance away. We both know I'm skirting around the truth. There's no one I trust enough to put as my second. Sam would be my choice, but with her across the city leaving her old life behind, I have to find someone else.

I should have made her my second over Colin all those years ago, but I doubt she would have taken the job. Plus, she wasn't trained enough to do the job. Back then, even Sam would have argued that Colin was the better choice. Blaming my best friend is an excuse. No one could have predicted he would fall off the deep end, fucking our entire world in the process. It doesn't help that I never wanted to put a target on Sam's back. I've spent my entire life protecting her however I can, but it's never enough.

"I understand that, but perhaps at least a third. We need someone other than Victor fucking Smith to take over should you need a break," Ren says, turning away.

"I don't need a break, fucker. I'm capable of running my side of the river," I call after him.

"Perfect. You can start any time, then."

He disappears from view, and I pull the door shut, scowling. I don't drive myself often these days. It's more of a hassle than anything. More often than not, I'm being carted to and from a gala or meeting I never wanted to attend in the first place. I take the long way home, just to prove to myself I'm not rushing back to *her*.

Crossing the river to the south of the city as the sun sets, I slow, taking in the destruction of our warehouse. Shattered windows and pockmarked concrete are the only signs something went down here. Thankfully, I got here early enough to waylay the police. The chief tried to cajole me into letting them come down, but he still had enough sense to listen when I told him to fuck off.

The next neighborhood over is even darker than the Barrens. No one lives down there, not even squatters. It's a dead space. The residents of the Barrens gathered closer to the center of the city when the Guild came through, so this area has been empty for the past year.

I catch a glimpse of light, deep within the buildings, close to the river, but it winks out as I blink. Now that the Guild has been pushed out, it's possible people are wandering back in.

My phone buzzes as I wind through the suburbs, but I keep driving. The last thing I need is to deal with another crisis, especially while I'm driving. As I pull into the driveway, I'm met with Moss's scowling face. He crosses his arms, leaning against the fountain. The urge to keep circling and blast back into the city rolls over me, but I park, pushing from the car.

As much as I want to avoid whatever shitshow Moss is about to clue me in on, I need to check on Lacey. She wasn't exactly pleased when I left her this morning. Placating her with a couple books I found didn't work. Hopefully, the snacks I had delivered did the trick instead.

"What is it, Moss?"

"Couple things, boss, and you're not going to like any of them," he warns, glancing around.

"Get on with it. I need a shower and dinner." I copy his stance, leaning against the hood of the car.

"More activity in the south. Some weird shit is going down."

"I was just there. Everything was quiet."

"It's more on the King's side, but whoever it is, they're bleeding into the Barrens."

My mind skips back to the light I saw in the dead zone. I wouldn't think anything of it usually, but stacked with everything else, it feels like more than a coincidence.

He's staring at me with an expectant look.

"What else?"

"Something happened earlier. I had a couple of the new guys on the north side of the house. Not much activity up there. They didn't check in. The cameras went down on the west side and then the fire came, surrounded the eastern side of the forest, but there wasn't a fire. False call."

"For fuck's sake. Why the fuck didn't you call me?" I bark out, stomping toward the house.

Moss calls my name, but I keep going. Someone is fucking with us, and I don't have time to hear his excuses.

"Goddammit, Mason. Just fucking stop," he yells, voice echoing through the night air. He's never raised his voice to me, understanding the hierarchy within our organization. Moss has always been respectful, loyal almost to a fault. I spin, more out of shock than anything else.

"What?"

"The girl you've had holed up there?"

Ice flows through my veins. I thought I'd kept her presence from everyone. Leave it to Moss to know and not say a fucking word. I don't acknowledge his words, neither confirming nor denying Lacey's existence.

"Boss, she's gone."

Fourteen

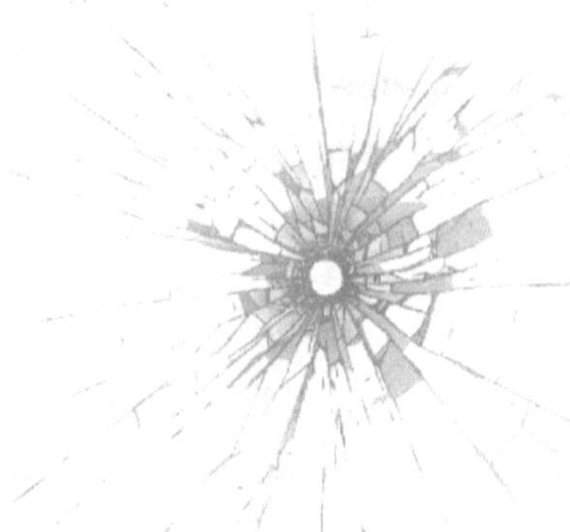

I'm glad Mason gave me sweatpants. They're the only thing keeping me warm at this point. Although, with the rain rattling the tin roof high above me, I doubt it'll last long. After two days down here, the fabric is caked in mud from the hole. I don't imagine they dug it themselves. The men who grabbed me don't seem the type to do manual labor. I spotted a pile of dirt before they tossed me down here, a shovel stuck in it as if they'd just finished.

Mason's words seep into my brain, that he was a much more benevolent captor than others. I should have listened. After his reaction in the bathroom and then leaving me alone for the rest of the night, I couldn't take it anymore. I should have stayed put. Instead, I decided to make my escape through the tunnels. I swear I bumbled around in the dark for hours, winding around corners and tripping down stairs that came out of nowhere.

When I finally found a door to the outside, I was immediately met by the grinning face of a man who looked like he wanted to eat me. The snarky comment he made about this being his lucky day was a little much, but it barely phased me, seeing as how this is exactly how my fortune has been recently. I was in no condition to run, especially after the workout I gave my freshly healed ankle. I wouldn't have made it to the trees, anyway.

A bag was shoved over my head, zip ties were lashed around my wrists, and I was carted off to this shithole. It's literally a shithole now since I've been peeing in the far corner. The smell mingles with the dirt, invading my nose, and I bury my face into my arm. Mason's scent has long-since vanished from the fabric of the shirt he stuck me in. Its loss is almost as painful as the throbbing of my ankle.

Clumps of dirt rain down on my head and someone barks out a laugh. Glancing up, I track the hunk of bread someone tosses over the edge. It thumps at my feet, and I snatch it up before they can cover it with more mud. The first night I tried to scramble up the sides when I thought they were sleeping. The walls crumbled in my hands. I barely made it off the ground, much less the eight feet it would have taken to crawl out of here.

"Wouldn't want our little hostage to starve," a gravelly voice calls and the others laugh.

I've counted five of them so far, although I'm sure there are others. No one's stepped up as the leader yet, which probably should worry me, but a numbness has seeped into my mind. I expected questions, but all I've been met with is taunting.

If they think someone is coming to get me, they'll be sorely mistaken. Maybe they think they can ask for ransom, but they don't know who to ask. They did take me from Mason's house, so they probably demanded it from him, and he said no. I wouldn't expect him to. We don't know each other. Not really. Spending two weeks together in a semi-hostile situation doesn't mean he'll come for me.

Wiping off the bread as best I can, I rip off a small chunk and shove it in my mouth. It's hard and tastes like sawdust, but I'm not about to starve myself. This is only the second piece of bread I've received. I probably should only eat half, but my stomach is cramping. A small water bottle I've been trying to conserve is tucked under my shirt, half full. I've given up trying to figure out how long ago my last real meal was, especially since Mason served it to me.

An ache rumbles in my chest, and I stuff the last piece in my mouth, chewing slowly. He's the only thing on my mind lately. My life was filled with a whole lot of nothing before we were thrown together. Reliving the last two weeks is the only thing that's kept me from breaking down.

"She's too quiet," one of them murmurs. "Should we ask?"

"No, wait for Razor."

I snort, covering the sound with my arm. Most of the people in the lower gangs pick their own nicknames and the fact he picked that one is ridiculous. He probably thinks he stumbled onto something there. I almost dismiss him as a threat until I remember I'm still at the bottom of a muddy hole dug in a metal lean-to shed with no hope of escape.

"I'm sick of waiting for Razor. Why is he even in charge?"

"Because he's the one who knows how to get a hold of Drake. Don't worry. We'll be rewarded. Maybe he'll even give us a taste before he deals with her."

A shudder runs through me, revulsion threatening to expel the bread I just ate. This exact conversation happens almost every night, with various players swapped out. The answer is always the same—wait for Razor—whoever the fuck he is. I haven't seen him, or at least he hasn't introduced himself. I don't know whether or not to be worried about that.

Rolling my neck, I try to ease the tension in my shoulders, and my greasy hair falls over my face. I wish I had a hair tie. I wish I had a toilet. Hell, if I'm wishing for things, I might as well wish my way out of here. Part of me still hopes someone will stumble upon us. I don't know exactly where we are, but it's probably not in Synd. The noise from the city's traffic is nonexistent, even when the rain isn't thrashing against the metal.

A phone blares over the storm and one of them steps away. I should probably figure out their names, but I can't be bothered. Thankfully, I've been able to detach myself from the fear that should be engulfing me. They haven't done much other than throw me down here and not feed me enough. I can ignore their jeers and threats.

That's enough, the voice in my head murmurs. Swallowing hard, I pull out the water bottle to take a sip. Soon enough, the despair will crash through me and I'll lose it, but it won't be tonight. I've made it this far without breaking down. After two days, though, I wonder how long I'll have to stay strong.

"Oh little mouse, are you stuck down there? Should I help you get out?" someone jeers.

I don't even bother to look up. They'd probably try to kick dirt in my eyes again.

There's a grunt and I peek at them as a shovelful of dirt cascades through the air. I duck, but it lands on my head. Dropping the water bottle, I curse, scrambling to get it before all the liquid runs out. There's only a mouthful left, but I slam the cap on, anyway.

"Oh, did you drop your water? So sad."

Gritting my teeth, the need to mock him rides me hard. It's like he's parroting bad movie lines, spewing them at me as if they'll upset me. I refuse to let them get to me. Mouthing off the first day didn't go well. I spent so much time with Mason not caring whether I snapped at him, I did it without thinking.

Another clump of dirt hits my back and I bow my head. Wrapping my arms around my legs, I strive to make myself as small as possible, but it doesn't do anything. Dirt continues to rain down on my body and a sob crawls up my throat. Shuffling closer to the edge doesn't help. When I stand, a rock hits me in the head and I finally break, crying out as I crash to my hands and knees.

Raucous laughter drowns out his voice, but I'm sure he's spouting more bullshit. Blood trickles down my temple. Crawling to the far edge, I curl into a ball as they bury me alive. I don't know how long it lasts, but tears stream down my face. Sinking my teeth into my arm, I hold back the scream begging to be let out.

I thought I could handle being in this hellhole, but my sanity is slipping in the wake of my imminent death. I can taste it in the dust coating the back of my throat. It shimmers around me, threatening to pull me into a black void of nothingness. Dying always seemed like a far-off thing I didn't need to concern myself with. Yet here I am, counting my breaths, wondering which one will be my last.

A crack of thunder rattles the metal high above my head, then the night falls silent. I hesitate, too afraid to lift my head. I'm convinced as soon as I do, another clump of mud will be flung at my face. After what feels like forever, I peek out of the safety of my arms. No one is there. The handle of the shovel lies just on the edge, as if he threw it down and bolted.

Sitting up, I brush the clumps from my lap before standing. I tip my head back, searching for any sign of life. Maybe they were scared of the thunder and ran. Eyeing the handle, I contemplate whether I'm strong enough to jump for it. With my luck, I'd end up breaking my ankle for real. Maybe they've left me here to die of starvation. My stomach cramps at the thought, and I wrap my arms around my middle, curling into my body.

"Dead yet?" A voice rings out, tinged with laughter.

Straightening, I back into the wall. There's not enough room to run from him in this small space. I've only seen this one once before, the day I was taken. His grin held a cruel edge that still rests there. Out of all the men who took me, this is the one I fear the most. His scarred face holds a history of violence I never want to learn.

"Still nothing to say? Too bad. Maybe I could have helped you, had you only asked."

Pressing my lips together, I stare at him. I refuse to fall into his trap. I'm sure he'd help me from this prison and then torture me or...

I cut off the thought, not wanting to even imagine the horrors this man would engage in. It's too much for my mind to handle. I've survived by assuming that they're a ragtag group of men who don't really know what they're doing. Latching onto their "boss," whoever he is, as the villain allows me to tamp down my terror. If they're not the ones I have to worry about, I can get out of this hole and escape. I'll run as far as I can, never stopping.

My ankle gives out and I wobble, sinking to my knees. Even if I could escape, I doubt I'll be running. They'd catch me long before I reach any semblance of safety.

A cloth sack lands in front of me. My skin itches just imagining it over my head again. Glancing up, I catch the man's dark eyes as he raises an eyebrow. The rain eases, settling into a pitter patter against the roof.

"Put it on. We're moving."

He walks away, and the rumble of a vehicle echoes through the night. I don't know how they're going to get me out of here. When they caged me, they threw a rope over the edge. I could have refused, but I'm sure one of them would have pushed me. I'm weak from lack of food, barely enough water to survive, and being in a fucking hole for what feels like forever. Even in the best of times, I doubt I'd be able to climb a rope.

The man appears again, gripping a ladder. He scowls when he spots me staring up at him.

"Put the hood on or I'll leave your ass here to rot, no matter what anyone else wants. Or maybe I'll just shoot you instead."

He sets the ladder down, pulling a gun from behind his back. When he points it at me, I flinch. Sucking in a deep breath, I pull the hood over my face. How the hell am I supposed to see the ladder when my face is covered? He probably didn't think that far ahead. The night fills with a rattling clang, and I stumble upright.

Cool metal bites into my palms and I start to ascend, peering from the bottom of the sack to place my bare feet firmly on the rungs so I don't slip. I swear it takes me five minutes and then rough hands snatch at my wrists, hauling me up. He doesn't wait for me to get my bearings or get my feet under me, electing to drag me along, muttering all the while.

Twisting my arm, I attempt to free myself, but the frigid barrel of his gun presses into my neck. Every muscle in my body locks up, panic overriding any rational thought.

"You run, I shoot you. You scream, I shoot you. You do anything to piss me off, I shoot you. Understand?" he growls in my ear, hot breath through the fabric making my skin crawl.

Swallowing hard, I push down the nausea, letting it rest next to the terror and despair. He gives me a little shake before I'm stumbling along next to him again. I almost cry out when my shins crash into metal, then cough as the exhaust fumes choke me.

He shoves me hard, and I barely catch myself before more hands seize my arms, dragging me inside. Rope digs into my skin as they lash my wrists together. A door slides shut, and I tuck myself into the corner. There aren't any seats in the van, at least none that I've crashed into when I was in here before.

As we start to move, it hits me how doomed I really am. I should have let him shoot me. I should have run when I had the chance. My arms were free, the hood a small barrier between me and sight. That small opportunity I let slide by because I was too afraid. Even though I should have known it was my only chance, because no one is coming to save me. And I just blew my moment to save myself.

Fifteen

Mason

Frustration bleeds through me, seeping into my bones and making me question everything. Throwing my phone down, I grip the back of my neck. I've been searching for Lacey for nearly a week, but there's no sign of her. She's disappeared into the bowels of Synd, and I've barely kept my rage in check since. I slam my hand on the desk, sucking in a deep breath to calm down. Shaking my head, I turn on the computer, hoping someone found something I missed.

Moss keeps harping on me, questioning whether she was rescued or kidnapped. I admit it's a little too coincidental—catching her skulking around my house, spying on what we're doing, then vanishing two weeks later. Rage and doubt are my constant companions. I should have kept my guard up, kept a better eye on her, or put someone else in charge of keeping an eye on her. I never would have been able to put her in the basement holding cell deep below the foundation of the Byrns' mansion.

I haven't been there since I stumbled upon Sam about to cut Colin's throat. I didn't know Colin had aligned with the

Guild, selling us out to spur me into overthrowing the Kings. I didn't know we were no longer fighting for the same side. I didn't know my second had threatened and kidnapped her. But I trusted my sister, as I always have. I chose her in that moment, and I don't regret it. I never have. Sam seems to think I feel some sort of guilt, or blame her for his actions, but all I taste when I think of him is betrayal. I hold plenty of guilt for other shit, but not because of him.

Even if I could have stomached going down to the holding cell, I never would have put Lacey down there. From the beginning, my gut told me she wasn't a threat. I tried to convince myself she was, but it never felt right. Regardless, unearthing her secrets became my obsession, driving me toward some purpose I still can't define. Now I'm a jumbled mess, searching for an explanation for her disappearance.

Moss thinks I'm lying to myself, chasing after an illusion of who I want her to be instead of who she actually is—a traitor. Even if she fucked me over, the worst I'll be able to bring myself to do is send her away. I've made it clear to Moss that no one touches her. Though if she's spilling vital information to our enemies, we're going to have more problems.

I pull up the cameras, switching over to code to search for discrepancies. I can decipher just enough to be dangerous, but rely heavily on Ren and Nemesis for these types of things. The hacker hasn't been answering my texts, the last message mocking me every time I open our thread. Reaching out to Ren isn't an option I want to explore. He'll spill to Sam, who will suddenly be ridiculously interested in my affairs, which will bleed over to the others. Too many people already know about Lacey's existence, and I refuse to be forced to explain myself about why I'm so set on finding her.

Scrolling down, my eyes snag on a string of numbers that don't belong. Something is blocking the camera feed from around the time Lacey vanished. I'm afraid if I delete it, the entire footage will disappear. This is my last hope of figuring out what happened. Short of sweeping the whole city, there's not much more I can do without some sort of tip coming in.

The door to my office bursts open and I flinch as Alex strolls in, kicking it shut behind him.

"What's up, buttercup?" He collapses in the chair across from me, grinning per usual.

"I'm a little busy, Alex."

"Course you are. Might have some intel for you, though, so whenever you're ready."

He folds his hands over his stomach and gazes out the window, as if he's perfectly content to wait. I've never known him to be anything other than overflowing with energy. Most of the time, he's bouncing in his seat when he has something to say. Today, he tips his head back as his eyes fall closed.

"You're not taking a nap in my office."

"Seem to me like I already am," he murmurs.

Rolling my eyes, I focus on the screen in front of me. I flip to the cameras, squinting at the screen as I lean in close to search for anything I've missed before. Guards patrol on the edge of the property. My car pulling out of the driveway is barely visible. Nothing is amiss.

I sigh, skipping the footage back to the beginning, searching every angle on the north side of the house. All of them cut out at the same time, flickering back on after five minutes. I haven't found anything on the ones positioned on the west side. I have no doubt they slipped into the tree line at the back, so I'm grasping at straws now.

Going back to the code, I highlight the section I'm contemplating taking out. Alex's hand shoots across the desk, hitting the delete button before I can stop him.

"What the fuck, King," I cry, leaning back from the desk as I wait for the entire program to crash.

"Seemed like you needed a push."

I return to the cameras, my heart thudding rapidly in my chest. I skip ahead to where they previously cut off and relief floods me as it plays through. Guards run toward the front of the house, and though there's no sound, I can almost hear the alarms ringing through the air.

"What's that?" Alex says from directly behind me.

"Would you back the fuck off?" I snarl.

I contemplate elbowing him in the stomach, but he'd probably just laugh. Still, I rewind the footage, pausing when he jabs at the screen.

"I don't know what you're pointing at," I grumble, tilting my head as I study the frozen image.

"That's hair, right? Or maybe a dog? Could be a squirrel, but black ones aren't usually found around here." He leans over my shoulder, tapping the keyboard, and the frame skips. "What's that?"

"Shit," I mumble, starting the sequence over.

Ice flows through my veins, numbing my body. When I loop it for a third time, I realize my hands are trembling, and I clench them into fists. It's not much to go on, but Alex is right. At the edge of the frame, black hair with a streak of red whips around. A few seconds pass before someone's elbow pops onto the screen. Another couple seconds pass and a hooded head tips into view.

Lacey was kidnapped. From my home. She must have found the secret tunnel tucked away in Sam's bedroom. Unless someone from the inside helped. It doesn't matter. She was stolen away, in broad daylight, and I wasn't here to save her. Regardless of how we started, I failed to protect her. Overwhelming guilt gathers in my chest, threatening to suffocate me. It's a familiar feeling, reminding me of all the people I've let down over the last year.

Alex slaps my back, jolting me back to reality. "Breathe, man."

Pushing back my chair, Alex grunts when I run into him. I slam my laptop shut before rushing for the door, intent on finding Moss. He's the only one who knows about Lacey, and I need more men to help me find her.

Alex skids in front of me, holding his hands out. "Whoa, Byrnsie."

"Don't fucking call me that. And get out of my way. I have shit to deal with."

"I realize you have some squirrel hunting to do, but I swear this is important."

"Make it fast," I snarl as my palms itch to throw him out of my way.

"Okay, so, I caught sight of Victor. He was meeting with someone in the alley behind L'endroit Chic."

"You realize that just means 'the fancy place' in French, right?"

He grins. "I'm well aware. Anyway, I couldn't get a good look at the other guy because I got a call from a contact in the Barrens. Someone is moving down in no-man's-land. Looks like they're trying to take over some old office buildings, maybe a warehouse or two. I think it's the same people who have been fucking with our shipments."

"Why the hell are you telling me instead of Shane?" I ask, shifting from one foot to the other.

I wish I could throw his ass out, but I'm still trying to play nice. The vise around my heart squeezes the longer I stand here. I've wasted too much time going back and forth on whether she was taken or she turned on me. My thoughts turn dark, imagining everything they could be doing to her. Lacey found every single button I have and mashed them all at once. I can only hope they haven't broken her so badly she'll never call me out on shit again.

Alex's hand lands on my shoulder. "Mason, it's on your side of the river. That's why I came to you."

I nod slowly, my vision unfocused as I piece together all the information. Something is still eluding me. Finding all the pieces will be a bitch, but Lacey is my top priority right now.

"I'll deal with it," I say, and Alex gives me a look. "Don't. I said I'll fucking deal with it, and I will. Now, get the hell out of my way."

He steps aside, opening the door as he goes. I practically run into TJ, who's loitering in the hall. I gesture for him to follow me, trusting that Alex can find his own way out. A year ago, I never would have let him wander around my house. Hell, even a week ago I wouldn't, but only so he wouldn't stumble upon Lacey.

I shove out the front doors, contemplating if the two incidences are connected. Stopping at the back corner of the guard shack, I wait until Alex drives past us, waving like he's in a parade. Scowling, I catch Moss's eye through the window, and he sends the younger guy with him on rounds.

"Boss, Ren King was here. Said there's some activity on the south side."

"Alex just told me," I say.

"This is beyond the city limits in the forest down there. One of their guys was running a shipment and spotted a van on the road to the old substation. Might be linked to your girl," Moss says.

My stomach flips at his words, even as I remember that she's not truly mine. I may be planning on rescuing her, but after that she'll want to run for the hills, I'm sure. This kind of life isn't easy.

I glance at TJ, who wisely keeps his mouth shut. Shaking my head, I try to erase those thoughts from my mind, but they're lodged in now. I don't know her. Half the time I thought she was in league with the people fucking with us. We don't have a future, which is exactly as it should be.

"I need some guys—the more experienced and loyal, the better."

A little of the tension bunching my muscles eases as they both nod. If I didn't have them to rely on, I would have given up a long time ago.

"How many?" TJ asks, pulling his phone from his pocket.

"A dozen. I want to keep this as quiet as possible. I don't know what we'll find when we get there."

"We going to the Barrens?"

I nod, watching as TJ's fingers fly over the screen. "We're moving tonight."

"Might have a problem with that," TJ mumbles, and I raise an eyebrow. "We have that big shipment of weapons coming in to make up for the ones that have gone missing. We've got most of the guys down at the Depot to receive it. I can pull them, but then we run the risk of someone else snatching them—again."

"Plus, pulling off whatever operation you have in mind might take time. I'd rather take an extra day than walk into a trap," Moss adds, crossing his arms.

Frustration rolls through me, and I shake out my hands. Weighing the risks between saying fuck it and going tonight, or waiting is harder than I would have thought. I can't allow more supplies to be stolen. We're already short as it is, with shipments being waylaid left and right. But them moving Lacey to another location terrifies me. The longer she's in their hands, the more she suffers—the more opportunity they have to pull information from her in the worst ways possible. There are too many variables to do both.

"Pull Rigger and send him to me. Tomorrow at nightfall we move." I track TJ as he pivots, starting back for the house.

"Problem, Boss?" my head of security asks.

"I'm sending Rigger to check out the south side. I have a hunch whoever took her was moving her to no-man's-land."

Moss leans against the side of the building, tucking his chin to his chest. I can practically hear the gears turning in his head. Usually, I respect the process, appreciating that he takes time to think through each scenario. Now, I'm two seconds away from walking. After so many months of stagnation, I finally have a purpose. The desire to do something, anything, is hounding me.

"It still may be a trap," he says gruffly.

"I'm well aware."

He raises an eyebrow before glancing at my hands, balled into fists at my sides. Uncurling my fingers, I shove them into my pockets. It hits me that I'm waiting for his permission. I haven't felt this way since I was eighteen, so unsure of myself as I begged my men to follow me. I spent so long convincing them I was fit to lead and I'm right back where I started. It's why I let Victor do so much in the beginning. I'm paying the price for those decisions now. I didn't have experience before, but I do now.

I clear my throat, narrowing my eyes at him. "We're moving tomorrow, regardless of whether it's a trap. I need answers, and she's the only lead I have."

Moss snorts, shaking his head. "Sure, Boss. Whatever you say."

Stalking back to the house, I don't bother to respond. The words would stick in my throat, anyway. He'd see right through me if I denied his assumptions. Agreeing with his silent accusations isn't something I'm prepared to do.

I should just let her go, leave her to whatever fate she's destined for. In the grand scheme of things, she's a small part, but in the last two weeks, she's wormed her way in. I'm riding a razor-thin blade between saving her for my own selfish reasons and breaking the choke hold she has on my mind. Before I make any rash decisions, I have to talk to her.

The only reason I'm so wired to find her is to discover what she's told them. Glancing back at Moss, I find his eyes still on me and I realize I'm not fooling either one of us.

Sixteen

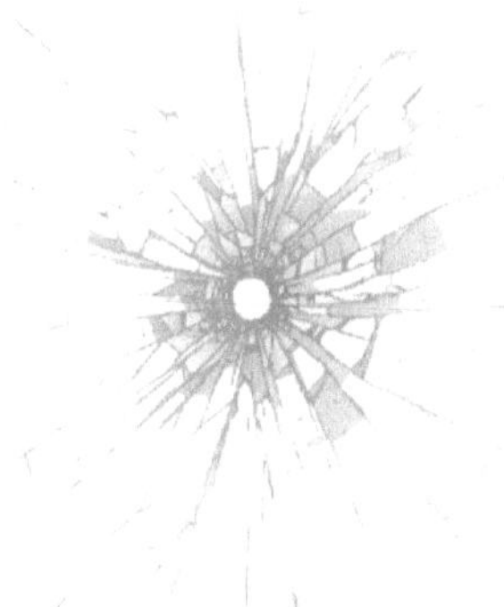

Lacey

My body won't stop trembling. Pain radiates up my leg, but I've mostly ignored it. I'm more concerned with the fact I can't stop shaking. It's not that cold in here, though with the sun dropping, I'm sure I'll freeze again. I just got over whatever infection I had when I was caught by Mason and now my body is battered and bruised all over again. This time it might actually put me in the ground.

Fear trickles down my spine, filling up my pores one by one. I didn't realize what true darkness was until they stuck me in this room. When I was in the hole, at least during the day, a muted light shone through the cracks of the metal. This room is a downgrade in that respect. Occasionally, the light in the hall will shine under the crack of the door. Those moments are few and far between, though. I no longer know what day it is in this forgotten space with no windows, and I'm losing time bit by bit.

I expected a bullet or a beating once the van I was stuffed in stopped. Except there was nothing. No speaking, no orders, no questions. I was shoved into this room and left to rot for I don't know how long. I don't even want to think about the other possibilities they might have planned for me. The five men I counted before have doubled. More come every day, including the mysterious leader, Razor.

He's standing in the doorway now, the light outlining his slight figure and casting his face in shadow. It's blinding after so long in the dark. He tosses me a piece of bread and I try to hold back, but I snatch it up. Shoving the food in my mouth is difficult with my wrists bound, but I manage. Gagging, I scoot into the corner. They can't come up behind me if my back is to the wall. I wish I wasn't dependent on them. Fuck. I wish I wasn't here.

I wish I was back at Mason's house. I may have accused him of kidnapping me, but he was right. This is worse than anything he put me through. He took care of me, even with all the questions. Part of me wonders if he set this up, orchestrating an elaborate plan, but I dismiss it. Even after the moment we had that ended with him giving me the silent treatment, I still don't think he put me here. The idea is laughable, if I was in any mood to laugh these days.

I didn't think I'd ever be in a position like this. I'm not that important. Maybe that doesn't matter. My connection to Mason might be all it took to put me in their line of sight. If I could go back, I wouldn't change a thing except I never would have run. I'd reveal all my secrets to him, if I could go back.

Tears fill my eyes, streaking down my face as I gnaw on the hunk of stale bread. After I broke down in the pit, I stopped worrying about whether my tears would be used against me. Everything is used against me, so what does it matter?

"You know, we could just starve you until you give up what you know," he says.

His voice is jarring, high-pitched, bordering on whiny. I keep quiet, eating faster so he doesn't take what little food I have left. By the time they decide to give me water, I'm dizzy, with a constant headache, and I'm pretty sure my stomach is actively eating itself.

"He's not coming for you."

I know he's not. It took me longer than it should have to realize they think Mason will rescue me. In the hole, I thought they asked for ransom and were sorely disappointed. Clearly, he didn't answer their demands, if they ever made them in the first place. I'm not surprised. We have no connection. No one is coming for me. I'm on the verge of telling him to just get it over with. There's no reason to keep going at this point. I doubt I'll be able to escape them. I no longer have the strength to even try.

"I don't understand why you protect him. He clearly feels nothing for you."

I bite the inside of my cheek, longing to scream at him. No one, including Razor, has asked me anything. They throw out their threats and mock me, but they don't ask any questions. It's as if he wants me to guess, giving up whatever knowledge I possess. Maybe he doesn't know what to ask and that's why we do this song and dance several times a day.

"It's been nearly a week and yet it's business as usual on the east side," he sneers, crossing his arms and leaning against the door frame.

I almost break then, all while filing away the information he's letting slip. A week. Almost half the amount of time I spent locked up, being taken care of, coddled, in the Byrns mansion.

Even if Razor knew I was an asset to the Byrns mafia, I still wouldn't tell him anything. I don't owe Mason, or hell, even the Kings or the Reapers, anything. Until Mason found me in the woods, we had a strictly business relationship. Fuck, it wasn't even a relationship. It was a transaction. And a lopsided one at that. Even so, I wouldn't tell this man anything. That's not the way I operate.

Now that I've spent time with Mason, seen who he is when no one else is around, I won't betray him. Our rocky start notwithstanding, I won't repay his kindness by outing him to this man, regardless of what I'm facing. I'm sure the torture will start soon. I won't last. I'm hoping I'll pass out before I can reveal anything that will damage him.

Ducking my head, I slip the last of the bread in my mouth. My jaw hurts from chewing, but I force it down. I can't afford to waste any sustenance. I don't know when I'll be fed again. I jolt, banging my head against the wall, as light flashes off the blade of a knife seconds before the edge is under my chin. Swallowing hard, I push back, but there's nowhere to go.

"At what point are you going to understand we have the power here?"

I've never been this close to him before. Now I can pick out every pockmarked pore on his face. The flecks of green woven into his brown eyes doesn't make him any more human. They're dead—soulless—with an edge of mania lining them. I couldn't answer him even if I wanted.

He sways, knees pressing into mine, and the blade nicks my neck. The wound stings as a trickle of blood tracks down my throat. I can feel it soaking into my torn shirt—Mason's shirt.

"We can do so much more than hide you in the dark…starve you," he murmurs, trailing the tip along my jaw and across my cheek.

I try to keep as still as possible, but every muscle trembles, worse than before.

You could end it now…

I suck in a shuddering breath at the thought. I could lean into the blade. I could kick out, hoping I'd die in the ensuing battle for the knife. I'm not stupid. I wouldn't win. I would bleed out on the concrete floor of this dingy office building.

There is no grand escape plan like I had at Mason's, even though I only tried to leave that once. My phone was in the woods, and I had the brilliant idea to find it. But I wanted to stay. I'd take Mason's snarky attitude and soggy sandwiches over this any day.

"Why don't you be a good little bitch and tell me how to get to Mason Byrns," he murmurs, brushing the knife along my cheekbone and settling under my eye.

I flinch and it nicks my skin. Swallowing hard, I turn my face to the side, but his hand wraps around my throat. He squeezes, cutting off my air, and my feet slide along the floor in my attempt to get away. I'm afraid to use my hands, bound as they are.

The pressure eases enough for me to gulp in a single breath before he slams my head against the wall. My vision blurs. My stomach rolls. My head pounds. I stop fighting. Bringing the knife back to my face, a smirk appears on his lips as he picks the perfect spot to begin.

A yelp escapes me before I clamp my lips shut as he pushes the tip deeper right below my eye, dragging it down my face. I've never experienced this type of pain before. It feels like I'm being filleted alive. My body heaves with the force of my sobs, though I know it'll only make things worse. Tears drip on his hand, mingling with the blood he's taking from my body. As he reaches my jaw, he flicks the tip and I jerk to the side, droplets of blood splattering across my face as my eyes fall closed.

"A little reminder. This is the least we can do. Remember that the next time I ask you a question, little bitch."

I don't see the blow coming as he lashes out, slapping me and I fall to the side, another cry leaving me. The door shuts, followed by the thud of a lock, echoing through my battered body. I don't know how long I lie there, wallowing in what my life has become, but eventually I push myself upright, my bare feet slipping across the tiles as I do. My face is on fire, overriding every other ache I had before.

I need to stop the flow of blood still coming from the wound, but there's nothing in this room other than me and a bucket in the corner that reeks of stale pee. There's not a lot of it, since they rarely give me water. It doesn't help the nausea building in my throat.

Gazing down at my black shirt, I gather the hem and try to rip it. It takes longer than it should, but eventually the fabric gives. Balling it up, I press it to my face gingerly, sobbing when the pain intensifies. My stomach cramps, the bread sitting like lead. I pant, attempting to breathe through the nausea. I was already on the verge of passing out from starvation and can't afford to puke.

I can't tell if it helps, but as numbness sets in, I press harder, if only to give myself something to focus on. I can't feel the tips of my fingers. My toes went numb a long time ago, back when I was in the pit.

Honestly, it was my fault. This whole situation is a result of my stupidity and poor choices, starting with my foray into the woods and ending with me in this barren room. Looking back, though, it started long before I snuck into the forest.

It started with jealousy, leading me straight here. I should have left well enough alone. I'm exactly where I should be—deserving all the pain and suffering, if only to atone for my behavior. Stalker is too tame a word for what I was doing. And I'm reaping every seed I've sown. I didn't deserve the kindness Mason freely gave me. I didn't deserve any of it.

Even knowing all this, it doesn't stop the ache in my chest or the panic from flooding my veins at the thought of Razor returning. Regardless of whether I deserve to pay for my sins, I still can't accept that this is my fate. The restraint is suffocating. If Razor keeps carving me up, I won't last long. The only reason

I've made it this far is because of fear and exhaustion. I wasn't fully healed when they kidnapped me, and the added stress on my body makes it that much worse.

I dip in and out of consciousness, never knowing how much time has passed. I won't call it sleep, since my body is still strung tight, anticipating the next round of pain. The flames licking at my face are a constant reminder of the danger I'm in.

At first I thought I was tough, since I didn't react like all the women I've watched in movies. They freak out and end up making silly mistakes everyone can see but them. It wasn't until I'd spent so long in the dark, I realized my brain just shut down. I'm not strong—I'm numb.

Someone kicks the door and I jolt from my half-conscious state, pushing upright to huddle further into the corner. The coolness from the tiles under me helped my burning face, and its absence sends another bolt of pain through me.

My limbs shake as the voices outside start yelling incoherently. I strain to hear what they're saying, but the wood separating us muffles everything. Fireworks resound through the space, cutting off their tirade. It's long past any holiday, though, and then it hits me. Not fireworks—gunfire.

Someone is shooting. I have no idea where the noise is coming from. Honestly, it could be Razor doing some light housecleaning. Maybe someone pissed him off and he decided to float them. There's always been a line between what I know and what I've experienced, which makes this whole situation strange for me to grasp. I understand the workings of the underworld, but I've never been so close to it before.

I know the Kings and Byrns are in the mafia. I know they control those at the top who are in positions of power. I know they kill people who threaten their position within Synd. Most of all, I know they're dangerous. But I've witnessed it all from behind the safety of a computer screen. Hell, I've helped them in most of the endeavors they've engaged in over the years. I've never been in the thick of it, an outside player they probably forget about as soon as I've done my job. I don't blame them. I'm not important enough to remember.

Another round of gunfire ricochets through the air and I slide my arms around my legs, pressing my chin to my knees. It hurts, but the pain grounds me in the here and now. The bloody rag I made rests at my feet, and I focus on the dark splotches covering it.

My wound has stopped bleeding for the moment. At least I think it has. It stretches with each muscle twitch. Before long, I'm sure it'll break open and start again. I can't bring myself to make another bandage. Exhaustion rolls over me, but I force my head up as feet pound past my room. The sudden activity isn't something I've experienced since I've been here.

I crawl toward the bucket, the overpowering scent making me gag, and I swallow hard. I resort to breathing through my mouth, but it doesn't help. The container is the only defense I have, other than maybe taking off my shirt and strangling any-one who comes in. If I was barely able to rip the fabric, there's no way I'm strong enough to accomplish choking someone with it, especially with the zip ties circling my wrists. Sam Byrns could pull something like that off, but even if I wasn't weak from hunger and blood loss, I still wouldn't be able to do it.

Silence falls, which is more terrifying than the noises from before. Full darkness plunges into the room as the light in the hallway winks out. Part of me wishes I knew what was happening, but the other half knows that my ignorance is bliss.

I scooch closer to the bucket until it's within arm's reach. The idea of throwing a bucket of pee has nausea crawling up my throat. I don't know if I can bring myself to do it. At least I'm next to the door now. Anyone who comes in will only see an empty room unless they come inside.

"Get the fuck back," a deep voice bellows into the dark.

More gunfire pops through the air, then a silence so deep descends, yet all I register is the ringing in my ears. A shudder runs through me at the realization it doesn't matter who it is. No one is coming for me. And I can't even bring myself to blame them. I'm nobody—a ghost of a memory that will fade from the world, leaving nothing in its wake.

No one is coming for me.

Seventeen

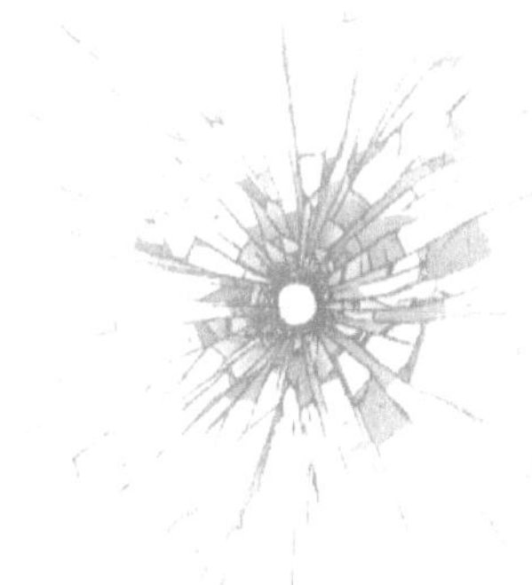

Mason

We've been at this for twenty minutes, and yet we can't find a way in. This would be so much easier with more men, but I'm hesitant to call in backup. The few guys I enlisted for this mission are loyal enough to follow me into this foray without a second thought. They do as they're told. Calling the Kings or Helms is out of the question. They'll have questions I don't have answers to yet.

"You going to tell me who these guys are, Mason?" TJ wheezes as he ducks behind a low wall next to me.

"They're our enemy. That's all you need to know." I may trust these guys with my life, but I haven't told them why we're here either. At least not the real reason.

"Well, Rigger is down. Got shot in the leg, but everyone else is still in position. Are we storming or..."

TJ's eyes meet mine, awaiting my orders. He knows the alternative is negotiating and we rarely play that game. Very few situations call for it. Negotiation spells weakness and we are anything but weak. Complacent at times, perhaps, but never weak. Victor fucked up more than some deals when he took over. He made us appear weak. Regret that I haven't done more to rectify his fuckups slams into me.

"Information. This is bigger than them fucking around down here. They're probably the cause of a lot of the issues with the lower gangs and missing product. The deals we're on the verge of losing will fuck with the entire economy. I want to know what the fuck they want and who they're working for. Make it happen."

"Might be hard, since we started with bullets first, but okay. You don't think they're working alone?"

I raise an eyebrow before peeking over the wall at the dark building. It's small, more of an abandoned storefront, but it's set up the same way as our distribution spaces. It's seen better days, like all the places in the Barrens. In fact, most of the ones lining the river further north are in better condition.

These men have to be in league with someone else. They're too disorganized—chaotic—to pull off what they've accomplished so far while not having any defense to speak of for an attack like this. Unless they assumed we'd never find them. The chaos we've been dealing with is calculated, unlike this gang.

"No, I certainly don't," I murmur, glancing at my phone as TJ pushes to his feet and crouches behind the bricks. "TJ, don't shoot the woman. I need her."

"Your woman?" He raises an eyebrow.

"Don't start. We have business from before…well, we have things to discuss." My heart pounds, the ache flaring in my chest. He nods before disappearing into the dark.

Ten minutes later, his text pops up, directing me to a side entrance. Easing through the darkness, I take in the silence blanketing the air. My suit is wrinkled from crouching behind a fucking wall, but I needed to dress the part, especially since these men seem to not know who I am.

Brick, one of my top guys, is waiting for me, and he kicks in the door at my nod. He ducks through first in case these fuckers don't respect protocol. I won't take the risk of getting shot again. Usually, I would have sent my guys in to drag them all out and demand information while they knelt in the gutter, but I don't have enough men with me to accomplish that without too many losses on both sides. I'm not willing to put them at risk like that.

The space is set up like an office with a reception area at the front, windows lining the space, and rooms trailing off a hallway in the back. Half a dozen ragged men litter the space, dressed in black with guns hanging from slack hands. I don't bother with them, searching for the leader. They all eye me warily, no one stepping forward, and I grind my teeth. I raise an eyebrow as a short, skinny man steps up, sneering.

"I believe you have something of mine," I say calmly, straightening the cuffs on my suit.

He barks out a laugh. "I doubt that, Byrns."

"Good. You know who I am. That certainly saves us some time. Who are you?"

"None of your fucking business. You came onto our territory. Get the fuck out."

I snort, glancing around. Not only is he delusional, he's also scared. A stronger man would have already shot me. This man only holds a knife, hanging limply at his side, though the blade has red streaking it. He might be the leader of this ragtag group, but he's not a threat to me.

"I think you're mistaken on how it works here in Synd. This city is mine. You bow to me." Tucking my hands in my pocket, I rock back on my heels as his face flushes.

"What the fuck do you want?"

"I won't repeat myself."

He barks out another laugh, the sound grating on my already frayed nerves. We don't need all of them to have our questions answered.

Glancing at Brick, I catch his eye, and he nods. Running my hand through my hair, the night lights up and the men drop one by one. Blood sprays across on the white tiles, and I step back to avoid the mess. Only one remains, the leader, and the knife clatters from his numb fingers, taking in the carnage around him.

"Any last words?" I ask, and I catch the tensing in his limbs. I doubt he can give me anything to solve the many issues plaguing us right now.

He doesn't have time to run as I pull my gun and shoot him in the forehead. He crumples, red seeping into his clothes from his compatriots' bodies. A slow stream of blood trickles from the hole, dripping to mingle with the pool spreading across the tiles. Less than five minutes was all it took to neutralize them. Brick moves to the door to signal to the others as I stalk down the hall, kicking open doors as I pass.

They're all barren spaces, devoid of furniture and people. I loop around to the other hallway and start the search all over again. Several of the rooms on this side hold evidence of the men lying in the front area. Tables and chairs, half-played card games, and random cots litter the spaces. They're dingy and a sour smell floats in the air.

I slow the further I travel down the hall, searching for evidence. They had to be working for someone, but I don't find anything at first glance. I'll have to send someone down here to go through the place before we burn it. This is one of the few times I'm thankful this building is on the outskirts of the Barrens. Fewer questions are asked when emergency services are called down here.

The last room looms and my breath quickens. There's always the possibility she's not here. Maybe she was—a clever ploy to throw me off. Something pulls me along, a feeling flipping my stomach and urging me forward.

Instead of blasting my way in like I was before, I push on the handle, but there's no give. Shoving my shoulder into the wood, it cracks, but still doesn't open. I step back and slam my foot into the door, once, twice, and finally it splinters apart.

Lifting my gun, I peek from the hallway into the darkness. The light above me flickers on, illuminating the corners of another barren room and disappointment crashes through me. Heaving out a sigh, I start to turn but whip back when the smell hits me. The other rooms were sour with sweat and stale cigarettes, but this room is rank. Burying my nose in my elbow,

I lean into the room, not willing to step fully inside. It smells like they used this place as a bathroom. Nasty fuckers.

Something shuffles against the tiles, and I step over the threshold, lifting my gun. The stench is overpowering, and I gag, swallowing hard to keep the bile down. A bucket sits in the corner. I'd put cash money this is where the odor is coming from. Why they'd use a bucket instead of using the bathrooms I passed while searching, or hell, going outside, doesn't make sense.

Brick calls for me. I glance behind and catch a dark pool of liquid on the floor. I assumed it was something nasty I wouldn't want to examine, but I see it's actually dried blood. Whatever they did in this room isn't something I want to examine further. Stepping toward the door, something shifts behind me, and I spin.

Tucked behind the door, barely visible, is Lacey. I almost don't recognize her with her head bowed and muddy arms wrapped around her legs. I imagined this moment every day over the past week. The rage I felt before I knew she was taken dominated how I thought this would go. It drained away when I saw the footage, replaced with a sense of urgency. Now, all I have is a crushing weight in my chest. The barrel of my gun dips until it's hanging by my side.

And then she lifts her head.

I barely recognize her. Dried mud streaks across her arms and covers her lank black hair. I can't even make out the red anymore. The clothes I lent her are in tatters and splattered with dirt and blood. It's her face, though, that has my gun clattering to the tiles. A deep, angry wound runs from just below her eye down to her jaw. Red trickles from it, dripping from her chin, keeping time with the silent beats pulsing through the air.

Guilt crashes into me at the sight of her, and I fall to my knees. She was taken, most likely beaten, and fuck knows what else. Rage sweeps through me again. I should bring the assholes back to life and kill them again. Torture them slowly instead of giving them the quick deaths they met minutes ago.

My trembling fingers reach for her, and she jerks back, tears filling her eyes before splashing down, mingling with the blood on her face. Her entire body shudders as she lists to the side. I don't know how she's still conscious. A lesser person would have succumbed to the pain long ago.

Footsteps race down the hall and she tenses, scooting closer to the bucket, and my heart cracks. All her sass and sarcasm has been bled from her drop by drop. I can't imagine what else they did to her.

A week is a long time to be kept somewhere. The wound looks fresh, though. If I can get her to the doc, maybe he can fix her up. I should call him, but my first priority is getting her out of this hellhole.

TJ skids to a stop in the hall, and I throw a hand up to stop him. I don't know how she'll react to a stranger coming in. Her green eyes are blank now, but fear flashed in them when she spotted me. Who knows what they told her about me? They may have said I was the one who ordered her here, to be cut up and terrorized. I don't want to rush this, but we have to move.

"Mason, we need to go. Nicki was just here," TJ murmurs, peeking around the door, eyes widening when he spots Lacey.

"Get the rest out. Leave the car."

"I'm not leaving you. I'll meet you outside," he says and disappears back to the front.

Lacey's forehead rests on her knees again, as if she's too tired to hold it up anymore. My palms itch to gather her in my arms and carry her from here, but she might fight me, or spiral. I don't want to make it worse.

Crouching, I tilt my head to scan what little of her body I can see for more injuries. Other than her bruised ankle, there are none visible, which doesn't mean much, but it's something.

"Lacey?" I whisper and she peeks at me, dull eyes finding mine. "We need to go. Can you walk?"

She doesn't move, not even a blink. Shock is a strange thing, but I don't think that's what's happening here.

"Kitten, I'm going to take you home."

I'd like to wait, but if Nicki is telling us to get the hell out, things are serious and we need to leave. Now. Nicki leads most of the Barrens and her intel is never wrong. We don't have the time to do this slowly. I can repair any damage I cause later, when she's safe. None of this would have happened had I just let her go that night in the woods. Regret swirls within me, and I tip my head back.

"I'm going to pick you up now. Don't freak out," I murmur, shuffling toward her.

"Why?"

I freeze at her gravelly voice. It sounds like she hasn't spoken the entire time she's been here, and my stomach rolls, even while pride swells in my chest. I'm sure they tortured her, demanded answers to questions she didn't have, and from the way her voice sounds, she never said a word. Her eyes stab into mine, no longer blank and lifeless. Accusation swims in them, and I deserve every bit.

"Why what?"

She coughs, wincing before asking, "Why are you here?"

There are so many ways to answer. I could tell her the men who took her were our enemies. I could say I'm here to save her. Neither of those are the truth, not really. I came because I was worried—worried she would talk, that she was hurt, that she had duped me. Her supposed betrayal was a knife in the gut, even though rationally I understand she owes me nothing. When I saw the video, guilt at not finding her sooner twisted the blade, sending lashes of pain throughout my body. There are so many reasons I came, but none of them matter now. All that matters is keeping her safe.

"I'm here to bring you home."

Eighteen

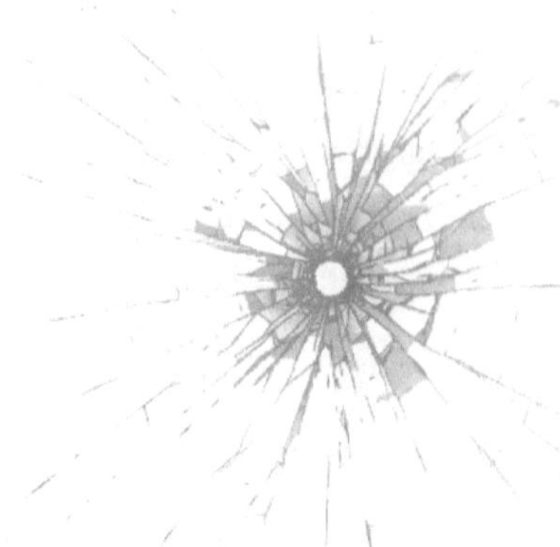

Lacey

Twilight sleep. That's what the doctor keeps muttering to Mason when they think I'm not awake. I don't know what it means, but it feels appropriate. I still don't know what day it is. Most of the time I'm dipping in and out of consciousness, hoping the darkness will drag me down for good each time, but I always return to the land of the living—to pain and heartache and regret. I could handle the constant pain if it wasn't for the regret.

Life shouldn't be this hard. I was fine until I got caught up with the mafia. The irony isn't lost on me. It's as if I'm living in a movie, though I didn't realize it would be so painful. They always make it seem like getting shot or hurt is badass. They recover and live to fight another day. Reality is much worse.

Still, the pain is the least of my concerns. My face is still on fire most of the time, only the shadows of my dreams easing it, but in those murky scenes is a new kind of pain I never anticipated.

The leader who cut me—Razor—lives in a space in my mind, ambushing me every time my body demands rest. Thousands of scenarios play out, and yet I always end up in that hole, his face swimming through the shadows. And then there's pain. So much pain.

"Lacey, wake up." Mason's voice floats through the gloom. I can't see his face, but he's here—somewhere. "Come on, Kitten. Come back. You're safe."

Jerking back, terror floods my body. I can't trust him. Not in this dream. He's not him. I stumble through the trees, which appear one by one in my path, crashing to the ground and pain radiates through my cheek. Looking up, Razor brandishes a knife, psychotic grin in place. A silent scream escapes me, and my eyes fly open, revealing Mason's concerned face.

"Sorry," I gasp, turning my face away, the sheets brushing against the bandages covering my cheek.

"Don't be. It'll get better," he murmurs, jostling my body as he pushes away.

Glancing around the familiar room, I brace myself for someone else to appear, but no one is here except us. I thought he'd set me up in another room. Instead, I'm tucked away in his bed. A computer graces a table under the window now. I imagine he works there while I'm sleeping. I heard him tell the doctor he was worried about leaving me alone. Why he cares enough is beyond me, but I don't.

Inside I'm dead, leaving a vital piece of myself in the van when they snatched me, another in the hole, more in the room. I dropped a trail of breadcrumbs made up of my essence for someone else to find, but they stole them, refusing to give them back. They're lost in the winds of pain and trauma, leaving only a kernel behind to wink out in the dead of night. A small flame of who I am rests deep inside my soul, waiting for someone to feed the ember and bring me back to life, but they never come. Mason's words of safety aren't enough to breathe life back into me. I'm waiting for the final blow, delivered with a manic grin and a bullet.

"Not enough," I mutter under my breath, eyes falling closed again.

"What's not enough? What do you need?"

He's closer, murmuring the questions in my ear, and I shiver, both from the action and the stab of fright snaking through my body. I didn't hear him come back. I wish I could sink back into the darkness, even if I'm met with more nightmares. At least there I can convince myself I might never wake up.

"Nothing," I wheeze, turning my face away.

"Lacey, we can't keep doing this. I need you to get better."

I snort, but the move sends pain through my face. Everything hurts these days, and it makes me want to curl into a ball or beg for him to end it all. Yesterday—I think it was yesterday—I asked him to let me go, but he pretended he didn't hear my words. We both know if I leave, I'll never survive. I'm too…broken. Even I know it.

"Why? Why do I need to get better, Mason?"

It's the one question I haven't asked. In fact, I've barely said anything since he brought me back. I passed out on the car ride here, cradled in Mason's arms the entire time. Bits and pieces of the next few days are etched in my brain like snapshots of time, all of them horrific.

Numbness set in after that, protecting me from the poking and prodding, from the screaming and thrashing. At one point, I'm pretty sure Mason held me down as I screamed, begging for a release only death can deliver.

I wasn't ready for the answer before, but I'm to the point where I no longer care. His words can't hurt me anymore. Nothing can. I brace myself anyway, for the damnation his answer will visit upon me. He'll tell me he needs information, though I know nothing. He won't believe me, like before. I'll be stuck in this in-between space that doesn't have an end.

"Because I can't live seeing you like this," he murmurs, but I must have heard him wrong.

We mean nothing to each other. I'm the foolish person who was stalking him in the most ineffectual way possible. It's probably creepier since I started watching the Kings first. I could always say it was because I was worried about their security, but it was jealousy at the heart of it.

I thought it was longing, but after spending almost two weeks in his house while I was healing, I realized how envious I was of their lives. They have each other and I have no one, and honestly, I thought if we could just stumble upon each other, everything would change. Now I realize it would be useless. I was never meant to be a part of their world, especially with how broken I am, both inside and out.

"Can I go?" I whisper, swallowing the sob stuck in my throat as tears fill my eyes.

"You can go back to sleep. I'll be here when you wake up."

"When can I go home?"

"Just…stop. You can't take care of yourself right now, Kitten."

"I don't want to sleep. I want to go home."

Misery crashes into me. I'm sure I sound like a whiny bitch, but he's only delaying the inevitable. If I'm here, he's forced to take care of me and that's the last thing I want. He shouldn't be forced to stay by my side, nursing me back to health yet again. It's my fault I'm in this position. If I had stayed in my lane and been honest with myself, I wouldn't be a burden on his life.

He sweeps into view, planting his fists on his hips and glaring.

"Fine. You want to go home? Then go. There's the door," he growls, sweeping out a hand.

Pushing up, I can't hold back a groan, and he raises an eyebrow, as if I've made his point for him. I'm out of breath by the time I lean against the headboard.

"Why don't you ask me what you want to know? Then we can be done with this."

"Done with what? We're not doing anything."

"Exactly," I snap. Confusion floods his face and I wince.

"What the fuck are you talking about?"

I wave away his words. "I don't know why they were there. I don't know if they were acting alone or not. All I know is they were asking questions about you. They mentioned the Kings at one point, but that was in passing. Most of the time I was in the hole, and no one said anything to me, so that's what I know." His face falls the longer I go on, but anger flashes in his eyes when I mention him. "I didn't say anything. The entire time, I never said a word."

His head dips, chest heaving, and I wait for the end. I can taste it in the air.

"Hole?"

"Huh?"

"You said you were in the hole. What the fuck does that mean?" He doesn't lift his head, just stares at his feet.

"Oh…I, uh, the hole. It was just a muddy hole. I don't know. I couldn't see anything other than the ceiling. It was dark."

"That doesn't make any sense, Lacey. A muddy hole in the floor of a building? Are you sure? I swept that entire place and there was no hole. Were you in the forest?"

"Why do you care?"

"I need to be able to find it again."

My heart skips a beat. Of course he'd want to see it. He'll probably tell the Kings and the Reapers, and everyone can use it when they have someone who needs a little light torture. I'm not stupid. They're criminals, dressed up in fancy clothes and slapping on civilized faces for the masses.

Underneath, dwelling in the shadows, they're the bad guys of the story. At best, I'm an accomplice to that, though I never put too much thought into what they did with the information I feed them. I ignored any whisper of morality, mostly because I justified it. The people they were taking down were corrupt—dirtier than they were. But that's only what I see. Maybe in the dark of night, all it would take is an insult for them to snap and throw someone in the river.

Shaking my head to rid myself of the thoughts swirling through my mind, the wound on my face pulls and I grimace.

It's strange to forget a huge bandage covering my cheek, but I do it more often than not. I'm not thinking clearly. I haven't been since Mason carried me from the darkness.

"Tell me you won't use it."

"For fuck's sake. No, I'm not going to use it. But we might be able to find who *is* throwing people down there. It may lead us to whoever they were working for," Mason says, running a hand through his dark hair.

It's the response I hoped for. I need to recenter myself, remember he's not like the men who took me. I accused him of kidnapping me, but he was right. Mason treated me differently. He took care of me, fed me, clothed me. Sure, he asked questions, but I never felt threatened. It was the only reason I was able to give him attitude. When I was in the room, surrounded by evil, I never would have spoken to them the way I spoke to Mason. I was reminded quickly to keep my mouth shut. I would be more disfigured than I already am. Swallowing back the tears, I remind myself that despite Mason's kindness, I'm still just an unfortunate piece in a puzzle he's trying to solve.

"I don't know where it is. They put a sack over my head, tied my hands, and we drove for a long time. When they pulled me out, I passed out. I don't remember getting to the building. The ride back here is the only reason I know where it is. I can't tell you anything."

"What else did they do?" he asks in a strained voice.

"Nothing. Just this." I gesture to my face. It's the truth, though he doesn't look like he believes me. I'm sure he thinks

I was raped, but they didn't seem interested in threatening me with that.

"Did they…"

"No. I swear I didn't tell them anything. I didn't say any-thing."

Coughing, I curl into myself as my ribs ache. This is the longest conversation I've had in almost two weeks, and my lungs no longer know how to function. He rushes forward, shoving a bottle of water in my direction. When my chest no longer feels like it's trying to collapse, I twist the cap off and take a sip.

"I'm calling the doctor again," he mutters, pulling out his phone as he paces away.

"Don't. I'm fine," I wheeze. "I'll go and you won't have to deal with this."

The explosion is slow as he spins and chucks his phone against the wall. It bounces innocently to the floor, but his body un-ravels, crumbling to the ground as he grips his hand and roars. My heart leaps in my chest, and I pull myself across the bed. There's nothing I can do, since I don't understand his reaction, but I still crawl to him. I pause when I'm close enough to touch him. I open my mouth, but he groans, so I snap it shut.

"Why is this happening?"

"What do you mean?"

"Nothing. Absolutely nothing," he rasps, pushing to his feet. He's out the door, the beep of the lock resounding through the sudden silence.

Nineteen

Mason

"Byrns, what the fuck is going on over there? I thought you were looking into the shit going down in the south?" Shane grumbles.

I'm stuck in another meeting with the Kings, though nothing has changed since the last time I was here. A wave of déjà vu rolls through me and I pull out my phone, shooting a text to Moss to check on Lacey. I didn't want to leave her in the first place, but she was sleeping. She pretends to be asleep most of the time and I let her. Every time I walk into my room, the knife in my heart twists a little bit more.

I should have gotten to her sooner. If we would have moved when I first found out she was taken, she wouldn't have the physical evidence of my failure etched into her skin. The more I try to help her, the further she slips away.

"Shit is going down in the Barrens, but it's not spreading anymore. They've gone into lock down. Not much else I can do there. The lower gangs are doing the best they can to hit back at whoever is targeting them. I'm pulling guys off the Depot to help down there, but I refuse to spread us too thin," I say, glancing at my phone again, sighing when Moss's text comes through telling me she's fine.

"Our shipments are still going missing, but things have slowed down at least. What about yours?"

"It's a shitshow. Other than Young, my contacts in Harris have completely ghosted me. I'm scrambling to find someone to replace them. Rima is in shambles, so I'm looking up north. Helms might need to reverse his lines. Where's Sam?"

"She's with Alex dropping Emma off in the mountains," Ren says, not bothering to look up from his tablet.

With all the shit happening lately, I completely forgot about Shane's younger sister. The city isn't a safe place for a four-teen-year-old, especially one who's related to a mafia boss.

"Do we have an update on the Guild? Out of everyone, this situation is feeling uncomfortably similar to the months leading up to them coming to Synd," I say.

"It's not the Guild," Ren murmurs.

I roll my eyes, not bothering to ask him to elaborate. He's not one to withhold information, but asking will only annoy him, and I still won't get anything out of him. I wish shit would just magically work itself out.

Taking over ten years ago was hard, since none of us knew what the fuck we were doing. We were all in the same boat, but we dealt with our shit and worked our way back. For a long time we thrived, even though it was hard. The last few years, our lives have been one disaster after another, and we can't seem to catch a break.

"Well, someone is trying to come in and fuck with our city," I say.

"Not necessarily Synd. Whoever they are, they're concentrating on the east side. None of the Barrens on our side have been hit. Most of the missing shipments are ones that came through Byrns's territory. They probably assumed it was yours. Someone is targeting you specifically," Ren says.

"Well, fuck my life."

The door swings open and Sam strolls in, plopping down in the chair next to me. She grins, propping her elbows on the table. Ren glances up for the first time since I've been here, the hint of a smirk playing on his lips before he concentrates on his tablet again. Relief flashes in Shane's eyes before he drops his gaze to the paperwork spread across the table.

"So…anything new I should know about?" she mutters from the side of her mouth.

"No. Why?" Pulling out my phone again, I scan the emails I'm still neglecting. Most of them are from Grayson and get progressively more clipped with each passing day.

"I heard from a little birdy you've got someone hidden away over there," she murmurs.

I can't stop the twitch that rattles through me, and I glance at Shane and Ren.

"Don't worry, I didn't tell them. But…"

"Don't start, Sam," I mumble.

"Come on, Mase. I want to meet her," she hisses.

"Meet who?" Alex says, and I jolt, practically upending the chair.

"No one. Stop being nosy, Alex," she says.

My phone buzzes, pulling my attention away. TJ's text is garbled and riddled with typos. He fought tooth and nail not to get a phone, but necessity and all that. Replying, I shove it back in my pocket.

There's no reason for me to still be here. I don't have time to sit around and wait for them to get their shit together. I won't ask for help either. They're dealing with enough on their own, especially Sam. Between helping Mac deal with her brother's disappearance, and then Sam's friend in the Barrens getting stabbed, she hasn't been in the right head space to help me. I don't blame her. I won't ask her, anyway. Sure, I hire the Wraith for jobs, but asking my little sister to help me solve the problems piling up on my side of the river feels weird.

"Well, smells like cum in here, so I'm gonna go," Alex says, then laughs while flipping us off and the rest of us scowl.

"Fucking gross, Alex," Shane shouts after him.

Pushing to my feet, I make my way around the table, intent on following Alex's exit.

"Where the fuck are you going, asshole?" Shane calls, and I flip him off over my shoulder too.

"Let us know if there's news, Mason," Ren says, but he still sounds distracted.

Small footsteps chase after me and I slow until Sam falls into line next to me. Neither of us says anything as we wind our way through the halls. In fact, we're almost at the front door before she stops me with a hand on my arm. She stares at a small door under the stairs before she shakes her head.

"Do you remember when we were kids?"

"Not much. I mean, we didn't exactly have a normal child-hood."

"We thought it was normal, though."

I sigh, ducking my head. "You might have. I didn't, but that's not surprising."

"What do you mean?" she asks, leaning against the banister.

"You were young. And a girl. Dad didn't exactly keep you in the loop. I did what I could so you wouldn't have to see the things I did."

Sam scrunches her nose, pursing her lips. "Didn't work out too well, did it?"

"I mean, you think you had a normal childhood, so I'd say I did a pretty good job."

"Are things…better?" Her brown eyes find mine, laced with pain.

"I'm working on it."

Other than the breakdown I had the other night with Lacey, who definitely didn't understand what the fuck was happening, I've been too busy to think about anything other than my world crumbling around me. Having to save Lacey gave me something to focus on, not that she realizes it. And I don't plan on telling her anytime soon. She's got it in her head that I care if she handed over information. I wish she would have, if only to save her the pain she's suffering now. The more she told me about what happened, the deeper I fell into my guilt. I couldn't hold it back and I lost it. We still haven't talked about it. We probably never will.

"Do you wish sometimes it would have been me?" she whispers.

Seizing her arms, I shake her a little and her startled eyes flash to mine. "Don't ever fucking say that again. I would shoot Colin a thousand times over if it meant you lived. Fuck, Sammy."

Gathering her in my arms, I hold her. I can't stop the trembling in my limbs, even as she wraps her arms around my waist, face pressed to my chest. We haven't hugged in months, fuck, maybe years.

This world doesn't encourage weakness, and that's what our relationship is seen as. Our father always had the plan to sell her off for some alliance, like they used to before. I didn't dispute it, but I did everything in my power to make sure it didn't happen. My stomach turns when I remember Colin was my back-up plan. If Dad ever made the move, my best friend was the one who would get her away, take her anywhere but here. All to save her from a life of pain. The coup over a decade ago was a silent blessing for Sam, even if she never knew it.

"Mase," she says, voice muffled from my suit. "I wasn't talking about that." Pulling from my arms, she grimaces. "I was actually wondering if it would have been better if I was the one who…took him out."

"Either way, the answer is no. It was my responsibility, regardless of what led up to it."

"You know you don't have to do it all alone, right? I mean, I can help." She tucks her hands in her hoodie, but I know she's twisting her fingers together. It's a nervous habit I thought she'd done away with years ago, but lately it's coming out more and more.

"Fine. If you insist, I need someone to get the police chief in line. I know you talked to him, but he's pissing me off. He keeps calling and emailing and he's driving me up a fucking wall. Nemesis couldn't find anything on him—said he was clean, but I don't believe it. He's gotta be hiding something. Figure it out and I'll give you a cookie." I smirk when her eyes light up. She always was one to be bribed with food.

"Okay, but it'd better be a good cookie." She grins before loping away, waving as she disappears into the darkened house.

Another wave of déjà vu hits me as I make my way down the front stairs to my car, except this time, Alex is leaning against the hood. Part of me wishes I could just drive away. He's no longer grinning, which is why I stop in front of him. It's rare he's not smiling and cracking a joke or dropping some random fact.

"What can I do for you, Alex?"

"You know when you were down? And we were trying to figure out what the hell was happening and shit kept going sideways?" he asks, arms crossed and staring at his feet.

"Not really. As you said, I was in a goddamn coma."

He waves away my words, glancing at the fountain. Or maybe he's looking at the hippo, still front and center in their driveway. It's worn now, the gold muted even as the last rays of the sun catch the metal.

"Back then, I kept grasping at anything to keep going. It felt like everything was piling on and nothing was going right, and then Sam was shot, and then she was just…gone. And during it all, we were battling a ghost we couldn't see, much less find. I felt like I was fighting fifteen battles at once. And then it was over. I mean, the Night Slayers coming through and that whole deal with Willow and her stalker was a thing, but it felt like we could breathe a little, ya know."

"Okay. Why are you telling me all this?"

"Shit feels like it's starting over, minus you getting shot, of course. But it feels like we're getting hit from all sides and no one sees it. There's something out there, and we're missing it. Like a ghost is haunting us, and we won't know they're real until they reveal themselves."

He meets my eyes, concern lining them. I chose not to find out more about what happened when the Guild came through, other than what I needed to know to fix shit. I didn't want to hear about how their relationships grew with my sister. It's awkward enough as it is, since not many know she's with all of them. Every party or gala I go to, I end up fielding endless inquiries about them, so much so I've avoided going all together.

"I'll figure it out," I mutter.

"Victor's been doing some shady shit."

"When is he not?" I scoff, crossing my arms as my chest tightens. I need to get back to Lacey. This time, I really am rushing home to her.

"More so than before. He's been meeting with the police chief. But then he disappears every time. I've tried following him, but with Nemesis off on some random ass vacation, I can't really do more to find where he's going."

"What do you mean, she's on vacation? I've been trying to get a hold of her for weeks now."

He snorts. "Course Ren didn't say anything. Got a message a couple weeks ago that she'd be off the grid for a while. No clue when she'll be back. Personally, I think she was sick of his shit and bounced."

"Well, that's just fucking great."

"She ever fix your camera situation?" he asks, tipping his head back and pushing off the car.

"Yeah, seems like it. Said she did the last time I heard from her."

He nods, walking past me toward the house. I track him until he's at the front door.

"Alex." He turns, raising an eyebrow. "I might need your help with something."

"Does it involve beating the shit out of someone?" he asks eagerly, hustling back down the stairs.

"I don't care what the fuck you do, but I think it's about time we get rid of a nuisance."

Twenty

Lacey

The walls are bleeding.

The rational part of my brain tells me I'm wrong, but that doesn't mean I can convince my eyes of the truth. Tracking the crimson trails, I wonder, if I got out of bed, would it transfer to my hands? Would it cover me, coat my arms, seep into my skin? Or would it disappear, vanish into the recesses of my mind, only to return when I retreated?

A knock at the door has me blinking rapidly, and the blood recedes. I don't bother answering whoever is on the other side of the thudding. They'll figure out pretty quickly Mason isn't here. I should get up and shower, but the last time I tried, I ended up curled in the corner, still clothed, trying to escape the spray. Mason found me and freaked out. I didn't know why until I could hear myself muttering over the roar in my ears about the blood. Nothing like bathing in blood.

Another knock has me rolling my head toward the door, eyes fixating on the handle, but it stays put. The beep from the keypad has me blinking again, but I still don't move. I've only seen one other person in here. I don't remember his name. His eyes were filled with pity. Deciphering why was a lesson in patience for me and I didn't like what I found.

The door swings open and the last person I ever expected steps through. She hasn't changed in the weeks I've been missing from the outside world. Same wavy auburn hair and laughing brown eyes, though they're muted today. Dressed in all black, per usual, she peeks around the door, eyes skipping to the closet, then swinging to the bathroom before finally settling on me.

Tilting her head, she scans me from head to toe. "Well, they certainly did a number on you, huh?"

Rolling my head away, I make sure the walls are the correct brown, no red in sight, before turning back to her. I'm splayed out on the bed, ankle wrapped again and in the same shirt and sweatpants Mason dressed me in when he brought me back. I don't remember him doing it, and I assume the other clothes were burned. Even after the shower, I refused to change. He wrapped me in towels to dry me off and set me next to the fireplace. I roll my eyes, thinking of the ridiculousness of having a fireplace in a bedroom.

"Fucking rich people," I mutter.

"Uh, noted. You don't like rich people. Got it. I've been told I'm super down to earth, if that counts?"

"Is that a question or a statement?"

"Ahh, okay. So, shit's a little shitty right now for you."

"You could say that."

She hops up on Mason's makeshift desk, tucking her legs under her and pulling out a bag of pretzels. Staring at them and then at me, and she tucks them away.

"Guess you know who I am. Don't worry, Mason didn't rat you out. TJ told me you were here. He was worried about…well…pretty much everything. I figured you could use someone else to talk to other than my grumpy brother."

"I'd rather not talk to anyone, but I doubt you'll listen," I sneer.

There was a time I would have given anything to have this conversation. All I wanted was a chance. Not like this, though. Not when I'm stuck in a bed, too afraid to get out in case the floors floods with blood. Not when I'm shredded and broken, inside and out. Not when I've finally seen the errors of my ways and all I've received from them are pain and heartache.

Fuck, I'm morose.

"Well, then."

"Sorry," I whisper. "I'm not usually…never mind. What did you want?"

She raises an eyebrow, glancing around again. "Lots of things I want, but I'm not sure you're in the right mindset to answer my questions."

"Try me," I say, closing my eyes. The red tinging my vision was enough of an indicator it was about to start raining.

"In no particular order: what happened while you were kidnapped, who took you, did they say anything about someone else, and how do you know my brother?" She grins when I peek at her. "Just those to start."

"I'd rather not talk about what happened, I don't know who they were talking about. And I don't know your brother."

It's not a lie, per se. Admitting I was stalking him and then got caught because I'm shitty at it will only hand me a one-way ticket to smother-fest. Or stabby time. Whichever she's in the mood for.

"Hmm, see, I know you're lying, but I also realize how traumatizing it can be to be in your position," she murmurs, a haunted gleam entering her eyes as she looks away.

It's morbid curiosity that has me asking, "How do you know I'm lying?"

"Mason isn't exactly the warm and cuddly type. He never rescued kittens or helped old ladies cross the street. But here you are, seemingly a complete stranger, saved from a demon's clutches and set up in his room—in his bed—to heal. In fact, he's at the fucking store right now, buying snacks. Don't ask me how I know that and *please* don't tell him. However…" she pulls out the word, eying me, "Mason Byrns does not snack."

"Who the hell doesn't snack? Everyone snacks." I bite my lip, wishing I would have kept my mouth shut.

"I know, right?" she cries, throwing her hands up.

"I see what you're doing," I mutter, and she tilts her head. "You're trying to connect so I'll open up. You could just threaten me instead."

She sobers, brows pulling low, and my stomach flips as the red mist gathers in the corners of the room.

I sigh, closing my eyes again. "I *may* have been in the woods, and Mason *may* have caught me. I *may* have rolled my ankle and he *could have* been asking me questions he didn't believe the answers to. Then I was kidnapped, and I'm pretty sure he thought I was with them, but I wasn't."

"No, you certainly weren't," she murmurs.

"You've got to be fucking kidding me. I told you to leave it the fuck alone, Sam." Mason's voice cuts through the air, slicing into my already frayed nerves, and I shiver, slitted eyes ping-ponging between them.

"Actually, I believe you said, 'Don't start.' As you can see, I didn't start anything with *you*. I went straight to the source." Sam smirks.

"Get out. She doesn't need you coming in here interrogating her," he growls, dropping a bag on the end of the bed. I'd put money that it's filled with snacks, just like she said.

"Dammit, Mason. I wouldn't bust in here and start demanding answers she's not ready to give. How fucking terrible do you think I am?"

"For fuck's sake, Samantha, I wasn't saying you would. But she also doesn't need you in here trying to be all buddy-buddy with her. You can't force people to be your friend."

"I can at least give them the option. It's fucking hard to meet people, if you haven't noticed that being cooped up in this house all by yourself." She gives him a withering look.

"I have plenty of friends."

She hops down, crossing her arms, foot tapping against the hardwoods. "Oh yeah? Name one."

I clear my throat, but neither of them acknowledges me. They're glaring at each other, waiting for the other to break, until Mason throws his hands up, muttering something about that not being the point. Stomping into his closet, he slams the door behind him, and I jolt, the sound echoing through the air like a gunshot.

"Sorry 'bout that," Sam mutters, running her hand through her dark hair.

"I'm sure it's weird having siblings."

It's the only thing I can think to say. I just wish they would both leave. No, I wish *I* could leave. I'd hole up in my house and pretend the world didn't exist, imagine the last couple weeks were a weird dream and nothing has changed. I could go back to work, living in the shadows of their existence without ever actually stepping foot in their world again. My fingers brush the bandage covering half my face, and I remember that's wishful thinking. I'll never be able to go back to ignorant bliss. Whenever I leave here, I'll be gone for good. My stomach flips and a pulse in my chest aches, traveling to my head to take up residence.

"You're an only child?"

"Sure," I mutter.

The last thing I'm going to do is reveal my life story to her. Something as innocuous as whether I have siblings could be the difference between remaining a ghost or someone digging into my past. I've scrubbed that person as best I can, but I'm sure some trace of her exists somewhere in the world. The fact I gave Mason Byrns my real first name was a step too far. I hadn't said it out loud in over a decade until he demanded one and my actual name slipped out. I wish I would have made up one.

Sam sighs, bringing my attention back to her. "We're not the enemy. You know that, right?"

"Doesn't really make a difference."

Her face falls and guilt stabs me in the gut. "Can I get you anything?"

"Can you convince your brother to let me go home?"

"I'll make you a deal. If you're better in a week and you don't look like you're going to waste away into nothingness, I'll smuggle you out."

"I'm not going to…"

I can't even finish the lie. My plan was to skip town and run as far away from Synd as I could, but now? I doubt I'd make it out of town, not because of the mafia leader who's clearly hiding in the closet, or from the assassin staring at me like she wants to save me from myself. I won't make it out because as soon as I get home I'll wallow in my own misery until I'm a shell of myself with nothing left in my life but a jagged scar to mark my time here.

"I'll check on you later. Just…don't do anything stupid. Shit might seem shitty now, but it'll get better. Things are—" She clears her throat. "Getting weird out there. I don't want you caught up in something that has nothing to do with you."

She pounds on the closet door before tiptoeing to the window and slipping out. I should probably act surprised she's essentially scaling the side of the house, but I don't have it in me to pretend anymore. Keeping in all the secrets I know about them is exhausting, and I'm already existing on a wisp of will to live right now.

"She didn't say something stupid, did she?" Mason asks, voice floating from across the room.

I shake my head, not bothering to open my eyes. If I pretend to sleep, maybe he'll leave me alone. Bags rustle at the end of the bed, and I roll away from him, swallowing the groan crawling up my throat when my bandaged cheek presses into the sheets. I roll to my other side and tears slide down my face. Keeping my eyes shut tight, I rub the wetness away, but they don't stop.

Mason's hand brushes the hair away from my forehead before the warmth disappears. Bereft. That's what I feel when he leaves. I don't know if it's him or merely the presence of another person—the knowledge that someone knows where I am. Someone is pretending they care. My heart won't survive if I entertain the idea of him worrying about me. Instead, I sit in the gray area of not knowing.

The bed dips behind me, and I freeze. I don't want to change bandages or be poked and prodded. I don't want to be reminded of the bruises painted across my body. Usually, he tries to check my injuries when I'm sleeping. Sometimes I pretend I am, just so I don't have to deal with it. He catches me every time.

My muscles tense when his arm slides around my waist, tucking me close to his body. Pressed to his chest, my back warms, easing the tension in my body bit by bit. I should pull away or tell him I'm fine. Instead, I sink into the darkness, begging the nightmares to leave me be for one night.

Twenty-One

Mason

Sleep lifts slowly from my mind, and it takes me a minute to figure out what's different. Lacey's body molds to mine and she sighs in her sleep. She's the only one I've had next to me in bed. Ever. I don't want to burst the bubble of safety we've fallen into.

Last night was the first time she didn't thrash through her nightmares. I've tried to get her to talk about them, but she pretends not to hear me. I can't imagine what she's reliving in her head, unable to escape. When I found her in the shower, muttering about blood, I realized I was in over my head. The shit I went through is nothing compared to her trauma, regardless of whether or not I grew up surrounded by death.

There's only so much I can do, but when I found her silently crying, I couldn't help myself. Sliding next to her was like a part of me slotting into place. I tried to ignore the peace swirling around us, but I also didn't retreat. I wish I could say I slept as soundly as she did, but I kept waking every hour, panic dousing me in flames until I felt her body next to mine. My dreams were plagued with loss and frantic searching for something I couldn't remember. Then I'd stumble upon her mutilated body and jolt awake.

"You can let go of me," Lacey whispers.

Draped across my chest, hand resting on my heart, she doesn't move. Flexing my hand on her hip, I don't bother answering. I'll keep her close as long as she'll let me. It's the only way I'll be able to keep going at this point. Something has shifted between us, even if she doesn't feel it yet. She's too deep in her despair to notice anything else, and I hope I'm able to lead her back into the light before she disappears completely.

Guilt is my constant companion these days. I should have let her go when I first found her in the forest. I should have kept her safer. I should have noticed the signs that she wasn't in league with anyone—trusted her when she told me who she was. I should have saved her.

The weight on my shoulders is a constant reminder that, though she's relatively whole physically, mentally I failed. I wasn't fast enough. I didn't try hard enough to find her. I was so caught up with seeking proof, I didn't listen to my instincts. She needed me, probably thinking no one was coming for her. She's a shell of herself now. Every snarky comment wormed its way under my skin, and now that they're gone, I realize how much I miss it—miss her.

"Mason…" she murmurs, ducking her head and wisps of her hair tickle my cheek. "Just let go."

Dropping my hand, I huff out a breath. My chest aches and I attempt to rub away the pain, but it doesn't help. I track her as she scrambles from the bed, teetering as she stands. My palms itch to steady her, but I'm sure she'll push me away. I should let her go home, but the unknown threats seeping into my territory are enough for me to keep her here as long as possible. Selfishly, I don't want to let her go. Rubbing my hands down my face, I try to scrub away the emotions roiling inside of me.

The bathroom door clicks shut, and I sit up, setting my feet on the cold floor and resting my elbows on my knees. Checking my phone, I'm reminded of all the things I'm neglecting. Moss's latest update is another three hits in the south. TJ is yelling about some shipments going missing. There's a missed call from Sam and Pinch, our numbers guy. I debate all of three seconds before I text Pinch. His response is almost immediate, and I let out a soft curse.

"What's wrong?" Lacey's soft voice floats over me, easing some of the tension in my shoulders.

I almost confess all the issues I'm dealing with, but pull back at the last second. "Business."

"Oh, okay." The dejection in her voice is evident, and I open my mouth. "Will you take me home now?"

Rage bubbles up inside me. I'm going to assume it's rage. If it's something else, I refuse to name it. It's the only question she's ever asked. I've barely been able to get anything out without her bringing up going home. I've tried to give her time to open up. I don't want her leaving with her mind broken, but I can't keep her here forever. Refusing to acknowledge that she just asked me what was wrong, and I brushed her off, probably isn't the best course either.

"Yeah, sure. Go ahead." My tone is flippant, overshadowing the other emotions. "I'll call you a car."

I catch the shock splashed across her face before I push to my feet, heading for the door. I'm done fighting her. I'm done keeping her safe. She's made it clear she's not my responsibility, and I need to start listening to her. I'll have to deal with the guilt later, after she's gone.

"Wait, that's it?" she asks as I reach the door.

"Were you expecting something else?" I ask, glancing over my shoulder.

"I just…" Her hand reaches up, stroking the bandage. "I, uh, I need pants."

My eyes flick down, taking in her bare legs. Fading bruises still mar her skin, along with the wrap on her ankle. She doesn't need it anymore, but I haven't told her. She's walking fine now, other than the aches and pains plaguing her. Shaking my head, I realize I've been staring at her body for longer than necessary, and I pull my eyes away.

"There's some in the closet. I'll be in my office when you're ready."

I walk out before anything else slips out. There's nothing to say, anyway. I don't even understand why I care so much. I'll chalk it up to the guilt and eventually she'll fade from my mind. With all the shit going down, she won't live there indefinitely. She'll be a distant memory before long. If I repeat the words enough, maybe I'll believe them.

I'm almost to my office when I remember she has no idea where I went. I pivot, marching back the way I came. When I pass the main hallway overlooking the front door, I spot Victor locking the front room he's taken over. He's still in one piece, so I assume Alex hasn't visited him yet. I gave King free rein, but I have a feeling he'll toy with my uncle before finally ending things. If it goes on too long, I'll have to step in, but not yet.

By the time I reach my bedroom, I'm seething. I jam in the code and burst through the door, practically taking it off its hinges. Swiveling my head back and forth, I scan the space, searching for her dark hair. The sheets are still rumpled, matching indents on the pillows, and I peer into the bathroom, but it's empty too. Sucking in a deep breath, I turn for the closet, praying she didn't decide to wander off on her own. The familiar rush of panic wells up in me. Pushing open the door, it creaks, sending a shiver down my spine.

"Seriously? You couldn't wait like all of five minutes?" Lacey shrieks, snatching up a shirt to cover her chest, but not before I caught the flash of metal. How I missed a nipple piercing is beyond me, but now I can't stop staring.

She clears her throat, and my eyes tick up, taking in her flushed face. My mind blanks and I stutter back a step. I can't remember what I was upset about a moment ago.

"At least you got your spark back." I smirk, but it falls when she widens her eyes.

"What the hell are you…you know, never mind. I have to…finish getting dressed." The breathlessness in her voice gives away how much I've affected her. Or maybe it's just the fact I walked in on her half naked.

The thought pulls me up short as my eyes wander down her body. There are so many reasons I should walk away. Each one of them skips away in the wake of her swaying toward me. She shakes her head, and I see my window of opportunity rapidly closing.

"You realize I've seen you naked before, right, Kitten?" I murmur, stepping closer.

Her mouth falls open before she snaps it shut, scowling. "And so you thought it would be okay to burst in here without so much as a knock?"

"Couldn't be because I was worried, could it? Or because I thought you had disappeared. Or that someone had found you. None of those things crossed your mind, did it? Besides, I think you've forgotten that this is my room," I snap.

This isn't the time for this conversation with her half dressed and still dealing with the aftermath of her captivity. I can't stop the words from pouring out, though. The days have bled together as I've tried to pull her back from the edge. And at every turn, I've failed. I can't keep doing this. She doesn't owe me anything. We aren't anything but two people thrown together in a strange situation no one could predict.

"And what if I did? I'm not the one who put me in here. All I've asked for was to go home. I didn't ask you to keep me or save me or help me. I didn't force you into this. No one told you to worry about me." Her chin trembles as tears fill her eyes and all my defenses fall in the wake of her misery.

"You didn't have to," I shout, thumping my fist against my chest. "It's my fault you were there. Of course I would worry about you."

Understanding dawns across her face, and she pulls in a shaky breath.

"It wasn't your fault. This"—she gestures to her bandaged face—"all of this is my fault. If I didn't come here, you never would have met me. None of this would have happened. We would have stayed strangers, the way it's supposed to be."

My throat closes and the world around me spins. This is what she's been keeping from me, and I hate that I've forced it from her. Curling my hands into fists, I resist the urge to gather her up, refusing to let go until she sees the truth—that none of this is her fault.

"I don't care."

"I know. You don't owe me anything. You've helped me more than any reasonable person would. And I won't be able to repay you for that, but you have to let me go."

"I don't care," I repeat.

A single tear tracks down her face and she nods. Shaking my head, I step closer. The words I want to say won't come. I want her to fight me, yell at me, berate me. Whatever it takes to snap her back to who she was before. I want her to stay with me, as ridiculous as that is. We have nothing except deception and trauma binding us to each other. Still, I can't let her walk away, even though I know it's inevitable.

"I don't care—" I start, and she slashes her hand through the air.

"You don't have to keep saying it. I hear you loud and clear."

I step close enough to place my hands on the wall on either side of her head. "I don't care if you think it was your fault. It wasn't. I don't care if you think no one should worry about you. Doesn't change the fact that I do. I don't want you to be in my debt. I don't want you to run off to wherever the hell you live and think that no one cares, because I do."

"Why?" she whispers. "We don't know each other. We're nothing. I'm noth—"

I lean in, our lips a hairbreadth apart, and she falls silent. Resting my forehead on hers, I close my eyes. Somewhere along the way, I saw Lacey change. She's no longer the woman sneaking around my property. But I still can't figure out why it matters if she's here or not. The only thing I can point to is she gave me something to focus on when the rest of my life was filled with apathy. And that isn't enough of a reason.

"Take a shower and then I'll take you home," I mutter, pushing away from her.

I'm almost to the door when a black dress shoe flies past my head, thumping into the door. Whipping around, I gape at her. A flush covers half her face as she seethes.

"Did you just throw my own fucking shoe at me?"

Tipping her head up, she narrows her eyes. "Damn right I did."

"Why?"

"For being a fucking dumbass. Now get the fuck out." She raises the other shoe, cocking her arm back.

I pivot, ripping open the door to retreat. Seconds after I slam it closed, a thud reverberates through the wood.

What the fuck.

Twenty-Two

Lacey

I've been hiding in the bathroom for almost an hour. I keep expecting Mason to bust down the door, demanding to know what I'm doing. Pressing my ear to the wood, I strain to hear him on the other side, but I'm pretty sure he left. I should have stopped myself. Revealing shit to Mason wasn't in the plan. Hell, I don't even have a plan. Not really. It's a loose idea of keeping my shit together while the world goes up in smoke around me.

The steam from the shower I just vacated still billows through the air, fogging up the large mirror. I wipe it away, wishing I could erase my thoughts as easily. His words from before wash over me, coating my skin. I pretend the flush covering me is from the shower instead of him almost kissing me.

Swiping the bandages from the counter into the garbage, I finally glance at my reflection. My wound stands out against my flushed skin, an angry reminder of my captivity. The doctor said I'd always carry a scar, but it should fade with time. How much time, he couldn't say. Maybe one day I'll think it gives me a devil-may-care look, but not today. Right now, I want to wash it away as effortlessly as I did the sweat clinging to my body under the hot water.

A shiver rolls through me, even while wetness gathers between my legs. All I want to do is go out there and demand he keep going. It's an exceptionally bad idea. I'm playing with fire, an inferno that will engulf me if he uncovers my secrets. I don't have many, but they're not small ones by any stretch of the imagination. With no way of knowing how he'll react, I should have stopped him long before we got to this point.

Our lives are weaving together in a way that will hurt to extricate myself from. Ripping myself away from him will be painful, but necessary. Leaving could have saved me a world of hurt. Refusing to sleep in his bed would have been smart, too, even if the nightmares don't consume me as wholly when he's holding me. The longer I stay here, the more I realize how much I'm relying on him.

A knock on the door has me jerking around to snatch up my clothes. The last thing I need is Mason to barge in on me half naked again. Either all my insecurities will fall from my mouth without warning, or I'll throw another shoe at him.

"Just a minute," I call as I struggle with the leggings Mason handed me earlier.

They're long enough, but they don't fit right. I wish I had my sweatpants. The thought pulls me up short when I remember that those aren't my clothes. The sweatpants I've been wearing are Mason's. By the end of the day, I'll be in my own things since he's suddenly so keen on getting me home.

An ache blooms in my chest. For all his words of comfort, he freely admitted to the guilt riding him. I can't be responsible for distracting him from what he needs to do. And I need to get back to my job or start packing. I don't know how I'm going to move all my shit from Synd. Maybe I'll just abandon it and buy new equipment.

Huffing, I tug the door open, finding him sitting in the chair across the room, phone in hand. He glances up when I pull it shut behind me, leaning against the wood.

"Ready?" he grunts, fixing his gaze over my head as he pushes from the chair.

"For what?"

He shakes his head, sighing. "I'm taking you home. Let's go."

He makes it all the way to the hidden panel in the corner of the room when he glances back. I'm rooted to the floor, stomach rolling. I don't know what I expected, but this wasn't it. After asking for this almost every day, now that it's here, it doesn't feel real. I won't admit how much I hate this, but I don't belong here.

For some reason, I expected Mason to fight for me—to beg me to stay, which is ridiculous and irrational. We're clearly meant to go our separate ways. I can't help myself, though, as I wrap my arms around my stomach to stop myself from touching the scar on my face again. It burns, but that could be the blush on my cheeks.

"Anything else?" I ask.

He turns, planting his hands on his hips and a blank mask covering his face. "What do you mean?"

"You were adamant I was some mole, infiltrating your organization to take you down or some shit. Then I get kidnapped, and you found me"—I grit my teeth as he scowls—"saved me, whatever. Then you send your sister in here to interrogate me under the guise of becoming my friend. And now that's it? I'm just free to go? You don't have any other questions you want to throw at me?"

"I didn't ask Sam to come here. In fact, I told her to back off, so don't put that shit on me," he snarls.

"What about that episode in the closet? You going to explain that away, too?"

He ducks his head, mumbling, "I wasn't thinking clearly."

I rear back as if he's slapped me. I don't know how to respond, but he's obviously waiting for one. Swallowing hard, I gather the pieces of my life scattered at my feet. No use leaving them behind for him to find.

His phone chimes, pulling his attention from the floor, and he curses. "I don't have time to explain shit to you, so start moving or I'll throw you over my shoulder and toss your ass out. Then you can walk home."

Gnawing on the inside of my cheek, I keep my retort inside. I don't have any other option than to follow him into the tunnels. I expect to come out in the garage or outside, but instead we come to another hallway.

Sunlight streams from the opening, blinding me after several minutes in almost complete darkness. Mason saunters into the room, collapsing into a chair behind a desk, booting up a computer. My fingers tingle and I lean back into the safety the dark provides.

"Get in here. I need to do this first," he grumbles, pointing at the chair across from him without looking at me.

"I thought you were calling me a car?"

"Change of plans," he mumbles.

I shuffle inside, shutting the panel behind me before perching on the edge of the chair. I don't want to stare at him while he works, so I gaze around his office. Usually, I'm peeking in from the outside. This is like a glimpse behind the curtain, at the inner workings of a man who's always been a bit mysterious. Even though I've spent the last few days in his bed, this seems more intimate.

Floor to ceiling bookcases line the wall behind him, stacked full of books, random snapshots of his life framed in front of them. Sam's smiling face is in most of them, all with her stuffed into a black hoodie or t-shirt. The society girl doesn't live within these walls. I wonder how many people are allowed to see her without the mask she plasters on at galas and clubs.

A globe sits in the corner, looking oddly out of place. It's fancy, while the rest of the space is comfortable and cozy. There's not much more to look at. I wish I could wander around, perusing the titles behind him, but one glance at his scowling face, and I decide against it. He'd probably bite my head off. He's done a complete one-eighty, as if his confessions in the closet were all for show and he's back to normal now.

"What the fuck," Mason mutters, eye fixed on his screen.

He grabs his phone, grooves rooted between his eyes. "What the hell is going on, Pinch? There's no fucking way you lost a million fucking dollars. Fucking find it or they'll be finding your body in the river."

He slams the phone down, immediately seizes it again, and swipes across the screen, sending a message, and then calls another person.

"Where the hell is our shit, TJ? This is the sixth one this week, and it's a fucking Tuesday." He pauses, pinching the bridge of his nose. "Then send our guys instead of hiring this shit out. I'm sick of putting out fires. We're losing money hand over fist. I'm not going to put up with it anymore."

He slams the phone down again and I flinch. His eyes shoot to me, and he sighs. Tipping my head back, I bite my tongue. I don't know what's going on, but I could help. Losing money, shipments going missing, and fuck knows what else, are my bread and butter. This could be my last hurrah for them, solving the mysteries, and then I'll disappear. At this point, Ren will have received my auto-message that I'm off-grid. It wouldn't be that strange for me to never come back. They'll assume…nothing. They'll probably only notice because they'll have to find someone else to do their behind-the-scenes dirty work. Maybe they already have.

"Sorry, I'll take you home." He pushes from the chair, making his way back to the panel, but I'm frozen to the chair, staring at the computer. "Lacey."

"I could help," I say. I almost wish I could stuff the words back in.

"No, you can't. This goes beyond a few web searches. Doesn't matter. I've got someone." He grimaces, and I wonder what just went through his mind.

"Except I'm right here, offering my assistance. If you don't want me to help, just say that, but don't insult me while you do it. Just because I'm a woman doesn't mean I don't know what the fuck I'm doing."

His eyebrows disappear under the flop of chestnut hair that's fallen over his forehead. "I wasn't saying that. This would require you to know more about the businesses we're involved in, and I'd rather not suck you in more than you already are."

"You mean you don't want me to spill your shit to whoever grabs me next. If I was able to keep quiet while this happened"—I gesture to my face—"then I think you can trust me."

His jaw clenches as his fingers curl into fists at his sides. A worm of doubt inches through my brain, knowing I'm lying to him with every word I speak. This is probably the worst idea. The offer sits between us, withering away the more time passes. I open my mouth to rescind my proposal when he throws his hands up, grumbling under his breath.

"Go ahead. I'm sure you won't even be able to get into the system. And not because you're a woman, but because the person who set it up is extremely proficient at this kind of thing."

He waits until I've taken his seat before collapsing into the one I vacated. The password box blips on the screen, and I sit for a whole minute before I bypass the whole thing, and I'm in. I leave most of his personal shit alone. I've never looked at it, even though I have access. Just because I can, doesn't mean

I should. I'm sure at least one of them is terrified I'm hacking into all sorts of places, but I've never done it. Ethics don't come into play often in my job, but looking at them felt like a line I wasn't willing to cross.

"Which do you want me to look into first?" I ask, pulling up another program.

"You're in?" He burst from the chair, rounding the desk to lean into my space. "How the fuck did you do that? Find out where my money went."

It takes me five minutes to follow the trail of withdrawals and bank transfers before I sit back.

"What is this?" he asks, squinting at the screen.

"An offshore account. Managed by one Marcus Erickson. Any idea who he is?"

"Maybe. Sounds familiar, but I don't know," he mutters.

"Like a lyric you heard in a song long ago, but you can't remember the title?"

"Exactly."

He's still staring at the screen, as if the guy will pop out and tell him who the hell he is. Usually, I give them the information and then sit back. What they do with what I give them isn't my business unless they ask for more, but this situation isn't standard. Not that what we all do, by any stretch of the imagination, is normal.

"Can you find him?"

"Probably, but it would take awhile." Time I don't have, apparently, because he straightens, pulling out his phone again to send a text. I duck my head, if only to stop my eyes from wandering. "It's probably an alias. Anything else?"

"Shipments."

"What about them?"

"Can you figure out what's happening to them? They're disappearing without a trace." The excitement in his voice is palpable as he leans over my shoulder. I pull up another screen to check cameras on the south side. "Plus, there's a bunch of shit going down on the south side of the city. Can you…"

He stops so suddenly, it takes me a minute to realize he didn't finish his sentence. I glance from the corner of my eye, then whip my head around when I find his dark eyes blazing. Leaning back slowly, I drop my hands to my lap.

Instead of retreating, like I expect, he leans closer, growling, "How'd you know where to look?"

"What do you mean?"

"You started looking up the cameras in the south before I told you where the shipments come in. So, tell me, Lacey—who are you working for?"

My breath hitches as he steps back, casually tucking a hand in his pocket. The move is more menacing than it should be and damn if I don't fucking light up like a firework exploding across a dark sky. This is absolutely the wrong time for this. I should not be turned on by the power written into the lines of his body.

He raises an eyebrow, and I wouldn't be surprised if he's gripping a gun in his pocket. My eyes dart down and then my cheeks flame when I realize it looks like I'm staring at his crotch.

This is not the time to be having my body perk up as if we didn't almost get down and dirty two hours ago. I can't even see anything anyway since he's covered in pants.

"I work for myself."

"Is that so?"

"Okay, that sounded bad. I know what you're thinking, but—"

"Do you now?"

He narrows his eyes, and I finally start to feel the butterflies in my stomach. They're not the happy ones I've previously had. Now, I'm nervous he'll actually shoot me. Or lock me away, just like the others did. The trembling starts in my hands, running up my arms until my entire body is shaking uncontrollably. I blink and a halo erupts around his head, deep red and shimmering. When my eyes fall closed, images filled with darkness and pain flash across my vision.

Opening them again, the walls are bleeding, and I jolt, the chair tipping back. It rights itself, and I bury my head in my hands. Digging my fists into my eyes, I wish I could will away the mirage. I may know I'm hallucinating, but I'm not going to admit it out loud. I don't know how to stop it.

"Don't think that'll work on me now. You're clearly an amazing actress. Tell me who the fuck you work for." Mason's voice filters through the void, but I can't reach him anymore.

My eyes are dead weights in my head. Lightning strikes and my face bursts into flames. Time warps, and I weave in and out of consciousness. When I come to, a wailing echoes through the room. Hands brush against my skin, leaving ice in their wake. Smacking them away does no good. Even I can tell my movements are erratic and disjointed.

My mind clicks back to reality, and I realize it's me who's screaming. Curled on the floor, my body aches everywhere that's not on fire. I can't imagine what I look like, freaking out and losing my mind. His words no longer register through the throbbing in my head.

The darkness lapping at the corners of my mind becomes a tsunami, engulfing me and dragging me under. I don't know how long I'm out, but when I come to, I'm no longer on the chair. I'm not even on the floor. Instead, I'm tucked in his bed, shivering, though several blankets are stacked on top of me. Sunlight streams through the open curtains, but I think it's lower in the sky. Mason is propped up against the headboard, his hand buried in my hair. His fingers flex when I peer up at him, but he doesn't wake up.

My entire body aches, but I doubt I have any new injuries, at least. I'm not sure what happened, but I've seen enough medical dramas to realize I'm reliving the nightmare of being kidnapped. How I would even explain that to Mason isn't something I want to think about. He clearly doesn't want to know anything other than who I work for, which is ironic.

I snort, then suck in a breath and hold it until my lungs are screaming. Letting it out slowly, I peek up, meeting Mason's brown eyes. His fingers flex again, digging into my scalp before he tugs them away. Swinging his legs over the bed, he stalks into the bathroom, slamming the door behind him. Seconds later, he whips it open again, poking his head out.

"Don't fucking go anywhere," he growls, swinging it closed again.

"Like I would," I mutter, my voice raw.

"Heard that," he yells before the water turns on.

Groaning into the pillow, I roll toward the edge of the bed, sliding to the floor. My legs give out and I end up on my knees. Resting my forehead on the mattress, I wait until my head stops reeling, sighing when I finally don't feel like I'm going to puke. When I turn my head, laying it on the comforter, my cheek screams in protest and I switch sides.

As soon as the world stops spinning, I'll run. Well, probably not run, because I'll end up hurting myself again, but I'll stumble my way out of here. I just need a minute.

"Least the walls aren't bleeding anymore," I say under my breath.

"What the fuck does that mean?" Mason's low voice rumbles through my body.

"Nothing," I sigh, burying my face in the mattress again.

His muffled footsteps come nearer, and I tense.

"Who do you work for?"

"I work for myself."

"Sure," he sneers. "Is anything you told me real?"

"I didn't lie to you."

He won't believe me. I'm so exhausted at this point. We've come full circle, from him dragging me into his house, refusing to believe me, to coming to some semblance of a truce, then back to him thinking I'm his enemy. What's the point of even trying anymore?

"Fine. We'll see how you feel about the truth after a little time down in the cellar."

He reaches for me, and I scramble back, knocking into the nightstand and the lamp clatters to the floor.

"I work for you, asshole." The words tumble out in my haste not to be put back in a hole. Covering my head with my arms, I curl into a ball, and images flick at the edges of my vision.

"What?"

"I fucking work for you," I cry, tears streaming down my face. "I swear I work for you."

Twenty-Three

"What does that mean?" I ask after Lacey stops rocking.

The first time she said it, I dismissed her words completely. The shock is still wearing off and I'm not sure which way to go now. I was convinced she was faking when she was muttering about blood, but I doubt she could fake passing out. Throw in the tremors and I'm questioning whether I was right in my accusations. Even if she wasn't in league with her kidnappers, there's no reason she should know about our operation. It's not a huge stretch that she'd know I'm in the mafia. Anyone who dug deep enough would be able to figure it out.

It's ludicrous to assume she works for me, but she's so adamant I'm questioning everything. My organization is huge, spanning the entire east side of the city until running into the Reapers in the north. I couldn't even begin to know everyone who does business for the Byrns family. The hierarchy is in place for a reason, taking the stress off me to deal with inane issues, and leaving them to the people down the line.

"Lacey, what does that mean?" I ask in a low voice, crouching in front of her.

Her arms are over her head, as if she's protecting herself from the outside world. I'm afraid to touch her at this point. Even when I suspected her of being a mole, I didn't touch her. I don't know if it's because I'm losing my edge, or because I didn't want to hurt her. I'm torn between demanding answers and accepting she might be telling the truth.

"I can't…I shouldn't…" she wheezes.

"How do you know about the shipments?"

She dissolves before my eyes, gasping for breath as she trembles. When I can't take it anymore, I reach out a hand, brushing her arm. She doesn't pull away, hiccupping as her tears subside, and I keep skimming my fingers across her soft skin. After another minute, her muscles ease and she heaves out a sigh. I know why she freaked out. As soon as I mentioned locking her up, she lost it. That's not the reaction of someone who's faking.

"Lacey," I murmur.

"What?"

"Tell me." It comes out soft, nothing like the hard tone I was striving for.

"I just do some security work for you. It's nothing."

Narrowing my eyes, I tug her arm away until I can see her tear-streaked face. Bright green eyes stare back at me, widening the longer I stare.

"Don't start lying to me now," I growl.

"How do you know I'm lying?" she whispers, a tremor in her voice.

I open my mouth, snapping it shut when nothing comes out. It might be the tilt of her mouth or the reddening of her cheeks, but there's something there that wasn't before. All this discovery points to is that every time I questioned her, demanding answers, she was telling the truth. Guilt swirls through my gut and an ache starts behind my eyes.

"What do you know about what's happening in the south?"

"Nothing. I've been here for the last three weeks, remember?" The snark is back in her tone, but at least she's no longer cowering.

Sighing, I rock back on my heels, tipping my head to the ceiling. I can tell she's holding back, but the what is elusive, tickling the back of my brain, refusing to come to the forefront. If I could figure that out, this whole process would be a lot easier. I could make plans and decisions, and everything would go back to normal. What normal is now is a mystery, but I'm not going to focus on that. I can't plan for the future without knowing, though.

"Do you work with Nemesis?"

It's the only connection I can imagine she has to me. I always thought the hacker worked alone. Watching the flush travel up her neck, and disappearing under her arm, it hits me.

"You've got to be fucking kidding me," I whisper, scrubbing my hands down my face.

No one has met the hacker unless Ren has been keeping shit from us. I've never even heard her voice before. We communicate through texts and email, though Ren talks to her on the phone. I should have suspected Lacey was Nemesis from the beginning. Why, though, I don't know. It wasn't obvious. She never gave herself away. There must have been something I missed. I should have figured it out.

"I'm not..."

"Don't. Just...don't," I snarl, as my feet carry me from the bedroom.

Slamming the door behind me, I slip my phone from my pocket, but I don't know who to call. There's a reason she didn't say anything in the first place. Wanting to keep her identity a secret isn't surprising. I doubt even Ren, who's closer to her than anyone else, has met her. I can't wrap my head around the fact that she's actually Nemesis.

I blast back through the door, intent on questioning her more, but the room is empty. Panic spears through me, making me stumble over the rug. A door slams down the hall and I quickly push my own closed. Stalking to the closet, I pause in the doorway.

Water is running in the bathroom, and I spin toward it. I stop when my hand rests on the knob, sanity flooding back in. I shouldn't ambush her. The last time I walked in on her naked ended with me almost kissing her. My cock hardens remembering how she shivered, desire in her eyes, before I walked away.

Stepping back, I shake out my trembling hands, then my eye catches on the panel leading to the tunnels. It's mostly closed, but the nearer I get, the more certain I am it's not latched completely as it should be. I can't remember if I shut it when

I carried her here from my office. I was too conflicted by her panic attack and betrayal to pay attention.

I stalk to the bathroom and burst through the door, shattering the lock along the way. A scream rings out as I scan the room, finding Lacey cowering in the corner, arms covering her head again. My heart skips and my stomach flips. Rushing to her, I crash to my knees, gathering her in my arms. She fights me, but quickly dissolves into tears, tremors wracking her body.

Murmuring into her hair, I rub her back, trying to right the wrongs with my caresses. In the short amount while we've known each other, I've fucked up royally multiple times. My volatile emotions have swamped my ability to see things clearly and make the right decisions. Long before Lacey showed up, I was broken. I wasn't fooling anyone, but I thought if I acted like things were normal, eventually they would be.

Fingers curling in my shirt, she shudders. The sigh I let out ruffles her hair, and the strands tickle my cheek. I wish I could take away her pain, which isn't something I think I'll ever be able to do, especially since I'm responsible for some of it, if not all. Comforting her, helping her, should come from someone else—someone she knows. They'd be better equipped to heal her. Someone who's crumbling can't fix another broken person. It never goes the way one thinks it will.

Shaking the hazy memories from my mind, I tuck my hands under Lacey's body and stand. She jolts in my hold, clutching me tighter, and her fingernails dig into my skin through the fabric. The bite of pain is enough to center me and solidify my resolve.

Instead of lowering her to the bed, like I want, I set her in the chair. It's not as comfortable as the bed would be, but she's not injured, other than the ones already peppering her body. The jagged scar gracing her face is a stark reminder of what she went through.

"You need to move—leave Synd. You should tell Ren you're leaving, or he's liable to track you down," I say, crossing the room to put as much distance as possible between us.

Leaning against the wall, I shove my hands in my pockets so she won't see them curling into fists. I shouldn't be having such a visceral reaction to her leaving. We barely know each other, plus she's safer as far from this city and me as possible.

Whoever is coming won't distinguish the innocent from the guilty. From the evidence of their crimes until now, they'll only ramp up, taking shit further than I'll be able to handle. Before long, I'll have to call in the Kings, maybe even the Reapers. I'm hesitant to ask for their help after everything they've gone through already. If I could have pulled myself from the dark hole I found myself in after I took Colin out, we wouldn't be here at all. The blame lies squarely at my feet, all from a single bullet.

She tucks her head between her legs, and I wait until the color returns to her face before I clear my throat.

"Ren King doesn't know who I am," she whispers, and I turn away from her tear-streaked face.

"Doesn't matter. You're close with him. He'll—"

"Am I? Because from where I'm sitting, you all know each other. You're friends and are there for each other. I'm just the person you call when you need a fix, or a save, or disaster strikes and you have nowhere else to turn," she snarls.

"Bitter much?"

"Fuck off. You can tell him whatever the hell you want, but I will not be calling him to tell him some sob story. He wouldn't care and I don't blame him. So, are you taking me home or am I walking?"

"Can you walk? Because I'm pretty sure I've been carrying your ass everywhere the last two fucking weeks," I scoff.

The way she see-saws between vulnerability and pure audacity is giving me vertigo. I can't help but snap back when she tells me off as if I'm some random guy on the street instead of a mafia boss. Most people are afraid of me, even if they don't know what I do behind the scenes. No wonder Sam stepped back from the spotlight. At first, I thought it was because she was trying to hide the fact she's dating three men, but now I wonder if she was just tired. I don't blame her.

Lacey—Nemesis—has always known who I am, including everything we're engaged in. No wonder she didn't care about snapping at me. We already have a relationship, regardless of what she says. As our secrets are revealed, a weight lifts from my shoulders, clearing my vision, and exposing the path we need to take, no matter how much I hate it.

"Do whatever the fuck you want," she sighs, head thumping against the wall as her eyes fall closed.

The dark rings under her eyes are pronounced. Her nights have been interrupted by nightmares, but I didn't realize how much they were affecting her until this moment, as the will to keep verbally sparring with me drains from her before my eyes. I open my mouth before I can change my mind.

"You're paying for the lamp, by the way."

She groans, rubbing her hands down her face, flinching when she hits the still-healing scar.

"I'm not paying for shit. It's your fault it broke, anyway."

"My fault? You're the one who knocked into it," I say as she glares at me.

"Because you were an asshole."

"Don't worry, I'll just take it out of your next job," I say, smirking, then sober. "You don't have anywhere to go, do you?"

"Does it matter? I'll figure it out." She waves a hand lazily, eyes still firmly closed.

"And what happens when you get there? Set up shop again? Start hacking for someone else?" Spotting her green eyes peeking out, I raise an eyebrow. "Or have you made enough money off us you'll just retire on a beach somewhere? Live out the rest of your days drinking dirty martinis and suntanning?"

Her mouth drops open and she snaps it shut, shaking her head. "Do I look like someone who likes the sun?"

She doesn't, but I'll keep goading her until she admits she has no fucking clue how she'll survive outside of Synd. I may not have used her hacking skills until a few years ago, but Ren has been working with her for almost a decade. This is her home, whether or not she wants to admit it to me. Her safety depends on her leaving, but if she can't take care of herself when she's gone, then the point is moot.

"Tell me, Nemesis"—she scowls at the use of her alias—"what were you actually doing in the woods that night?"

Twenty-Four

Lacey

L*acey*

Lying is such a strange thing. On the one hand, it's hard keeping track of the storyline one weaves, all while making it believable. On the other hand, it's incredibly easy. Being truthful requires a vulnerability I'm never quite ready for. In reality, one is giving a piece of their essence, exposing parts of themselves for others to judge. Apparently, I'm not very good at lying to Mason. If I reveal to Mason the reasons I was in the woods that night, I'll be admitting my own hubris.

I thought I fixated on them because my work creates a solitary existence. It's not like I can do the job with other people around. Even if they knew I was a hacker, I'd never be able to show them my true self, regardless of the circumstances. It would expose me more than I could afford. The mafia families may control the infrastructure from the mayor to the lowliest clerk, but that protection doesn't extend to me. Once again, I am on the outside, barely on the fringes.

Sighing, I drop my arms to wrap around my waist. If I squeeze hard enough, it might stop my stomach from rolling. Puking on his rug would only make shit worse.

I should have left when I had the chance. I shouldn't have offered to help. Hell, I should have stayed as far away from Mason fucking Byrns as possible. I thought if I just had an in, everything would fall into place and my life would change. And it did, just not in the way I expected.

I realize if I would have stayed away, I wouldn't have met Mason, had a small glimpse into his world, but I also wouldn't be scarred. Mason never said, but I overheard him and the doctor talking when they thought I was asleep. The doctor was adamant I would carry a physical reminder of my time in that office building forever. I just wish I could erase all evidence of my kidnapping from my body. I didn't realize how many other injuries I carried until Mason started counting the various bruises gracing my skin.

I jolt back to the present, realizing his face is stony now instead of the cocky tilt he had when he asked.

If I ignore him, eventually he'll get exasperated enough to leave. He'll scowl and march from the room and I can slip out the panel. Eventually, I'd make my way outside. I won't risk the hallways. I may have never met Victor Smith, but I watched him slowly dissolve the Byrns name while Mason was in a coma. I did what I could to mitigate the effects on the financials, but there was little else I could do. There may have been more than a few text messages I intercepted from him. He's still here. In this house. I won't risk running into him.

"Why haven't you killed Victor yet?" I murmur.

His head whips up, and his hand curls into a fist as a flush crawls up his neck. "What do you know about him?"

I don't understand his reaction. I thought the others would tell him what Victor did while Mason was out of commission. I shouldn't be the one who reveals all his uncle's transgressions. I certainly shouldn't have asked him about it, especially so callously.

"I'm sorry. I thought you knew…"

"Knew what? What do you know, Lacey?" He pushes from the wall but doesn't come any closer. I tense regardless.

"I don't know anything. Are you taking me home now?"

I push to my feet, sidling toward the door. He eyes me, and I turn toward the exit. When I glance over my shoulder, he's crossed the room, stopping right at my back. Sucking in a deep breath, I try to put some distance between us, but he grabs my arms. Leaning in close, his breath ghosts across the shell of my ear and every nerve ending in my body lights up.

"If you won't tell me as Lacey, then tell me as Nemesis. What do you know about Victor?" he murmurs. In any other circumstance, the move would be erotic.

"A lot, but it's not my place. You should ask the Kings. Or Sam."

He sighs as his fingers squeeze my biceps. "They don't know anything, at least since I came home. So, start talking."

Nodding my head, I tug from his grasp, and after a moment of hesitation, he lets go. The rollercoaster I've put my body through, or rather my mind, is taking its toll on me. All I want to do is sleep for three days in his ridiculously large bed and pretend the outside world doesn't exist. Unfortunately, I doubt Mason will leave me alone long enough.

Instead of falling into the cloud of blankets, I drop back in the chair, tucking my legs under me before propping my elbow up and resting my chin in my hand. He sways, looking a little lost, before he plops down on the edge of the bed. His head drops in his hands, and he rubs them over his face. I don't want to be the one to start. Hell, I don't even know where to begin.

"What do you want to know?" I ask after a whole minute of pretending I'm not watching him.

"What's he been doing?"

"A lot of meetings. Random ones that seem like accidents, but really aren't."

"What does that mean?" he grumbles.

"He'll go out to lunch and happen upon high-up people, like the police chief or businessmen. Never any women, of course. They pretend like it wasn't planned, but he's not very good at being sneaky."

"Like when we met?" Piercing me with his dark eyes, I straighten.

"That wasn't planned. I mean, I was hoping…working."

"And when I asked you to find, well, you?" The corner of his mouth tips.

Huffing, I turn away to gaze out the window. "I scrubbed my image from the cameras. Why did you even want to find me?"

From the corner of my eye, I catch his scowl, and my stomach tightens. It doesn't matter. I don't care what his reasons are because they no longer matter. They've obviously changed drastically. Indecisiveness swims in his eyes, but I'm sure they'll take a deep dive soon enough. The longer we talk, the less he'll be intrigued by me, if there was anything there in the first place.

Blinking back tears, I mumble, "Never mind. I don't know what else Victor is doing, but he's been moving money around his personal accounts. I was in the middle of tracking them when…well, you know."

"When you started stalking me?" He swipes a hand across his mouth, but I can't tell if he's smirking or frowning.

"Bold of you to assume I started that night." I tip my chin up, challenging him to question me on it.

He shakes his head as he pushes to his feet and prowls to the window. The move is predatory, almost lethal as he slips his hands in his pockets, and I shiver. Tracing the lines of his body, a thrill rolls through me, and I scold myself, not that it helps.

Unraveling from the chair, I tiptoe past the closet. If he turns on me, I want the quick getaway. At this point, I no longer know where I stand. Honestly, I never knew where I stood with him, but the stakes didn't seem quite so high before.

Mason's voice rumbles out as my hand slides along the panel, searching for the latch. "Going somewhere?"

"I'd rather not get shot in the head, so I figured I should have a plan."

He doesn't turn from the window as he ducks his chin to his chest. "So, you planned to get in one of the tunnels and make me rescue you again?"

He swings around, leaning against the wall. "I saved you from breaking your ankle, even though you fought me every step of the way. Then I saved you again when you wanted to skip out, even though you weren't capable of feeding yourself. And do we really need to go into afterward? I hardly think so."

"You want to compare notes on how many times I've saved your ass? Pretty sure I'd win."

When he chuckles, ducking his head, a thrill shoots through me. I can't keep doing this, if only because I've been through the fucking wringer already. Any more and I'm liable to burst into a billion pieces with no possibility of putting myself back together. I don't even know if I care. I'm jumping between wanting things I shouldn't and not giving two shits what the hell happens to me.

I grind my toes into the floor, tucking my hands behind my back so he won't catch me twisting them together. "Well, you're being fucking obtuse so…"

"*I'm* being obtuse? You can't figure out if you're staying or going. One minute you're running away and the next you're—" He straightens, his scowl back in place, and marches to the bathroom, slamming the door behind him.

"Not helping your case there, buddy!"

Rolling my eyes, I sigh as I resume my search for the hidden latch. Actually, I can't remember if it's a secret button or a latch or if I should just dig my nails into the edge and pry it open. My stomach flips when my finger catches on a dip next to the panel. It looks the same as the rest of the wall, but the slight indent gives it away.

I glance behind, but the bathroom door is still firmly closed, and no sound comes from behind the wood. When I lift my hand to brush the hair from my face, I realize I'm trembling. This feels like a mistake, but I'm out of options. I can't stay here, regardless of everything before. Staying here would mean admitting I need help. It would require me to demand answers to questions I'm not ready to ask.

The depression in the wall gives easily, and the panel pops open, revealing ever-tapering shadows marching down the stairs. I stand before the darkness for a full minute before I come back to reality. I'm stalling, waiting for Mason to come barreling after me. I want him to stop me. I want him to admit he wants me to stay. I want him to want me. Clearly, he's not going to. Once was enough for him.

Every time he slips, he stalks away—out of the room, away from me, out of my life. It's where he belongs. After spending the last few weeks here, going through everything I have, it's obvious I don't fit. I knew I wouldn't, but that kernel of hope burned brighter. Now it's just an ember, threatening to wink out in the first step into the void in front of me.

"Seriously? I leave the room and you're ready to jump ship?" Mason growls.

Glancing over my shoulder, I find him only a few feet from me. "You left. Figured I should make myself scarce."

"Any idea how the hell you're going to get there?" he sneers. "And don't think I forgot you still haven't answered my questions."

"Well, it's pretty fucking embarrassing. I just wanted to see what it was like to be a part of something. Whatever. It doesn't matter. I shouldn't have been there. Hell, I shouldn't even be here right now. So, why don't you take me home and we'll forget"—I freeze before I say something I'll regret—"everything."

"And you'll disappear? I'm assuming you don't need any help with that."

He slips past me, avoiding my eyes, and I slowly follow. As he pulls out his phone to light the way, I glance back once at his bedroom, a foreboding swamps my senses. I pad down the steps after him. The further we go, the louder the silence engulfs the space, leaving a yawning chasm between us, and I'm left wishing I could banish every voice screaming that I'm making a huge mistake.

Twenty-Five

Mason

For the sixth night in a row I'm parked outside Lacey's house, hidden in an alleyway so she doesn't spot my car. The irony of the situation is not lost on me. When I dropped her off, she said it would take awhile for her to pack up her things and skip town. She also said she wouldn't tell me when she left.

"Poof, I'll be gone. Like the shittiest magic trick in my arsenal."

"Do you actually know any magic tricks?" I asked.

"A magician never reveals their secrets. You should know that."

Then she grinned and skipped into the house, as if her ankle wasn't killing her. I caught the wince as she passed the kitchen window before she closed the blinds. Not to mention her grin didn't reach her eyes.

Since then, I've either had someone stationed outside her house or I've been here myself. Sleeping in my car isn't exactly the greatest, but I'd rather put up with a sore neck than wake up one day to her being gone, or dead. Besides, keeping an eye on her eases the guilt that's my constant companion these days.

My phone buzzes and I jolt, straightening in my seat. Her house has been dark the entire three hours I've been here, but she's in there, I can feel it. The screen lights up, and I sigh as I answer.

"What do you need, Ren?"

"Why the fuck are you whispering? You on a stakeout or something?" Alex's voice rolls down the line and I pull the phone away.

"Why are you calling me from Ren's phone?"

"Long story. It fell in the river."

"Super long story. Could you tell it again? I'm not sure I caught it all."

"Fuck you, man. Listen, where are you for real? I got some shit we have to go over and I'm not doing it over the phone," he says. Ren bellows Alex's name in the background, and a door clicks shut.

"Did you steal Ren's phone? You realize he's going to know every fucking thing you did with it, right?" I chuckle.

Out of all the Kings, Alex might be my favorite. Over the years, I've rarely seen him without a smile on his face, except when his family is threatened. I've also witnessed when he's gone berserk, like a couple of months ago, when someone thought it would be wise to fuck with Sam by grabbing her ass. The guy was carted out with more than a few broken bones while Sam sat by smirking.

"Why the fuck you think we gotta meet in person?" No way am I going to have him breathing down my neck about my special little assignment.

"Where you at? I'll come to you."

Squinting at Lacey's house, I debate whether I should call someone to take over so I can meet Alex or just play it off when he gets here. The last thing I want is a bunch of fancy-ass cars tooling around her neighborhood. It'll only draw more attention, but I've never had anyone else out here at night. Knowing my luck, or rather hers, that would be when someone comes for her. I don't want to keep him waiting, either. I give him the address of the house next to me and he laughs.

"What the hell are you doing in that neighborhood? Are you actually on a stakeout? I'll snag some of Sam's snacks and be right there." A pounding on the door echoes from the background, followed by Ren's angry voice.

"Don't drive one of your shinies. Take a car or something."

"Yeah, yeah. I got you." His laughter cuts off abruptly when he hangs up.

My grin slides from my face as I sober, remembering how empty my house is now. I didn't realize how accustomed I'd become to coming home to Lacey. It might have been a weird situation filled with sharp retorts and sarcasm for days, but at least there was someone there. She woke me up in a way I didn't expect.

Admitting how lonely I've been since I dropped her off doesn't change my mind. I was right to let her go. And she clearly had no problem leaving. Whatever was forming between us was too volatile to last. I still haven't decided whether I wanted it to go beyond two people thrown into a situation. Not that it matters, since she's skipping town.

And Lacey and Nemesis are the same person.

I shake the thought away. I'll keep her secret from the others, mostly because I don't want to deal with their whining, which is exactly what will happen. Her being Nemesis doesn't change much anyway, at least not for me. When I look at her, I don't see the hacker—I see Lacey, the spitfire who threw a shoe at my head. I rub the ache in my chest, resting my head back.

Doesn't matter either way, I remind myself.

Ten minutes later, there's a knock on my window, and I snap upright to see Alex's grinning face leaning down. Rolling my eyes, I throw my thumb at the passenger seat. I should pay attention to my surroundings or I'm going to get shot. Again. Alex slides into the seat, dropping a backpack at his feet.

"What's up?" he asks, slapping his legs and turning to me.

"Nothing. What did you need?" I keep my eyes trained on Lacey's house. I can't afford to get distracted again, least of all by Alex King.

"Shit, son. We really *are* on a stakeout. Hot damn, I'm glad I brought some snacks. Sam almost cut my dick off when she caught me sneaking out the back door with this." He unzips it, revealing a plethora of baggies filled with everything from trail mix to brownies.

"You've got to be kidding me. Alex, this isn't a stakeout. Tell me what's going on and then get the fuck out of my car," I grumble.

"Where the hell did you pick this beater up? Clearly, you're trying to blend in. That suit isn't helping, by the way."

I'm not surprised he's completely ignoring my questions. Alex does what he wants, often going off the rails on his own tangents, with no regard to what everyone else is doing. Thankfully, he gets shit done most of the time, even if it's in an unconventional way. A lot of people think he doesn't have two brain cells to rub together, but he picks up on details others wouldn't notice. He just chooses not to say them out loud unless absolutely necessary.

Sighing, I lean over and snatch a baggie from him before ripping it open and throwing a handful of cheese crackers in my mouth. He snorts, grabbing his own, and we spend the next few minutes in silence.

"You going to tell me what you've found?"

He hums, tilting his head back and forth. "Don't have much. I haven't had a reason to get close lately. We've got some shit going down. Seems whatever was concentrated on your side of the river is starting to bleed over to the west side. We're mostly handling it, but doesn't leave a lot for extracurriculars. Vicky's been a little elusive, but once I find his pattern, should be easy to squeeze the turnip," he says, then stuffs an entire brownie in his mouth.

"Squeeze the turnip? That doesn't make any fucking sense." The curtains flutter and I lean forward, squinting. I don't know if I'm hoping to catch a glimpse of Lacey or praying I don't. I'd rather her not find me watching her house like a creeper.

"What are we looking for?" Alex whispers, eyes fixed on her house.

"Nothing. What are you going to do with him?" I murmur. I shake my head when I realize I'm whispering, too.

"Seems like we're definitely on a stakeout, but whatever. I was going to have a little talk with him first. I think he's doing some shady shit, yet no one can tell me what. Plus, the police chief has stopped calling. Don't know what you said to him, but he's being sneakier than before," he mumbles.

"Sneakier or just learned who's in charge?" I'd rather not talk shop right now. I want to deal with Victor and then kick Alex out so I can stalk Lacey in peace.

Is it really stalking if it's to keep her safe?

I shake the thought away, resigning myself to sitting here with Alex and dodging his questions about the real reason I'm parked in the middle of a residential neighborhood in a beat-up car watching a house that for all intents and purposes looks empty. Maybe he'll assume it's a safe house. It's plausible and he'd probably leave it then.

The sharp rap on my window has me practically jumping into Alex's lap. His gun appears, pointed straight at Lacey's annoyed face. She doesn't even flinch when he pulls the hammer back.

"Shit, Alex, put that away, for fuck's sake."

Shoving his hand aside, I wait until he flips the safety on before I roll the window down. She leans into the car, raising an eyebrow as she takes us in. A jagged pink line runs from just under her right eye down to her jaw and my gut twists. I glance away but can't keep my gaze away from her for long. Her absence for the last week has felt like a lifetime, and I've hated not knowing what she's doing.

"Someone cut up your pretty face, sweetheart. I hope you returned the favor," Alex quips, grinning.

"Didn't need to. He was already dead," she deadpans. "There a reason you two are hanging out across from my house? Pretty sure stalking is illegal."

Her eyes meet mine, and the ache in my chest pulses. "You'd know all about that, wouldn't you?"

Smirking, I force my muscles to relax one by one. I can feel Alex's eyes swiveling between us, deciphering the situation he's stepped into. The last thing I'm going to do is explain to him the convoluted circumstances we've created. I'd never hear the end of it. It's bad enough Sam knows about Lacey. She's texted at least a dozen times, asking me when she can come over again. I don't have the heart to tell her why she can't. I'm sure Lacey wouldn't want me to spread around her departure, anyway.

"You should be gone by now. What's the deal?"

She rolls her eyes, propping her chin in her hand. "You shouldn't be parked outside my house. What's the deal with *that*?"

Facing forward, I stare at her house, refusing to answer. Even if Alex wasn't here, I wouldn't admit I'm worried about her. She may be able to scrub her existence from the internet, but from people's minds is a different story. I'm sure whoever is still wreaking havoc in Synd hasn't forgotten about her. I'm convinced they're biding their time until she slips up and they can grab her again, forcing me to make decisions I'm not ready for. Hell, I don't even know who I'm up against yet. Taking out Razor and his gang wasn't enough. The more I dig, the more I'm convinced I need Nemesis. But asking her means putting Lacey in danger, and I can't stomach it.

"Why are we forcing her to leave? She in with them?" Alex's gun wavers as he tips it toward her.

"Knock it the fuck off, Alex. She's not…I mean, she's fine. Don't worry about it."

She grins, reaching her hand through the window. "Hi, I'm Nemesis. Good to meet you."

Alex's mouth drops open, and he blindly shakes her hand. Still gaping, he drops his grasp on her and pats his pockets, never taking his eyes from her. I've never been more thankful his clumsy ass dropped his phone in the fucking river. He'd be calling the rest of them in a heartbeat and then I'd have to deal with the fallout, which is exactly what I've been trying to avoid.

"Thought you didn't want anyone knowing? Dammit, Lacey, you just gave your identity to the biggest fucking gossip in Synd," I snap, squeezing the steering wheel to keep myself from strangling her.

"What's it matter? I'm skipping town soon, anyway. In fact, it's pretty fucking freeing to tell someone instead of them torturing it out of me."

"Wait, wait, wait"—Alex holds his hands up, shaking his head—"I thought you said you were Nemesis, but he just called you Lacey. And torture? Please tell me you didn't pull that shit, Mason."

"You didn't honestly think my actual name was Nemesis, did you? Come on, Alex. I'm smarter than that and so are you," she scoffs.

"I didn't torture you. Don't spread that shit around," I mumble.

She rolls her eyes, sighing. "Metaphorically speaking."

"That doesn't make any sense," I say as Alex shakes his head.

Alex thrusts his finger at me. "How the fuck does he know your actual name?"

"Would you calm the fuck down? This isn't a big deal. You handled the news of Sam being the Wraith perfectly fine, from what I've heard, but you're going to freak the hell out now?"

Throwing his hands in the air, he scowls. "And now you've told her Sam is the Wraith. Seriously, is there anything you *don't* know?"

Lacey tilts her head, tapping a finger on her chin. "Nope. I mean, sure there's things I don't know, but secrets like that? Yeah, I know all those ones."

He grins, a gleam entering his green eyes. "So, you can tell us who dropped the hippo off in our driveway?"

"I refuse to get involved in your ridiculous pranks. Don't even ask. This one"—she throws a thumb in my direction—"already tried that. Anyways, I'm going to need you two to clear out. You stick out like sore thumbs."

"Hey, I dressed the part. It's this one who doesn't know not to wear a suit to a stakeout."

Gritting my teeth, I suck in a deep breath. "For the last time, it's not a stakeout. We're not in a fucking cop movie. Now, how about both of you get the fuck away from me and go back to what you were doing?"

"So testy. You getting—" Alex says.

"Do not finish that sentence or I'll drown you in the river," I snarl.

Lacey's hand lands on my arm, patting me, and my entire body lights up, sending licks of flames through my blood. She's mocking me, shushing and murmuring, "There, there," as if I'm a toddler having a meltdown.

I don't shake her off. I don't want to. This might be the last time we talk. It was hard before, dropping her off at the door I'm currently staring at and knowing I wouldn't see her again. Now, it'll be excruciating, and I can't even react since Alex is grinning next to me.

"So tell me, Nemesis, Lacey, wait, which do you want to be called?" He screws up his face as he snatches up a bag of trail mix, scrunching his nose before he drops it and snags another brownie.

"Whatever is fine. Mason's the only one who calls—never mind. Nemesis is probably easier to keep track of."

"Gotcha," he says around a mouthful of chocolate. "Got a couple questions for ya. How'd you two meet? And does Ren know who you are? Like, really are? Or is this asshole the only one? Oh, and why the hell do you have to leave? Ren's been freaking out for weeks now, locking himself in his office and mumbling under his breath. Hell, the other day Sam walked in completely fucking nak—"

Slamming my arm into his neck, I trap him against the seat, and he coughs. I'm not pressing hard enough to cut anything off, but it's enough for him to stop talking.

"Think hard about what you say about my sister, Alex." Slowly I lower my arm, and he rubs his neck before shoving the rest of the dessert in as if nothing happened.

"Sorry, forgot who I was with." He smirks and then swipes it away with his hand.

"Try to keep it in mind next time," I growl, wrapping my hands around the steering wheel again.

Lacey leans down, her finger tapping along my arm as she contemplates Alex.

"Unfortunately, this isn't a slumber party where we trade our deepest, darkest secrets."

"I'm going to be honest, Nem, I don't get why you're keeping shit from us. Protecting Mason, perhaps?" He grins at us as I press my lips together. "Promise I won't tell a soul. I mean, other than Sam, because she can always tell when I'm keeping secrets, and she's fucking terrifying. Come on. It's the least you can do."

"Sam's met her," I mumble, and Alex crows, as if this is a huge revelation. He starts babbling about how he knew it and how he's going to call her on shit, but I've stopped paying attention.

Lacey's eyes glaze over, as if she's not really seeing Alex's animated movements. The warmth of her hand slips from my arm, a chill running through me at its loss. Leaning forward, I catch her eye, and I swear I catch the nightmares dancing through them, ensnaring her mind and forcing her to relive the hell she's been through.

"Kitten," I murmur. "What is it?"

Fear flashes across her face and she steps back, hands dropping from my window. She turns, dashing for the darkness behind us, away from her house. I'm out of the car before Alex realizes what's happened, and his shouts chase me through the dark, fading the farther I descend into the blackness. Something spooked her, or she's locked in some memory, and I can't leave her. Dragging her back to reality won't be easy, but I have to try. As I dash into the night, I realize I never should have let her go home. Even if I catch her, I'll never be able to keep her. She's not mine, no matter how much I wish she was.

Twenty-Six

Lacey

Thankfully, I know my neighborhood like the back of my hand, so navigating it in the middle of the night isn't hard. The absence of a moon isn't helping, though. I skid to a stop when a knee-high fence appears out of nowhere. Footsteps crash through the night, coming closer with every passing second, and I leap over the spikes. They're my downfall, as my pant leg catches on one and I crash to my hands and knees. Dew seeps into the fabric along with the pain radiating through me. I've healed a lot in the last week, but I'm still not a hundred percent.

Mist lashes across my back, as if it's laced with acid. The blood flooding the car followed me, lapping at my shoes now. Logically, I know there's nothing there, but I can't rationalize illusions from reality. It wasn't what made me run. No, I took off when Alex's face morphed into Razor's, after he told me not to protect Mason. My fight or flight took over, forcing my feet as far from him as I could. I didn't have the chance to get away before, but I won't let the opportunity pass me by this time. Half of my brain knows it's Mason chasing me, but I can't wrap my mind around reality.

A scream escapes me when a strong arm wraps around my middle, hoisting me upright. I fight until Mason's autumn scent seeps into my pores, calming my tense muscles, and I go limp. The blood eases, gently coiling around our feet before ebbing away to soak into the grass. Rationally, I understand it's only an illusion, but convincing myself of that right now is hard. Sucking in a deep breath, my eyes flutter shut as the heat from Mason's body eases the panic in me. When I open my eyes, I spot Alex, concern written all over his face.

"She okay?" He's not loud, but his voice carries through the night, and I wince.

The last thing I wanted was for someone else to witness me breaking down. It's hard enough with Mason, but at least he understands why. He's been there from the beginning. Alex, on the other hand, has known me for all of seventeen seconds and I'm already a fucking mess.

"There goes my reputation," I mutter, my voice cracking.

"I don't think he'll hold it against you, Kitten," Mason whispers in my ear, and I shiver at the intimacy of the act.

After a week of wallowing in the absence of his arms, to be in them again is surreal. I cling to him, digging my fingernails into his skin, but he doesn't complain. In fact, he sighs, as if he's reliving the moments as well.

Shaking my head, I push against him, urging him to release me, but he tightens his hold. "Mason, he'll say something."

"Don't fucking care. Just don't make me let you go yet," he murmurs, burying his nose in my hair and breathing deeply.

"Seriously, if I need to call someone, I don't have a phone, so I'd need to go back or something. Someone's gotta tell me what to do," Alex calls, swaying from side to side.

"She's fine. Just a little flashback. Why don't you go back to the car?"

"Flashback of what?"

Mason sighs, dropping his arm and stepping in front of me, as if that'll stop Alex's questions. Rolling my eyes, I poke him in the back, and he snarls over his shoulder.

"Knock it off. Like you said, I'm fine now." Stepping next to him, I cross my arms as if I can protect myself from the inevitable conversation. "I ran into a spot of trouble and have some lingering effects from it. They're getting better."

"Liar," Mason breathes. "And a spot of trouble? I hardly think being kidnapped, held in a fucking hole, and then having your face slashed up is a 'spot of trouble,' Lacey."

He glares at me, and I smirk. "Still not scared of you, Mase, but good try. Everything is fine, Mr. King. They're dead, so they won't bother me anymore."

I refuse to acknowledge my pounding heart or the nausea burning in my gut. If I fake bravado long enough, maybe it'll seep into me and be real. Nothing good will come from admitting I'm still terrified most of the time. I locked myself in my basement for three days when I came home before I ventured back upstairs.

Mason might have thought he was being sneaky, but I spent most of the time waiting for him to appear, spying on him as he kept watch from across the street. Panic would swamp me every time he pulled away, though I tracked the others he sent in his stead. I won't tell him any of that. He's still set on me leaving, but I haven't had it in me to make any plans.

I'm afraid I'll spend the rest of my life looking over my shoulder for the next disaster to strike, so I might as well do that from here. With my cover blown, I might be forced to. I trust Mason to keep my alias quiet, but he's right, Alex King is a big ole gossip when it comes to his family.

"And what happens when the people they worked for come after you, huh? Think they'll just leave you be because you're locked away in your house? Or do you perhaps think they might just kidnap you again and then I won't be there to save your ass?"

Fists clenched at his sides, panting, he's embodied the epitome of a mafia leader, but underneath the rage lies a kernel of fear. It's in his eyes, blowing out his pupils so the brown is overrun by blackness. It's in the flare of his nostrils, as he snatches at the remainder of his control over an impossible situation. One I've put him in, with no care as to how it affects his life.

"This is all my fault," I whisper, and his face falls. "I'll be gone by tomorrow night."

I turn, stepping gingerly over the fence. I don't know how the neighbors haven't come to see what the commotion is about, but the houses stay dark as I plod back to my place. Mason and Alex's raised voices chase after me, but I keep my pace steady. I won't run again unless I'm forced, and I won't wait for them to talk me out of it. Hell, they'll probably agree with me.

Staying in Synd will only distract Mason from what he needs to do. Even if my house is safer and I'm an expert at disappearing behind a computer screen, he'll never be convinced I'm capable of taking care of myself. Raging at him won't do anything other than force him to fight harder. It's in his nature—his blood. I'm not a problem to be fixed or a loose end to be tied up, but that's how he sees me. Leaving is the only option I have left to keep him safe.

If I stay, I'll only be a burden. He'll eventually tire of the responsibility. My being here will eventually put Sam at risk, which Alex will have a problem with. I don't know what would trigger a scenario like that, but from where I stand, the possibility is enough to force me onward.

"Nemesis," Alex calls, and his heavy footfalls slow as he steps into place beside me. "I don't know what's going on, but I'm pretty sure you should stay."

I stutter to a stop, biting the inside of my cheek before I answer. "I realize my leaving will leave you guys high and dry, but I'll set some things in place for Ren before I go. Help mitigate the fallout."

He runs his hand through his hair, glancing back to where Mason is presumably still waiting. When he turns back, he's scowling.

"That wasn't the reason, but whatever. If you fuck off to somewhere, who's going to protect you?"

"I hardly need protection. I'm capable of taking care of myself."

His eyes catch on my still-healing scar and his brows pull low. I'm sure he thinks I'm incapable of a lot of things, first and foremost keeping myself safe. My security has always lain within my ability to hide in plain sight. This wound on my face will make that harder, but at least I can still lurk behind a screen.

"What about Mason?" he murmurs, tilting his head.

His words pull me up short, and I scramble for the right response.

"What about him?"

"Don't tell me you don't see it," he scolds, crossing his arms. "And if you leave, it'll only get worse."

"You all will be fine. You don't have to convince me I'm important or some bullshit. Ren is more than capable of dealing with things."

"Shit, you really don't see it, do you?" He sighs, scrubbing his hands over his face.

I refuse to admit I know exactly what he's talking about. Without the entire story, Alex can't even begin to comprehend why entertaining the idea of Mason and I being together would be disastrous for both of us, but especially me. There's too much guilt, and I don't have enough to offer someone like him.

"I can take care of myself," I say, tipping my chin up as my heart breaks a little more.

"And when you fail?"

Seething, I open my mouth, stabbing my finger into his chest.

"Lacey," Mason says, and I turn away from them both, furiously swiping at my eyes.

"Alex, get in the car."

Alex sighs before edging around me. He stops, looking down at me, and I tense. "Go easy on him, Nem. He's been through a lot. There's something there. Don't fuck it up. He's different and I'm pretty sure that's because of you."

He walks away before I can respond, and I keep my eyes on him until he slips into the car. I doubt Mason heard what Alex said. I'm not even sure what he was getting at with the last bit, but that may be because I don't want to. If I look at it too closely, I might find something I can't handle. Or maybe something I'm not ready for yet.

"You going to take off again?"

"Not in the way you mean. Was there something else you needed?" I ask, keeping my eyes trained on the back of Alex's head. I'm pretty sure he's snacking again, and I swallow down a chuckle. Now is not the time to lose it over a brownie.

"Don't do that. We've been through enough where we shouldn't have to hide behind formal words and business transactions."

"This isn't a business transaction. And I'm the last person to use formal words, Mr. Byrns."

I can't help myself, and a small smile forms when his snort rings out between us. Stepping up beside me, his hand brushes my skin and then his fingers tangle with mine until they're laced together.

"I can't keep doing this," I whisper.

He's yanking my emotions around, his words saying one thing and his actions another. All it does is send me into a spiral of self-doubt. I didn't think we'd ever be standing here, halfway through the middle of something neither of us wants to define. And in a matter of minutes, it'll be ripped apart, and I'll walk away forever.

I can stand here a bit longer. I can carry this memory with me to another city. At this point, I wouldn't have to work again. I could do exactly what he said and retire on some beach and drink dirty martinis. Read as many books as I want or…I search my mind for something else. Shit. I don't have any hobbies. Hell, I barely read. I don't have time. Retiring sounds fucking boring.

Setting up in a new city and creating a new identity will keep me occupied for a few months, but I doubt I'll ever fully move on from Synd. I've spent the better part of my adult life here, helping the leaders who live in the shadows. A part of me will always be here. I'll never be able to move on, especially from the man standing next to me, which is entirely ridiculous.

"You could—"

"Don't. Don't say something you don't mean. Don't come here and fill my head with things when not even five minutes ago you were spouting all of the dangers of staying here. It's not fair. We don't owe each other anything. The shit we went through doesn't connect us in some mystical way. In fact, we never would have even crossed paths had I kept a sane thought in my head. You need to stop sitting outside my house. You think you're doing something, but it's only making me more of a target. I've prepared for shit like this, so I'm well equipped to keep myself safe. I'll be gone by tomorrow."

"But—"

I untangle my fingers from his. "Go home, Mason. Do your job. Keep your family safe. Stop thinking about the what-ifs and worrying about me."

"Can't just turn it off, Lacey. Doesn't work like that. Even if I could, I wouldn't want to," he says gruffly.

Huffing, I cross my arms before swinging around. "You realize it's the guilt, right? That's all this is. There's no reason for you to care about me. I'm some crazy person who was quasi-stalking you and got caught. If I would have been kidnapped from my own house, there'd be nothing for you to feel guilty about. It'll drift away like the fog on the river, evaporating with the morning sun. But I have to actually leave in order for that to happen. So, let me go. Your life will be easier when you do."

I turn away before he spots the sheen in my eyes. I wish it was different, but I can't change the circumstances now. It's too late for grand declarations and wild promises that would probably turn out to be hollow.

Once inside, I refuse to peek out the window like I did a week ago. I refuse to give in to the pain of watching him drive away and out of my life a second time.

Twenty-Seven

Mason

Ren settles in the seat across from me, setting his mug down carefully before meeting my eyes. The coffee shop is practically empty, but I tucked myself in the corner by the back door for a reason. I had hoped no one would find me, or at least I'd be able to make a quick getaway out the door leading to the alley. It has nothing to do with this being the table where I first saw Lacey.

"You're being morose lately, Byrns. Sam has asked that I speak to you about it, but let's pretend I did, and we'll get on to more important business," Ren says, pulling out his tablet from the bag hanging off his chair.

"Fine by me," I say, waving my hand as I lean back.

"Alex said you might have something for me?" He cocks an eyebrow.

Fucking Alex. It was hard enough to convince him not to say anything about Lacey's secret identity, but skirting around the truth of everything that's transpired between us was worse. He kept asking questions I didn't have answers to. Didn't help I had to drive his ass home, either. It gave him way too much time to worm shit out of me. Threatening him with a bullet in the head only made him laugh. I'm sure Alex told Ren some vague shit, and I'm dealing with the aftermath.

"Not sure what he's talking about," I hedge, glancing over the menu hanging above the counter. One of the baristas gives me a half smile before turning away, shooing the rest of them into the back. "Did you have them clear the place?"

"No, but there may have been an article published today about me. I'm sure the rumor mills are turning," he mutters, eyes fixed on his screen. "What do you know about Nemesis's whereabouts?"

My heart skips a beat, and I cross my arms to cover the tremor in my hands. I've done what she asked, staying away from her house for the past three days. Coincidentally, I haven't slept since then either. Instead, I spend the nights either searching the Barrens or tracking the shadows cast by the moon across my ceiling.

"Why would I know where she is?"

He sighs, finally setting his device on the table as his gray eyes pierce me. "Why do you consistently insist on doing things by yourself, Mason?"

"Clearly, I don't since I've been working with you three and the Reapers for almost a year. That's more than we've done since the attempted coup."

"I realize the loss of Colin was a blow you weren't expecting. Especially after such a long era of peace within Synd. We anticipated the transition of not only your hierarchy, but your personal life as well. We've tried to support this…phase, in whatever way we can, but we will not step in and usurp your position. No matter what bullshit Shane has spouted. His methods may be archaic, but underneath all of his bluster is concern."

Carefully, I keep my face blank throughout his speech, but bark out a laugh when he mentions his brother. "Shane King doesn't give two shits about me. I don't expect him to either. The only concern he has is for how my decisions will affect his side of the river and Sam. Those are the things he cares about. If I wasn't tied to him through my sister, he would have floated me long ago, I'm sure."

Ren nods and I'm pretty sure he's biting the inside of his cheek. "I'm not the one to convince you of Shane's motives. However, I do know him better than you. Now, let's cut the bullshit. Tell me where Nemesis went. Alex isn't exactly subtle, but somehow you instilled some loyalty within him, which is fucking annoying. I've become worried about her, which is not something I anticipated, so if you could clear things up, I'd appreciate it."

Staring at each other, I debate how much I should reveal. Lacey might not want anyone to know her extracurricular activities, but Ren won't let this go. He'll keep digging until he either loses his mind or finds the truth. It's rare he shows emotions or admits he cares about someone beyond his circle.

"She doesn't think anyone will remember her," I murmur, and his eyes widen.

"What a ridiculous notion." He taps his finger on the table. "Wait, she told you that? When?"

"A lot has happened in the last few weeks. However, she's already left Synd."

He pushes back from the table abruptly, upending his chair in the process and the wood clatters across the tile floor. Bracing his hands on the table, he looms over me, snarling. "What the fuck did you do?"

"Ren." Sam's voice rings out sharply from behind him and he straightens, face smoothing into a blank mask.

Snatching up his tablet, he pivots, marching toward the door. Their fingers brush as Ren passes and the tension in his shoulders eases. The tinkling of the bell on his exit is a sharp contrast to his outburst. Sam's eyes track him until the door whooshes shut, and she weaves around the tables toward me. Settling into Ren's vacated chair, she props her arms on the table and glares at her folded hands. The missing barista pops up a minute later, placing a mug next to her elbow and then scurries away.

"You going to tell me what's going on or do I have to keep piecing shit together like some fucked up puzzle?" she asks before taking a sip.

My stomach tightens. "What'd you tell the Kings?"

"Seriously? I can't deal with another pissing contest, Mason," she breathes. "Just tell me what's happening."

Tipping my head back, I suck in a deep breath and proceed to spill the entire story of the last few weeks. I leave out the way my feelings toward Lacey have changed, morphed into something I don't even understand anymore. My emotions are too tangled up with guilt and trauma to understand clearly, anyway.

Relaying to her what's happened takes the better part of an hour, and my coffee's gone cold by the time I'm done. Miraculously, Sam stays quiet while I'm speaking, only occasionally tapping her nails on her mug. Halfway through she sighs so aggressively I expect her to slither from her chair, straight to the floor.

"Sam, this needs to stay between us," I say.

She huffs, spinning her empty mug on the table. "I don't like keeping things from them, especially Shane."

"Bet he gets pissy, doesn't he?" I chuckle, but she doesn't join in.

"How about you let me handle my relationships with my guys, and we'll go back to pretending I'm not involved with three men?"

"Fuck, Sam. It's going to get out eventually. In fact, there's more than a couple articles speculating on it. Who fucking cares? Your life is your own, so just fucking live it."

I've never told her so plainly before that I don't give a shit who or how many she's with. If anyone talks shit about what she's doing, they'll only do it once. Whether the Kings or I get to them first is the question. Eyeing Sam, I realize she'd probably get to them before the rest of us even knew it happened.

Her brows pull low and she scrunches her nose. "You honestly don't care?"

"I'd rather not have this conversation, because I don't like thinking about you with anyone. But, no, I don't care. Clearly, it's the best scenario for you, since they're in our line of work. Plus, anyone can tell they love you, so again, I don't fucking care. As long as you're happy and all that sappy bullshit. Can we stop talking about this now?" I grumble, spying tears in her eyes.

I didn't realize she put so much stock in my opinion. In my mind we had an unspoken agreement to never talk about it. Now, I'm curious how often she's worried about what I think. I wonder if she'd care if I was with Lacey. Gritting my teeth, I push the thoughts of her aside.

"Okay, onto your issues, of which there are many. A plethora. A multitude, if you will," she says.

"Did you get a word of the day calendar or something?"

She grins before her face sobers. "So, the woman I met at your place is actually Nemesis, who we've been working with for years. She's also been spying on you and then she got hurt, then she was kidnapped, and then you saved her before finally convincing her she needed to skip town for her own safety. And now she's gone, which means Ren is freaking out and you're heartbroken. Did I get that right?"

"I'm not fucking heartbroken. It was a business decision."

Snorting, she waves her mug in the air, as if that'll magically make more coffee appear. "You practically bit my head off the other day. Nemesis is more important to you than being merely an asset. And Ren doesn't have many people he clicks with. He considers her a friend, even if he's never said anything. Stands to reason she's more than just business to all of us. You know she scolded Ren after he admitted to fucking with the cameras when I was dealing with the police commissioner last year?"

"I didn't. She's a pain in the ass most of the time, so that's not surprising. This conversation is moot anyway, as she's gone. I have no idea how I would even get a hold of her, even if I wanted to. Which I don't. I need to focus on cleaning up my territory and find out who the hell is fucking with me."

My phone vibrates, and Sam's eyes drop to it on the table. A smirk rolls over her face before she pushes back and makes her way to the counter, then starts chatting with the barista who magically appears.

Snatching my phone up, time slows as I read the message once, then again. The device slips from my grasp, clattering across the table. Grabbing it again, I stare at the screen, not really seeing the words. I jolt when it vibrates again, another message popping up.

"What's going on?" Sam's voice sounds a million miles away.

"I have to go. I have to…" Pushing to my feet, I can't take my eyes away from my phone. "Sorry, Sam. I'll call you."

Brushing past her, I start for the door, pivoting when I'm halfway there. Sam's eyes widen as I blow past her for the back entrance. When I finally look up, I find three men loitering around my car, clearly trying to boost it. I've been driving the beater I swiped from one of the warehouses for almost two weeks. It's not worth shit, but it allows me to blend in most of the time. Alex may have been right when he said I shouldn't wear a suit, which is why I'm currently in a hoodie and jeans, but I wish I'd worn something more intimidating today.

"Get the fuck away from my car," I bellow, slipping my phone into my pocket.

Tucking one arm behind me, I grasp the handle of my gun, hoping I don't have to use it. I'd rather not have to deal with a clean-up in the middle of the afternoon. One of them takes off, bolting for the mouth of the alley, and disappears around the corner. The other two, though, aren't as smart. Instead, they square up, and one of them pulls a gun.

"Piece of shit car. I'm sure you can afford to give it to us," he says, his weapon hanging loosely by his side.

"You *really* don't want to fuck with me," I growl.

I barely stop myself from rolling my eyes when Sam's slight figure appears behind them. A crazed grin graces her face and I sigh. She's itching for a fight, for whatever reason, and while I would love to give her an outlet, I'd rather not deal with the aftermath.

Shaking my head, she pouts, but doesn't stop moving in on them. She slips a knife from her sleeve before she crouches behind a dumpster, peeking over the top and wiggling her eyebrows at me.

"You could make this easier and give us the keys," he asks, his nasally voice echoing off the buildings.

"You could just walk away. That'd be the easiest solution." Slipping my weapon from my back, I point it at him and he jolts. "If you're going to pull a gun, be prepared to use it, dumbass."

His friend jumps forward, knocking into him, and his weapon bounces on the concrete as he crashes to his knees. The friend reaches for the car door, as if it'll open if he just tries one more time. Rolling my eyes, I take one step and the alleyway lights up, a blast of fire exploding from my car and knocking me back. Heat engulfs my body, my head bounces off the ground, and the world goes dark.

Twenty-Eight

Lacey

Smacking myself is not the way I wanted to wake up. Groaning, I rub my eyes as I sit up in bed. Alarms blare around me and the flashing light in the corner of my makeshift room pierces me. I knew I should have chosen something else to make sure I woke up when someone approached my house, but this was the easiest on short notice.

Grabbing my tablet, I pull up the cameras for my front door and groan as I flop back. Alex King is standing on my doorstep, pounding away. The consequences of my missteps are piling up. Letting a leader of the mafia know where I live is just the latest one. I don't even know why he's here. This was exactly the reason I laid the trail of my departure from Synd.

Rolling out of bed, I pull on a pair of sweatpants. After putting in the code to stop the incessant blaring, I tromp up the stairs. I'd love to think he'll wander away, assuming I'm gone, but the determination on his face says otherwise. Swinging open the door, he braces his hands on the frame and glares down at me.

"Can I help you?"

"Thought you fucking left?" he growls, and I straighten my spine.

Gone is the laughing man from the other night. So is the somberness gracing his face from when he was advising me to stay. He looks pissed, but underneath is a layer of concern. He's panting, face flushed.

"I doubt that's the reason you're pounding on my door at four in the afternoon."

"You need to come with me. Now. Shoes," he barks, pointing at my bare feet.

Crossing my arms, I tap my foot. "Want to tell me why? Or am I supposed to just fall in line because you yelled at me?"

"For fuck's sake, it's Mason. He needs you, so get the fuck going or I'm throwing you over my shoulder and carrying your ass to him." He pivots, marching back to his car. "Two minutes!"

His attitude leaves something to be desired, but I don't doubt he'd make good on his threat. Before I slam the door, I watch as he paces next to his car before getting in and resting his head on the steering wheel. His behavior twists my stomach into knots. Mason should have received the text messages by now. Which means he realized it was me and he's pissed. The last thing I want to do is have him freak out because I didn't actually leave Synd. I could lock down my house, stop interfering in their business, and wait until everything blows over.

Instead, I grab a hoodie and slip on my flip-flops. It's not warm enough for them, but I don't have the energy to find socks. At the last second, I grab my backpack filled with clothes and toiletries. I packed it when I decided I was staying in Synd.

I never want to be stuck without clothes again if I can help it, no matter how comfortable Mason's are.

Throwing my tablet and a phone inside and zipping it closed, I set the codes to lock down my house. Slipping out the front door, I wait for the thud of the locks setting before making my way to Alex's car. He barely waits for me to close the door before he takes off, weaving through the streets. When we hit the river, I wipe away the sweat gathering on my palms and hold my breath to calm my racing heart.

"Thought we would be going to the Byrns estate."

"They're at our house," he mutters, jerking the wheel to pass someone.

Their horn blares as we race past, and I wave while they flip us off.

"You realize it won't help anyone if we're wrapped around a pole, right?"

"Shut the fuck up. I left her to come get your ass, so why don't you show a little gratitude," he snarls, gunning it when we hit their street.

"Wait, who? What the hell happened?"

Glaring out the windshield, he presses his lips into a thin line and then cranks the wheel and we bump up the driveway. Slamming on the brakes, he throws himself from the car, not waiting for me, and I scramble after him. I haven't been here in months and certainly never inside, and my nerves double.

Darkness swallows me when I step through the door, and I blink to clear the spots from my vision. Alex has disappeared into the massive house, leaving me to wonder what the hell I'm supposed to do. The Kings' house may be identical to Mason's, but that doesn't mean the rooms are the same. Bouncing on the balls of my feet, indecision licks through me until a flash of blonde hair whips around the corner.

"Hello, Lacey? Or do you prefer Nemesis?"

The woman is short, and that's saying something, as I'm not exactly tall myself. I should ask who she is, but I already know. Willow St. James came to Synd only a few months ago and fell in with Hawk, the Reapers vice president. She had troubles with a stalker, which pissed me off. It took me forever to find him, but eventually I did, thankfully before she was hurt.

Folding her hands in front of her, she tilts her head and I jolt, realizing she's waiting for me to speak.

"Lacey is fine. I was looking for—"

"I know. They're this way."

Hurrying up the grand staircase, we turn down a corridor. At the end, Ren is buried in his tablet, talking to Ryker Helms and Hawk. I rarely talk to either of the bikers nowadays, usually going through one of the Kings. They stick to their territory, but they've been mingling with the mafia leaders more and more lately.

Ren's head pops up when we get close, and he stares at me. I lift my hand but tuck it around my middle when he doesn't move. Willow steps up next to Hawk, wrapping an arm around his waist, and he drops a kiss on her head. I turn away, gazing around the hall. Anything to get away from Ren's searching eyes. I knew he was intense, just from our conversations, but experiencing it in person is a whole other level.

"So, can someone tell me what I'm doing here?" I say, my voice carrying, though I tried to be quiet.

"Alex didn't tell you?" Ryker asks, and now I have two intense men staring me down.

"Uh, no. He just threatened to toss me over his shoulder. Said something about Mason and then yelled at me some more, but he wasn't exactly making sense."

"You should tell her," Ryker whispers harshly to Ren.

Ren peers over his shoulder. "Why the hell should I do it? Alex should have told her."

"Because you know her better than the rest of us," Hawk chimes in and Willow smacks him.

"For fuck's sake, are you two bickering about who's going to tell her what happened? You're both ridiculous," Mac, Ryker's girlfriend, says from behind me.

She grabs my elbow and steers me toward the door, muttering under her breath. My eyes find Willow's wide blue ones and she gives me a look I can't decipher. Disappearing from view as we step through the door, we're met with Shane King's raised voice. Mac drops my elbow and stomps to a bed, where the rest of the people who run the underbelly of Synd are gathered. I have no idea where I am, but it's insanely huge. There are at least five doors leading to fuck knows where.

"If you would have just told us what the fuck was going on, maybe this shit wouldn't have happened," Shane bellows. "People keeping shit to themselves is exactly how things went to hell a year ago. I'm not about to go through another shitshow like that again just because you think you can handle this on your own."

A low voice mumbles from the bed, but I still can't see who's in it. I assume it's Mason, but why they're all in this room is beyond me. A conference room would be the better place if Mason was mad at me, like Alex's behavior suggested. Hell, even the kitchen would be a better place than a random bedroom. Unless Mason was hurt, but then the others would be freaking out, wouldn't they?

"Didn't ask…you've got to be fucking kidding me. Pull your head out of your ass and start asking for help before it's too late. Do it before one of us gets killed, Byrns."

"You realize I can't take you seriously with that shirt on, right Shane?" Sam's laughing voice floats over the crowd and Shane shifts, revealing Sam and Mason propped up against the headboard next to each other.

"Your fault I have it in the first place, Princess," Shane growls.

Ducking to the side, I step behind the open door. I shouldn't be here. Alex shouldn't have come to get me. This is clearly a family thing. I don't know what happened, but I probably shouldn't know either. The door pushes into me as someone walks through and I spy the back of Ren's head. When he glances around, I shuffle deeper into the corner, hoping he doesn't turn around.

He steps further inside and grabs Mac. "Where'd she go?"

I'm slipping around the door before she answers. The last thing I want is to intrude, and it feels like no one knows why I'm here either. If I can get away before Mason spots me, then I can pretend I was never here. I can hole myself up in my house, and next time I won't answer the door, especially not for Alex King. Ryker and Hawk are hunched over a screen with their backs to me, and I let out a small sigh.

I'm halfway down the hall when Willow catches me, falling into step beside me. "Are you okay?"

"I'm fine."

"You don't seem fine. You seem confused."

She gives me a small smile, brushing her hair over her shoulder before tucking her hands into the front pocket of her fluffy pink sweater. She looks out of place, surrounded by bikers in leathers, but somehow she fits.

"I didn't really get the story of what happened, so, yeah. I'm still confused. Doesn't matter. I think Alex overreacted in bringing me here."

"Oh, he definitely didn't. Mason was freaking out, saying he thought it was a decoy to get to you. Obviously, that wasn't the case, but he wouldn't stop yelling until Alex said he'd find you. Shane was a little salty since he was the last to find out who you were or rather, that Mason knew who you were? Sorry, I'm still learning everything here." She chuckles, glancing over her shoulder as we round the corner.

I let out a sigh as I spot the front door at the bottom of the massive staircase. "What was a decoy?"

"The car bomb."

She says it so matter-of-factly, her words don't compute at first. When they do, I miss the next step and her hand on my arm is the only thing stopping me from tumbling down the stairs.

"Car bomb? What the hell are you talking about?"

She winces, peering back to where we came from. "Sorry, I'm not...I'm probably not the one to explain this to you. I only know because I was with Hawk when Ren called. We were closer, so we got them."

"Them?"

I'm so lost at this point, I'm ready to race back up the stairs and demand someone give me a proper explanation. Pivoting, I'm ready to do just that when sanity rushes back in. It's none of my business. Mason told me to leave Synd and I didn't. If he's spouting off about a car bomb being a decoy to get to me, then he has to be pissed at me. I'm not about to get bitched out in front of these people. Especially if he's revealed anything about what I've done over the past year.

"You know what, never mind. I can find the answers myself. Just tell them I left for real this time."

"For real?" She tilts her head, and I shrug off the hand she still has on my arm.

"Yeah, I said I was leaving Synd and then I didn't. It's a lot of work to get all my stuff disconnected. Can't just pack a bag and be gone."

"Liar," Mason says, his deep voice resonating in my bones.

Automatically, my spine straightens and my palms tingle. Willow grimaces, stepping back and then hurrying up the stairs, leaving me alone with him. Peeking from the corner of my eye, I find him glaring at me, arms crossed over his bare chest, with a bandage wrapped around his shoulder. I close my eyes, as a wave of dizziness swamps me.

"Not my circus, not my monkeys," I mutter and spin to clomp down the steps.

"Seriously? Just going to walk away?"

At the bottom of the stairs, feet from freedom, I turn again. "I shouldn't be here in the first place, Mason. You're clearly fine, so I'm going to go."

"You didn't leave," he says, still planted at the top of the stairs, and I feel like we're a million miles apart.

"Like I said—"

"Cut the bullshit, Lacey. We both know you're not in there packing. You're too busy tracking down stolen money." He smirks as if he's won something.

Huffing, I roll my eyes. "As amazing as this little conversation is, I have to go. Glad you didn't get blown up."

He sobers and my stomach clenches. I didn't mean it so flippantly, but I can't afford to be dragged back into his orbit. Ever since we ran into each other in the coffee shop, I've been on a rollercoaster, never knowing which way was up. He turned my life upside down, and I can't figure out if it was for the better or not. It certainly wasn't for him if he's getting blown up and thinks it's because of me.

"This isn't over, Kitten. You're in this now, even more than you were before."

"I wasn't in anything before. I am exactly where I was, just a little more scarred now," I say bitterly, gesturing at the line on my face.

It's less red than before, but not enough. I'm surprised no one mentioned it when I got here. Stepping into their world has left me disoriented and scarred. That's what this whole trip has felt like—stepping into another world. In Mason's house, I was confined, sheltered, and kept apart. I wasn't in the middle of anything, spending most of the day by myself.

Here, with everyone's accusing stares boring into my soul, I realize how out of place I am. I'd never fit in with these people. They're a family, and that's not something one just steps into, demanding a place. Here they earn their spots. And I haven't. I never will. Which is why I kept asking Mason to let me go. I've always known I wouldn't fit.

Hurrying out the door, I try to slam it, but it's too heavy. Instead, it thuds behind me. With the sun setting, the bitter wind has picked up, and it sends a shiver rolling down my spine. At that moment, the skies open up, dowsing me in seconds, and a humorless laugh leaves me. The icy rain pierces my skin like an omen of worse things coming, hiding in the shadows, waiting for the opportunity to flood through the streets of Synd and whisk me away.

I don't know if I'd care if it did.

Twenty-Nine

"Lacey, get your ass back in here," I yell, but the door stays shut.

She probably can't hear me through the thick wood. Suddenly, rain lashes against the windowpanes and I rush down the stairs. I can't let her be caught in a thunderstorm. She'll probably get hit by lightning and then I'll have to revive her or some shit.

Heaving open the heavy door, I almost crash into her standing on the top step. She's already soaked, and I haul her back into the foyer. Shivering, she stumbles into me. I wince as her head hits my shoulder.

The explosion didn't do much, but when I hit the ground, my shoulder took the brunt of the impact. I wouldn't have even bothered wrapping it except for the road rash. If I had a choice, I wouldn't be at the Kings' house either. With Sam being knocked unconscious from the explosion, I wasn't going to take her home. The Kings would have killed me. Besides, this is her home now.

"You're going to get sick again, standing around in the goddamn rain," I grumble.

"Let me go, Mason. I need to get my bag, and then call for a car."

Her entire body shivers, teeth clacking together. I pull her back into my chest. She tugs, trying to get away, but I grip her tighter and she sighs.

"I won't freeze to death from two minutes in the rain. And I have clothes in my bag, which is in Alex's ridiculously expensive car. Plus, I'm already wet, so I don't really care about going back out there," she says, even as her muscles ease.

Releasing her, I step back, hoping she doesn't bolt. Or at the very least, she comes back if she does. When Alex said she was still in the city, I almost went after her myself, but I was torn. Leaving Sam when she's injured felt wrong. A visceral need welled inside of me to confirm Lacey was tucked away, safe in her house. Plus, I need answers only she can give.

I track her movements out the door as she dashes to the car, and then while she stomps her feet when the door won't open. Turning to me, she glares when I slide the keys from my pocket, smirking as I press the button. If looks could kill…well, I'd be dead several times over from her gaze over the past several weeks.

"You could have unlocked it before I got there, asshole."

Tracking rain on the rug, she pushes her wet hair off her forehead. Even looking like a drowned rat, she's still striking. Even with the scar running down her face, water dripping from the grooves, she's still captivating.

I've spent so long denying the want inside, I'm never sure how to respond. I no longer know why I'm fighting myself. Since she stumbled into my life, I'm more grounded. Looking back, I don't know if I've ever been this focused on something.

After the coup, I was surviving, doing what needed to be done for Sam, for the family, and for the city. Since the Guild came through, I just haven't given enough of a shit to deal with anything. Lacey made me feel something other than numbness.

"What would be the fun in that?" I start up the stairs but turn when she doesn't follow. "You coming?"

"I'm not going up there." Crossing her arms, she leans against the front door, but straightens almost immediately.

"Could we not do this? I'm fucking tired. Why won't you come upstairs?"

She sighs, glancing around. "Because I just came from there. And I'm sopping wet."

I smirk and she rolls her eyes. "I'm sure I could help you take care of that."

"What the fuck," she breathes.

I've spent the last few weeks denying that I want her, thinking I'm making the right choice. In reality I'm lying to myself, justifying why she's safer away from me. Being on the outskirts of our world affords her a layer of protection. The moment I brought her into my house, I stripped that security away without even realizing. I'm still torn between where she'll be safest, but I'm done tempering my words.

"If they don't care about blood splattered about, then they won't care if the carpets get a little wet. I can't carry your ass around right now, so you'll have to walk on your own two feet. I realize you're not used to that anymore."

"You are so fucking insufferable. Do you even hear yourself when you talk, or is it just a buzzing sound in your ears at this point?"

She stomps up the stairs, huffing as she pushes past me. Once at the top, she pauses. Clearly, she has no idea where to go, so I grab her elbow, guiding her past the hallway where everyone is gathered. I catch Willow's eye, and she shoos everyone inside the bedroom. Helms snarls, but Hawk pushes him inside before either of them spot us.

"Where are we going?"

"Somewhere you can change without a bunch of people waiting around for you to waltz out of the bathroom," I say, pushing open a door to what should be a bedroom.

Heaving a sigh of relief when I find it's stripped bare, I close the door behind us and lean against the wood. She spins in a slow circle before dropping her backpack to the ground.

"You going to leave, or are you expecting me to put on a show?" she asks, planting her hands on her hips.

"I wouldn't complain, but there is a bathroom behind you."

She scoffs, scooping up her backpack and marching for the door, then slams it once she's inside. I drop my hands to brace them on my knees. I kept up the ruse of being fine for long enough, but now my body is failing me.

Whoever rigged my car to blow didn't anticipate someone trying to jack it. Thankfully, I didn't lose consciousness for long and was able to make calls to everyone. Once I got to Sam, though, it became a shitshow. She was just waking up, and I happened to be on the phone with Shane when she did, which sent everyone into high alert. As if my car blowing up wasn't enough reason to panic. Although, events like this seem to be commonplace nowadays.

Weeks of peace are all we're afforded these days before another issue crops up. I've been running full steam for almost a year, though most of that has been spent healing my body or hiding from my problems. I just hope it's not too late to clean up my territory.

"Are you okay?" Lacey's voice floats over me, easing the tension gathering in my lower back.

Straightening, I take her in, swathed in all black, before saying, "I'm fine. Long day. Ready?"

"For what? No one's told me what's going on and I'd rather not be here anyways."

Dropping into a chair by the window, she pulls out a tablet, effectively ignoring me.

"If you don't know what's going on and you didn't want to come, why did you?"

Looking up, she raises an eyebrow as she purses her lips. "You say that as if I didn't have an angry mafia enforcer threatening to bust down my door."

"Well, if you don't care, then why'd you help with the money?"

Her eyes drop and her shoulders tense. "What money?"

"You realize I know your tells, right? Stop lying and just tell me what you did."

Sighing, she drops the tablet on the table and pulls out a phone. I wonder how many devices she's got stuffed away in her bag. It's jam-packed full of shit.

"It wasn't hard, but I still don't know who took it in the first place. Whoever it is, they're not ignorant, or at least whoever works for them isn't. The identity is buried under a bunch of VPNs and shell companies. So, it'll take awhile to figure out who they are." She squints at the screen and then her nostrils flare. "Holy shit."

Marching toward her, she doesn't look up until I'm next to her and fear swims in her eyes. The screen is playing the explosion over and over. It's surreal to watch my body fly back on repeat. Lacey taps the screen, and another shot of the alley pops up. She tries to angle it away from me, but I grab her wrist, watching as Sam jumps up and the blast hits her. She slams into the brick building, body crumpling to the ground. The dumpster is the only thing that saved her.

It's not until Lacey's other hand grips my wrist that I realize I'm practically grinding her bones together. Forcing my fingers from her, I step back. The video still plays on a loop, burning into my brain, and I know I'll be reliving this in my nightmares. It'll be added to the roster of other atrocities I watch each night. The only time I've had a reprieve was when Lacey was tucked next to me.

"Okay, so I'm caught up. The cameras are jammed before this, so I doubt I'll be able to see who's responsible," she mumbles.

"Why did they turn on after, then?"

I don't understand how most of this stuff works. Ren's explained it at least a dozen times since Lacey started tripping the cameras, but it never sinks in. This isn't my forte. It never bothered me, since I had Ren and Lacey—Nemesis—to answer any questions. Now I wish I had paid more attention. This is beyond the basics, though. Her fingers fly over the screen until she lets out a frustrated cry and throws it down.

"I can't find anything from here. They turned on because whatever triggered the mechanism, most likely the guy grabbing the handle, was set on a frequency that interrupted the signal that was blocking the cameras. I need to go home," she says, shoving her devices in her bag, and then pushing to her feet.

"Wait. What does that mean? I don't understand." Holding up my hands, I stop her from barreling me over.

"It means I can't work on a fucking tablet. I need my computers and they're at home. So, I have to go."

The bedroom door swings open, slamming into the wall, and we both freeze as Ren prowls inside. Lacey stares at him like a deer in headlights, and I step in front of her. Ren scowls, but I'm not about to let him go after her because he's jealous I found out who she is before him. It's not like we planned it, though he probably doesn't know that. I doubt Sam's been running her mouth, telling them everything I revealed at the coffee shop. She hasn't exactly had the opportunity.

"Get the fuck out of the way, Byrns. I'm not going to shoot her because she kept shit from me. She's a hacker, I expect such things. *You,* on the other hand, I can be pissed at, so tread carefully," Ren says as he advances on us.

"Mason, get out of the way. It's fine. Maybe."

"Not helping, Kitten," I mutter.

Ren rolls his eyes at my nickname for her. I don't owe him anything and she's never complained. He's just pissed he didn't figure shit out before I did. I'm not going to apologize for it. He'll just have to deal.

"Do you have any idea how fucking worried we've been?" Ren growls, and I glance at Lacey, whose eyes widen.

"Uh, excuse me?"

"You've been gone for fucking weeks, and all we've had is some bullshit auto-message about a vacation. No one knew where you were, we couldn't find you, and then you show up with *this* asshole."

"Today is really fucking with you, isn't it?" I chime in and he snarls at me.

He's usually calm and collected, playing his cards so close to his chest, he probably can't even decipher them half of the time. According to Alex, he broke when Sam wouldn't wake up after I shot Colin, but I was so out of it then, I didn't notice. This turnaround is freaking me out. It's been hard enough feeling like I'm on the outside of whatever bond they've formed. Even Helms and his crew are closer to the Kings now, and I've spent the last eight months in limbo, watching them from behind a sheet of glass, wishing it would shatter.

"Stop it. Both of you. This isn't helping anyone. Ren, I'm sorry for…well, whatever it is you're mad about. Mason, stop being a dick to him. He's clearly having a hard time evaluating the situation with Sam being hurt, plus probably taking on the extra workload I inadvertently left him. Now, will someone please take me home or should I call a car instead?"

"You're not fucking leaving," I yell at the same time Ren says something about her dropping off the grid.

"Stop. If you want answers, I need my computer. Clearly, I can't leave you guys to figure these things out yourselves, so I'll stay in Synd until this is resolved and then I'll—"

"You're not fucking leaving," I growl.

Ren's face reddens and I wonder if we've pushed him too far.

He turns to me, jabbing a finger in my chest. "This is all your fucking fault. If you would have just kept your area in line, we wouldn't be here. Sam wouldn't be hurt, and no one would be slowly dismantling our city. It would have been better if you had—"

"That's enough, Ren." Shane's voice cuts through the tension swirling between us.

Lacey sucks in a breath, stepping closer to me, and her hand brushes my arm. Ren's eyes gloss over, and he shuffles back, hands flexing over and over as he tries to rein in his emotions. His accusations aren't anything new. No grand revelations come from them. They're the same ones that have bounced around my own head for the last eight months. Ren merely said out loud what everyone else is too scared to, including me.

Ren shakes his head before meeting my eyes. "I apologize. That was out of line."

He pivots and stalks from the room, closing the door softly behind him. Silence descends, blanketing the space, as I struggle for a response. If I admit he was right, I'll be seen as weak. If I deny it, we all know I'll be lying. There's no way to get out of this without appearing as if I'm either a whiny bitch or a weak one, and in our world, neither is acceptable.

"Tell Sam to call me," I say as I grab Lacey's backpack.

"Fuck that. I'm not explaining shit to her. She wants to see Nemesis. Plus, I'm not cleaning up the fallout from Ren's inability to keep his thoughts to himself. Sam isn't going to be happy about any of this, and I refuse to be the one she takes shit out on." Shane plants himself in front of the door, as if that will stop us.

"I have to get *Lacey* home. There's nothing to explain. I have work to do, and so do you."

Shane runs his hands through his hair, clearly frustrated, but whether it's with me or the fact there are a dozen people in his house right now is debatable.

"*Lacey* can use Ren's system to figure shit out. And you know your sister isn't going to let this go. Sam's got some sixth sense on reading Ren. She'll get what happened out of him and then shit will hit the fan. I'm not cleaning up the mess. It's been a minute since she was pissed at me, and I'd like to keep it that way. We're finally in a good place and I won't jeopardize that for you."

"You mean you finally pulled your head out of your ass and stopped taking your own insecurities out on my sister?" I say, all the while knowing I'm deflecting.

I expect him to scowl or cuss me out, but instead his face drops, fear lining his eyes.

"You have no idea what it's been like here. We're all dealing with shit in our own way. Don't make the same mistakes I did, Mason," he says dejectedly.

Shane leaves, his usual cockiness drained from his gait. Lacey starts after him, stopping when she notices I'm not following. Tilting her head, she eyes me and my stomach tightens. I know what she's going to say before she even opens her mouth. She'll tell me Ren was wrong. She'll say it wasn't my fault. She'll try to convince me I did everything I could, all the while knowing I fucked up.

Thirty

Lacey

"Go. I'll catch up," Mason says.

He won't. I may not be able to read his tells, but the shadows in his eyes and the grooves in his face give him away. I'll walk out, expecting him to follow, and then he'll disappear. I don't know where he'll go or what he'll do, but it won't be what he needs. Ren's words will seep into him, solidifying everything he's already thought himself. I'm sure he expects me to counter what Ren said, but I can't. And I can't walk away without him.

"He's partly right," I murmur.

His head whips up, surprise splashed across his face until it smooths into a blank mask. "I'm aware."

"I said 'partly.' You didn't listen to the pauses in between his words."

"Pauses literally mean there's no words, so I don't think I missed anything," he says gruffly.

"You did, but that's okay. If you had asked for help in keeping your side of the river in line, things would have been easier. And we both know Sam didn't get hurt because of you. He's pissed at himself for not being there to save her from being injured. Which is slightly different than the guilt eating away at you, but similar enough. Which means he's pissed, not at you, but at himself because he sees the guilt in you, and it resonates with him. Not an easy thing for him to wrap his mind around."

"And that's my fault?"

"No, but it explains why he's so upset and lashing out at you. Mason, no one wishes—"

"Stop. I'm not doing this with you. We don't have time to hash this out, and it won't change things anyways. Besides, I have more important things to worry about."

He pulls out his phone, but I can tell he didn't even turn it on. He's shutting down, pushing me out. We may bicker more than normal, but I thought we were getting somewhere. Where is unclear, but it's slowly ebbing away as Ren's words stab through the shield he's built around his heart. I thought…it doesn't matter what I thought.

"Fine. Go ahead and sulk. Be the martyr and leave everyone else to clean up the mess. Have fun with that," I say bitterly, stomping out the door.

It would be so satisfying to slam the door behind me, but I don't. I make it all of five feet before I realize I don't have my backpack. I left it behind with Mason. The last thing I want to do is slink back in there to get it. I can't leave it behind, though. Replacing the tablet and phone would be annoying.

I also left my wet clothes draped across the bathtub. I was going to ask for something to put them in, but now I'm wondering if they'd even have a plastic bag. They're rich enough they probably just buy a new garbage can every time it gets full. I snort, remembering I'm rich too, mostly because of them. I've spent the last five years working exclusively for the Byrns and the Kings. Habits from my early years die hard, though.

Bouncing on the balls of my feet, I shake out my hands and then march back inside. Mason is nowhere to be found. My backpack sits forgotten by the table.

I glance inside the bathroom as I pass, but he's not there either. I scan the room, searching for a hidden panel, but nothing pops out. He must have slipped into the tunnels. There's no way he went out the window, especially with his shoulder injury.

I zip up my backpack and sling it over my shoulder, glancing around the room again. Sighing, I make my way out the door. When I come to the hallway I should turn down to meet the others, I stop. I could go down there, smooth everything over, and ask to use Ren's computer.

Then again, I could just keep going, straight out the front door. I doubt anyone would notice at this point. They have enough going on without me interrupting them, forcing everyone to focus on me instead of what's important.

Hurrying past the opening, I skip down the stairs, almost tumbling when I miss one. I latch onto the banister to stop my descent and then slowly continue. I'm almost there when a door slams from within the house, and I jump the last couple steps. When I land, my ankle gives out, and I hop the last few feet. Thudding into the wood, I slide down as I pant, rubbing the pain away.

"Where's Mason? And what the hell did you do to yourself?" Shane calls from inside the dark interior of the house.

"I didn't do anything, and I have no idea where he went. I'm sure he's still here somewhere. Might want to search the tunnels first."

"Does everyone know about the fucking tunnels? What's the point of having secret passageways if everyone knows about them?"

"I don't think it's common knowledge. I only know because of the schematics. I don't have anyone to tell anyways."

His face falls into a scowl, ice-blue eyes piercing me, and I freeze as I struggle to push myself up. I forgot who I was talking to. I've become too used to Mason, who isn't intimidating to me in the least. He is to others, but not to me.

Shane King, on the other hand, is just as scary as the first time I saw him. Technically, we've never met, but my first job with the Kings resulted in me watching Shane shoot someone in the leg, and then the hand, and then the head. It was intense, but at least I knew what I was getting into then. I stayed, even after watching him dump the body in the river, knowing the guy he'd killed was a thousand times worse than them.

"How do you have the schematics of my house?" His voice is deadly, cutting through me and my cheeks flame.

I roll my eyes, then duck my head, hoping he didn't see. "It's in the job description. It's not like I'm sharing it on the internet."

"It's a good thing you're on our side then, huh?"

Reaching down, he holds his hand out. I hesitate, then place my hand in his, letting him pull me to my feet.

"Did you hurt your foot or something?"

"Twisted my ankle. It's fine. I'm just going to get going. I'll figure out what I can about the explosion."

Digging around in my bag, my phone and tablet are both missing. I paw through the clothes, but they're not here. I huff, checking the side pockets, even though I know I didn't put them there. Dropping to my knees, I toss my clothes out one-by-one, becoming more frantic by the second. It's not a huge deal if they're missing. No one can get into them, but it's a pain in the ass to replace them. Plus, I'll have to take the time to download all the data to a new device.

"Fucking Mason," I mumble.

Shane's hand falls heavily on my shoulder, and I jerk away from him so hard, I crash into the door. I forgot he was here, watching me freak the fuck out and talk to myself. I'm used to being alone, where no one questions me when I start muttering random things. My own company has been perfectly fine for years, and now I'm being forced to interact with people who probably don't even like me.

"Are you okay?" he asks, hand still outstretched as if he'll haul me back to my feet.

"I'm fine. Everything is fine. Can you call me a car? I just need a car."

Scrambling to shove the pieces of my life back into the bag, I hope it settles my thoughts as well. It mirrors my emotions—chaotic, disjointed, and messy. As I stare at the remnants of my life strewn across the expensive rug, I realize how off-kilter I've been since I met Mason in the woods. But more grounded as well. I couldn't set myself straight since everything hinged on him. I can't keep living my life, waiting for him to figure out what he wants. It's clear I'm merely an annoyance in his world, one he never planned, nor wanted.

"Nemesis, what did Mason do?"

Shane's voice is no longer the hard growl of a mafia leader, but rather the soft flow of coercion wrapped in manipulation. I refuse to give him more fuel to attack Mason. I won't hand him a reason to doubt Mason's leadership.

"Nothing." I suck in a deep breath, finally meeting his eyes. "Actually, he did everything. He took care of me when I was hurt, even though he had every reason not to. He saved me when he didn't have to. He could have left me—he *should* have left me, but he didn't. I won't be the cause of his downfall, so you can just go back to your family and leave me be."

Shane lifts his hands, leaning back on his heels. "I wasn't accusing either of you, Nemesis. But you're pretty worked up over—ah. I get it."

He nods, as if he has it all worked out. I don't understand what big revelation just dawned on him, but I'm not about to ask, either. He can live his life with his perfect little family, running his perfect little area, and loving his perfect little woman. The thoughts burn to ash in my brain as I realize how jealous I sound.

Shane King is not responsible for how my life has turned out. He deserves the happiness he's living. I've watched the progression of their rule from afar and I could tell how hard things were—how lost they were—until they found the glue that bound them together in Sam.

"I'm going to get going. If you find my shit, just toss it. Tell Ren not to bother trying to hack in. He won't be able to, though I know he'll try, regardless. Better to just not tell him about it, so it doesn't send him over the edge again." I push the last bottle of shampoo into my bag.

"Lacey Ann Nemesis, where the hell do you think you're going?" Sam barks from the top of the stairs, and I sigh, dropping my chin to my chest.

"Not my name."

"Well, obviously." I can practically hear the eye roll in her voice. "You seriously weren't even going to check on me? I thought we were friends."

Peeking at Shane, I find him staring at the rug, a small smile playing on his face. When he pushes to his feet, his eyes meet mine and he shakes his head before bounding up the stairs. Sam scowls as Shane mutters something, but the frown morphs into a grin as he gently wraps his arm around her. I look away, not wanting to intrude on their moment. From the shadows under the stairs, Mason's dark eyes meet mine and my chest tightens, butterflies erupting in my stomach.

We stare at each other, neither willing to break the connection. At least that's what I hope he's feeling, too. There's something tying us together, regardless of how much we fight it. I wonder if I would have felt its tug, cinching around my heart tighter and tighter the further I ran had I left Synd when I said I would. If I stay, will it be a constant reminder of what

I could have had, if circumstances would have changed just slightly? One decision to go right instead of left, one choice to stay instead of leave, one promise made in the dead of night, with only the stars to witness them, could have changed our entire trajectory.

"Did we miss it?" I whisper, not caring whether he can hear me or not.

He tilts his head, eyes burning into my soul. I blink and the flicker of hope extinguishes as Sam stomps down the stairs. I hold Mason's gaze as he lifts my phone. He's cut off from me as Sam steps into view, but she glances behind as she does.

"Mason, what the hell are you doing creeping under the stairs? Frickin' weirdo." She turns back as he steps out. "You're not actually leaving, right? You haven't even met everyone. Come on."

Grabbing my hand, she pulls me after her. I barely keep my feet under me as we make our way to Shane and then down the hall. I tug, but she doesn't loosen her grip. Gritting my teeth, I follow her. I'm sick of being pulled back into their world with no explanations. I'm tired of witnessing something I'll never have. I'm exhausted with the push and pull of Mason and his damn indecisiveness. Every time I try to distance myself, to do the right thing, they drag me back, and I'm forced to see how much I don't fit yet again.

I expect to be led to the same bedroom, but she leads me through the halls until we're in front of a set of double doors. Shane pushes through first and the cacophony of voices grows louder. Everyone stops as we step through and I freeze, tugging my wrist from Sam's grasp finally.

"Well, this is fun," I mutter, leaning back.

"Get in the room, Lacey," Mason mumbles, his hand landing on my hip to guide me inside, and a shiver rolls through me.

"Don't boss me around, Mason."

Stepping from his hold, I make my way to the least intimidating person in the room—Willow St. James. I drop into the chair next to her, not realizing my mistake until it's too late. Mason lowers himself on my other side, and I spin my chair away from him. He snorts and I purse my lips instead of letting the snarky comment sitting on my tongue fly.

"Does it itch?" Willow asks as the rest of people start their own conversations again.

Running my finger along the almost-healed scar, I wonder how noticeable it is. Half the time I forget it's there these days.

"Not anymore. It did in the beginning. How's your wrist?"

Shock spreads across her face before she smiles. I'm sure she didn't expect me to know about the injuries she sustained when dealing with her stalker. I'm sure there are a lot of things I notice that they don't, which only solidifies the idea that I'm an afterthought in most of their minds. Which begs the question—why am I here?

"It's good. Twinges sometimes, but honestly, it wasn't that bad. At least now, between Hawk and me, we always know when it's going to rain."

Mason's fingers brush my leg. "Lacey, if you're going to be here, then you're all in. You won't be able to leave."

"What are you going to do? Kidnap me? Again?"

"I doubt it would take much to convince you to stay," he murmurs and his hand trails up my leg before his fingers dig into my inner thigh.

Biting my tongue, I squeeze the arms of the chair to stop myself from clamping my knees together. He's playing some game I can't hope to win. He's back to being wishy-washy, bouncing between flirting with me and running away when shit gets too hard. He's playing with fire and I'm pretty sure I'm the only one who will get burned.

Thirty-One

Mason

"Mason, we're all a little busy, but maybe you could pay a-fuck-ttention, yeah?" Shane booms from the other end of the table.

Pulling my eyes away from Lacey is harder than I thought it would be. I keep my hand on her leg, if only to make sure she stays put. Every time I turn around, she's trying to slip away. Regardless of whether she wants to, she's in this now. Her skills aside, I've realized I don't want to let her go. I certainly don't want her leaving Synd.

"Stop being an asshole, King. Last I checked, we're on the same level, so you can quit acting like you're my boss."

"If you'd run your shit, I wouldn't have to act like your daddy, would I?"

"Stop bickering. You sound like children. We have serious issues to discuss, so let's focus on them instead of whatever tête-à-tête is happening over there," Ren says, his voice even now.

He seems to have gotten a grip on his emotions, at the very least. Catching Shane's eye, he shakes his head, and I glance away. I'm not about to call Ren out in front of everyone, but eventually we'll have to address it.

When Lacey skipped out before, I couldn't help myself. I snatched her phone and tablet and slipped into the tunnels. I needed a minute to set things straight in my mind before I faced her again. Even if she left the King's house, her devices would have given me an excuse to go to her place. It was my way in, to convince her to stay, preferably with me.

I don't like her being in that house alone without me. It's irrational and doesn't make sense. There are dangers hiding within the shadows of my own home. Living without her isn't an option right now, though. It's selfish, but I clearly I won't be able to think straight if she's sequestered in her house. Lacey isn't used to being immersed in our world. The dangers surrounding us aren't ones she can hide from behind a screen.

Wandering around the tunnels, I realized the way I'm doing things isn't working. She centers me, clears the fog from my mind, and makes me want to try. Pushing her away didn't work, so I'll do what I can to keep her by my side. We'll deal with the rest of our shit when we're in the same house again.

Lacey's fingers dig under mine, and I squeeze her flesh.

"Would you let go?" she mutters from the corner of her mouth.

"Nope." I smirk before turning to Shane. "I've got a concentration of men in the south. Whoever is trying to move in has some level of awareness. They're staying out of the Barrens.

Nicki won't even return my calls. The one and only time she answered, she cussed me out in another language."

"My fault. She's pissed the police chief is talking about cleaning up the Barrens and we haven't done anything," Alex chimes in as he passes a brownie to Sam.

Sam grins and I flex my fingers, earning a huff from Lacey. It's hard not to see the differences in my sister. She was listless before with no direction in life, and then she met the Kings. I wasn't around when she fell for them, but seeing her now is completely different. *She's* different. The Kings changed her, filling in the gaps trying to sneak through, and lighting her up from the inside, much the same way Lacey has me.

"They're talking to you," Lacey hisses, and I pull my gaze away from Sam.

"We'll need more men along the river then, but I doubt the residents down there will allow it. I'm not concerned about them. They can take care of themselves, as we saw with the Guild. However, our shipments are now being disrupted. They're small incidences. Normally, I would chalk it up to our typical loss on such products, but coupled with the issues within your territory, I'm inclined to believe they're connected," Ren says as he swipes at his tablet screen.

"Safe houses are being hit," I say and every head whips to stare at me. "All of them have been empty so far, but it's only a matter of time before my people get caught in the crossfire."

"What else?" Helms growls.

He's usually silent in these meetings, preferring to observe and then go off and do his own thing. We're more alike than I want to admit.

"I was missing some money, but it's been returned. My shipments have almost completely dried up. And my people are being targeted. I imagine we're dealing with the Guild again. They're clearly pissed about not being able to take Synd the first time, and they're back to finish the job. I'm sure it's salt in the wound I'm not six feet under, too."

Lacey makes a sound in the back of her throat and Helms's eyes track to her as he raises an eyebrow in question.

"It's not the Guild," Lacey says, leaning forward slightly. "They're holed up in Rima now. They don't divide their resources between two cities and they won't start now. They didn't even bother putting their headquarters in Synd, probably biding their time before establishing their base here. I'm not saying they don't have a part in the shipments going missing or whatever, but they're not targeting you guys."

Alex's elbows thump on the table as his eyes narrow. "But how do you know?"

"Seriously, Alex. We're not doing this again. I refuse to have this asinine conversation with you every time Nemesis is brought up," Ren grumbles.

"I know because I'm good at what I do. Plus, I live in Synd too, so it stands to reason I would care whether it was overrun with criminals." She blanches, cheeks reddening as Alex smothers a grin with his hand. "I mean, like actual criminals. Fuck, you know what I mean."

Willow pats Lacey's arm, muttering something I can't hear. Conversations pop up between the others as the meeting devolves into chaos. Alex's animated voice rises above the others, teasing Sam. Helms and Hawk are whispering together as the Reapers' president's arm sits possessively on the back of Mac's chair. They've all seemed to find their place within this world, settled into something more. Their lives changed and I'm still here, waiting for whatever they have to slap me in the face. Flexing my hand again, I ease my grip, rubbing my thumb in light circles, and Lacey's breath hitches.

Lacey leans in, whispering, "Can I go now?"

"Yeah, let's go," I murmur, standing, and the conversations swirling around us dissolve into a quiet hum.

"Going somewhere?" Shane asks as he leans back in his chair.

"We're not accomplishing anything sitting here. We're going home. I'll let you know what we find, and we can make a plan, if needed," I say, settling my hand on Lacey's back to guide her from the room.

"If needed? You can't be serious. We're already deep in the shit, Byrns. We need to come up with a plan now, not when the fucking city is burning around us," Ren sneers.

"Don't fuck with me, Ren. I've had a shit day, and I still have more to do. I didn't say anything before, but I won't be so lenient next time," I say as I push Lacey toward the exit.

When I kick the door shut behind us, she steps away from my touch. Uncurling my fingers, I eventually push them into my pocket, hiding the evidence of my anxiety from her. I stay a step behind as she navigates the halls of the Kings' mansion as if she's been here a million times before. She didn't spend much time outside of my bedroom, but apparently studying blueprints gave her a sense she knows where everything is. Or maybe she just memorized the route to the conference room.

"Mason!" Sam's voice echoes down the hall, and I glance over my shoulder.

I can tell she wants to run, but her brief bout of unconsciousness is slowing her down. I grab Lacey's arm, pulling both of us to a stop. She groans under her breath, but I keep my grip on her so she doesn't disappear again.

"Seriously? Were you two running or some shit?"

Sam braces her hands on her knees, sucking in deep mouthfuls of air while she pants.

"We were walking at a normal pace, Sam. What did you need?"

I'm not about to go back and listen to the Kings bitch about what we're going to do. Half the time our meetings devolve into them making plans for a dinner or how they'll get out of the next gala. They invited me in the beginning, but as the months wore on and my answer never changed, they stopped asking.

Sam lifts a hand, a set of keys dangling from her finger. She glances up when I don't grab them and shakes them. After I snatch them, she straightens.

"What's this?" I ask.

"They're car keys, dumbass."

Rolling my eyes, I sigh. "No shit, Sam. What am I supposed to do with them?"

"Maybe you should give them to Lacey. She'll know what to do. You're supposed to take Alex's car so you don't have to call one. Honestly, none of us wants you relying on someone else to drive you right now. Today was not fun and I'd rather not repeat it," Sam snaps, crossing her arms.

Lacey twitches in my grasp before settling and I peek at her. She stares at my shoulder, face emotionless.

"Yeah, okay," I say, slipping them in my pocket.

Dropping Lacey's arm, I pull Sam into a hug. We're not huge on affection, but before I was shot, neither of us felt like we needed to. After we both tiptoed around each other so much, it never was the right moment. We've been walking on eggshells whenever we're in the same room, always wondering what will set the other off.

"Don't disappear on me again," she whispers into my chest, and I squeeze her a little.

"Same. Love you, Sammy," I murmur, dropping a kiss on her hair.

She still smells like smoke and burnt rubber. Neither of us had a chance to shower in the scramble to figure out what the hell was going on.

Releasing her, I turn and grab Lacey's hand, sighing in relief she stayed put, though her chin is tucked against her chest. We're almost around the corner when Sam clears her throat.

"Love you too, Mase."

I lift a hand in response, not bothering to turn back. I'm lost in my thoughts and before I know it, we're sliding into Alex's expensive car. Mumbling under my breath, I press the button on the dash, and it roars to life before the engine settles into a purr. Thankfully, the rain has stopped, since I have no idea how to turn the wipers on, although his car probably can sense it and turns them on automatically.

"Fucking shinies," I mumble.

"Shinies?" Lacey's voice is jarring after so much silence.

"It's Barrens language. They call fancy cars shinies. Makes sense, since they're all polished, but their vernacular bleeds into ours some."

"Oh yeah, I forgot," she mumbles.

Rolling out of the driveway, I turn the car toward Lacey's house. I may not want her staying there anymore, but she'll need to gather her stuff. Plus, I need the time to convince her my place is safer than hers. I'm sure she'll argue, and I'll probably end up pulling a muscle wrangling her back into the car, but at least I'll know exactly where she is from now on.

"Vernacular is a pretty big word."

I catch her smirk from the corner of my eye as we stop at a red light. "I'm a pretty smart guy."

"Oh, for fuck's sake. Did you pick that up from a rom-com? Or was it on some website full of pickup lines? News flash: those don't work on women."

"Good thing I'm not trying to pick up women then, huh?"

She snorts, turning to look out the window. The light turns green, and I ease us forward.

"Turns out I already picked up the one I want," I murmur, glancing from her to the road.

"I'd rather not—wait, did you seriously turn your stupid pick-up line into another line?" she scoffs, turning her bright eyes to me.

"I thought it was particularly clever, but go ahead and mock me all you want. I'm not exactly well-versed in this type of thing."

At this point, I'm just glad we're broaching the subject. Hopefully, it'll make the conversation about her staying with me smoother, though I doubt it. I fully expect her to fight me on my plan.

"What's 'this type of thing'?"

"Flirting or whatever."

I resist the urge to look at her again and concentrate on navigating the slowly darkening streets in the setting sun. This isn't how we usually are. Our conversations are full of sass and sarcasm, both trying to one-up each other with whatever comeback we can think of. Even while she was sick and delirious, there was an edge to our words.

"Or whatever," she breathes, more a statement than a question.

I park in the same alley I watched her house from the week before. Not much has changed, except there's a shimmering within the windows that wasn't there before. Squinting, I can't make out what's blocking the view. I watched her before, puttering around the kitchen or sitting on the couch. Part of me wanted to run in there and force her to hide away and the other held back, since I knew beyond a shadow of a doubt she was safe within her walls while I was there.

"What did you put on your windows?"

"Steel shutters. I locked it down when you stopped stalking me."

Doubt shatters my resolve that my house is the safest, but I slough it off. Even if she was locked away in a bunker, I still think the best place is by my side. Besides, I won't be able to function not knowing where she is.

"Let's go pack your shit."

Thirty-Two

Lacey

"Excuse me? Where the hell do you think you're going?" I cry, scrambling after Mason as he gets out of the car.

"I'm going to help you pack."

He tugs me across the road, head swiveling as he scans the neighborhood. I'm not particularly happy with being yanked around like I'm a toddler who takes off when they see something shiny, but I've missed the connection. I've gone so long being alone, I didn't think it would be that hard to go back to a solitary existence. Yet the short time staying with him made me aware of my loneliness.

"You realize you're waffling, right?"

"If you want waffles, you'll have to talk to Helms. He's perfected them."

"You've got to be fucking kidding me. That's not an answer. You keep saying I need to leave and then you turn around and want to what? Flirt with me? That doesn't make sense. I didn't pick you up at the Morning Brew, intent on a hot date."

Angling my body to hide the keypad from him, I punch in the code. He snorts, but I push through the door without commenting. I expect him to have some snarky comeback, yet he merely follows me inside. I set the alarm, trying to ignore the fact that he's the first person to step foot inside my home. With my parents being out of my life and barely ever leaving the house, therefore having no friends, I've never invited someone back to my place. The very few times I've hooked up with someone, it's been somewhere else. A random bathroom or a shitty hotel has been the most common, but honestly, it's been years since I've hooked up with anyone other than my favorite toy.

"Don't touch anything." I mutter, dropping my backpack by the door. "You'll probably make the walls crumble around us."

I trip over the words, changing them halfway through my sentence. No reason to remind him of the events from earlier.

"You don't have to do that, censor yourself because my car got blown up. But back to our previous conversation…"

Glancing over my shoulder at him, he licks his bottom lip before spinning slowly to scan my living room. The barren space only holds an old couch, with worn blue carpet. I don't even have a TV. If anyone came over, they'd assume I was destitute.

Walking into the kitchen, I pull open the fridge, if only to hide behind the door. I'm not hungry, which is good since I don't have much food here. I've been having food delivered to the house two blocks over when I remember to eat.

Peeking over the top, I track him until he steps out of view into the hallway. My bedroom is back there, but there's nothing in it. He won't be able to get into the basement. He'll ask about the heavy door locked with another keypad, but hopefully I can put it off as long as possible.

My stomach tightens as I imagine letting him into my private space. I spend most of my time in down there. Just like my house, no one has ever infiltrated my sanctuary. That's exactly what it is for me—a sanctuary—a place I can retreat to when the world is too much. I understand computers. No one bothers me. No one judges me. Online, I can be whoever I want, and if someone pushes back, I can just invent someone else. The anonymity I find within the numbers is a peace I've never found anywhere else.

Except that's not true. When I was staying with Mason, I never had to be someone else. I learned young to mask who I was, because I was always too much or not enough. I never understood what they meant when they said I was strange. Mason never shied away from me, no matter how annoying I was.

My parents wanted me to be the perfect daughter, even if they never wanted a girl. I had to act a certain way, speak a certain way, be a certain way. Eventually, they wanted me to be invisible in plain sight. As long as I didn't interrupt the perfect little world they carved out, I could stay. The moment I no longer fit the mold they forced me into, when I overflowed the hole they dug for me, I was no longer useful. It happened long before I realized. I was too young to fully comprehend that they didn't love me.

I spent years chasing their affection with nothing to show for it in the end. Good riddance.

Mason knocks on the door frame, and I jump back, slamming the fridge to cover my surprise. Being lost in my own memories of what my parents put me through is not where I want to be when there's a freaking mafia boss in my house.

"You okay?" he asks, concern flashing in his eyes, and I turn away.

"I'm fine. You can't really expect me to pack my shit up right now."

"I won't make you pack alone, if that's what you're worried about," he says.

I'm ready to stab him, even though I probably would miss and hit my own leg or something. I used to know how to defend myself, but as the years passed, I lost a lot of skills. Now I'm wishing I would have kept it up. The weapons I bought five years ago are stuffed away in a closet downstairs, collecting dust. Since the last thing I want to do is touch a gun, knives seemed the way to go. The scar on my face tingles, and I wonder if I'll even be able to pick up a knife anymore.

By the time I'm done contemplating whether I still have any muscle memory left, I've lapped the room three times. Mason's eyes track my movements. Crossing my arms to cover my trembling hands, I lean against the counter.

I've always been on the outside of their group, always in the shadows of their world. Getting involved with Mason in any capacity would be not smart. But I can't stop from imagining what it would be like. Not just sleeping with him, but truly being a part of something more than what I am. It's the reason I stalked them in the first place, to feel like I belonged.

It didn't work.

"I can do this on my own, Mason. You don't have to babysit me. I realize I didn't leave before when I said I would, but I will now. But I also have to look into the car bomb and whatever else Ren's been blowing up my phone about before I go. So, why don't you head home, and I'll message you when I'm done." I duck my head, staring at my toes poking from beneath my sweatpants.

"Oh, you misunderstand, Lacey. You're going to pack the things you need. You're going to put them in my car. And you're going to stay at my place. Preferably in my bed, but I'm open to negotiations on that."

Whipping my head up, I study his smirking face. I can't tell if he's joking or serious. Either way, it would be a very bad idea. Besides, sleeping with him was never in the cards, even if he has been dropping hints all day. If I stay at his house, engage in whatever extracurricular activities he has in mind and then something goes wrong, I wouldn't be able to just leave. I would be stuck. I shake my head as my eyes fall closed. Thinking about it now means I'm already expecting things to go poorly.

"And then what?"

He straightens, suddenly serious, as if he didn't expect me to consider it. Maybe he was joking and I'm too obtuse to catch on. His flirting earlier was subpar at best. It's entirely possible he didn't mean for me to literally stay in his bed.

"What do you mean?" he asks, mirroring my stance on the opposite counter.

"I'm assuming you want me at your house to make it easier to operate and exchange information. When all of this is settled, what happens then?" I hold my breath until my lungs are screaming as he stares at me.

"I want you at my house for my sanity, Lacey. You're not an informant I'm going to shove into a safe house. You're not an asset to be protected. You're—" Mason grunts, struggling for the words. "—Important."

"I'm actually both of those things—an asset and an informant. I'm also a hacker who's been working for your families for almost a fucking decade. You can't separate those things from me as a person," I huff, tucking my chin to my chest again.

"The fuck I can't. Okay, sure, you're important as a hacker, but even if you weren't, I'd still want to protect you. And I can't do that when you're here and I'm there."

I throw my hands up. "But I don't need to be protected! Look around you, Mason. I'm in a literal goddamn fortress. I have so many security systems in place, along with fucking bulletproof shields over every possible entrance. Even if someone could get past all of that, which they can't, they'd never be able to do it without my knowledge. You realize I knew every time you sent someone here, right? Every single time you pulled into my neighborhood, I knew. Not my street. Not across from my house. My fucking neighborhood. And do I really need to remind you I've never been kidnapped from here? Your house, though, well, for all its secret tunnels and fancy locks, I was still taken. I bypassed your cameras for *months* without you realizing."

He quirks an eyebrow. "If that's your argument, you might want to rethink it, since *you're* the one who put in our systems."

I let out a strangled cry, spinning around to brace my hands on the cool tiles. I hate them. The pattern, the grooves, the cracked caulk between them grates on my already frayed nerves. Rubbing a finger along the edge of one, I scrunch my nose.

Mason's hands land next to mine, a second before the warmth of his body pressing into my back seeps into my skin. I tense, then all the fight goes out of me and I sag into him. Sighing, he rests his chin on my shoulder, and I close my eyes.

"We don't have to have it all figured out right now, Lace," he murmurs.

"Don't call me that," I mutter, tensing again.

"Why not?"

I contemplate not saying anything. We could stay in this bubble we've randomly found. I could pretend this is normal, imagining we lead boring lives with no threats and our biggest problem is his pathetic pickup lines. We'd never bring our pasts into it or talk about anything other than what was for dinner. That shit doesn't happen in regular people's lives either, though.

"It's what my parents used to call me. I'd rather not have to hear it again," I say matter-of-factly.

"Okay," he says before pressing a kiss to my neck.

I twitch before turning my head to look at him. A soft smile pulls at his lips, as if his actions are the most normal thing in the world.

"What the hell was that?"

"You don't want to be called Lace, I won't call you Lace. I'm partial to Kitten anyway and you've never said anything about it, so I'll just stick to that one. You'll have to tell the others. I'm not about to argue with anyone over it. They'll think it's coming from me and do it just to spite me."

He pushes back, wandering toward the living room. I follow, if only because I think my brain has short-circuited. I've found Mason Byrns has that effect on me. One minute we're yelling at each other and the next he's holding me. I don't know what to do with that.

"I wasn't talking about my name," I say, leaning against the door frame as he wanders down the hall, stopping in front of the door to the basement.

"Where does this lead?" he asks, knocking his knuckles against the metal.

"Great. We're ignoring me again. Perfect. That's just the basement."

"Just the basement, huh? Nothing down there? Except none of your computers are up here. So, they must be down there. Oh, and your bed hasn't been slept in for a while, so you're probably sleeping down there too. Do you have boxes?"

"Boxes?"

"For packing." He grins, throwing a thumb over his shoulder at the door.

"Seriously? Were you ever taught how to have an actual fucking conversation? Or were you taught to ignore everyone around you until they fell into line?"

"I'm the head of a mafia family, Lacey. Which do you think?"

"Gotcha. Well, let's have a quick tutorial. I ask a question, you answer it, we have a discourse only pertaining to that subject, and then we move on to the next one. And when I say I'm not going to pack my shit up and move in with you, your job is to fucking listen," I say, crossing my arms.

He stalks toward me, and I straighten, tipping my chin up the closer he gets. When his eyes dip to my lips, I step to the side, but he advances until my back hits the wall. His hand thuds above my head, and he leans close, caging me in. My breath hitches as I struggle to school my features into some semblance of neutrality. His smirk tells me I've failed.

"I did listen. I heard you when you called yourself an informant, devaluing who you are to me. I heard you when you said you didn't want to be called Lace. I even heard your silence when you didn't object to me calling you Kitten. I heard you when you objected to staying at my house, claiming you were safer here than with me. I also heard when you asked about what happens after we deal with this situation, but since I don't think you're ready for that answer, I left it. Just because I don't agree doesn't mean I didn't listen. I'm merely choosing you over your arguments."

Thirty-Three

Mason

"That doesn't even make any sense." She gives me a withering look even as her breath hitches.

"Let me be more clear then," I breathe, leaning closer. "You accused me of being wishy-washy, and I've decided I'm done with that. I want you. I want you in my house, in my arms, in my bed. All the other shit we can deal with later, but I want you and I'm done denying that I do."

Her tongue darts out, licking her bottom lip before she pulls it between her teeth. Running my thumb across the plump flesh, a flush sneaks up her neck to her cheeks, giving her a delicious glow. I sway, pressing my body into hers, and she whimpers.

"Any thoughts going on in that pretty little head of yours?" I ask, tipping her chin up.

"Why me?" she whispers, and my heart cracks.

"Because you woke me up."

I swoop down, covering her mouth with mine before she can respond, pouring everything into the kiss. Here, in this moment, it doesn't matter where the blame lies. It doesn't matter where we started. It doesn't even matter where we're going. We can figure it out later, when the dust settles and nothing else stands in our way.

Her lips part and I sweep my tongue in, sliding my hand into her hair to tilt her head. The moan she lets out reverberates in my chest and I groan, deepening the kiss. Her body molds to mine and her nails dig into my shirt, twisting into the fabric. She attacks the buttons, not bothering to undo them all. Easing back, I brush her hair behind her ear.

She traces one of my tattoos, following the swoops of the skull covering my skin, and I shiver. I nip at her earlobe as she melts under my touch. She's intoxicating in a way I've never experienced before. I skim my palm up her side under her shirt, basking in the feel of her soft skin.

"Mason, this isn't a—" Her breath hitches when my hand dips under her bra and I cup her tit. "Good idea."

"I think it's an excellent idea," I murmur.

"We're constantly at each other's throats," she says, even as she trails her nails down my body as far as she can with my shirt still half buttoned.

"Then we'll just have to occupy our mouths."

I capture her lips with mine again. She whimpers and I drink in each one, every gasp pushing me forward. This could blow up in our faces, but I can't think of a better way to go than when I'm deep inside her.

"Mason," she whines when I pull my mouth away, resting my forehead against hers.

"Last chance to back out, Lacey."

Her tongue darts out, sweeping across my bottom lip, and I groan.

"If you're in and want out, just say the word. But I won't be gentle with you, Kitten," I murmur, brushing my fingers along her jaw. "Say you understand."

"I understand," she whispers.

Brushing my thumb over her nipple, my nail catches on the barbell and she yelps. I don't know if I hurt her or not. She grabs the hem of her shirt, whipping it over her head, and then unhooks her bra, shimmying the straps down her arms until it pools at our feet. Her fingers dig into my hair, gripping the strands and yanking me toward her tit. I dip my head, pulling the bud into my mouth, flicking the metal with my tongue, and she moans. Pulling away, I skim my mouth along her skin to her other nipple.

"No piercing on this one?" I nip at the top of her tit, and she jolts.

"I freaked out after the first one," she says, her voice quivering as I swirl my tongue around the bud.

Her nails dig into my scalp, and I hum at the sensation. The only thing I want right now is to strip her down and fuck her against the wall. Nipping one last time at her nipple, I dig my fingers into her ass and lift her. She yelps, arms winding around my neck. Marching to her bedroom, I toss her on the comforter, and she shuffles back.

I grab the back of her knees and yank her toward the edge of the bed, legs dangling over the side. Propping up on her elbow, she glares at me as I sink to my knees before hooking my fingers into the waistband of her pants and tugging both them and her underwear over her hips.

"What the hell do you think you're doing?" she demands, clamping her knees together.

Sliding my hand into hers, I pull hard until she lands on her back.

"I'm going to bury my head between your thighs until you come all over my face."

Gripping her legs, I push them apart until she's spread out for me. Her huff turns into a squeal as I waste no time swirling my tongue around her clit. I groan when I realize how wet she already is, and I take full advantage, plunging a finger into her core. She squirms, moans falling from her lips as I pull it out slowly before adding another one.

"You're going to be a good girl for me, aren't you, Kitten?"

Her answer is another moan as I suck her clit between my lips. Her pussy flutters as I flick my tongue, her whimpers becoming the backdrop of her pleasure. When I hum, she clamps around my fingers, a low groan leaving her as she spasms around them. Slowing my pace, I ease her through her orgasm until her body is a trembling mess above me.

Pulling my fingers from her, I lick my lips as she gasps. The taste of her is just as intoxicating as the rest of her. She stares up at me, eyes half-lidded and filled with pleasure. A bolt of possessiveness rolls through me.

"Is this where I thank you?" She smirks, closing her legs, and I snarl. "You thought you'd make me come and I'd return the favor?"

Leaning over her, I plant one hand beside her head, my other trailing down her body. She raises an eyebrow, challenging me. Using my knee, I part her legs, slipping my hand between them to stroke her pussy, and she squirms.

"You can talk back all you want, Kitten, but you forget I can tell when you're lying. You want me to sink my cock into that wet little pussy of yours. You want me to fuck you until you can't remember your own name. I can see it in your eyes. Go ahead and be a brat but be ready for the consequences. I could leave you here, begging for release with no satisfaction."

She narrows her eyes even as she clamps her thighs together, trapping my hand. "You wouldn't."

"Try me. You brought out the claws, thinking there'd be no punishment. But I am very interested in how well I can make you listen."

Her mouth drops open and I swoop down, covering it with my own. Our tongues duel, fighting for dominance until she succumbs to me, moaning as she grips my wrist, fingers still buried in her pussy. Her hips move in time with my thrusts and her other hand grips my side, trying to pull me on top of her.

Ripping my mouth from hers, I bury my face in her neck. As I sink my teeth into the delicate skin, she tilts her head to give me more access. I lean back to admire the mark I've left, and my cock throbs.

Standing, I pull my fingers from her, and she cries out as I peer at her flushed skin. Her legs are open, pussy glistening, and I almost drop to my knees again, just to get another taste. Instead,

I pop my fingers in my mouth, meeting her gaze, which drips with desire.

"You want to come again? Then take these off," I say, gesturing to my clothes.

"You're asking me to undress you?" Her tone suggests I'm ridiculous for even asking, but a hunger rests in her eyes.

"Oh, Kitten, I wasn't asking."

We stare at each other for a good thirty seconds before she whines, slamming her hands on the comforter. Sitting up, she reaches for my shirt. I expect her to unbutton it the rest of the way, but she grips the sides and tears it open. A low rumble echoes from my chest, and I circle her wrists as the buttons ping across the hardwood.

"That wasn't very smart," I growl, forcing her hands to my pants before releasing her.

The back of her hand grazes my cock, and it takes everything in me to stay still. She does it again as she pops open the button and sits back. Gritting my teeth, I raise an eyebrow and she rolls her eyes. She shoves my pants below my hips and then leans back on her hands.

Wrapping my hand around her neck, I tug her closer. "You're playing a dangerous game, Lacey."

"I'm terrified," she murmurs, licking her lips.

"You should be."

"What are you going to do? Spank me?" She bites her lip as if the idea excites her, and my craving for her expands tenfold.

"You going to behave?" I ask, and she shakes her head. "Have it your way, brat."

I step back, dropping my hand to my pants and shoving them the rest of the way down. My underwear follows and she blushes. I tip my chin up and she scrambles further onto the bed. Taking one final look at her, I latch onto her ankles and flip her.

"What the hell, Mason?"

Her muffled cry has me grinning as I smack her on the ass, leaving a pretty pink handprint behind. She shrieks, trying to roll, but I clamber onto the bed, straddling her legs. Stroking my cock with one hand, I caress the mark with the other. The sight of her flushed skin is almost too much.

"Still going to be a brat? Or should I continue?" I trail a finger across her skin.

She turns her head to the side, blowing the hair out of her face. "I don't see how that's supposed to get me to stop."

Tipping my head back, I swallow my moan. This is exactly how I imagined she'd be, fighting me every step of the way in the best way possible. Her body trembles beneath me as my hand connects with her skin again and she curses, wiggling as I stroke the red mark left behind.

Leaning down, I cover her body with mine. I brush my lips over her cheekbone. She's whispering something under her breath, almost too quiet to hear, but it's one word on repeat—please.

"Oh, Kitten, don't worry. I'll give you exactly what you're begging for," I growl.

Her hips buck, attempting to dislodge me, and I drop more of my weight on her, keeping her in place.

"I do not fucking beg," she snarls.

A low chuckle leaves me and I push up, spanking her once more. She thrashes in my hold, her voice caught between a hiss and a moan. Dipping my fingers between her thighs, I let out my own curse when I find her drenched. Lacey might fight me, but she wants this as much as I do.

"Do not move," I command before pushing off her.

"You're an asshole," she breathes, but she stays put.

"Good girl," I murmur, spanking her again, and she cries out, desire lacing her tone.

Yanking her hips up, I leave her face buried in the mattress. I rub my cock over her entrance, and she pushes back. Draping my body over hers, I cup her tits, squeezing before I pinch both of her nipples. She squeaks and then her hand sneaks between her legs. I grab her wrist and think about pulling it behind her back, but I need both of my hands to fuck her properly.

Sitting up, I line myself up with her pussy, pushing the tip in as she shudders. "You're going to take my cock, and as a reward, I'll let you come all over it."

"Fuck you," she spits.

Slamming into her, the rest of her reply is lost in a low moan. Whether they're mine or hers isn't clear—probably both. She quivers beneath me, her pussy clinging to my cock. Digging my fingers into her flesh, I roll my hips, reveling in the feel of finally being deep inside her.

She squirms in my grasp, and I pull out slowly, then thrust into her. Picking up my speed, I don't give her any time to recover as I pound into her, the heat from her pussy enveloping me. Her fingers dig into the sheets as she thrashes, pushing back in time with me.

An ache builds deep in my gut, but I refuse to come without her falling over the edge, too. Sliding my hand along her thigh, I slap her ass and she screams into the sheets, her pussy clamping around me as she comes. Grunting, I fuck her through her orgasm until I follow her into oblivion. Flames lick through my veins, leaving ash in its wake.

Covering her body with my own, I wrap my arm around her waist and tip us to the side, fused together. I'm not ready to leave her heat. She's still shivering in my grasp, clinging to my arm. When she finally settles, a whine leaves her as I slip from her pussy, grunting at the loss. Closing my eyes, I breathe in the scent of us, and another missing piece deep within me slots into place.

Thirty-Four

Lacey

"Shit," I mutter as I slip from Mason's arms.

He mumbles something, fingers grasping for me, but I slide from under the comforter he must have pulled over us. I dash for the bathroom in the hall, heat flooding my cheeks. I've never had someone fuck me to sleep before, but apparently Mason's cum has a magic potion in it or something. Glancing at the clock on the wall as I pee, I realize two hours have passed and I groan.

Finishing up, I stumble over the threshold. My legs are like jelly, barely able to carry me back to the bedroom. He's thrown off the comforter, only a thin sheet covering his hips and one arm rests over his eyes. My gaze trails down his body, following the ink until it disappears under the fabric. Rubbing my hand against my cheek, I run it down my body before shaking my head and dropping it to my side. Just the sight of him gets my blood pumping and wetness gathers between my legs.

"Can I help you with something, Kitten?" he says, breaking the silence and my eyes dart to his.

My breath catches as he slides his hand down below the sheet, clearly gripping himself, and I shudder. My own hand circles my throat as I lick my lips. He tugs the covers aside, and it slithers from his hips, revealing his cock, already thick and hard.

"Come here," he grunts, and I shake my head. "Oh, Lacey, you saw what happened last time you didn't obey me. Now come over here and ride my cock."

I shudder as my fingers flex against my throat. Spinning, I take off for the door. For some reason, I want to see how far I can push him, how hard he becomes when I do. His growl chases me down the hallway, followed by his bare feet thumping against the carpet.

A cry leaves me when his arm seizes me around my waist and he crowds me against the wall, trapping my body with his. My nipples harden as they meet the cool wood, and I rest my forehead against it, waiting for his next move.

"Did you think you could run from me? Did you think I wouldn't chase you? Catch you?" He adjusts his hips, lining himself up with my pussy. "Did you think you could get away?"

I squirm, trying to take him in. "Please."

It comes out with a gasp as my resolve crumbles, scattering at our feet. I don't fucking care. I just want him inside me again. His lips brush my neck as his other hand reaches around to circle my throat.

"Good girl," he groans, thrusting into me hard. I moan, clamping down on him.

He freezes deep inside me, then rolls his hips. I push back to entice him to move. A shuddering breath leaves me the longer he makes me wait.

"Mason," I whine as I thump my forehead against the wall.

"Beg," he grunts, guiding my chin up with his thumb, and I tip my head back.

"Fuck you," I gasp, and he pulls out, then surges into me again.

"Try again, Kitten. Beg like I know you want to."

I grit my teeth and his hand at my waist trails down my body until his fingers find my clit. His movements are agonizingly slow, building me up, but not enough to send me over the edge. He pulls his cock out, surging back in, and I whimper, holding back the words I know he wants to hear. Every time I get close, he eases off, rubbing along the sides until I'm panting with need.

"Stubborn little thing, aren't you?" he murmurs. He pulls completely out of me, removing his hand, and steps back.

"You've got to be fucking kidding me," I wheeze, resting my forehead against the wall.

He slaps my ass and I groan, my pussy clenching around nothing. Leaning in, he bites my shoulder, then presses a kiss to the marks I'm sure he's left behind.

"If you want something, beg for it. If not, then I'm sure you can take care of it yourself."

"Please," I whimper. His hand slides up my body, pinching my nipple. "Please fuck me."

As he rolls the bud between his fingers, I push back, and his cock slides between my ass cheeks.

"Better, but not quite. Try again."

I let out a strangled cry and his hand dips down to my clit again.

"Please fuck me hard. Make me come." The words are ripped from me, stated through gritted teeth.

"There it is," he breathes. "Turn around."

I spin, almost tipping over in my haste, and he steadies me with a hand on my waist. Picking me up, he slams me against the wall, surging into me in one stroke as I wrap my legs around him. He does as I asked—begged—fucking me hard and fast. My nails dig into his shoulders, leaving half-moon circles behind, but he doesn't complain.

"Play with your clit, Lacey. Come all over my cock," he pants, eyes fixed on where we're joined.

Dropping my hand, I press my clit, rubbing it. My pussy spasms and I close my eyes. He drops his head, sucking my nipple in his mouth, and stars explode behind my lids. I pulse around his cock, and he groans my name as he comes, jerking inside me.

Our gasps fill the hallway, echoing through the empty house. Lifting his head from my chest, he eases my feet to the ground, slipping out of me. Wetness coats my thighs, dripping down my legs, and I stare at my feet.

The gravity of the situation floods over me, overwhelming my senses. There's a ringing in my ears and my stomach tightens. I just let Mason Byrns fuck me. Twice. Even while I was watching him, I never thought we'd be in this position.

When I glance up, he's already walking down the hall back to the bedroom and my heart drops. After everything, he just strolled away as if none of this matters—as if *I* don't matter. His words seemed to hold a promise, but now I'm not so sure. Maybe this was nothing more than a quick lay. After everything we've been through, it doesn't fit, but he still vanished.

Glancing toward the bedroom, I listen for any indication that he's coming back. When he doesn't, my heart cracks a little more. I should have anticipated this. I should have stopped things before we slept together. I should have known as soon as he got what he wanted, everything else would disappear. He never promised me anything.

Swallowing hard, I resign myself to picking up the pieces alone. I sigh, shuffling to the bathroom and flipping the lock behind me. I can't face him right now, not while I'm dealing with the consequences of not protecting my heart.

Cleaning myself is my first priority, and then I can address the elephant in the room. Maybe he'll slip out while I'm in the shower, remembering all the reasons he didn't want to keep me in the first place. At least then I can get to work.

A sob catches in my throat and I shove my fist in my mouth. Doubling over, I squeeze my eyes shut, wishing I could stop the pain rolling through me. It shouldn't hurt this much. Sleeping together doesn't mean he owes me anything.

I straighten, sucking in a deep breath to center myself and letting it out slowly. The water is cold when I turn on the shower, heating up slowly as the pipes knock around in the wall.

He knocks on the door and the knob twists as I stare at it. "Lacey, open the door."

Wincing, I step into the shower instead, letting the hot water cascade over my body. Usually I wash my hair first, but I grab my soap first, scrubbing away the existence of us from between my legs. He knocks again, but I refuse to open the door. Dealing with him means admitting I made a mistake, and I hate making mistakes.

The wood cracks as a deep thud echoes through the space and I jump, my feet almost slipping from underneath me. Cursing under my breath, I lean out of the shower and flip the lock. He busts inside as I close the door, reaching for the shampoo.

And then he's there, seething as water splashes across his bare chest. At least he put his pants back on. He stands there, staring at me like I've grown a second head. No, as if I've tricked him in some way. I'm not the one who started this. I was content to let him go, ignoring all the feelings bubbling up inside me. He was the one who said he wanted more, demanded I pack up my things, convincing me I'd miraculously woken him up.

"You want to tell me why you locked the door?" he demands, crossing his arms over his very naked chest, reminding me I'm not wearing any clothes.

I cross my arms, covering my breasts as his nostrils flare. Having this conversation while I'm naked isn't ideal, but apparently I have no say in the matter.

"Because I'm cleaning up. Now, can you close the door? You're letting all the warmth out."

Narrowing his eyes, he scans me, fixating on my legs. "There a reason you scrubbed away all the evidence of me from your body?"

"I'm on birth control," I snap, and his head whips up.

"I wasn't…I'm not…what the fuck, Lacey. I wasn't worried about that," he snarls.

"Then what the hell is so important that I can't shower in peace?"

I need to get him out of here before I break. Standing in front of him now after he walked away minutes after making me come so hard I forgot how to breathe is killing me slowly, robbing me of any remaining dignity.

He sighs, dropping his hands to grip the shower door. "Finish your shower and then we'll talk."

"We don't need to talk. Just go home, Mason."

Turning away from him, I hold my breath, shoving my face under the spray. Hopefully he'll leave, and if he doesn't, then the water will wash away my tears and he'll be none the wiser. The shower door creaking is the only warning I have before his arms wrap around my waist and he presses his chest to my back. I jolt, tipping my head back as I furiously wipe my face.

"What the hell are you doing?" I sputter as he presses a kiss to the side of my neck.

"I'm not going home without you. Made that pretty clear," he grunts, reaching around me to grab my body soap.

I snatch at it, knocking the bottle from his hand, and it bounces around our feet. "You're not using my soap. And you're not taking a shower with me. Get out."

Leave it to Mason to piss me off as soon as my emotions get the better of me. At least it makes it easier for me to ignore the ache surrounding my heart. If I snap at him enough, maybe he'll finally leave shit alone. I can go back to…nothing. I have nothing but work to go back to, which will tie back to Mason. I'll never be free of him. My days will be filled with awkward texts and this pain. I refuse to go through this forever.

"Here I thought giving you a multitude of orgasms would sweeten your disposition. Can't say I'm disappointed, though," he chuckles, reaching for my shampoo instead.

I spin, pressing myself against the wall, the handle digging into my back. He raises an eyebrow at me before pushing his sweatpants down his hips. He's not even wearing any boxers and his cock springs free.

"How the hell are you still hard?" I ask, face flushing as soon as the words pop out.

He smirks, a dimple gracing his cheek. "Guess you just have that effect on me."

Turning, he sets the bottle at his feet, giving me an amazing view of his toned ass, and I almost groan out loud. Covering my mouth, I tip my head back. I obviously can't be trusted around him since a tingling starts between my legs. After years of pleasuring myself, my pussy gets one taste of Mason's cock and nothing else will do. Traitor.

"Fine, let's just have this conversation now, then. We fucked. You walked away. Now you can leave," I say to the ceiling.

His fingers grip my chin, tilting my head until we're staring at each other.

"Is that what you want?" he murmurs.

"Does it matter?"

"Of course it fucking matters," he snarls, stepping into the spray, crowding into my space. "I didn't walk away. I went to find something to clean you up because I'm not an asshole."

"Debatable," I mutter, trying to turn away, but he grips me tighter.

"You're coming home with me, Lacey. Whether you stay in my bed or not is entirely up to you, but I'm not allowing you to stay here alone."

"Allow me? You don't have the right to *allow* me to do anything, Mason Byrns."

He smirks, leaning closer until our lips brush. "How can I not have rights to something that's already mine?"

He presses his lips to mine, sweeping his tongue in my mouth as his hand grips my waist, fusing my body to his. His cock slips between my legs. He slides his hand over my wet skin, grinding his hips into mine, and I whimper when he hits my clit. Like all the other emotions suffocating me, I'll deal with his possessiveness later. Standing in my shower, I give myself over to the sensations he's building yet again in my body.

The longer he holds me, the more I realize how completely and utterly fucked I truly am when it comes to this man.

Thirty-Five

Mason

"Open it, Lacey," I grumble, leaning against the wall next to the basement door.

"I'm getting to it."

She's not. She's staring at the keypad, probably contemplating whether she's capable of showing me her inner sanctum. The parts of her house I've seen so far aren't personal, but this feels like it is.

"I promise I won't steal anything."

She scoffs, punching in the numbers, and the door unlocks, revealing a wooden staircase. Lights flash on as she tromps down and I follow. The basement isn't exactly finished with its concrete walls and curtains sectioning off areas of the room. She cringes when I glance at a makeshift bed shoved in the corner. Pushing through the fabric is like entering a whole new world.

The computer screens lining an entire wall blink on. One screen flashes a welcome message with a list below it. Leaning in, I try to read it, but she steps in front of me, glaring.

"This isn't a museum and I'm not a tour guide, so don't expect me to explain what I'm doing. You'll stand in the corner and keep your mouth shut."

She pokes me in the chest, and I capture her wrist, bringing her hand to my lips and kissing her palm. She rolls her eyes, tugging from my grasp, and I grin. This is much better than whatever the hell I was doing before. The moment I decided she was mine, something settled inside me. The guilt hasn't diminished, but there's a certain peace from just knowing she'll be where I can see her.

An alarm sounds and she drops into the chair, spinning around and staring at the screen. I shuffle closer, but I can't make any sense of what she's looking at until she pulls up a camera at the end of her street. It vibrates, flashing white every few seconds, and a curse falls from her lips. Her fingers fly across the keyboard and another screen pops up with another angle. Three more boxes flash into existence and then they all go dark as a deep rumble echoes through the space. The ceiling shudders and then another boom hits us.

"Lacey, what the fuck is going on out there?"

I'm sure she's expecting me to keep my mouth shut, but we clearly have bigger problems thundering toward us, quite literally. Sitting idly by while she searches through images isn't going to help my anxiety.

An eruption flares from the corner of one of the screens and then goes white. Seconds later, the sound rolls over us, the explosion causing the house to sway under the heatwave blasting through the neighborhood. I throw myself toward Lacey as the metal beams above us groan. Her cry rings through the space as I tackle her out of the chair, tucking us under the desk.

"What the hell is wrong with you?" she shrieks.

Her voice is muffled against my chest, and I press into her, waiting for the ceiling to collapse on top of us. The room falls silent, nothing but our harsh breaths filling the space. Pulling back, I scan her face before peeking out of our small bubble of safety. I don't know much about the structure of houses, but I'm not taking any chances with Lacey's life. I was careless once before, and she bears the scars from my inaction. Guilt eats away at me, turning my stomach, and I shove it down. I don't have time to think about all the things I should have done before to protect her. I won't make the same mistakes twice.

"Would you get off me? The ceiling is reinforced, just like the door. They could blow the house above us and we'd be fine," she cries, shoving at my chest.

"Shit fails all the time, Lacey. I'm not going to risk your life just because you say it's okay."

I groan as I stand, the ache in my muscles from earlier coming back full force. Wincing, I fall back into a chair as she scrambles out to check the cameras. Fingers flying across the keys, she pulls up a mess of code lines, squinting at the screen. Even if she wasn't moving so fast, I still wouldn't be able to keep up with what she's doing.

"What happened?" I mumble, rolling my shoulder to alleviate the pain shooting down my arm. I don't regret any of the escapades we engaged in earlier, but my muscles are protesting.

"That's what I'm trying to figure out," she mumbles. "Got it. What's this place?"

Pointing to the screen, she finally meets my eyes. Swallowing another groan, I push to my feet and shuffle closer to study the address. My breath hitches when it finally clicks.

"That's one of our distribution centers. One of my men—" I clear my throat as I slide my phone from my pocket. "One of my most trusted men runs it. What happened?"

A few more clicks and she pulls up a video, playing it on a loop.

"It's gone," she whispers.

I can feel her eyes scanning my face, boring a hole through me as I process what I'm watching. The familiar apartment building sits innocently, then it explodes, over and over. One minute there and the next—gone. My eyes are glued to the image, burning it into my brain.

TJ has been running that area for decades, long before I took over the Byrns family. He's always stayed in that building, running guns, and training prospects within its walls. I'm sure it won't sink in the place is gone until I see it for myself.

My phone slips from my grasp, snapping me out of whatever trance I'm in, and I scramble to grab it, snarling when I find it in Lacey's hands. She drops it on the desk, holding her hands up. My chest tightens and I slam my eyes closed. Ten seconds is all I take to pull my shit together. It's just a building. I have no reason to believe there was anyone inside.

The thought has me snatching up my phone and pulling up TJ's number. Lacey turns to the screens again, running some program I can't hope to understand, and I pace away. The line rings, over and over, mocking me with its dulcet tone. His voice mail picks up and I hang up, immediately connecting the call again.

"If he was there, his phone wouldn't ring," she murmurs and I turn back, finding her watching me.

"Unless someone took his phone before they blew the goddamn building up," I snap, dialing again. And again. And again.

I give up, pulling up Moss's number. Thankfully, it clicks over almost immediately.

"Boss."

I turn away from Lacey, schooling my features. "Where's TJ?"

"Hold."

Anxiety rides me hard, but a bolt of gratitude shoots through me. I never have to explain shit to my men. They take my orders, do their jobs, and I rely on them to get it done. Dealing with the other factions within the city drains me. Shane argues every point, wanting an explanation for every decision I make.

Maybe because you're shit at making decisions recently.

The voice in my head sounds suspiciously like Sam, and I push her from my mind. Spinning back around, I find Lacey with her hand over her mouth, staring at a photo of Willow St. James, Hawk's woman. Why she's bothering with the Reapers doesn't make sense.

"What are you doing, Lacey?" My tone has an edge of accusation in it, but I can't hide it.

"Um, we might have a problem," she says, glancing over her shoulder.

"Boss? He's on a run to the south. You want me to get him on the line?"

"Do it. Tell him to call me immediately."

"Yes, sir. Anything else?"

I hesitate, studying Lacey's face. I don't know if I can protect her and my territory. Clearly, she has a set-up here. Just the thought of leaving her here, though, sends a bolt through me. She was right. There's no way we can move all this equipment in my car. I'll have to get some guys over here to deal with it, and even then I don't know when she'll be back up and running.

"Lock it down. Level two. Full protocol. I'm sending an address. Get a team here to move shit to the house."

Lacey's cry of outrage drowns out most of Moss's answer, but I assume he's agreeing, so I hang up. She explodes from her chair, waving her hands wildly. The sounds coming from her are unintelligible and the corner of my mouth pulls up before I can erase the emotion.

My phone rings and I hold up a finger. I spin, having to hide from her before she can catch the full-on grin plastered across my face at her reaction. Relief floods me when TJ's name flashes across the screen seconds before I answer.

"TJ, where are you?"

"On our way back from a run. Listen, the driver was acting twitchy. Said he thought he was being followed, but didn't have anything conclusive," he says, voices colliding in the background.

"TJ, it's gone." I don't know how to tell him. It's his home, his entire life was there. I've never known a time he didn't run shit from there.

"What's that? Would y'all shut the fuck up? I'm talking to Byrns, motherfuckers," he yells and the others quiet immediately.

"They blew up the apartment building. It's gone."

There's a beat of silence, and then he lets out a soft curse. "Who?"

"I don't know."

It kills me I don't have answers. I hate admitting I don't know what the fuck is going on. Whoever is coming after me isn't just targeting me, they're coming after those under my protection. I can't keep reacting to things. Finding whoever is behind this needs to be my top priority, right after Lacey's safety.

"I'm sure you'll figure it out. Say, can I stay at your place?" He busts out laughing, his reaction punching me in the gut.

"Yeah, of course. We're locking down. I'll talk to you when I get back," I murmur.

"Mason?" Lacey calls, and I turn as TJ hangs up.

The screen is filled with so many boxes, I don't know where to look first. The video of the apartment is frozen in the middle of the blast, and I glance away, focusing on Willow's face instead. I don't know how she's involved, but clearly Lacey thinks whatever she's found is important.

"What'd you find?" I grunt, fixating on my phone.

I need to get home as soon as possible. Locking down isn't something I take lightly. The fact Victor didn't shut down when the Guild came through was just one of the reasons I'm done with his bullshit. I make a mental note to call Alex and tell him to get his ass in gear dealing with my uncle.

"Are you even listening to me? I can't do this all by myself, Mason," Lacey seethes. Her voice filters through the haze clouding my mind.

"I'm dealing with some shit here, Kitten. Sorry I can't give you my full attention the second you want it," I snap, firing off a text message.

"Don't turn on me, you asshat. I'm trying to help you here, and this is important," she snaps, pointing at the image of Willow.

I bow, gesturing for her to continue, and she scowls. I stay where I am, though. If I get any closer to her, I'm liable to snatch her up and channel all my anxiety into fucking her. The more time I spend with her, the more I want her. I'm convinced if we can just get over all the bullshit, we'll be fine. I'm no longer concerned with the aftermath. No one batted an eye when Alex brought her to the Kings. They were more put out I discovered her identity before they did.

"Are you going to explain what you're talking about, or can I go back to locking down my territory?" I raise an eyebrow, and she flushes.

"Someone is looking into her. They're digging into her past. Not much to do to fuck with her now, since she's under the Reapers' protection."

I sigh, toying with my phone, debating who to call about this. Willow might be Hawk's, but Helms is the president.

"I'm assuming we don't know who?"

"Obviously, or I would have told you. The more concerning issue is the police in Rima are searching for her in connection with her stepfather's disappearance." She spins around, leaning back in her chair.

Ducking my head, I cross my arms, staring at my feet, but not really seeing anything. My thoughts are jumbled, each one vying for attention. Half-plotted schemes and retaliations pop into focus before drifting away as I dismiss them one by one. There's only so much I can do from here, even with Lacey's set-up. I need to get home, call a meeting, deal with my men, start protocols, and prepare my territory for a war we've apparently been waging for much longer than I thought. Whoever is behind this seemed to be targeting only me, picking off pieces of my life and not caring who was caught in the crossfire. Fucking with Willow, though, brings the Reapers to the forefront.

"Do we think it's the Guild?"

Rage courses through me, followed closely by guilt. I should have been there before, helping the others deal with the Guild. Instead, I was lying in the hospital, no help to anyone. I've been trying to handle everything by myself, as if I could make up for my absence by doing it alone. Now all I've done is put us in a worse position than before.

"There's no indication they're behind this. I think it's one person orchestrating everything, but Mason, this is something that's been planned for a while. There's no way all these things could go wrong all at once."

"All at once?" I finally snap out of whatever trance I was in, her words barely filtering through.

"When I was…taken, a bunch of other shit happened too. The apartment building being blown, along with your car earlier. Plus, the supply chains are all messed up. Nicki said Oracle is rampant in the Barrens again. This isn't an isolated incident. They're systematically dismantling the city, starting with you. They've started fucking with the Reapers. The Kings will be next. This is going to get a whole helluva lot worse before we have all the pieces to this puzzle."

"Pack whatever you need, clothes and shit. I've got guys coming for this stuff," I say, waving a hand at her computers. "We'll find a place at the house for it all."

"I can't do my job from your house, Mason. I don't have the time to set it all up again by myself."

I nod, pressing my lips into a thin line before pulling up a contact in my phone. It rings once, twice while Lacey eyes me. Relief sinks into my bones as it connects.

"Ren. I need your help."

Thirty-Six

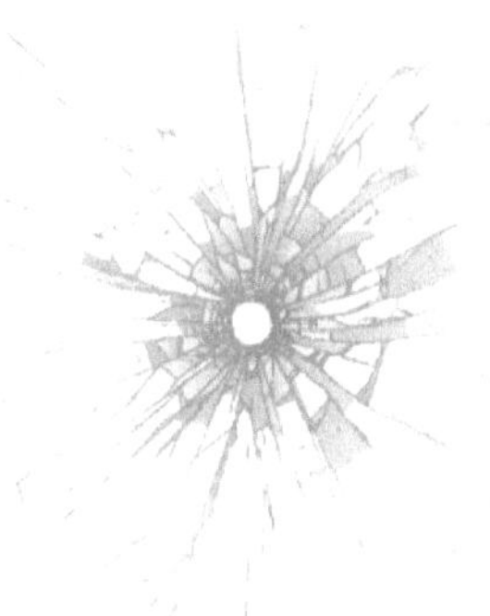

Lacey

I huff, a scowl permanently etched on my face. My mother's voice floats through my memories, telling me my face will stick that way if I keep it up, and my lip curls. I slump further down the wall, arms aching from crossing them so tightly against my body. One of the guards gives me a small smile as he passes and I snarl, causing him to jump before scurrying away.

Good.

"Would you stop scaring my men?" Mason mutters, stepping in front of me.

"Would you stop bossing me around?" I snap, clenching my teeth so hard my jaw aches.

He steps into my space, straddling my legs with his own and leaning in close. My breath hitches, but then I mentally slap myself and scowl again. Ever since he informed me I didn't have a choice on whether I was coming here, to his house, regardless of my excuses, he's been glued to my side. On the car ride over, after I hastily threw some clothes in a bag, he kept sliding his hand along my thigh and holding my hand.

As he runs his nose along my jaw, I freeze, holding my breath.

"I think you like when I boss you around."

"I think you like when I decide not to listen," I say before pressing my lips into a thin line.

His low chuckle ghosts past my skin, sending goosebumps down my neck. I don't know what change he went through, but the differences are stark. Indecisiveness guided his every move before, preying upon both of us, until…somewhere between leaving the Kings' house and my own, maybe. Or maybe when we fell into bed together.

Apparently, losing that one particular building was the cat-alyst for him, forcing him into the position of a leader. That change filtered over into his treatment of me. We still have a lot to deal with between us, but we don't have time now. I'll table it for later when we're not in the middle of a crisis.

"Kitten, you realize I took it easy on you before, right? Your brattiness is going to get you into trouble. And I can't wait to deal with it," he murmurs, nipping at my lobe before pulling back, and I catch his smirk.

His phone rings and he answers, walking away. I resume my scowling. Pressing my thighs together, I try to will away the desire. It's no use, and I thump my head against the wall. Another guard brings in another computer screen, tripping over absolutely nothing, and I squawk, blasting off the wall as if I'll be able to save it.

An arm wraps around my waist and my mind blanks. Dark-ness bleeds over my vision and the wound on my face burns. Crimson drops hit the floor, streaming down my face and drying on my neck, leaving an incessant itch in its wake. A bolt of lightning hits my chest and I explode, kicking and clawing at my captor. My throat aches, but no sound hits my ear. It's as if the world has turned off with the flick of a switch.

Whipping my head back, the band around my waist tightens as someone curls their body into mine. A sob bursts from my lips as I fight the blackness threatening to sweep me under its waves, drowning me beneath the surface of sanity.

The band around my body releases, and my lungs expand as air rushes down my throat, searing my insides with flames of terror. My body convulses, knees cracking as I hit the ground, dirt my only companion. My blood shivers within my veins, the vibrations shattering the hold on my mind and a blood-curdling scream forces its way from deep within my soul.

"Get the fuck away from her," someone roars, and I flinch.

Warm hands cup my face, and the scent of autumn fills my nose, invading my mind. *Mason,* my mind whispers, urging me to trust the safety his name invokes. Another sob leaves me, and the world turns back on.

Groaning as the lights stab into my senses, I slam my eyes shut. My body sways, and I pull in a deep breath to steady my racing heart. I squint through the red haze floating through the air until Mason's face fills my vision. It's then that I realize I'm shaking. Not shivering, not trembling, full-on quaking, rattling my bones with the force rolling through my body.

"Breathe, Kitten. It's not real. Focus on me," he whispers.

"You're real," I choke out, shards of glass filling my throat.

"That's right. I'm real, and I won't leave you. I'm right here."

The haze retreats in the wake of his words, the rest of the room coming into focus. An ache sets in my muscles, and I can practically hear my bones creaking. Glancing around, I realize we're the only ones left. All the guards have cleared out, except for Ren hovering by the door as if he's some bouncer. Mason's fingers on my chin guide my gaze back to him, concern lining his brown eyes.

"Are you with me?" he murmurs, brushing his thumb across my cheek.

I nod, not willing to risk opening my mouth. I'm afraid I'll start screaming and never stop. Ducking my chin to my chest, I concentrate on filling my lungs with a scent other than freshly turned dirt.

Now that I'm no longer blinded by panic, I realize it all was a flashback invading my mind and taking over my reality. Shame sends a flush to my cheeks, and I pull my face from Mason's grasp before shuffling back. It's bad enough I'm having these hallucinations in front of Mason and then Alex, but now Ren has witnessed it as well. How will they ever trust my work if they know what a mess I am?

"Lacey," Mason whispers, his voice laced with regret.

I shake my head, stumbling as I push to my feet. Spinning for the door, I stop short before pivoting toward the bathroom tucked away in the corner of the room. This isn't one of the massive spaces I stayed in before. It's an office more than anything, and the bathroom reflects that, a sink and toilet take up most of the space.

Shoving the door shut, I lean against it, as if I could stop them from coming in, but I don't move. Sliding down the wood, tears streak down my face. I'm just glad I kept them at bay long enough to retreat. The last thing I need is to cry in front of them, too.

Their voices slip under the door, a low murmur of words I can't make out. My mind skips to each toxic thought, wondering what they're saying about me. I wish I was home, locked away in the safety of my basement, and pretending the outside world can't touch me. It wouldn't stop me reliving my time in the hole, or the man who gave me a scar, but at least I wouldn't be embarrassed when I inevitably lose it.

I thought the few weeks would be enough to ease some of the nightmares, but now I'm convinced this will be my life forever. I'll spend my days pretending I haven't gone through anything horrific, and my nights locked in the nightmare of a world that no longer exists.

I jolt when someone knocks on the door, even though it's soft. Swiping my hands across my face, my fingers catch on the raised skin on my cheek, sending a shudder through me. When I stand, the world tilts and I grab the edges of the sink. I don't bother with the mirror. I already know what I look like—a complete mess.

"Yeah?" I rasp, the burn still present in my throat.

"Nemesis," Ren says, then clears his throat. "We should talk."

Sucking my lip into my mouth, I rack my brain for a way to get out of this conversation. Most of my equipment is already moved into the office Mason set up. It'll take another couple hours to move it back to my place, which is time no one can really afford. Watching them dance around the issue, admitting their mistake in moving me here, will be torture on a whole other level.

"Just put it all back. I'll figure it out," I call, tears filling my eyes again.

I may have fought Mason on staying here, gave him shit the entire time they moved my stuff, but a sense of relief had settled on me the minute I walked through the front doors. Several hours later and that relief is being ripped away, and the only person I have to blame is myself.

"That's not what we need to talk about. No one else is here, so you can open the door."

I was banking on him trying to kick me out, but the alternative is so much worse. I rip open the door, jumping when it slams against the wall.

"I'm perfectly capable of doing my job. But since you're the one who pays me, I'm more than happy to sever any ties we have and move on." The words burn coming out of me.

Ren tilts his head, and I glance behind him. The room is silent, devoid of life. Mason apparently abandoned me, not wanting to deal with firing me, if one could even call it that.

"I believe your thoughts are spiraling. How about instead of assuming you know what I want to speak on, you come out here and sit down?"

He steps to the side, gesturing to the computer chair already set up at the long table Mason dragged in here. My steps are wooden as I march past him and sink down. He pulls the other chair over and sits, facing me before propping his elbows on his knees.

"I'm sorry," he says, and his jaw twitches.

"Excuse me?"

"I'm the one who grabbed you. I was afraid you would hurt yourself if you tried to catch the monitor and I tried to stop you. I didn't realize you were prone to panic attacks."

"I'm not," I mutter, glancing away.

"Mason said these have been happening since you were kidnapped. You don't have to label them, but they're clearly affecting you. Eventually, you'll have to deal with the trauma you've suffered. However, I believe Mason is a calming force for you, so you might want to explore that more. If you need anything, you know how to get a hold of me," he says before standing.

He's almost to the door before I've recovered. "That's it?"

Ren turns back, raising an eyebrow. "Nemesis, we've been working together for years. While you may have assumed our relationship was purely business, most of us don't feel that way. Remember that the next time your mind tries to convince you that you aren't one of us."

Mason slips through as Ren exits, the door clicking softly behind him. Our eyes meet as he strides toward me, and the ache in my chest returns. Ren may have said all sorts of things I'm not completely ready to process yet, but dealing with Mason is a whole other layer.

I open my mouth, if only to fill the silence, when he swoops down and captures my lips. My gasp is caught between us, mingling with our breaths, as his tongue sweeps into my mouth.

Tugging me from the chair, he grips my hip, his other hand sliding into my hair. The ache from before falls away, replaced with the desire I shove down deep when I'm around him.

When his fingers tangle with the strands, angling my head to deepen the kiss, I shudder. All the roadblocks and excuses I've told myself shatter, drifting away like ash on the wind. I'm so consumed with the kiss, I'm thrown when he grabs my waist and sets me on the desk before stepping between my legs.

The next minute is a whirlwind of clothes being ripped off, scattered across the floor in our haste between more heated kisses. His pants are the only thing standing between us and I attack the buttons as he sinks his teeth into my skin, my trembling fingers slipping. Sucking on the mark, he leans back, admiring his work.

"Mine," he growls, low and dark just as the button slips out, and I shove his pants and boxers down his hips.

His cock springs free, and I lick my lips when he strokes himself and then tips my chin up to meet his darkened eyes.

"Something you want, Kitten?"

Biting my lip, I scrape my nails across his chest, leaving red streaks between the dark ink tattooed across his skin. I hook my ankles around his thighs, attempting to tug him closer, but he chuckles as his hand continues to move up and down.

A whimper leaves me when his finger dips between my legs, gathering the wetness there. He groans, tipping his head back when he pops it in his mouth. Swallowing hard, I wrap my fingers around his cock below his hand and squeeze, chasing the pleasure flowing across his face.

"I hate that you made me move here," I mutter, digging my heels into his ass.

He steps closer, releasing himself to wrap his fingers around my wrist.

"I hate what you make me feel," he grunts.

I scoot to the edge of the desk. His cock slips into me, and I shudder.

"I hate how much I want you," I gasp as my eyes fall closed.

"I hate how much I don't hate you," he growls, plunging into me.

We both freeze, breathless, as I quiver around him. My head dips, eyes fixed on where we're connected, and my breath hitches. Skimming his hands down my sides, he digs his fingers into my hips, and I glance up. As soon as our eyes meet, he pulls out and buries himself deep into me again.

Over and over, he repeats the move, slowly retreating before embedding his cock into me, stoking the flame inside of my gut until it's a raging inferno threatening to consume my very being. My nails dig into his skin, leaving half-moon circles in their wake, but it only seems to egg him on. He seems to thrive on pain. Admitting to myself I do too is harder than I imagined. Falling back on my hands, I groan at the new angle as he quickens his pace.

Grunting, he stops, buried inside me, then leans over my body. He nips at my neck before skimming his lips up my throat. I whimper as I wrap my legs around his waist, trying to pull him deeper, even though he's already fully seated.

"You going to purr for me, Kitten?"

"Careful," I warn. I'm sure the breathlessness in my voice undermines any force in my words.

He rolls his hips and I gasp, tipping my head back, knocking it against the wall. Flames of desire lick through my body and I shudder. His fingers wrap around my throat, squeezing. He pulls out, surging into me before stopping.

"I see my kitten's claws are out. If you're good, I'll let you come all over my cock."

I scratch my nails down his chest, meeting his gaze. "And if I'm not?"

His grin turns predatory, and I swallow as he squeezes my throat. "Then I'll put you on your knees and fuck this pretty little mouth of yours. And you'll take every fucking inch of me."

Thirty-Seven

Mason

"Psst."

Whipping around, I find Alex hovering next to a car swathed in shadows. I roll my eyes, tucking my phone in my pocket. After fucking Lacey into submission, I ended up hovering around her for the next several hours while she set up her equipment. For the last week, I've been sneaking in whatever time I can to sink back into her. I didn't want to leave her tonight, but Alex is a persistent fucker.

"What's with the spy shit? You could have just knocked, you know," I grumble, crossing my arms when I reach him.

"You're no fun. Besides, I'm worried our little friend might come home and see me. Might be suspicious." Alex grins, leaning against the hood of the old beater.

"And meeting in the shadows with a rusty-ass car in the middle of the night around the corner from my house isn't?"

He waves away my words before pulling out his phone and scowling and I wonder if he's going to lose it on someone. I've only seen him go feral a couple times, but it was enough. The dead look that enters his eyes is enough to deter me from ever getting on his bad side. Thankfully, it takes a lot for him to tip over the edge.

"Listen, I followed Vicky to some meet-up. I tried to get a picture of the guy he was meeting with, but it was too dark. They seem chummy, though. I think he's planning something, but I haven't found anything else. You might want to loop Nemesis in, see what she can find," he says, running his hand through his hair. "I'm not sure what else you want me to do unless you want me to float him. Sam might be pissed about that."

"I hardly think she'll be upset if Victor is no longer among the living," I scoff, glancing behind me to scan the street.

An itch between my shoulder blades sets me on edge. I don't like standing in the dark talking about shit like this. Anyone could be watching us, but I doubt they'd be able to overhear our conversation. Still not ideal. I wish I could skip this part and just have everything done with, but if Victor is planning something, I can't afford to kill him yet.

"Uh, Sam will be more upset she didn't get to stab him herself. Figured you knew that."

"I most certainly would." Sam's voice floats from the dark, and she steps into the moonlight filtering through the trees.

Alex grins, slipping his phone in his pocket, and loops his arm around her. Sam smacks him before pulling from his grasp while he chuckles. I didn't want to get my sister involved in this whole mess. It's a toss-up whether Alex told her about tailing Victor or if she just figured it out. She has a way of slipping into places she's not supposed to be. Those skills make her an excellent spy and assassin. Unfortunately, it makes it ridiculously difficult to keep shit from her.

"So did Alex spill the beans, or is he terrible at not getting caught?" I check the tree line again. I'd assume the feeling I had before of someone watching us was from Sam, but it's still there, worming into my brain.

"Neither. I'm just really fucking good at my job. One *you* prepared me for. Be nice if someone would keep me in the loop," she says, rolling her eyes.

"Couldn't be because I didn't want you involved," I mumble under my breath.

"Oh, fuck off. We're all waiting for our pound of flesh from Victor. You can't deny us the luxury of taking it personally, Mason. Pull your head out of your ass and let someone help you for once," she snarls.

"Asked Alex for help, didn't I?" I snap back.

Alex steps between us, holding up his hands. "Oookay, let's just take a step back. Fuck, I knew you two were siblings, but could you stop with the bickering? Geesh."

Sam throws her hands up as she spins around before ripping open the car door and sliding into the driver's seat. Crossing her arms, she scowls through the windshield, and I glare back at her. It's like we're petulant children again.

Alex turns to me, failing to see her sticking her tongue out at me. I'm sure Alex never has spats with Shane or Ren. He always seems to be the peacemaker. He clearly doesn't understand what it's like to have an annoying little sister. Emma is probably too young to really piss him off like Sam does me.

"We need to get into that room you were telling me about. I don't understand why you don't just bust down the door and pretend it was someone else. That's gotta be where he keeps all his little secrets." He pauses, looking back at Sam again. "You know who *could* get in there without being caught…"

"I doubt Sam would want to do that. She can barely handle being in my house these days," I mutter, pulling out my vibrating phone.

"Who's that?"

"No one," I say before slipping it back in my pocket.

Alex is a nosy little bitch, always wanting to know what everyone is up to. I don't think he does anything with the information. He just likes being the one who knows what's going on in everyone's lives.

"It's Nemesis, isn't it? I mean, Lacey. Sorry. She okay?"

"She's fine."

Sam climbs from the car, slamming the door behind her. When she stomps over to me, my mind flashes back to her at fifteen, trying to convince me she was trained enough, and she didn't need to go back to the mountain retreat. She wanted to hang out with her friends. I didn't have the heart to tell her they didn't care about her. Those kids only wanted to befriend her for what she could get them, which was status.

I was just starting to venture out into the city again, having survived the worst of the attempted coup aftermath. The final straw, though, was finding out the mayor's son had plans for her.

Sam could have taken care of it herself, but if I could help her avoid the whole situation in the first place, I would. I did. She just hated me for a while afterward. It was a hate I was willing to take.

"Listen up, buddy," she snarls.

"Buddy?" I ask, smothering my smirk and raising an eyebrow.

"You heard me." She pokes me in the chest. "I have just as much right to take that asshole out as you do. In fact, I'd argue I have more. That bastard—"

"We're not getting in a pissing contest about who he's fucked over more."

While she glares at me, I can practically see the gears working in her mind, trying to figure out which excuse she can fling out that'll convince me she should be the one to put a bullet in his brain. She'd probably smother him, or chop him into little pieces and feed him to a wood chipper.

"Where's Lacey?" she asks, narrowing her eyes.

"At home. If you really insist on helping, then find a way into that front room Victor took over and get us some information. And for fuck's sake, do not get caught."

"Except he's rigged every entrance," she mutters.

I spin, intent on going back to the house and slipping under the covers next to Lacey. Every night for almost a week, she's fallen asleep at the desk I set up for her. She whines whenever I carry her to my bed but hasn't told me to stop. She's exactly where she belongs. I didn't even give her a separate room. What's the point if she's going to be in next to me every night, anyway?

"Wait," Sam calls, rushing to my side. "Listen, don't freak out, but Nicki is pissed. She's thinking about locking down the Barrens. Oh, and there's a bunch of contacts in Harris who are pulling out. The shipments coming from Rima are all over the place. Some of them aren't getting here at all. Shit is falling apart and I'm thinking we might need to up the ante."

"I already locked down and started protocols. Not much more I can do unless we go full lock down. That would be catastrophic for the city. You know that."

My house comes into view, only a few lights shining from the many windows this late at night. Glancing at Sam, a memory hits me of us as teenagers walking home after I caught her sneaking out of the house. Dad was on a rampage, dealing with some fallout within the family. If he found out Sam had snuck out, I don't know what he would have done, but I was scared enough to go out and find her myself. This moment feels like then, when she was pissed at me, and I was trying to handle everything on my own.

"Shane's worried about you," she murmurs.

I scoff, side-eyeing her. "You mean he's worried about his territory. And you."

"I mean, true. But he *is* worried about you, too. He keeps asking if you're okay." She sighs, skipping in front of me and skittering to a stop. "You know we don't care if you're with Nemesis, right?"

"I'm not with Nemesis," I say, the words burning in my throat.

"Bullshit. Bet Lace would have some things to say about that."

"Don't call her Lace." My words come out harsher than I intend, but the sentiment still stands.

"Oohkay. That your little nickname for her?" She smirks, but it falls when I wipe my face of expression.

"I'm serious, Samantha. She doesn't want to be called Lace. It's none of your fucking business why. Again, I'm not with Nemesis, because when she's with me, she's Lacey. Now, if we're done discussing my love life, please get the fuck out of my way."

Her eyebrows pop up, and she purses her lips. I can tell she's dying to let some bullshit fly. She's practically bursting at the seams from holding back. Crossing my arms, I let her stew as her nose scrunches up. Alex snorts behind us, but we're locked in a battle of wills.

"Say your piece, Sammy, before your head explodes." I shake my head, waiting for the floodgates to open.

She shifts from one foot to the other, cracking her knuckles before she bursts. "Calling it a love life now? Pretty fucking bold, if you ask me."

Rolling my eyes, I shove past her. Peals of laughter chase me down the street, and I resist the urge to glance back. Just as I'm about to round the corner, I peek over my shoulder. Alex's concerned face is fixed on Sam, who's doubled over, clutching her stomach. A grunt escapes me when she crosses her legs and squeals.

"For fuck's sake, Bug. Do not fucking piss yourself," Alex bellows before scooping her up and throwing her over his shoulder.

The trees block them from view, although Sam's squawking floats on the wind, fluttering what few leaves are left. Autumn's fury is rushing away as winter sets in. I wish I would have grabbed a coat. Instead, I'm stuck in a fancy suit that doesn't protect me from any of the elements.

I didn't want to deal with anything other than the shit going down in Synd, but the mayor insisted we needed an in-person meeting. I'm still seething at the fact he didn't show up. Thankfully, Alex texted me, giving me an out, but if the restaurant manager had come over one more time to ask if I needed anything, I was liable to shoot him.

"Boss, we might have another problem," Moss calls as I pass the guard shack.

I stop, closing my eyes and pulling in a deep breath before pivoting. I just want one night where shit isn't going wrong. One night where I can seduce Lacey without interruptions. One night where I can pretend the world isn't burning around us.

"What is it, Moss?"

"Another safe house burned down. This time in the south. Feels like someone caught wind of where they are. Systematic and all. We keep having to shuffle people around."

"Anyone killed?"

"Nah. Whoever it is, they aren't targeting the ones that are occupied. Real fucking strange if you ask me," he says, crossing his arms and leaning against the door frame.

"I'll take care of it," I murmur, but it's become a rote response at this point.

The look he gives me tells me he knows I'm paying him lip service. There are so many things I'm supposed to be taking care of and yet they get buried under all the other tasks that are seemingly more important. I'm suffocating under the weight of everything I'm pretending to deal with. All I trade in are empty words.

"Lower gangs are starting to talk."

He says it like we haven't had this conversation twice this week. They've been grumbling for months now. Nothing is ever good enough for them. They all want more—more money, more territory, more of fucking everything. They clearly don't know how good they have it, even though I realize I've been slacking.

"Not my job to babysit them, but I'll talk to Rigger about it."

"Boss—"

"I said I'd fucking take care of it. Or fucking deal with it yourself," I snarl.

I stomp away, hoping he doesn't follow me. He's been pushing back more and more lately, and it's starting to annoy me. It's like everyone's forgot who the hell is actually in charge. They're cautiously testing how far they can step out of line until my patience runs out.

If it was just the lower gangs, I could go in and clean house. At every level, though, my men are muttering under their breaths, criticizing the decisions I'm making, and generally pissing me off. I barely understood what was happening a dozen years ago when the others rose up, attempting to overthrow the ruling families of Synd. Looking back, the signs were all there. And they're being repeated.

"Mason, we should talk," Victor says as soon as I step through the door.

It's long past midnight, and all I want is to go to bed. The days seem to stretch to impossible lengths, elongating and warping time to suit their own nefarious needs. And yet there isn't enough time to put out all the fires burning on the east side of Synd.

Sighing, I turn to him, taking in his haggard appearance before slipping my phone from my pocket and checking the text message from Alex.

"What is it, Victor?" I ask, fixing my eyes on the screen.

"Clearly, something is happening within Synd. I believe it's time we address it," he states, but I can hear the sneer in his voice.

"I'm taking care of it."

He straightens the cuffs on his suit, though it's hanging off his frame. Limp gray hair that's in desperate need of a trim lies across his damp forehead. Clearly, his health is failing, but maybe it's the guilt eating away at him. Betraying family isn't kind on one's body. I rein in my thoughts, reminding myself that I have no proof he's working against me.

"While you may think you're taking care of it, the sentiment doesn't always translate to actual action. Perhaps it would help if I took some things off your plate," he says, staring at my shoulder.

The fact he can't even look me in the eye as he's offering to oust me from my position as head of the family has me fingering the handle of my gun. I could shoot him right now, drag his body out the front door, and leave him in the gutter. I could bash his head against the wall until he stops trying to worm his way into my head, convincing me I'm not enough to rule. I could float him, and no one would miss him—not a single person would care.

Glancing at Alex's text message again, I push the thoughts of putting him six feet under from my mind. Alex says he'll take care of it, so I'll allow him to run with whatever he has planned.

"How about you let me dig the family out of the fucking hole you put us in, yeah? Because from where I stand, you did a fucking number on us that *I'll* be dealing with for years."

Spinning before he can respond, I walk off into the darkness of the house. I find Lacey fast asleep at her desk, the screens lining the wall dark. When I gather her in my arms, she doesn't wake. She curls into my body, sighing as I carry her to my room. My phone buzzes as I pull the blanket over her. Gazing down at her, I wonder if I can get away with ignoring the text message. It's probably Alex with some random fact or Sam begging me to let her take down our uncle.

Sighing, I stride into the bathroom, softly shutting the door behind me. I read the message twice before the words finally register. Thumb hovering over the screen, for a split second I contemplate responding, but then a curse falls from my lips. I can't involve anyone else in this. I need to right these wrongs by myself. Even as I stalk from the bathroom, I realize I'm officially fucked.

Thirty-Eight

Alarms hammer through my skull, adding to the migraine I've had since last night. Tonight. I have no idea what time it is. Moonlight filters through the curtains of Mason's bedroom window. Wracking my brain, I try to figure out how I got here. The last thing I remember was deep diving into Willow's past.

Whoever is tailing her is covering their tracks exceptionally well, which is annoying as shit. Sifting through the various factions who are searching for Willow hasn't been easy either. Speculation runs wild in Rima, but most of the media has bigger shit to deal with. Eventually, we're going to have to look into it, but we're dealing with enough as it is.

The thought pulls me up short. I don't know when I started lumping myself in with the leaders of Synd. I doubt Mason would mind. Not to mention Ren's comments about adjusting my way of thinking. They would probably insist I'm part of them, whether I admit it or not.

When the alarm sounds again, I'm pulled into full alert. I can't tell if it's coming from Mason's room specifically, or if the whole house is on lockdown. Mason talked about threat levels and protocols, but I barely paid attention. Finding out who is targeting Mason has taken up most of my time.

Scrambling up, I search for my phone, finding it on the bedside table. It rings as soon as I snatch it up, Sam's name flashing across the screen.

"Sam? What the hell is going on?" I ask, whipping my head around to find my pants.

Alarms blare in the background of the call, creating a pulsing within my skull. Dashing to the bathroom, I slam the door shut. Sam yells something on the other end I can't make out and then a door clicks shut, muffling the noise.

"Lacey? I need you to not be Lacey right now. I need you to be Nemesis," she says, steel lacing her voice, but a quiver comes through as well.

"What's wrong? What happened? I need to get to my computers."

Rushing from the room, I rip the door open, almost colliding with a guard. Stopping short, I scowl at TJ. I haven't had much interaction with him, and he's probably a perfectly nice person, but his presence tells me Mason isn't home. Mason has been leaving me alone more often, assigning someone to follow me around as if I'm not perfectly capable of taking care of myself.

"Willow is missing. She was supposed to go to the Raines's old house, but when Hawk got there, she was gone. They're searching in Reaper territory, but she's vanished. Hawk is freaking out."

"When?"

"An hour maybe? Helms has a hard time reaching out still. Mac called me when they knew."

"A fucking hour?" I yell, blasting through the door, TJ close on my heels. "What the hell is wrong with you people? You realize this makes my job harder, right?"

I swear it takes a bazillion years for my computer to boot up, and my leg bounces a mile a minute by the time it does. Sam yells in the background, something about protocols. As I pull up the cameras in Reaper territory, I make a note to fix the ones around their headquarters. With everything going on lately, it hasn't been on the top of my list. A lot of things haven't been making the cut these days. Issues that seemed so pressing before have taken a back seat, impatiently waiting their turn.

"Sorry, it's kind of a shitshow around here. This is like the third time she's been taken, so we're all just a little on edge."

"I was there, Sam. I was searching for that fucking car for fucking ever. And now here I am, scanning for another one. For fuck's sake. I'm ready for this shit to be done," I grumble as my eyes flit across the screen.

"You and me both, honey. But until we find Willow, nothing else gets done."

I huff, eyes catching a woman's blonde hair outside of a nightclub before they skip to the next image. Being shitty to Sam won't help anything, but at least she's not taking offense. I've spent most of my life hiding who I am from others because I was always on the outside of their circle. It's weird to clap back at her with no repercussions. Sam doesn't seem miffed or upset I basically just cussed her out. Then again, I sounded like an asshole, bitching about Willow being missing. She and Sam are friends, and yet I offered no sympathy.

"Shit. Sorry, Sam. I'll find her."

"What the fuck are you apologizing for?" she grunts, the sound of her footsteps pounding on the tail of her words.

"I didn't mean to be a bitch. She's your friend, so obviously you'd be upset she's been kidnapped."

Rewinding the video from a camera outside of Trigger's bar, I tilt my head as I replay it two, three, then four times. There's something about it that doesn't look right, but I can't put my finger on why. It's a completely normal car, driving past at night. In fact, there are several bikers leaning against the building who watch it with no reaction. Yet a voice in the back of my head is tapping at my brain, demanding I pay attention.

"Eck, let's not use the k-word. Little touchy around here. I'm surprised you throw it out so fucking casually, to be honest."

A car door shuts on her end, just as I pause the camera feed and zoom in on the back windshield of the car. Frame by frame I advance the feed, scanning the entire image. Shane's muffled voice filters through, yelling about sectors. I'm pretty sure he's talking to Ryker, but it could be Hawk.

"Didn't really think about it," I mutter.

"Seriously? Not like it was that long ago. I mean, if it were me—"

"Shut up," I murmur, squinting at the bright red lights. "I think…right there."

I watch it twice more from different angles before I'm convinced.

"Nemesis, talk to me," Sam says, a warning in her voice.

"She was in the backseat of a car about an hour ago."

I rattle off the make and model and then start searching the rest of the city for it. Chaos reigns on Sam's end as she conveys the information. Tracking the vehicle throughout the city, I lose it when they reach club row. Traffic is too thick to keep track of one car in a sea of them, especially since I'm guessing at how long it would take for them to travel from one point to another.

"They disappeared into the Barrens forty-three minutes ago on the east side. Close to the train station," I yell into the phone, trying to get Sam's attention.

"Fuck if that helps."

"Doing the best I fucking can here. The Barrens are fucking huge, so finding out where they popped out isn't exactly easy."

My fingers fly across the keyboard as the door next to me opens and I flick my eyes to the side. I don't have time to deal with anything other than this. After I find the car, I can look into who the hell took Willow. Unfortunately, it's not as simple as narrowing down her enemies.

The families of Synd are so intertwined now, the threat could be coming from anywhere. Unless her captor is one of her stepfather's friends, but I doubt he had people he would consider friends. He was the type to collect minions, using and discarding them at will.

TJ clears his throat and I roll my eyes. "I'm sorry to interrupt, but we have a situation."

"Kind of already dealing with one," I mutter.

"Who's that?" Sam barks.

"It's TJ. What do you need, Timothy James?" I ask, barely glancing at him. I've been trying for the last week to figure out what TJ stands for, but his poker face is on point. Even if I do guess correctly, I doubt he'll admit it.

"Not my name. When was the last time you saw Mason?"

"I don't know. Early afternoon maybe? Why?"

I've been holed up in here, doing my job. It's not all that different from when I was sequestered in my basement. Although now Mason will pop in, forcing me to stop whatever I'm doing to pay attention to him. I don't know what's going on between us, but I've stopped fighting the feelings swirling within me. I'll ride this train as long as he'll let me. I fought him long enough.

"He's gone. No one knows where he went."

Peering at him, his words filter slowly into me. "What?"

Concern flashes in his eyes. "Mason is missing."

"No, he's not. He brought me to bed," I murmur, a blush spreading across my cheeks. We never discussed what others know, but TJ's been around more than the others. He's not ignorant. "He asked you to guard the door."

"Lacey, no, he didn't. I was coming to see if he was with you. He's gone," he says slowly, as if it'll hurt less if he doesn't rush his words.

Shaking my head, I grab my phone, intent on calling Mason when I remember I'm still on a call with Sam.

"Sam, have you heard from Mason?"

The line goes quiet, only the faint rumbling of an engine filtering through. A soft curse echoes through the phone before the line goes dead. My heart jumps into my throat, and I scramble to the bathroom.

Crashing to my knees, I dry heave, body convulsing as I try to expel the knowledge swimming in my mind. Willow's gone, whisked away in the back of a car. Sam's bailed, probably not trusting me any longer. Mason's missing, whether to save Willow or because he's been taken too, I don't know.

"Get your shit together, Lacey. We need information, and you're the one who can get it. So, get done with puking your guts out and then get the fuck to work," TJ snarls from the doorway.

My phone rattles across my desk, and I dash into the bedroom, shoving TJ aside as I pass. Snatching it up, I answer without looking, sending silent pleas that Mason's voice will be on the other side.

"Mason?" Even I can hear the frenzied pitch in my voice, but I'm beyond caring.

"It's Alex. Sam is dealing with some shit right now. Lacey, you need to find them. If they die…we won't survive. Our families won't survive."

The line goes dead and my phone slips from my numb fingers, clattering to the floor.

Thirty-Nine

Mason

Frustration winds its way through my body in the same way I navigate the streets. I turn down yet another alley identical to the last one. The darkness of the Barrens infiltrates the air, smothering my senses.

Getting away without anyone noticing was harder than I imagined it would be. It's been years since I've snuck out of my own house. I rarely needed to resort to such extremes, and nowadays, I do whatever I want. Until now.

I'm sure Moss has a detail on me, tailing me whenever I leave the house. He probably thinks I didn't notice the random men following me when I was watching Lacey's house. I just didn't care enough to say anything. Their presence was a comfort in a way, knowing they were there if shit went down.

Glancing around the desolate landscape of abandoned buildings reaching up to the night sky, I shiver. I feel exposed. I thought I was independent, but I haven't been truly alone in years. It hits me that the only person I'd really want to be here would be Lacey.

Leaving her sleeping in my bed is one of the hardest things I've done so far in my life. I knew when I walked away, I very well may never see her again. But I'll never get to the bottom of things—never save Willow—if I don't. Deciphering the text message I received in order to find her is complicated. I'm still trying to figure it out.

I pull the slip of paper from my pocket, reading the message I scrawled hastily before I left. My phone is sitting on my nightstand. Lacey can track it, and I can't afford her interference. If anyone can get around the security systems Ren put in place, it's her. Hell, she's probably the one they came from in the first place. I can't save Willow, defeat whoever sent me the message, and keep Lacey out of trouble all at once. I'm only one man.

The convoluted directions I was sent are riddled with deception. They're throwing me off, probably to buy my enemy time. Even with the best instructions, navigating the Barrens at night is a feat I rarely have to tackle. Sam may flit around these areas like they're her own personal playground, but I'm not skilled enough to accomplish that. I respect their area and realize I am not the biggest nor the baddest person wandering around here.

Peeking into an abandoned storefront, I grit my teeth. The more time I waste, the less likely I'll find her alive. I'd rather not think about the aftermath if I don't get to her in time—if I walk away without Willow in tow. Hawk would kill me, and I wouldn't lift a finger to stop him. I'd deserve every hell he rained upon me. Part of me wishes I would have brought my phone to call him when I find her.

I stumble as my foot catches on a stray brick hidden in the shadows of a metal shack. Cursing, I glance back at the offending chunk of concrete, contemplating if going back and hurling it into the lean-to will make me feel any better. I dismiss the idea, turning to continue on my way, but stop short when I spot the office building ahead.

Whipping my head around, I realize I've made my way to the same spot I was standing in when Lacey was taken, back when I was fighting my feelings for her. Sucking in a deep breath, the image of her, bloody and starved, floats through my mind. I refuse to fail Willow like I did Lacey. Forgiveness wouldn't even be on the table at that point for me.

Willow isn't here. The directions, while confusing, never indicated this was where they're keeping her. Besides, between the pockmarked walls and the inability to defend the building, the kidnapper would be foolish to use the office space again. I stumble away, not willing to relive more of the past.

Twenty minutes later, I stand outside an abandoned building. It's smaller than the warehouses we use to hold the various goods we move throughout our territory and beyond. It's also flimsier, with walls made of thin metal that rattle with each gust of wind. Tipping my head back, I scan the roof, but it doesn't look sturdy enough to hold a bird, much less a human waiting to snipe me.

Skirting around the side, I find a small door tucked away in the shadows. The text message said to come alone and enter through the front, which means they assume I'll come through the back, so I'll take the side instead. When the handle slides easily, I hesitate.

This whole thing is a trap. I already know that, but there's little I can do about it. The warehouse is mostly dark, with only a single streetlight from outside streaming through the high windows. As I step inside, I scan the space.

There's no sign of Willow, but that doesn't mean she's not in one of the rooms scattered around the perimeter. The space is split in two, with a wall dividing the room. I pull my gun from my back, holding it loosely at my side.

I clear the front of the building, peeking through the dark windows. I find empty offices, devoid of everything but dust and debris. For a warehouse in the Barrens, it's fairly clean. Most of the time, these buildings are overrun with people seeking shelter from the cold descending upon the city. I'm on the south side of Synd, though. Most gather closer to the center of the Barrens, near the Egg.

"Why don't you stop sneaking around and come join us, Byrns," a gravelly voice echoes around the building.

His features are hidden by both the shadows dancing around the room along with a dark hood. Stepping sideways, he disappears from view. Gripping my gun tighter, I slide against the wall, straining to see around the corner. I spot Willow first, tied to a chair with a gag in her mouth. She doesn't look worse for wear, but that doesn't mean much.

Ever since she came to Synd, I've noticed a slow change in her. We don't exactly hang out, but when we cross paths, she seems to be a little more confident, more outspoken than before. A determined glint flashes in her eyes before she rolls them. Between Sam's training and Hawk's influence—his love—Willow has more of a backbone now.

The man finally comes into view from behind her, as a row of lights flare to life, temporarily blinding me. I raise the gun, training it on him, but he tsks, resting the barrel of his own weapon against the side of her throat. If he pulls the trigger, it might not kill her, but I'm not willing to take that risk.

He smirks, tugging down his hood, and I narrow my eyes, studying him. I realize he's not much older than I am. Sharp cheekbones are covered by a neatly trimmed beard. His blond hair rivals Willow's for brightness, though his is cut shorter, disheveled locks falling across his forehead. He's what Sam would call a pretty boy.

"Mason Byrns. It's been quite a long time," he murmurs.

Willow rolls her eyes again, leaning away from the barrel. I catch her eye, subtly shaking my head.

"Do we know each other?" I ask, shuffling to the side, and he smirks.

Shooting him in the head would be the best course of action, but his finger rests on the trigger.

"Hmm, once upon a time."

Willow gasps around the fabric, dropping her chin to her chest and wiggles. The man growls, digging the barrel into her neck, but she doesn't stop, and my stomach tightens. She spits out the gag, clearing her throat as she lifts her head.

"His name is Roman Drake," she says, wrinkling her nose as she twists her head to eye the gun. "And I highly doubt he's going to shoot me."

Drake's face morphs into a scowl, and he lifts the gun, pointing it at me. I mirror his movements, but Willow's revelation tickles something in the back of my brain, begging me to remember.

"I'd say this is nothing personal, but it entirely is," he says.

Willow tips her chair back as he pulls the trigger, knocking into Drake's legs, and his shot goes wide. She falls back, the metal chair crashing to the floor, and her head bounces off the concrete. Drake's gun skitters across the floor, and he scrambles into the shadows as I take a shot at him.

"Fuck," Drake bellows.

An explosive thunder eats his curse, and the walls around us crumple, hissing from the encroaching flames permeating the air. Another explosion rocks the building and I'm thrown off my feet. As my gun clatters across the floor, I scramble to my feet, only to fall again. One blast rolls into the next one, a continuous stream of fire detonating around us.

When I crash to the floor a third time, my head bounces off the concrete, leaving a ringing in my ears. Willow's eyes bore into mine as she lies across from me, still tied to the chair. Smoke pours into the space, dousing us in shadows seconds before my eyes fall shut. Her muffled scream is the last thing I hear before the world goes black.

Forty

Lacey

Small fires wink through the dark the closer we get to the Barrens. I've never been to this section of the city. The Barrens aren't exactly a place I stroll around on the weekends, even if I did leave my house. Once upon a time I flitted around the outskirts, but it's been years since I have. This area of Synd is a land of its own, with its own set of laws and its own punishments meted out with brutal efficiency. Most people in Synd pretend this place doesn't exist.

My problem lies solely in the fact that the Barrens freaks me the fuck out. I'm always afraid I'll get lost or I'll stumble upon the wrong person. The Barrens aren't forgiving, and I'm not skilled enough to defend myself in that situation. People from here live life one foot in the grave, and they fight like it too.

I should have driven myself. Instead, I'm stuffed between Ren and Hawk like a pimento inside an olive in the backseat of Shane's car while Sam frantically searches the streets for any sign of life. The tension has only grown the closer we get to where the car holding Willow disappeared. I couldn't give them a more concrete answer, which Ren sneered at, but since he didn't even notice the car in the first place, I brushed him off. He can be pissed at me all he wants. That doesn't make me incompetent at my job.

The familiar feeling of loneliness swamps me as Ren shifts closer to the door. I doubt he could get any farther from me without climbing out the window. I don't know what his problem is, unless he's still pissed that Mason discovered my identity before he was able to figure it out. He hasn't said anything to me since they picked me up.

I tried to get TJ to take me instead, but he refused, citing something about holding down the fort. We're already in partial lockdown, even though it's been quiet since Mason brought me to his house. The Byrns estate is crawling with guys patrolling the grounds. I doubt anyone could slip through the lines.

Shane eases the car into an alley, blocking the slight orange glow from up ahead. Whipping my head back and forth, it takes a minute to realize the rest are tumbling from the car as another vehicle pulls up behind us. Alex King and Ryker Helms step out, nodding to me as I follow Hawk's form before he can slam the door behind him.

Ryker snatches Hawk's arm before he can take off into the dark, likely losing us in the process.

"Get the fuck off, Helms," Hawk growls, swinging his fist toward Ryker's face, but the Reapers' president blocks it.

"You can't go tearing off without a plan. We'll find her," he promises.

I step away, letting them have whatever privacy I can give them. Shane calls to Helms and does some weird hand gesture. Stepping farther into the shadows, I glance behind. I might not want to slip off on my own, but none of these people are going to want me to be a part of their group. They'll be forced to watch my back, which only puts everyone else in danger. Finding Willow is their priority. Sam point blank told me when they picked me up that Mason probably snuck off and will be pissy when he gets home to find me gone.

"Shane, you can't go alone. At least take Alex with you," Sam says, exasperation bleeding into her tone.

Alex is too busy checking his gun to notice Shane is already striding away until Ren smacks him in the back of the head. Alex bounds after Shane and then skids to a stop. He spins back, racing to Sam and kisses her hard before disappearing from view.

Ren tilts the tablet he's been glued to toward Sam, and they whisper back and forth. Glancing behind again, I realize the alley is a dead end. Shane parking here probably wasn't the best idea, but he's already gone. And I'd never tell him he fucked up by not giving himself an alternative exit. I shouldn't be the one bringing it up.

"Kinda fucked up, didn't he?" Mac murmurs, and I whip around to face her.

"Who?" I'm striving for an even tone, but it comes out breathlessly, as my heart pounds in my chest. All I want to do is rush off like Shane did and try to find Mason.

"Shane. He shouldn't have boxed us in without another escape route," she says, waving her hand at the car.

Hawk slips away, and Ryker glances back at Mac before following his second. I assumed Mac would go with them, but I guess we're dividing groups down the line. Sam and Ren are still deep in discussion over whatever is on his screen. I thought everything would be a frenzied rush, like when they picked me up. Even then, it was a controlled chaos with lots of yelling over each other.

"Did they give you a gun?" Mac asks, turning back with a sheen in her eyes.

I wonder how hard it is for her to see her boyfriend walk away, knowing she might never see him again. Whenever I watched them, I always assumed they had perfect lives. Their world was complete. I didn't think about the constant danger they deal with. Staying with Mason means I'll probably be in the same boat.

"I don't need a gun," I mutter. "Maybe I should stay with the car, just in case."

She raises an eyebrow, scanning me from head to foot. "I'm sorry, sweetcheeks, but you're going to need a gun, even *if* for some asinine reason we *actually* let you stay with the car. Which we won't. Not after all the shit that's happened over the past, what, year?"

"Not to mention my brother would murder me if something happened to you," Sam calls out, not even bother to turn around and face us. I didn't realize she was paying attention.

"I doubt it would be that drastic," I mutter, leaning against the wall.

The brick is sticky, and I jerk upright, brushing the debris from my shoulder. The confidence that usually swamps me when I'm standing in front of Mason has fled, right along with him. Mac is looking at me like I've lost my mind, which only makes my awkwardness more apparent. I don't know where to put my hands, and it's possible I'm breathing weird. My stomach flips when Ren trains his eyes on me.

Sam swings around, planting her hands on her hips. "Lacey Nicole Nemesis, knock it the fuck off."

"Uhh, that's not my name."

"You're trying to get out of shit, but Mason came for you, so here's your chance to return the favor," Sam says.

I snort, rolling my eyes. "He didn't come for me. In fact, he actively kidnapped me. And *then* he came to kill me until he figured out I'd been kidnapped. Again. I've fucking been kidnapped twice in like, what, six weeks? So excuse me if I'm not feeling very hero-y about the whole fucking thing. I'd like to help Willow, but my place is not out here in the Barrens, playing at being a badass. Plus, no one knows where the hell Mason is. For all we know, he could be back at club row, meeting with some rando or something."

I tuck my hands under my arms to stop myself from waving them around some more. Mac's mouth hangs open, but I didn't say anything that wasn't true. Although maybe they didn't know any of the shit that just spilled out of me. I didn't think I was pissed at Mason for the shitshow my life has become. After my outburst, I might have to admit I'm a little bit angry with him. Doesn't mean I won't go tearing off to find him.

"He's not out fucking some random woman, Nemesis. Even if he wasn't enamored with you, that's not his style," Ren grumbles, tucking his tablet under his arm.

"That's not…that's not what I meant. I was talking about a meeting or something. He disappears and then comes waltzing back in like nothing's wrong."

Mac snorts, running her hand through her hair before shaking out her long, dark locks. "And yet them disappearing at the same time is a little suspicious, don't you think?"

"The chances of him being with Willow are slim, if not impossible. And if I go racing around the Barrens in the middle of the night with you guys, I'll only be slowing you down."

I no longer know where my argument is going. Do I want to be stuck alone in a car? Absolutely not. Do I want to admit that Mason is most likely bleeding out somewhere, waiting for someone to save him? The question sends a shiver down my spine, and I wonder how pissed Mac would be if I puked all over her boots. Glancing at her face, I expect not too happy.

"Don't be naïve, Lacey," Mac sneers, narrowing her eyes as she pulls a gun from her back, holding it out to me.

Swallowing hard, I wrap my hand around the handle—butt—whatever it's called. When she lets go, I almost drop it, my hand instantly slick and the nausea I was holding at bay wells up, threatening to choke me with its vileness. I don't do guns. My mind drifts back to my daggers, tucked safely away at my house. Everything happened so quickly when Mason moved my shit to his house, I didn't even think about bringing them. As I gingerly hold the gun, I desperately wish I would have remembered to grab them, even if I probably wouldn't remember how to use them.

"Seriously? Friendly fire is not a joke, Mac." Sam stomps over, ripping the gun from my hand before shoving a sheathed knife at me.

"Who the hell doesn't know how to use a gun?" Mac scoffs, throwing up her hands.

"Normal people, Mac," Ren says, smirking. "Let's go. We're wasting time."

Mac waits until I've taken a few steps and then falls into step behind me. I hate they feel like I have to be monitored, but it's probably for the best. I'm only going to be a burden if someone attacks us. Although, with these three, anyone would probably think twice about tussling with them.

The buildings seem to suck all the moonlight from the night. After five minutes, my muscles start to ache, they're so tense, and I'm flinching at every sound. At least I'm not making any noise. I'm pretty sure Ren would shoot me himself if I was.

The further we travel, the more Sam's demeanor changes. I've only ever seen her become the Wraith through the lens of a camera. Watching it happen in real time is something completely different. Her entire body morphs, silent feet sliding in and out of shadows. I expect her to vanish into thin air between one blink and the next.

"Anything from the others?" Mac whispers, stepping next to me.

I turn startled eyes toward her, but her head is angled at Sam. Of course she wasn't asking me. I slip my phone from my pocket anyway, glancing at the screen before I put it away. Searching for anything would be pointless since there's nothing to look for.

Peeking at the others, I realize I've fallen behind as they murmur, heads tilted together. I use their distraction to pull Mason's phone from my pocket. I found it on his side of the bed when I frantically searched for my shoes.

I want so badly for him to be off at some meeting, or hell, even fucking some random woman, rather than what all the pieces add up to. Logically, I know he left his phone on purpose. He snuck past all his guards, giving them the slip in the way only he could. He went off to save Willow, assuming whatever happened to her was his fault—his responsibility. Convincing myself otherwise is difficult and I'm not successful in the slightest, but at least it stopped me from puking in the car.

His phone is blank, even after I bypass the security systems. No texts, missed phone calls, or emails. It's as if he scrubbed the device before he took off, playing at being a hero. Why he felt the need to do it alone plagues the others, especially Sam, but I know why he did. The inherent need within him to fix the wrongs he's supposedly done over the past year has saturated his every pore. It's the reason he keeps saving me, even when I don't need it.

"Keep up, Lacey. I'm not going to spend time hunting your ass down when you wander off," Ren whispers harshly.

Huffing out a sign, I glare at his back. I think I preferred when he was ignoring me. With every biting remark he throws at me, I'm reminded of how much I don't fit in with these people.

When I imagined infiltrating their group, I thought it would be different. Actually, I couldn't even picture what it would be like, since I never thought it would happen.

Sam slows, falling into step with me. I can feel her eyes on me as we plod along, weaving between buildings and pausing at crossroads. I have no problem letting them lead the way. This is how we've operated for years, except now I'm left trailing behind them rather than tracking their movements through the cameras. If I was home, I'd be twiddling my thumbs anyway, since the Barrens don't have any eyes other than the contacts Sam has cultivated over the years.

"They don't blame you. Not really. You know that, right?" Sam murmurs, sidestepping a chunk of concrete littering the alley we're picking our way through.

"Could have fooled me," I mutter.

Ren glances back, glaring at me, as if I was any louder than Sam. Rolling my eyes, I tuck my hands in the front pocket of the hoodie I stole from Mason.

"Mason going out on his own is totally something he'd do. None of this is your fault. You just got caught in the middle. Unless you're keeping shit from us." She says it more like a question, rather than a statement.

There's a tinge of hope within her voice, as if everything would be easier to swallow, easier to deal with, were this centered on me. I suppose if it was about me, then they could wash their hands of it, run me out of town or hell, even float me down the river and be done with it.

Their lives would go back to normal, with my involvement only being a blip on the radar of their otherwise perfect lives. Although, over the last year, it's been anything but smooth sailing, but I'm sure they thought the hits would stop coming by now.

"No one knows me. I'm a fucking ghost. Unless I pissed off another hacker, but they wouldn't come after you guys. They'd decimate me online, destroying my entire alternate identity with a couple strokes on a keyboard."

"If you're a ghost, then couldn't someone drag you back to the world of the living?" She flips a knife around, her hands and eyes constantly moving, assessing the shadows as if she can see through the darkness.

"Ghost probably wasn't the best word to use. More like I'm dead. I even have a certificate to prove it."

Ducking my head, I hide my grin before wiping it away. Mason would have laughed, but Sam stays silent, probably processing what I said.

Sam grabs my arm, jerking me to a brick wall and putting her fingers to her lips. Ren peeks around the corner up ahead, but my eyes catch on a flicker of light, distorted through a window on the building we're facing. Sam slides around me, and I tilt my head, standing on my tiptoes.

Glancing up, I spy barely visible billows of smoke in the moonless night sky. I suck in a deep breath, an acidic burning of plastic and motor oil filling my nostrils. When I reach out for Sam, though, my hand meets the rough brick of the building. I do a double take when I find myself alone. All three of them have disappeared down another alley, slipping between the buildings, leaving me behind.

I hesitate for ten seconds before I take off for the burning building. There's no reason to believe Mason is in there. I don't possess the same skills as Sam, or the common sense of Mac, but something within me is screaming to go faster, push harder.

A beast unfurls within me, urging me onward, and I let it take over, flooding my limbs with fire. If Mason is in there, dead or dying, I'll burn the fucking world to the ground to find those responsible.

Forty-One

Mason

Smoke pours from several holes punched into the metal walls, fire licking along the wood making up the offices. Ears still ringing, I push to my hands and knees, almost collapsing to the concrete again. A metallic taste lingers in the back of my throat and I swallow hard. With smoke filling the space, I can barely make out Willow's unmoving form. My muscles scream as I crawl toward her.

The ropes securing her to the chair have chaffed her wrists, angry abrasions circling them. They're the least of my worries, though, as she coughs. I have to get her out of here before whatever explosive gas they used damages our lungs. With trembling fingers, I work at the knots as my head swims.

"Fuck," I grumble when they slip from my grip again.

Small hands knock mine out of the way, and I sway as I turn my head. Blinking rapidly, I try to erase the image of Lacey next to me, untying the rope much easier than my attempt. Her face is covered with a black bandanna, but I'd recognize her eyes anywhere.

"What the fuck are you doing here?" Accusation fills my voice, but processing her presence is hard with my head floating above my body.

"Saving your sorry ass, it seems," she growls, glaring at me.

"You're supposed to be safe."

"And you're supposed to tell someone when you go gallivanting off into the night, but we can't have everything we want now, can we?"

Willow's body slumps to the floor, dirt-streaked blonde hair spilling around her head. Reaching for her, Lacey knocks my hands away again, snarling at me before she gestures over my shoulder. Drake's unconscious body is sprawled across the floor, gun inches from his fingers and blood seeping from a gash on his forehead.

"We leaving him or what?"

For a split second, I hesitate. I should leave him to burn. I should let the building collapse on his body, snuffling out his life. Hell, I should let the gas infiltrate his lungs, poisoning him from the inside out. Instead, I push to my feet and stumble toward him. Tucking my arms under his, I tug him toward the closest hole in the building.

Lacey staggers as she picks up Willow's body, almost dropping her before she sets Willow on the floor again, mimicking me instead. Willow may be short, but Lacey isn't much bigger. The metal around us groans, urging us to move faster. The last thing we need is four of us dying in the Barrens, especially with no answers about who the hell is behind this, because Drake can't be working alone.

After the disjointed conversation I had with him, I doubt he was the one who set bombs to take out the warehouse. He's been meticulous in his quest to take me down. He did a piss-poor job. If he would have dismantled my territory more and then taken me out, it would have made more sense. Instead, he jumped the gun, vengeance getting the better of him.

"Drop him. We have to lift them through the hole," Lacey says when I attempt to step through the jagged opening.

We work together as the smoke thickens. Once I'm free of the hole, Lacey steps out, holding Drake's legs as the building sends out a final warning into the night.

"Faster," I breathe.

My lungs seize, and I adjust my grip on Drake's shoulders as a coughing fit overtakes me. As the support beams crumple, the screech of metal echoes through the streets, smoke surrounding us in seconds. Dropping to my knees, the dizziness in my head overwhelms me. Lacey's panicked voice rises above the noise, but it's muffled by the ringing in my ears. At least we were able to drag Willow far enough away to protect her from what's bombarding us now.

"Lacey," I wheeze, and her hand brushes my cheek.

Her eyes find mine and the world goes dark once more.

The dulcet tones of my sister are the first thing I hear when I swim from the darkness. She's cussing someone out while the groaning of hot metal makes up the background of her tirade. When I groan, rolling onto my back, my lungs seize again. I can't pull in a full breath, and my eyes fly open.

Stars blink into existence in the sliver of sky between the buildings. They're tiny pinpricks, surrounded by the black night. The space in between reminds me of the darkness I was immersed in minutes ago, and part of me wishes I could fall back into the comfort of those shadows. Life was a lot easier when I wasn't aware of what was going on around me.

Lacey's scowling face fills my vision, and a small smile tugs at the corner of my lips. Her eyes soften and then she's shoved aside, Sam's snarling face taking her place.

I follow Lacey's form as she tucks herself against the metal building. As she crouches, resting her forehead on her clasped hands, a bolt of déjà vu hits me. She lifts her head, our eyes meet, and my stomach turns. The blood might be gone, the jagged scar prominent against her skin, but the terror of that moment remains. A shudder runs through me as her gaze, dripping with remorse, finally breaks free of mine.

Sam hits my shoulder and I focus on her. "Knock it the fuck off, Sam."

"Do you have a fucking death wish? Who the hell goes off on their own? For fuck's sake, Mason," Sam snarls, pacing as she shakes out her hands.

I may understand why she's lecturing me, trying to expel the pent-up anxiety riding her, but she pisses me off at times like these. The lines of our relationship were always blurred, me being her older brother as well as the head of the family. She never quite knew when she should act like a subordinate. It's not in her nature to give in, especially to me. It's what makes her good at being the Wraith, and why she can hold her own with the Kings. Still fucking annoying.

Pushing up onto an elbow, I glance at Lacey before turning back to my sister. More people emerge from the shadows, collecting around Willow, who's thankfully sitting up, though she seems disoriented.

I clear my throat. "Where's Roman Drake?"

"Who?" Shane asks as he holds out his hand.

Gripping it, he pulls me to my feet, waiting until I stop swaying before he lets go.

"The man we pulled from the building." I rub my hand across my forehead, trying to ease the headache plaguing me.

"We propped him over there." He points beyond Helms and Mac. "Still hasn't woken up. He the one who kidnapped Willow?"

I turn away, stumbling my way to Lacey. Until I can finish my conversation with Drake, I won't let anyone interfere with his fate. Hawk would shoot him before he even woke up. Actually, there's very few people present who would spare him. Alex keeps stealing glances at him, a curious look on his face.

Crouching in front of Lacey, I brush the back of her hand and she jolts. My legs give out and I land on my ass. Her head shoots up, and she reaches out a hand, dropping it before she touches me.

"Are you okay?" I mumble, my words sounding garbled.

"Shit. Okay, we need a doctor. I think they're taking Willow back to Reaper territory." She pushes to her feet, stuttering toward Shane, but stopping short when Ren joins him.

"Lacey, what's going on?"

"Nothing. I just…you need a doctor. Do you want to take that guy back with us?"

She glances down at me, her face curiously blank as if she's scrubbed all emotion from her body. When she tucks her hands into the front pocket of her sweatshirt, I realize why it looks so familiar.

"You're wearing my sweatshirt," I murmur, even as a throb of pain stabs into my temple.

"It was the only thing I could find on short notice," she whispers.

Shaking her head, she marches off toward Sam, who's deep in conversation with Alex. They have a hurried conversation, but even that is too long. Darkness licks at the edges of my consciousness. Fighting against the pull, I rest my elbows on my knees, panting my way through the pain.

"I've got it, Shane. For fuck's sake, lay off," Alex shouts, shaking free of Shane's grasp.

Marching toward Drake, he scoops up the man's prone body, throwing him over his shoulder before disappearing around a corner. Hawk follows, Willow tucked safely in his arms. As they pass, Willow catches my attention, widening her eyes before Hawk's body blocks my view.

I'm hoping that means she hasn't said anything about Drake's involvement in her kidnapping. She didn't seem overly concerned when she was tied to a chair, but she's been taken twice, maybe three times now. I can't remember. Those instances were much worse than what we just went through. There are still too many unanswered questions floating through the air for Hawk to go floating him.

Mac waylays Lacey, tugging her off to the side. Mac's face goes from hope to concern to anger. She hisses something I don't catch and stomps away. Mac gives Sam a hurried wave before Helms pulls her away.

There are too many people loitering about. Not only because we're in the Barrens, but also because their voices are like anvils in my skull. Lacey trails behind Sam, then falls even further within the shadows as Ren stalks over as well. The look he gives her borders on hostile. Ren hasn't exactly been accepting of Lacey coming into our world, but I thought after he spoke with her when she moved to my place, things would settle down. Too many other issues stand in our way to address what the hell is wrong with him now. Besides, I'm pretty sure if I open my mouth, my lungs will fall out.

"Get up. We got a car a couple blocks from here and I'm not carrying your ass like a damsel in distress," Shane says. Sam's hand shoots out, smacking him in the chest. "What? Dumbass walked in here alone, he can walk out alone."

He saunters off, Ren prowling along after him. Sam stops, worry lining her eyes. I wait for her to say something, but she just sighs before walking away, and I wonder if it was actually disappointment etched on her face.

"She's just worried about you," Lacey murmurs, helping me to my feet.

We're both unsteady and the move almost sends us crashing to the ground. Leaning on her is the only option at this point since I'm barely holding on to reality.

"Getting shot wasn't so bad now that I've been blown up twice," I say with a chuckle.

"Not funny, Mason. Unless I can start joking about being kidnapped twice."

I sober, squeezing her shoulder. "Too soon, Kitten. Too soon."

Forty-Two

Lacey

Three days. That's how long it takes for Mason to start speaking in coherent sentences again. By the time we left the Barrens, his speech was slurred and erratic. Once we got back to his house, he could barely walk a straight line. Thankfully, it was only a concussion, along with a few bruises and cuts. Today, he's taken to whining, and I'm three seconds away from pulling my hair out.

"Fine. Do whatever the fuck you want, Mason. But Shane is about ready to bust down the door just to figure out what the hell is going on with Roman Drake, and I doubt he'll stop if I'm standing in the way," I say, throwing up my hands as he sits on the side of the bed.

"Shane's not going to run you over to get to him." He pushes up, wobbling on his feet before plopping back down. "He's an asshole, but he's not that kind of asshole."

"If you'd tell me what went down, I could probably help. Oh, and everyone wants to know where Victor is. And what is up with Alex? He keeps dropping by and poking around, as if he'll uncover some grand secret or something. He wants to talk to Roman as well." I list off everything I've been keeping from him.

Mason drops his elbows onto his knees, scrubbing his hands over his face. He's obviously not ready for all of this, but we really can't wait. Shane keeps calling, progressively getting more upset with every text. I stopped answering last night, which was not the right move.

"Sam's called like thirty-seven times," I murmur.

"Little busy trying to make the world stop spinning, Lacey."

I sigh, tipping my head back. "If you could just tell me what to do, maybe I could actually help instead of playing bodyguard."

"You can't help. I'll take care of it," he says, pushing to his feet again.

He takes two steps before his hand shoots out to steady himself. Resentment wells up in me and I tap it down, settling it right next to the despair and jealousy.

I've become his gatekeeper, hiding him away from the Kings and the Reapers while he recovers. Which only puts me on their shit list more than I already was. The last call I had with Mac, she ended up hanging up on me. She managed to tell me Willow was fine, but she's pissed for other reasons I haven't told Mason yet.

"Where is he?" Mason asks, pulling me from my thoughts.

Leaning against the doorway to the bathroom, I'd think he was trying to talk to me, but I'm pretty sure he needed a break. He's not even facing me.

"TJ wanted to put him in a bedroom, but Moss stepped in and threw him in the dungeon."

"We don't have a dungeon." He clears his throat, doubling over as a coughing fit overcomes him. I take two steps, but he's already waving me away. I stick my tongue out at his back.

"I saw that."

I throw my hands up again, then stomp from the room, leaving him to figure out how to get off the toilet by himself. I resist the urge to slam the door behind me as I catch TJ's eye. He's posted against the opposite wall. Again. Every time I've stepped foot from the bedroom, he's been here. When he's sleeping isn't a topic I've broached, mostly because I'm afraid of the answer.

"He need help in there?" he asks, glancing up from a tablet I'm not entirely sure he knows how to use, and raises an eyebrow.

"No idea. He's out of bed without puking so…"

Crossing my arms, I lean against the door while I scan the hallway. I won't admit I'm waiting for the thump on the other side of the door, telling me Mason has fallen and needs me. I'm jumpier than usual, even after being kidnapped. I expected to feel some sort of way when Roman was brought here, but I've been distracted by taking care of Mason.

During the quiet moments, I'm struck by how not concerned I am with him. The one thing Mason told me before he passed out was Roman Drake's name, which opened a whole new world of information for me to track down. Most of it is from almost twenty years ago, but I'm finding more shit than I ever thought I would about the families who run Synd. Just not shit that is going to help us. When I fell in with these people, I didn't look further than the attempted coup. Now that I'm digging into the past, I've learned a lot about their history, even if it is disjointed.

"Drake wants to talk to you," TJ says, breaking the silence.

"Are we calling him Roman or Drake? Because they're both first names and it's freaking me out."

He lets out a short laugh. "Depends on how long he lives, I suppose."

Huffing, I push off the door to make my way to the kitchen. I swing around before I reach the stairs, calling out, "Why me?"

"No idea. Don't go alone."

Rolling my eyes, I stomp down the steps. When I reach the bottom of the staircase, I jump back as someone hammers on the massive front doors. I shouldn't answer it, but Moss pulled a lot of the men from the interior of the house to patrol the grounds.

Resigning myself to playing hostess, I pull open the heavy door. Alex's concerned face peers down at me before he wipes the expression away, a false smile taking over.

"What's up, Nemesis? Mason here?" He glances over my head, searching for fuck knows what.

"He can't come out to play today. He's sick," I deadpan.

It takes him a good ten seconds and then he laughs much too hard, throwing his head back. Tilting my own, I study the dark rings under his sunken eyes, the green muted. I'm pretty sure the ghost of a bruise kisses his cheekbone. When he's finally done pretending I'm the funniest person on the planet, he fixes his gaze behind me again.

"We got some questions only he can answer. Hawk isn't letting anyone near Willow right now."

"With good reason, I'm sure," I murmur, but he's clearly not listening to me.

He leans away, glancing around as if someone is going to burst from the bushes before he ducks his head. "Listen. I need your help. Can you get me access to Drake?"

"Well, this is refreshing."

"What's that?"

"You coming out and asking to see him instead of dancing around the subject." I rush to finish as he opens his mouth. "It depends on what you want from him."

He finally focuses on me. "What do you mean?"

"Do you want his beating heart sitting in the palm of your hand, or are you going to calmly ask him questions?"

Alex drops the dopey grin he plastered on, smirking. "I can promise you I will not kill him or even rough him up."

"Fine, but if anyone asks, I took you for protection," I mutter, swinging around and leading the way toward the kitchen.

I'm sure there's another entrance somewhere, but this is the route they took when they dragged Roman's unconscious body through the house. No guard haunts the room like TJ does Mason's. I don't know if that's because they can't imagine anyone breaking out or because they don't want anyone getting suspicious. Either way, it leaves the way clear for us to sneak through the panels and down the stairs.

Pulling in shallow breaths, I try to calm my racing heart. The scent of dirt fills my pores, infiltrating all my senses, and I blink away the images flashing in front of my eyes.

I can't afford to lose it down here. This isn't the same hole I was thrown into. The stone making up the whole of the hallway is enough to tell me it's not. I purposefully scuff the soles of my shoes against the ground, just to remind myself of that fact. I'm glad I had the foresight to wear my sneakers instead of going barefoot like I have been lately.

When we round a corner, I spy a guard I don't know posted outside. He tenses when he spots Alex prowling along behind me. I wave him aside, but his wide eyes are fixed over my shoulder. I glance behind, and Alex makes the same motion I did. The guard can't be more than eighteen, and I almost feel a little sorry for him. He trips over his own feet to comply with Alex's silent demand, and I can't help but roll my eyes. I cover the keypad as I punch in the numbers. Moss didn't want to give them over, but TJ slipped them to me "just in case."

The heat radiating off Alex is suffocating as he steps closer, and I wonder if I fucked up by bringing him with.

"Has he been conscious?" he asks as a soft beep echoes off the stone.

"Yeah. The doctor said he would be fine as long as he's not tortured. Apparently the explosives were far enough away from where they were it wasn't that bad."

"Tell that to my pounding head," a deep voice rolls through the room as the heavy metal door swings open.

Alex pushes past me, and I tense, waiting for the sharp report of a gun. I slam the door shut, the locks engaging a split second later. If Alex is intent on killing Roman, there's not much I can do about it, but now I've made myself an accomplice. My feet shuffle of their own accord, unsure on whether I should call the guard or try to stop Alex.

"Fuck your pounding head," Alex snarls before slamming his fist into Roman's jaw.

He eases back, hands clenched at his sides, as if he can't decide whether to hit the man again. His entire body is trembling as Roman wheezes, head hanging.

A low chuckle fills the room before Roman spits onto the floor. When he lifts his head, grinning, his teeth are painted red. A trickle of crimson leaks from his split lip. He looks terrible, dirt and soot still streaking his face and covering his light blond hair in a sheen of gray. A deep gash across his cheekbone stands out against his pale skin, highlighting the sharp grooves of his face.

"Thought you weren't going to rough him up?" I mutter from the corner of my mouth.

Alex turns, a ferocious grin splattered across his face. "Whoops."

Glancing back at Roman, it's obvious no one allowed him to change before he was dragged down here. His clothes are in tatters, shirt hanging in strips off his body. I can't even tell what color his pants are anymore, unless they were always black. I shudder when I notice the bolts securing the chair to the floor.

The rope they used to tie him is thin, and he obviously tried to escape the bonds, if his raw wrists are any indication.

"You can do better than that, King. Thought you were an enforcer? Oh, wait. That's Ren. You're just the pretty face they put in front of the cameras, aren't you? In case no one has told you, you hit like a bitch." His voice is gravelly and I'm pretty sure there's a rattle coming from his lungs. Whatever the explosion did to him, it clearly fucked him up more than Mason.

"You say that like it's an insult." Alex grins, but there's a manic edge to it.

When Roman's piercing blue eyes find mine, my heart races. It's like he's staring into my soul, hoping to drown it in blackness to match his own. His gaze darts to my scar and his lip curls.

Breaking the connection, I shuffle back, intent on the door. I no longer care if Alex kills him. He deserves it for all the shit he's put them through the last few months. It hits me then that this is the man who orchestrated my kidnapping. He's the reason I spent however many days and nights in a muddy hole, cold and hungry. He's the reason I was starved, left to rot in a room with only a bucket. He's the reason I'll carry this scar on my face for the rest of my life, however long that is.

The urge to hit him overwhelms me, and I curl my hands into fists. Alex punches him in the stomach, taking Roman off guard, and a satisfied smirk pulls at my lips.

"Why were you meeting with Victor?" Alex says calmly, his tone at odds with the fury rolling off his body.

"Who says I was meeting him?" Roman sneers. Apparently, even evil men have their limits when it comes to creepy old dudes.

"This can go one of two ways..." Alex starts, picking up a hammer from the table lining the wall and flipping it in his hand.

"Why don't you tell Mason Byrns that you've been consorting with his illustrious uncle in the darkest parts of the night? Or better yet, you could tell his woman." Roman turns his gaze to me again.

I don't know what's going on, but I won't be caught in the crossfire. I'm already teetering on the edge of skipping town again. The others clearly don't want to rely on me anymore.

Finding out my true identity was too much for them, and now my greatest fear is morphing into reality. I fucking hate it. This is why I stayed on the sidelines, content to watch them from afar while they went about their lives like a happy extended family. Sure, there was heartache and a bit of suffering along the way, but...I cut off my thoughts when I realize I'm bordering on sentiment. Next thing I know, I'll be expounding on life being about the friends we make along the way or some bullshit.

"Going somewhere, Ms. Webb? Or should I call you Nemesis?"

I freeze, hand outstretched toward the door. I scrubbed that name from every conceivable place. The only way someone could find my surname is if they've been tracking me for years—from the beginning. Yet this mysterious man, who's been harassing the whole of Synd, and Mason in particular, somehow stumbled upon my name. I wasn't prepared for this type of attack. There's no way I can school my face to play it off like I don't know who he's talking about, but I try anyway.

"Not sure who the hell you're talking to," I sneer, but even I can hear the lie in my words.

Stepping back, I blindly reach for the keypad, wondering if I can input the code without breaking eye contact with Roman. He tracks my every move, and I catch Alex's confused look from the corner of my eye. I don't have time to explain my reaction. Roman's accusation that Alex is in league with Victor is, at best, ridiculous. There's no way he'd betray his family, especially Sam.

"Of course," he murmurs.

"As enlightening as this conversation is, I don't have anything to say to you."

He tilts his head, eyeing me. "I'm sure you don't. Not yet. What happened to your face?"

My body jolts back, head smacking into the metal door. Roman's face dissolves into one of alarm, but that doesn't make sense. He knows exactly what happened to me under his orders, I'm sure. I won't allow this man to make me question my own knowledge.

Unless it was someone else.

The thought rattles in my mind, latching on, and refusing to leave. I let the silence descend around us like a heavy blanket, smothering my senses. A red mist floats through the air between one blink and the next. I slam my head against the metal again, trying to dispel the illusion.

Several weeks have passed since I've experienced one of these episodes. I thought they'd fled, along with my determination to leave Synd. Even when Mason went missing and Willow was taken, I was fine.

The harder I fight to keep the blood at bay, though, the more forceful it becomes. I spin, no longer concerned with turning my back on two men who may or may not be conspiring against the mafia.

Jabbing a finger at the keys, it flashes red. Again. And again. Each time it spells out my demise in flickers of ruby, like flecks of blood coating my fingers. Sliding to my knees, I squeeze my head as pressure builds inside my mind, screaming at me to run, but fear douses me in ice.

A high-pitched ringing pierces the air and I open my eyes, only to find rivulets of blood streaming down the walls, gathering in the cracks of the stone before pooling at my knees. My face burns like acid is searing away the skin where the gaping wound once was. I dig my nails into my scalp, squeezing my eyes shut. When I open my mouth, no sound comes out, but my soul screams, releasing the poison drowning me.

Forty-Three

Mason

Slumped against the vanity, I swing my head to the bathroom door, contemplating life. I want to shower, but the effort it would require is probably hiding underneath the bed, which is all the way in the next room. I'm sure I'd keel over if I tried to get clean by myself, anyway.

Lacey left at least twenty minutes ago and hasn't returned, so I think I'm on my own. The fuzziness in my head hasn't completely dissipated. It reminds me of when I woke up from the coma.

At the time, my mind was a stark wasteland filled with nothing but that I needed to race home. I, in fact, did not race, as my body was not capable of moving faster than a snail's pace. Then shit hit the fan, and I was left to pick up the pieces of a split-second decision.

I jolt, almost tipping to the side, when something hits my bedroom door. It sounds like someone is slamming a body against the wood. Then the beep of the keypad laps under the bathroom door before footsteps pound through the bedroom.

I don't have the energy to do more than turn my head as Alex bursts in. Frantically searching the space, his eyes finally settle on me, and he scowls.

"Don't know what the fuck you're doing, but you've gotta get up. Now." His words filter slowly through the haze, but I still don't understand.

"When did you get here?"

My words are slow, but no longer slurred. Doc said I had a concussion, but clearly the gas from the explosives fucked me up. I've had plenty of head injuries before. They're unavoidable in my line of work, especially since my father saw fit to put me through initiation with guys who beat the shit out of me regularly just for being the heir to the Byrns family.

This is nothing like those times. It's as if the rational part of my brain is locked in a cage, screaming to get out, but I can't find my way through the muck blocking my way.

"We don't have fucking time, Mason."

Alex rarely uses my given name, and I tilt my head, trying to read the emotions dancing across his face. He reaches down, sliding his hands under my arms to haul me to my feet, but I'm dead weight. I can't get my limbs to obey. Collapsing to the floor again, I sprawl across the tiles, blinking away the spots dancing in front of my eyes.

"What's the hurry?" I ask when my vision clears.

"It's Lacey. Something happened when we went to see Drake." He crouches in front of me, mouth set in a firm line.

"Who?" My stomach rolls when he yanks me up.

My feet shuffle for a second before my legs remember how to work. Or maybe it's my ankles that are lying down on the job. They only really have one task, but I'm about to fire them. I snort as the thoughts roll through my mind, right along with the nausea in my stomach.

"Roman Drake, dickhead. Seriously, what the hell is wrong with you?"

Tucking an arm around my waist, he guides me slowly across the bathroom. The name flips a switch in my mind, flooding me with half-forgotten information. All the notes I have from I was looking into our families' pasts are locked away in my office. I could send someone to get them, but for now I'll have to rely on my faulty memory.

"We played with a Roman," I mumble.

Alex sighs, trying to urge my feet faster. "Yes, apparently they were the other family that hung around a lot. I don't have a lot of the facts, though."

I stutter to a stop to catch my breath, leaning against the wall. I couldn't find much about the Drakes, but they were mentioned in a few of the newspaper articles I found. They must have been prominent enough if Alex and I remember Drake hanging around, but how important they were to the running of Synd, I could never decipher.

"Did you slam into the door?"

Alex is absorbed in his phone, fingers flying over the screen. He doesn't even look up when he mumbles, "You fucking locked the thing. Had to guess the passcode. You really shouldn't use Sam's birthday, by the way. Little on the nose."

"All the passcodes are her birthday. I couldn't ever remember any other ones when I took over. Nemesis told me to change them, but I've never had a problem."

He glances up, piercing me with a look. "You mean Lacey."

"No, I mean Nemesis. When she's in work mode, she's Nemesis. Any other time she's Lovely Lacey," I mumble as my eyes fall closed, a grin spreading across my face.

The muscles pull at my cheeks, as if they're not used to the action. Alex can scoff all he likes. He was smitten with my sister the first time he saw her, too. He probably doesn't know I watched him distract her at the gala all those months ago. There was something in his eyes or the spring in his step when he walked away—maybe both—that told me all I needed to know. I ignored it at the time, so wrapped up in my own shit. Our lives are hard enough without worrying about who can survive in our world. I'm just thankful Alex is there to take care of her—love her.

Lacey's image floats past my lids, solidifying for a second before dissolving into shadows. She fits in our world, even if she doesn't believe it. The others aren't helping. I thought it wouldn't be that big of a deal, but with the way they treated her in the Barrens, it might be a long time before they accept her. I wish I could bash their heads together and get them to hurry the fuck along with it.

When Mac came back to Synd, it was like Sam manifested a best friend. Then Willow swooped in, and they welcomed her with open arms. I sigh, realizing I may have to step back from whatever alliance they've set up and deal with shit alone.

Hopefully, I can convince Lacey to stick with me. I don't know what the hell changed with Sam, but I rarely understand what goes through her mind.

"Are you even listening to me?" Alex's voice cuts through my musings and I jolt upright, almost crashing to the floor again.

"Forgot you were here," I mutter. My brain skips back, processing what he said earlier. "Wait, what's wrong with Lacey? Why the hell did you take her to see Drake?"

I struggle to remain standing, and he rolls his eyes as he grips my arm to steady me. Even the mention of Roman Drake sends a white-hot rage through me. The only thing holding me back from carving him up like he had Razor do to Lacey is the fact he's an asset now. Plus, Lacey would probably kick my ass if I killed him without getting information from him.

"We needed answers. There's a lot of shit going on with Victor I haven't really told you about," he confesses as we start stumbling along again.

I hate that I'm in this position with a muddied mind and weak limbs to carry me through yet another crisis. It reminds me of the time after the Guild swept through. Too much time was lost relying on other people to do my job for me, and yet I'm right back where I was a year ago.

Closing my eyes, I lean against the door frame. I knew I was taking a risk enlisting Alex's help in dealing with Victor. The enforcer is a good guy to have in your corner, but he also sometimes goes off the rails. Now he's confessing that he's keeping shit from me. I'm out of the loop and shit is going sideways. All because I asked Alex to deal with my uncle instead of just taking care of it myself. This is why I never ask for help.

"Just start talking," I mutter.

He leads me to the bed and I drop, burying my head in my hands. Someone sighs behind me. I jump, whipping around to find Lacey, fast asleep behind me.

"What the hell happened to her?" I growl, watching her chest rise in fall in an even tempo, counting her breaths.

"Flashback or whatever, like she had before. She kept mumbling something about blood," Alex whispers, but she won't wake if she went through an episode.

Weeks have passed since she went through one, and I wonder what triggered it. I assume it was something either Alex or Drake did. I don't care who the fuck Alex King is to my family. If he hurt Lacey, I'll eviscerate him. I'll bury him so deep in the ground, hell will gain a new resident. I'll rip him to shreds with my bare hands, if only so he'll experience the same pain he's put her through.

Lacey's dark hair hides most of her face, and I brush it back from her forehead.

"What'd you do." It's more of a demand than a question.

"You sent me to take care of Victor. Found out he was meeting someone, right? Well, I think it was Drake. I waylaid Icky Vicky, asking him what the hell he was doing. I *was* about to slit his throat when he started spouting about how we didn't understand and things weren't as they seem."

"Why the fuck would you…you were supposed to fucking kill him, not engage in chitchat. Victor has clearly been working against this family for fuck knows how long, and you got roped into his manipulations."

Guilt rolls in my stomach and the pounding in my head resumes. With every word, Alex solidifies why my best course of action is to do shit myself. If I take care of it, then at least I know it was done right. More people make shit messy, and I still have to come in to clean it up.

"I'm not convinced. And neither is Sam. Didn't she talk to you?"

"No. I've been a little busy being blown the fuck up," I bellow, instantly regretting my outburst when pain stabs through my eyeballs and my ears ring.

This conversation is getting us nowhere. There's not enough information or enough players present to figure out what the hell is going on. As soon as I can walk without my body rebelling against me, I'll need to visit Drake. Maybe I can get some answers out of him that Alex couldn't.

"Did you get anywhere with Drake, at least?" I ask and Alex tenses, dropping his gaze before pulling out his phone. "You're shit at this. How'd you stand up to Victor when he was questioning you about Sam when he took over?"

A scowl blooms across his face as he finally meets my eyes. "Maybe 'cause I didn't give two shits about Victor fucking Smith or what he wanted with Sam."

"Aww, sounds like you actually care about Mason, Alex," Lacey murmurs.

Spinning, I almost knock her over again, and she rears back, scowling. Bloodshot eyes stare at me, her scar standing out against the paleness of her skin. She shakes her head, causing her dark hair to hide it.

"You okay, Lacey?" Alex whispers, as if he'll startle her if he speaks at a normal volume.

"I'm fine. Thank you for getting me out of there."

She stares at her hands, twisting them in her lap, and I push off the bed. They're both hiding something, but I don't know if I'm well enough to suss it out. Whatever happened in the basement freaked them both out enough to keep shit to themselves. I don't like that she feels the need to hoard secrets.

Almost two weeks have passed since I moved her into my house. I thought she was merely getting used to being here. Instead, she hides away in her office, speaking in half-formed thoughts and disjointed sentences. I never get the full story from her, which I thought was because she was so used to working alone, but she has the perfect opportunity in the palm of her hand, and she refuses to give anything up.

"Want to explain what the hell is going on here?" I growl.

Leaning against the wall, I hope my moves belie how exhausted I am, but the look of concern flashing across Lacey's face says otherwise.

"You should sit," she murmurs, glancing toward Alex.

I hold up a hand when Alex steps toward me. "Start talking or we're going to have problems."

Lacey purses her lips. "You're going to have a problem if you keel over too, but what the fuck ever."

"Drake knows Lacey's last name," Alex blurts out, turning wide eyes to her. She squawks, throwing a pillow at him.

She flings a finger in his direction. "Alex has been secretly meeting with Victor."

"It's not like that."

"What the fuck is going on?" I shout over their bickering.

They freeze, swinging guilty gazes at me. My outburst may have forced them to stop acting like children, but it also sends a wave of dizziness through my head. Swallowing hard, I wait for them to explain. One of them better start talking.

Alex points at Lacey. "My shit can be explained away, but hers? I dunno."

"What's that supposed to mean? Did you honestly think I didn't have a last name?" Lacey raises an eyebrow. They're lost in their own ridiculous conversation. I don't have it in me to stop them again.

"Cher and Prince don't have last names. Not exactly weird to assume you're like them."

"Famous people? That's who you're comparing me to? Name one other *normal* person who doesn't have a last name," she challenges, smirking.

A grin spreads across Alex's face. "Hawk. Ink. Blue. Hell, almost every single person in the fucking Reapers."

I cross my arms, snorting.

"Oh, you think that's funny? Mister 'I'll take care of everything all by myself,'" Lacey says, narrowing her eyes, and I sober.

"Somebody better start explaining what the hell is going on and why Drake seems to know so much about us or I'm going to—"

"What? You gonna crawl down there and interrogate him? You can barely stand, Byrns. Maybe you should just let us handle this. We're better equipped to deal with this than you," Alex says.

Lacey winces, throwing another pillow at Alex's head. Thumping my head back, I stare at the ceiling. He might be right. No matter how much I hate to admit it, if only to myself, that I might no longer be equipped to lead.

Forty-Four

Lacey

The haze is gone, leaving behind a heaviness in my limbs. Even a few weeks was enough for me to forget how exhausted I am after an…I still don't know what to call them. Episode is as good a word as any at this point.

Shivering, I pull the comforter higher. I need to get these under control before it puts me in danger. I'm surprised I was able to get away from the room in the basement, though it wasn't unscathed. I suppose I didn't save myself this time, either. Alex did all the hard lifting. I hate relying on other people, yet lately I'm constantly being put in a position where I have to. Or Mason won't take no for an answer, ignoring all my arguments in favor of his own plan. I haven't fought against him that hard, though. I've never had someone to lean on, making this new experience both amazing and frustrating all at once.

Being in the throes of a hallucination in front of Roman Drake was mortifying. I'm not trying to impress him, but I also didn't want him to see me in that weakened state. We're supposed to be strong. Now our enemy thinks he can get to me just by calling me by my last name and figuring out my alias.

I don't have time to dwell on the impression I made on Roman. Right now, I'm engaged in a silent argument with Alex King. Mason looks like he's about to pass out, yet he's still demanding answers. I don't blame him. He doesn't deserve to be kept in the dark just because he got blown up. Again.

"Why do you guys keep getting blown up?" I mutter.

"I dunno. Why do you women keep getting kidnapped?" Alex smirks, dropping the pillows I chucked at his head.

"I seem to remember *you* getting kidnapped, too." I smirk as his mouth drops open.

He holds up a finger. "*I* was caught—not kidnapped. There's a difference."

"Is there, though?"

"Would you two knock it the fuck off?" Mason groans, scrubbing his hands down his face.

Sighing, I glance at Alex again. "So, Roman Drake clearly knows who I am. I don't know how he tracked down my name, but I think he's been fucking with me. Or someone he hired has been leading me on a wild goose chase."

Alex's eyes widen when Mason pins him with a glare. "Uh, I already told you what I've been doing."

"Call Sammy. Hell, if the rest of them can keep their mouth shut while we're meeting, invite them too. We need answers, and we're not going to get them by gathering them bit by bit from random people," Mason grumbles.

"Go home, Alex. We can meet tomorrow after Mason takes a nap."

Mason drops his hands to glare at me. "For fuck's sake, woman. I'm not a fucking toddler."

Alex holds up his hands, backing away slowly. Instead of the door, he makes his way to the tunnels. I glare at Mason, wondering if I can get away with smothering him.

"You're a fucking ass, you know that?" I hiss.

"You're treating me as if I can't do shit, Lacey. I'm a fucking mafia boss, and you're telling me to take a nap."

"Maybe because you never take care of yourself. And you're going to end up in the damn hospital again." I slide from the bed, spinning around to point at him. "Don't ever call me woman again. Figure your shit out."

I follow Alex, knowing he's probably long gone by now, but I can't stay in that room another minute. Going out the bedroom door means running into TJ, who probably heard me yelling at Mason, and I can't face his judgment. I'll have to go back eventually, but I need time. Maybe I can snag a blanket from somewhere and sleep in the office. I'm hesitant to call it mine, since I have no idea how long I'll be staying.

It hasn't even been a month, but time warps in our world. Days bleed together until suddenly six months have passed and I'm looking up what the date is, searching for lost memories in the haze.

I snort and then miss the bottom step in the muted light. My arms pinwheel as my feet slip, and I slam onto my ass, bumping down two more steps before crumpling on the landing.

"Why the hell do I never have my phone out when shit like this happens?" Alex's voice echoes from below me.

Groaning, I cover my face, if only to hide the tears forming in my eyes. My tail bone is on fire, and I might have pulled a muscle in my shoulder. At least I didn't break anything this time.

"What the hell are you still doing here?"

"I was getting my shit," he replies, holding up a black brief-case.

"You look like a cartoon villain," I say as he waggles his eyebrows at me. "What are you hiding in the Byrns's secret tunnels, anyway?"

"I'm not hiding anything. I just fucking showed you, didn't I? Besides, this is just a briefcase full of chips. I stashed it down here the last time we came over."

"Uh, tortilla chips?"

He gives me a look. "Why the hell would I have tortilla chips in a briefcase? They're poker chips."

Heaving to my feet, I eye him. "That doesn't make it any better. Or make any more sense."

"You're not thinking of running, are you?" he asks, glancing up the stairs.

"He's not coming," I murmur, not bothering to turn and look for myself.

Mason never follows. He's too stubborn and set in his ways. An hour, a day, a week later, he realizes where he went wrong and then pretends it never happened. If we were in a normal situation, I would have walked a long time ago. But we're not, and I can't. I can only hope when shit settles down, he'll stop running, or at least run toward me instead of away.

"I'm going to check on him. See if he's okay," Alex says, adjusting his grip on the handle of his briefcase.

"I wouldn't bother. He's probably not even in there anymore. He disappears for a few hours and then he'll come back, not that anything will change," I mumble, bitterness swirling through my tone.

"Lacey," Mason calls and I tense.

I didn't say anything I wouldn't to his face, but it's still embarrassing. He's stopped talking about me staying here, probably assuming he doesn't have to now that I'm firmly entrenched in their world—in his house. Talking to him about the future is begging for awkwardness and heartbreak. I'm not ready for that conversation.

"What do you need, Mason?" I bite out, still facing Alex, who runs his fingers through his hair and then waves before tromping down the rest of the stairs, the darkness swallowing him up.

Spinning, I cross my arms and glare at Mason. Shadows dance across half his face, making it hard to determine where his head is at. The last three days had my brain yo-yoing between guilt and anger, never fully settling on either. I'm not equipped to solve the problems facing everyone.

Gathering the pieces of the puzzle is usually easy. Then I hand them all over to these men and they put it together. I was content with my role. I wasn't ready to take on a new one. Then I fell further into their world and I no longer had a choice.

"We need to talk." He turns, stalking away.

I should just leave. I should disappear into the shadows, just like Alex. I should get back to work, doing whatever I can to help them. Instead, I trudge up the steps, sliding into Mason's bedroom before leaning against the wall next to the panel. I'm sure there will be more yelling, or at least an argument, but I refuse to engage. I'm done fighting with him.

"This isn't working," he sighs, settling on the bed and dropping his face in his hands.

My heart leaps into my throat, and I tuck my arms around my waist. I may have fought him almost every step of the way, but I never thought he'd kick me out. I should have, though. With how everyone else acts around me, barring Alex, I'm surprised it took him this long to pull the trigger.

"I'll need help," I murmur.

"I don't care. Take whatever you want. We just need to deal with this. Sooner rather than later."

Tipping my head back, I thump it against the wood. I do it again, hoping the dull pain will stop the tears from gathering in my eyes. I fell for him, even while trying to protect my heart. It wasn't enough. He wormed his way in, sneaking tendrils into the cracks he forged, and now he's ripping them out. The process is violent and bloody, much like our lives as of late.

"Once I get set back up, I can go through the Kings," I murmur, trying to infuse my voice with a confidence I don't have.

He scrubs his hands over his face before running his fingers into his hair. I wait, but when he doesn't answer I huff out a breath and march to the drawer he dumped my clothes in. Tugging it open, I gather up the mess of things in my arms, unsure what to do next. I didn't think this through. Hell, I didn't even want my clothes in here. I knew this shit was going to happen. I tried to stay away, but he sucked me in, forcing me into his sphere.

"What the hell are you doing?" he barks, his bare feet slapping against the hardwood behind me.

"Getting my shit. Where are the bags you used?"

Shuffling toward the closet, I'm stopped when his fingers wrap around my arm and he tugs me back. Half the clothes tumble from my arms, and I squawk, dropping to my knees to gather them up.

"Lacey, stop."

Mason drops next to me, batting my hands away. I don't realize how badly I'm trembling until he links our fingers, my tears splashing across our skin.

Scoffing, I tug, but he doesn't release me. This isn't the way I wanted to do things. Walking away from something that never really existed shouldn't hurt this much. And I certainly didn't want him to see me like this. I've worked hard enough to play my cards close to my chest.

I rip my hands away, scrambling to get my shit before he can react, but his arms fold around me and I lose it. My body heaves, deep sobs shuddering through my body. This isn't just because I'm leaving, though. It's the pain and suffering, the torture and neglect, the utter exhaustion plaguing my body from the last few months.

"Lacey, talk to me." Mason's voice cuts through the despair hammering at my senses.

"Sorry. Fuck, this is not…I'm fine," I say in a strangled voice.

"I can't carry you back to the bed," he whispers, regret lacing his tone.

I pull from his grasp, scooping up the clothes and holding them to my body like they'll protect me from his words.

"I'm not exactly in the mood for one last fuck, Mason."

"One last…for fuck's sake, Lacey, I'm not kicking you out, but you can't keep shit from me."

"I told you."

"Not everything. We need to talk it out, and I can't very well do that when my head is swimming and I'm about to pass the fuck out."

He sways and my eyes shoot to his. The black of his pupils almost drowns out the brown, and an alarm in my head flips on. Dropping the clothes, I grab his wrist and yank him upright. The vein in his neck pulses out the timing of his heartbeats. I'm no doctor, but it's clearly running a marathon inside his chest.

When I ease him onto the bed, he falls back with a whoosh and his throat bobs. I don't know where to go from here. Today has been too much, and it's only noon. Between meeting with Drake and the shit going down with Alex, my own fights with Mason should take a backseat. They're not important in the grand scheme of things. Plodding along and hoping something will change is wearing on me, though. I'm barely sleeping, we're constantly bickering, and nothing feels right.

"Stay with me while I catch my breath. Then we can talk," he murmurs.

"You need to sleep," I say, even as I sink next to him.

Looping an arm around my waist, he pulls me into him. The tension eases from my body as his warmth seeps into me. He's right. Now is not the time for deep discussions about whatever this thing is between us. We can't go into all the shit going down. We can't make a plan. Until he's well, we're sitting ducks.

I concentrate on his heartbeat as it settles into a steady tempo, echoing in my ear. Closing my eyes, I match my breaths to the rising and falling of his chest. If this was all we were dealing with, we could survive. As problems stack on top of more problems, I don't know if that's a possibility any longer.

Maybe the Kings taking over wouldn't be such a bad thing after all.

Forty-Five

Mason

Standing in front of the bathroom door, I hesitate, dropping my hand to my bare chest. I should probably put a shirt on for this conversation. Yesterday was a shitshow in more ways than one. Between Shane bitching about how we're going to hunt down all of Drake's minions and my head still being a muddled mess, I don't have much left over for anything else. I need to make time for this, though. I suck in a deep breath to steady my racing heart before running a hand through my hair.

"Get your shit together," I whisper, knocking swiftly before I can talk myself out of it.

Water sloshes behind the door. "Uh, yeah?"

"Can I come in?" I ask and then clear my throat.

She says something else sounding suspiciously like "your house" and I roll my eyes. I close the door gently behind me after I step inside, hoping she doesn't throw a shampoo bottle at me. We slept most of the afternoon, but by the evening she disappeared into her office. It was late by the time she came back. Much too late to have a serious conversation. This morning she was gone by the time I woke up. As the sun sets, my mind is finally clear and while I may not be ready, it needs to happen.

"Glad someone is getting some use out of that thing," I say, eyeing the back of her head poking over the lip of the bathtub.

"Why is it so big? Wait, don't answer that."

I chuckle, skirting around to sit on the bench tucked along the wall next to her. Keeping my eyes on her face is hard, especially when the clear water laps at the tops of her tits. I duck my head, crossing my arms over my chest, and will away my hard on. It doesn't work. Not that I'm surprised. I'm always hard around her, even when she does shit that pisses me off. Actually, I ache for her then.

"Sam threw a fit that none of the tubs were big enough in the house. She took it upon herself to remodel. This is what she came up with. I assumed she'd only replace hers, but apparently she needed a backup. I never used it until after I was shot."

"What's it like to get shot?" Her face flushes, and she slides further under the water. "Sorry."

"Lacey, you can ask me whatever you want. I'm not going to…" I sigh. I don't even know how to finish the sentence.

"Get pissy and disappear for several hours and then come back as if nothing happened?" I can hear the dejection in her voice, though she's aiming for sarcasm.

I could snap back at her, pointing out all the hiding she does in her office behind a screen, but all I'm doing is projecting my own issues onto her.

"Getting shot hurt like hell. But then it was"—I close my eyes—"peaceful. Like some type of limbo, I suppose. Before that, I saw Sammy."

"Standing over you or something?" she whispers, as if I'll stop talking if she disturbs me too much.

"No. It was her when we were younger. Just a snapshot of a memory. And then I woke up."

She nods, tapping her finger on the edge of the tub while she stares off into space. I wish I knew what she was thinking. The entire past year has been dominated by those ten minutes, eating up my time and sanity. It wasn't until Lacey I truly felt like I was freed from the prison in my mind.

"Do you want me to leave?" she whispers, and I whip my head up.

"Why would I want you to leave?"

"Stop answering my question with another question," she snaps, covering her chest with her arms.

"No. I don't. Is that clear enough for you?" I snarl. "I moved you here for a reason, and it wasn't so I'd have a fuck buddy. You may have been safer at your place, but that doesn't change the fact I'd constantly have my attention divided between taking care of shit here and worrying about you."

She huffs, glancing away. "Well, I'll stop trying to leave then."

"What are the others saying?"

"A bunch of bullshit. Honestly, none of them really want to talk to me, but since I'm gatekeeping you, they're forced to. Shane's annoying, but I've been able to fend him off. Sam just asked if you were okay yet and then would hang up. You saw how Alex was. He's the only one who doesn't seem to care that I'm"—her nose scrunches—"here."

"That's not what you were going to say," I murmur, pushing from the bench and kneeling next to the tub. "You were going to say you're at fault, weren't you?"

Trailing my fingers across the water, I watch as ripples cascade over her, lapping at her skin. I skim my fingers along her arm and she shivers. Following the line of water along her chest, her breathing picks up until she holds her breath, and I pull my hand away.

"Answer me, Kitten."

"Maybe. No. I think they were happier when they didn't realize I was a real person."

I scoff, lacing our fingers together. "Of course you're a real person."

She shakes her head, squeezing my hand. "But Nemesis wasn't. Not to them. I was a faceless entity who never really crossed their minds. Gone as soon as my job was done."

"You were real to me. It's why I kept texting you, even when you wouldn't answer."

She sighs, a slight smile playing on her lips, and I grin. It falls from her face as her eyes meet mine.

"They'll never fully accept me. It wouldn't be like it is with Mac and Willow."

I hear the question in her statement, the warning hiding beneath her words.

"Doesn't matter. We'll cross that bridge when we get to it," I say gently.

She leans forward, pressing her lips to mine. When she tries to pull back, I grip the back of her neck, deepening the kiss. She whimpers as she tries to get closer, water sloshing over the edge of the tub and soaking the sweatpants I've been living in for the past three days. Wet hands press against my bare chest, and I release her, letting my palm chase the droplets rolling down her body.

"Shit, I'll get a towel," she says.

I laugh when she turns to get out of the tub, splashing more water over the sides. I don't care about the floor.

"Stop, Kitten. Before you slip and crack your head open." I stand, shoving my pants off and step over the side. "Scoot forward."

"You are not invading my bath," she cries, even as she makes room for me.

I settle in behind her, the warm water soothing the aches plaguing my body. I pull her back to my chest as I tip my head back and close my eyes. Her hands dip under the water, gripping my legs as she rests her head on my shoulder. Pressing a kiss to her temple, contentedness flows through me.

I take my time cataloging every dip and curve of her body, committing it all to memory. Gliding my fingers along her thigh, I hook them around her knee and move her leg over mine. She hums in anticipation as I continue to explore her flesh until I run my fingers along her inner thigh. I'm inches from her pussy when she grabs my wrist.

"We cannot do this in a bathtub."

"Do what?" I hum, letting my lips take over teasing her skin. Nipping at her neck, I lick the droplets, and her grip relaxes.

She grabs me again as I brush her clit. "Sex in a tub seems fun, but in reality, it's not."

"And you would know because..."

Her elbow jabs me in the stomach, the air rushing out of me as I wheeze.

"Because I'm a woman and have to think of shit like that," she growls, pushing my hands away.

She gingerly steps out of the tub, water streaming down her body, and I can't help but track the droplets rolling across her skin. Exploding from the water, I suck on her nipple, metal clicking against my teeth as I drink from her like a man dying of thirst. She sways, a cry falling from her lips as her hands latch onto my hair, holding me against her. I growl into her skin, running my hands along her sides.

She whimpers as I pull away. I plant my feet on the floor, splashing out more water. Gripping her sides, I capture her lips with mine, devouring her. I walk her backward until her back hits the shower, rattling the glass. She reaches down, gripping my cock, and I grunt.

Ripping my mouth from hers, I tip my head back as she strokes me. I'm sure my fingers are leaving marks across her skin, branding her with my touch. Dropping my gaze, I stare as she squeezes my cock, her thumb brushing over the tip, and I shudder. As I glance at her face, she smirks, then bites her lip.

My hand circles her throat, pressing her head back against the glass and her mouth falls open, desire dripping from her gaze.

"You like the control you have over me, don't you?" I growl, tipping her chin up with my thumb.

She pants, nodding as her hand continues to work me. It takes everything in me not to groan at the way she's playing with me.

"Drink your fill, Kitten. Because when I take over, you'll gladly give up every bit of that control, begging me to take this sweet little pussy of yours."

My other hand slips between her legs, and I swipe through her wetness. She squirms, chasing my fingers as I bring them to her lips.

"Open up," I murmur.

Her eyes widen before she obeys. Her hand stalls, clenching around me, when I slip my finger between her lips. As her tongue swirls around it, I realize it's been too long since I last tasted her. I grunt, tugging my finger from between her lips along with my cock from her grip.

Grabbing her ass, I pick her up, burying my face into her damp skin. Her legs wind around my hips, and I take her into the bedroom. I walk past the bed, stopping in front of the fireplace. Before Lacey, I never used it, but since she's come, I've lit it more often than not. The flames chase away the loneliness from the space. Although maybe that's just her.

"Down," I command, and she drops from my body.

"Do not tell me you're going to rile me up and make me finish the job myself," she snarls, planting her hands on her hips, her nipple ring glinting in the firelight.

I grin, grabbing the back of her neck and slamming my mouth onto hers before releasing her. Ripping the comforter from the bed, I take two pillows. I drop them at her feet before spreading the blanket in front of the fireplace. I point to the space I've created, raising an eyebrow when she doesn't move.

"Lay down, Lacey. Now."

She narrows her eyes before slowly lowering to her knees. I duck my head to hide my smirk.

"I didn't say on your knees. I said lay down."

Her bottom lip pops out, and I drop to my knees too, pulling it from between her teeth and nibbling on the flesh. She sways toward me and I push her back. Propping herself on an elbow, she glares at me. I lick my lips as her knees fall open. Grabbing a pillow, I gesture for her to lift her hips, then tuck it under her.

"You have that look," she accuses, even as her eyes glaze over.

Smirking, I dip my head, nipping at the soft skin of her inner thigh. "It's not fair that you tasted yourself before I did tonight."

I lick her pussy from core to clit and she yelps, falling back as her hips kick up. I do it again, if only to get another taste.

"Delicious," I murmur before sucking her clit in my mouth.

Her legs clamp around my head and then fall open again as she whimpers. I take my time, building her up and then slowing when she's close. After three times, she grips my hair, yanking my head up, and I grin.

"What the fuck are you doing?" she snarls.

I run my tongue across my lips, her taste making me groan.

"Payback, Kitten. Now let me get back to devouring you."

"Are you going to make me come?"

"Only if you're good."

Her hand goes slack, and I nuzzle her pussy, breathing in her scent and committing it to memory. Slipping two fingers into her, I swirl my tongue around her clit and her nails dig into my scalp. The pain spurs me on. I pump into her faster until she's panting above me, squeezing around my fingers.

Her thighs snap around my head as she sails over the edge, moaning out her ecstasy. It's one of the sweetest sounds I've ever heard and a craving to hear it again seizes me.

"I wanted to do this slowly, but I can't," I growl, crawling up her body.

Settling between her thighs, I slam into her, thrusting as deep as I can. Her back arches, eyes falling closed as a gasp leaves her, and I groan at the feeling of her clenching around my cock. I can't take my eyes off her. Beauty incarnate, exactly like this, when everything else falls away. Dropping to my forearms, I cover her mouth with mine, drinking in her whimpers as I rock my hips.

I pull out slowly, plunging into her again, and her hands grip my neck, holding on as I work us both into a frenzy. Running my lips across her flushed skin, I sink my teeth into her shoulder. Her next orgasm slams into her, taking me by surprise, and I grunt as she spasms around me.

"Holy shit," she breathes, writhing underneath me.

Pushing up, I grab her leg, bringing it to my shoulder. Her cries echo around the room as I thrust into her. I slide my hand along her body, toying with her piercing, and she squirms beneath me. Our eyes meet and her lids droop as she bites her lip. I tug it from between her teeth.

"I want to hear you scream my name as you come around my cock, Kitten."

Her entire body shivers as she meets my thrusts. Dropping my hand to her clit, I circle the sensitive bud, urging her on. Her fingers grab my wrist, directing my movements, and I almost come. Gritting my teeth, I drop my chin to my chest, but I can't hold back. I tense, my hips stuttering as I spill into her, filling her up.

"Don't you dare fucking stop," she groans, and I fold over her body, catching myself with my hand, her leg still pressed to my chest.

Her own hand dips down as she circles her clit, and I can't pull my eyes from the sight. Her tits bounce as I surge into her, and I pull one between my lips, scraping my teeth against her skin.

"Lacey, come for me," I growl into her flesh and her pussy pulses. "Now."

She shatters around me, whimpering my name. I linger inside her as she shudders through her climax. Her fingers are still circling her clit, and I brush my mouth over her skin until I reach her lips, capturing them with mine as she sighs. No matter what happens, I'll bask in the salvation I find in her eyes.

Forty-Six

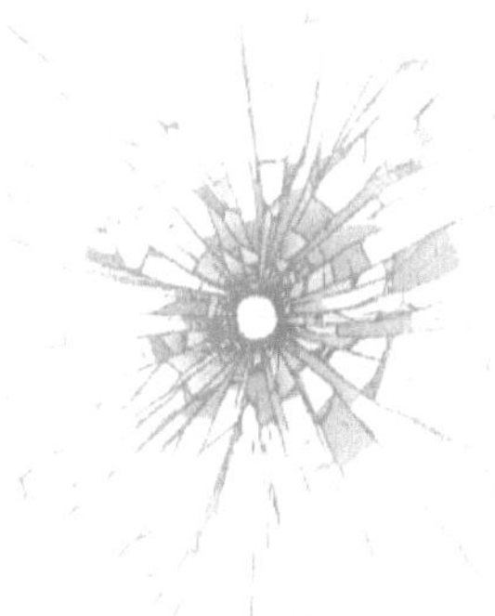

Lacey

My computer pings and I pull myself from my thoughts for at least a dozenth time. I can't concentrate tonight, which is not what I need right now. I sigh when I spot the alert for a couple cameras that are down. It keeps popping up at random intervals, like I've hit snooze on it. I don't want to turn it off, since I'll forget about it. Mason told me not to worry about them, since they've abandoned the warehouse.

I exit the screen, forcing myself to focus on the article in front of me. It mentions the Drakes all of three times, and I'm trying to read between the lines. Scattered across seven monitors are all the pieces of a very fucked up puzzle I can't seem to put together. I keep hoping I'll have an ah-ha moment and I'll spread the information in front of the group, and they'll finally accept me. Snorting, I realize how unlikely that is.

I don't care. At least, I tell myself I don't care. They can shove me aside and pretend I'm not useful as anything more than a source of information. They're kind of right, anyway. I don't bring anything other than my hacking skills to the table, except for Mason, I suppose, and even then, I wonder if I'm just a cure for his loneliness.

My mind wanders again as images from last night bounce through my head. Something switched in him, but I'm too worried about everything else to put a name to it. Once Mason realizes the others won't come around, I don't know what he'll do. Asking him to cut off the people who are essentially family isn't fair. I'd never put him in that position. Skipping town in the dead of night to spare him that pain doesn't seem like a better option either.

The click of the panel behind me has me grinning at the bright screens. Usually Mason comes through the actual door, but he's been sneaking through the tunnels for a "break," as he calls it. I'm not going to complain about the orgasms. Spinning in my chair, I search the shadows of the room, but it's not Mason standing there.

"Oh, it's you," I grumble, spinning back to the computers and pulling up a line of code. "Something I can do for you, Ren?"

"Nemesis," he says, sitting in the chair Mason usually uses. "We need to talk."

Glancing from the corner of my eye, I'm surprised he doesn't have a device in his hands. Every time I've seen him lately, he seems to be immersed in something on a screen. I thought that would help us connect, but I couldn't have been more wrong. He probably assumes I'm taking over his space or something ridiculous like that. As if I could ever replace his position in the Kings' mafia family.

"I'm all ears." Sarcasm laces through my tone, and his nostrils flare.

I'm sure he'll start spouting about all the shit Mason's not doing. If he needed me to hack into some place, he'd just text my work phone. Ren was the first one I gave my personal number to. He's had it for years and never used it, although maybe he did after my auto-message went out from my work line about going off-grid. Since I lost my personal phone in the forest, I just ended up getting a new one with the same number. It's been crickets from him on both devices, not that I'm surprised.

"A lot has happened in a short period of time."

I wait for him to continue, but he just sits there, staring at me as if I'm going to randomly absolve him of all his sins. I'm not a fucking priest—I don't need his confession. I purse my lips to stop myself from telling him to get the fuck out and talk to Mason if he's got shit they need to deal with. Instead, I opt for randomly changing the line of code in front of me.

"Your appearance was a shock, to say the least. I'm assuming you understand it's taken some time to adjust." He crosses his arms, dropping his chin to his chest, the action at war with his words.

"I doubt anyone has adjusted and I don't expect them to. Was that all?"

His head whips up. I turn my chair just enough so my eyes don't wander to him anymore. He'll huff and puff and then leave, and I can soak up the silence. I'd rather not have this conversation. There's enough to deal with, without hearing his reasons for being a dick to me, acting like I kick puppies in my off time.

"I don't know what the hell the others' problems are, and I don't really give a shit."

"Turns out neither do I." The lie burns to ash in my mouth and I swallow it down, letting it settle next to the jealousy and embarrassment.

The silence stretches until it taints the air between us. I've found people like to fill the quiet parts with whatever inane chatter they can think of until they're spilling all their secrets. Ren is a breed of his own. He's content to wallow in the stillness. We'll be here all night if someone doesn't break soon.

"I was worried," he mutters, as if the words are ripped from him without his permission.

"I had protocols in place. If I wouldn't have logged on, eventually you would have received instructions and your information would have been destroyed. No one would have known we had any connection," I state as my eyes glaze over, all while my fingers tap away.

"As if I give a shit about that. You going to keep changing the cursor color on every city employee's computer or have an actual conversation with me?"

I flush, biting my lip. I didn't think he would notice was I was doing. Not like I'd be able to concentrate on actual work while he's hovering.

"I was worried about you, Nemesis."

I spin, glaring at him. "If you were so fucking worried about me, then why the hell do you insist on calling me Nemesis? You know my fucking name."

He rears back, tipping the chair slightly. Grumbling under my breath, I turn back to the screen. I shouldn't have snapped at him. It only gives him more fuel to pass on to the others, and I already have the odds stacked against me.

"Because that's who you are to me. Not Nemesis the hacker. You haven't been that for a while. I thought you knew that."

"Nemesis *is* a hacker. You can't separate one from the other. Besides, I'm not someone you should worry about. Between you and Mason, I swear." I tuck my hands in the pocket of Mason's hoodie.

"I told you before, our relationship was never purely business. Perhaps for the others, but for us, it hasn't been that way for some time."

Shaking my head, my eyes catch on an alert I silenced. Grayson's on the move again, probably meeting with our enemies. He's becoming a thorn in our side. The model citizen he presents himself as must be a front, but hell if I can find out what he's hiding. It's starting to piss me off. Narrowing my eyes, I pull up the tracker on his car, letting it flash across the map of Synd. I'll check the cameras when he stops moving and hopefully get some answers.

"If you were so keen on being friends, then why exactly have you been an asshole since I showed up?"

There's no reason I need to know other than my own morbid curiosity. In fact, this entire conversation is terrifying and ridiculously embarrassing. I may not be able to decipher everyone else's reasons for shutting me out, but maybe Ren will give me some.

He clears his throat, hanging his head as he mumbles, "I don't have a lot of people in my life."

"Welcome to the club," I mutter.

He snorts, glancing up at me. "You're one of the few people I trust, Neme…Lacey. And when I found out all these people had met you and I was the last to know…I didn't know how to handle that."

"So, you took it out on me." It's a statement, not a question, but he hangs his head again.

"I suppose I did. Sam was not exactly happy with how I dealt with everything."

"Turns out I don't really care what Sam thinks," I snap, turning back to the screen to track Grayson's movements. He's still traveling, but I can't tell where the hell he's going.

"They'll come around. I'm surprised Alex has accepted you so readily. He's always been a bit—" He sits up, searching the ceiling for the right word, as if it'll drop from the sky and into his mouth. "Leery, I suppose."

"Of what? Me? I'm nobody. Sure, I have a lot of information, but it's not like I'm selling it to the highest bidder. I'm an asset and I'm perfectly okay with that," I say, but my heart isn't in it.

Ren gives me a look and I realize he knows I'm lying. Most of what I said is true, but I'm not okay with it anymore. Clearly, I haven't been for a while, since I spent almost the past year watching them, studying them, yearning for what they had.

Envy isn't exactly a desirable trait. I can't bring myself to be ashamed. If I wouldn't have wanted more, I never would have this time with Mason. He tipped my life upside down. While I probably would have preferred a different road to get here, I can't be upset by the results.

"Perhaps now is the time to stop lying to yourself, Lacey. Once we fix what's happening in Synd, you won't be able to go back to your life of hiding behind a screen," he says, pushing to his feet.

"I fully expect I'll be leaving Synd when this is all over, so there won't be any fear of me being shoved into the spotlight. I'm sure everyone will be happy with that," I say bitterly.

I pull up the camera outside L'endroit Chic, the fancy restaurant downtown, where Grayson's car stopped. The valet takes his keys as the police chief flashes his politician smile. Ren says something, but I've already checked out. There's another man who shakes hands with Grayson, but moves to get into his own car. Scrambling to hack into the cameras inside the building, my fingers fly over the keys. Knowing my luck recently, they'll be tucked away in a back corner where I won't be able to see anything by the time I'm in.

"Lacey, are you even listening to me?" Ren snaps.

"Yeah. No going back," I murmur, searching the video feed from inside the restaurant.

Ren leans next to me, bringing his face closer to the screen. "What are we looking at?"

I kick his shin with my heel, and he pulls back slightly.

"Don't block the screen, dumbass. That's obviously Grayson. I'm trying to figure out who he's meeting."

We stare at the feed as Grayson is led to the back, just as I predicted. The person is clearly a man, but shadows shroud his face.

"Come on. Come into the light, fucker," I mumble.

"Shit," Ren spits out. Pushing upright, he slides his phone from his pocket and texts someone.

"That's Victor, isn't it?" I ask.

I don't need his confirmation. I'm almost hoping he'll tell me I'm mistaken, and we can go back to searching for answers.

"It is. And he's clearly been missing since Mason went off on his little adventure. No one has been able to find him, as you know."

"Obviously. I've been trying to locate him. Mason has been in here at least half a dozen times asking if I have. There's other stuff going down too. I thought a lot of it would drop off once Roman was caught, but if anything, it's ramped up. Either he has someone else working with him or—I don't even know. Maybe he left them instructions?"

I thought having someone else in my space would be annoying, but having someone else here to bounce ideas off of, talk through shit, is nice. Mason tries, but he's got enough on his plate, especially the last few days being out of commission. Ren understands what I'm doing, how I operate.

"Orders. He would leave them orders, but I doubt he'll confirm our suspicions either way. We need to call a meeting, loop everyone in. There's something we're missing." He paces across the hardwoods, brows pulled low, as if he can figure everything out if he just thinks about it enough.

I spin in my chair toward him, holding my hands up. "You're going to have to stop throwing around the word 'we.' *You* can call a meeting. *You* can tell them what's going on with Victor. I'll keep trying to put the pieces together from here, but there's no way the others will let me into a meeting."

The panel swings open, revealing Mason's exhausted face, dark rings under his eyes. His eyebrows shoot up when he spots Ren, who either doesn't hear him or doesn't care to acknowledge him. Probably the latter.

"Regular party in here, hmm?" Mason says, a bite to his tone as he skirts around Ren and leans down, pressing a kiss to my forehead.

"Grayson is meeting with Victor," I whisper. "If someone can get down there quickly enough, we might be able to intercept him."

"We can't," Ren interjects, running his hand over his short hair. "I've already texted everyone. Sam said she'd try, but she's deep in King territory. I doubt she'll get there before he takes off. Can we track him?"

His eyes meet mine, and I shake my head. Mason's hand wraps around the back of my neck, massaging the tense muscles. My lids droop and I sigh. Ren stops pacing, tilting his head, and Mason steps away.

"I already have a program running facial recognition software and it hasn't picked up anything. It pinged the other day for

Roman as a partial match, but that happens sometimes. I think Victor is playing a game he's well-versed in," I say.

"He's been doing this a long time," Mason murmurs, glancing over his shoulder at the screens.

"I'm calling a meeting," Ren states, turning for the tunnels, stopping when he reaches the panel. "Remember what I said, Lacey."

I nod slowly as he slips into the darkness, the panel clicking shut behind him. I don't know exactly which part I'm supposed to remember, but I can guess. Glancing at Mason, I wonder if I'll be able to let him go, even if that's what's best for him.

Forty-Seven

Mason

"Tell me again why you insisted we meet here instead of your place," Shane spits out, leading Lacey and me up the stairs to the conference room.

"It's less likely Victor bugged your place," Lacey says.

After our fight a couple days ago, I expected her to talk about leaving again. She still hasn't told me her last name, but I don't care. That was never something I needed from her. We have a long ways to go, but there's little time these days for us to talk through what we are to each other.

"You can't sweep the place?"

"I could." She doesn't elaborate and Shane stops, spinning to face her.

"Going to explain why you didn't?"

"No." She glances at me and I nod, keeping my face impassive. "We'd rather not have to deal with everyone inserting themselves into the situation with Roman Drake."

I smother my grin behind my hand. It's the politest way I've heard someone tell Shane King to fuck off. He turns to me, raising an eyebrow, as if I'm going to step in.

"She speaks for both of us."

Lacey sucks in a breath, but I link our fingers together and pull her through the doors, leaving Shane to wonder what the hell my words mean.

"What the hell was that?" Lacey hisses, trying to tuck her body behind mine.

I don't blame her. The entire room falls silent, and the various factions eye us. No, not us—her. Sam tilts her head, zeroing in on our hands before her eyebrow crawls up her forehead. I wonder who got in my sister's head.

When they met, I thought they would get along, even if I didn't like it at the time. Normally, I would blame one of the Kings, but Sam has a mind of her own and she doesn't let them run roughshod over her. Her turnaround with Lacey suggests something happened between them, but when Sam glances at Mac, I wonder if it was the women who got involved.

Leaning down, I murmur, "Better they get used to us being a team."

"A team, huh?"

I grin at her before pulling her to a seat far away from Hawk. He's glaring at me like I personally kidnapped Willow. She's happily chatting away with Mac, no worse for wear. She doesn't even have any visible bruises. When she catches my eye, she gives me a soft smile and a little wave. My eyes skip back to

Hawk, and I decide not to return the gesture. Willow smacks his arm, and a heated discussion starts up between them.

"Have you talked to her?" Lacey says under her breath.

"No. I doubt Hawk will let her at this point. He blames me."

"That's ridiculous. How could you possibly be responsible for her kidnapping? It's not like Drake's only beef is with you. You're just the one he started with."

I wave away her tirade. We've already had this discussion. Rehashing it won't suddenly wake everyone else up. Until we have all the pieces, I'll be the one they blame. Explaining shit won't change their minds at this point.

"Byrns, you'd better start talking," Shane says, coming into the room, Ren in tow.

As they plop down, I notice the clear demarcation line they've set. Lacey and I are at one end of the table, three seats open on either side of each of us, while the rest cluster on the opposite end.

Glancing at Lacey, I sigh. She'll assume they're distancing themselves because of her. When we finally talked shit out, she told me all about how they acted on their way to the Barrens. At least they picked her up. Although, I don't know if they did that because of who she is to me or because she's a hacker.

"Go ahead, Kitten," I murmur, nudging Lacey's arm.

Digging her nails into her palms, she goes to stand, but I stop her. This isn't a class and she's not giving a presentation. She purses her lips to hide the trembling in her body, I'm sure. Wiping all emotion from my face, I stare over the other's heads.

"There are several fronts all converging on you at once, which will seriously divide your forces. Roman Drake is still in the Byrns basement and he's speaking in riddles. Victor is MIA, but apparently, he's been meeting with Grayson, who isn't talking. Someone should probably take care of that." Lacey falters, squeezing the arms of her chair until her knuckles whiten.

"Why is Nemesis the one giving us this information instead of you, Byrns?" Hawk asks, leaning back in his chair.

"Apparently, she speaks for both of them," Shane sneers, rolling his eyes.

The table falls silent as they all stare at us, various looks of hostility painted on their faces, except for Willow and Alex. The latter is avoiding everyone's gaze. Tilting my head, I wonder what happened. He never returned my texts on what the hell he was thinking. Gathering intel on Victor is one thing, but engaging is something completely different. With my mind a muddled mess a few days ago, I'm not sure I have the whole story from him yet.

"I told you I shouldn't have come," Lacey whispers, sliding down in her seat.

Pushing to my feet, I lean on my knuckles, pinning them each with a glare. "I don't know what the fuck your guys' problem is with Lacey, but you'd better get used to her being around."

"Or what?" Ren asks, tilting his head.

"Or get used to doing shit without us."

"Seems like we've already been doing that," Shane says, crossing his arms and leaning back in his chair.

Helms rolls his eyes as Mac leans over, whispering in his ear. He nods, never taking his eyes from me.

Ren sighs. "It appears as if you've been floundering for quite a while, Byrns. We've had to pick up the slack from your missteps more often than not over the last year."

"Couldn't have anything to do with the fact I was in a fucking coma for six months of that."

"Regardless, the number of times it's been requested we take over your side of the river is more than a little concerning."

Grabbing Lacey's arm, I haul her to her feet. "We're done."

The room explodes as the men burst to their feet, hands slamming on the table as they all start yelling at once. Lacey flinches, tucking closer to my side as I round the table.

Alex moves to block the door, concern etched on his face. He shakes his head when our eyes meet, as if I'll stay if only he asks nicely. I refuse to put Lacey through this bullshit. Piecing my life back together hasn't been easy, and it's like they thought I'd just bounce back. I'd wake up and miraculously be the same man I was before I was shot. Instead, I've been floundering as they watch from the sidelines, waiting for me to drown.

I won't continue to stand by while they're assholes to Lacey, either. They can come at me all they want, but she's done nothing but help us for years. I don't see why it matters so much that she's here instead of communicating through texts. They've made up their minds about her, but that doesn't mean I have to keep subjecting her to their shitty attitudes.

A gunshot ricochets over the mess of voices and someone screams as I spin, tucking Lacey behind me. Silence descends, revealing Helms, gun still raised in the air.

"Would you all shut the fuck up? You lot are goddamn embarrassing. How the fuck you were able to hold on to Synd and run shit ten years ago is a fucking miracle. Now sit down and let's figure shit out."

Sam drops to her chair, wide eyes staring at the biker. Mac smirks, spinning in her chair as she scans the rest of us. One by one, they return to their seats, until only Alex, Lacey, and I remain. Helms raises an eyebrow as he tucks his gun away. Lacey trembles behind me, resting a hand on my back.

"I hope you know you're going to pay for that, Helms," Shane mutters.

Looking every inch the president of an MC, he swings his eyes to Shane. "Is that so?"

A feral grin takes over his face, and I realize this is how he stayed in power at just nineteen, after his father died—through pure grit and determination. Throw in a little bit of that unhinged look and he didn't have to try very hard.

"Do you know how much it costs to fix a fucking bullet hole in this ceiling? You cracked the plaster, asshole." Shane swings his eyes to Sam, glaring, and she ducks her head.

"Bill me," Helms snarls.

"Is this normal?" Lacey whispers, resting her forehead between my shoulder blades.

"Totally normal," Alex says, grinning.

"Sit down, Mason. We're not going to solve any problems with you hovering by the door," Helms says, exhaustion bleeding into his voice.

Lacey tugs my shirt and I lead us back to our chairs, waiting until she's seated before sinking into my own. Alex lopes back, running his hand through Sam's hair before he sits next to her. The lines are still drawn in the sand, with us on one side and them on the other. I hate it.

Shane opens his mouth, probably to throw some more shit my way, when Hawk's smacks him, nodding at Helms.

"How much reach does Roman Drake have?" Helms asks, eyeing Lacey.

She glances at me before opening her mouth and then snapping it shut again. Tapping a finger against the arm of my chair, I wait, but she doesn't answer.

"Clearly, a lot, since our shipments are still going missing. Not to mention, random buildings are still being blown up," I say.

"Thought she was speaking for both of you?" Hawk sneers.

"Watch it," I snarl, leaning forward.

He scoffs and I think about adding how he's only here by our good graces, but I don't have it in me. I don't blame Helms. If I were in his position, I would have brought Hawk along too. On the rare occasion we met before the Guild came, I brought Colin. It didn't even cross my mind to allow Sam in the meetings. Back then I wanted her as far away from the Kings as possible.

Now that our families are working together, I've attended by myself, since my sister is firmly entrenched on the Kings' side, as she should be. Looking back, I almost wish I would have included Sam. Things might have gone differently if I would have treated her like a useful player rather than an asset to be brought out in the dark of the night.

"Fuck that. If she would have done her fucking job—"

Willow's hand on his arm has him stuttering to a stop, glancing at her. She shakes her head, and I swear they're having a silent conversation.

Willow turns to me. "Mason, I don't blame you or Lacey for what happened, or what you did after. I'd like to say you saved my life, but I got the impression Roman didn't want to kill me. He seemed to want to talk more than anything. I get the feeling he's...lonely. Clearly, he has a vendetta against you all, but he's also gathering information. He asked me a lot of questions. It wasn't until I refused to answer that he gagged me."

"He was taunting Alex," Lacey murmurs, eyes skipping to the enforcer.

"That doesn't surprise me," she sighs. "He actually asked me if I would feel better being in the back of the car instead of the trunk. And then asked if the ropes were too tight. At one point he apologized."

"For what?"

"Embroiling me in all of this." She takes a deep breath. "I'd like to see him."

Hawk jumps up, chair tipping back. "Absolutely not."

She flips her hair over her shoulder, then glares at him. "I didn't ask you, Hawk. Sit down. If I want to talk to him, and Mason says I can, then I will. And you will *not* be going with me. You can wait outside in the car. I'll even crack a window for you."

Sam snorts, covering her face, and Willow smirks, then wipes it away. She turns back to me, expectantly.

"He's not going anywhere. I don't see why not," I say slowly, watching Hawk from the corner of my eye.

It'd be just my luck for him to shoot me for not taking his side. I waltzed into an obvious trap to save Willow. I'm not about to let her be harmed in my house. Explaining that to him won't accomplish anything. She clearly needs the opportunity to stand on her own two feet without Hawk interfering.

Willow tips her chin up. "I'd also like Lacey to come with me."

Forty-Eight

Lacey

Mason scowls as he tugs me from the car. I barely clear the door before he slams it shut, yanking me behind him. Clamping my lips together, I let him manhandle me all the way inside. I expect him to disappear once we clear the doors, but he pulls me all the way to his bedroom, kicking the door shut behind me before stalking for the bathroom.

After Willow dropped her bomb, the meeting dissolved. There's so much more we needed to talk about, but everyone started yelling again. This time, no one stopped us when Mason tugged me toward the exit. Sam's eyes followed me the whole way. I half expected someone to chase us down, but the house was silent while we navigated through the twists and turns and out the front door.

"You realize you said it was perfectly safe for Willow, but as soon as it was me, you flipped shit."

"I fail to see how you are going to make this any better, Lacey," Mason growls as he paces the tiles.

"Why are you hiding in the bathroom?"

"Because I'm not about to rage in my office where everyone can hear me," he mutters, low enough he probably assumes I can't hear him.

Rolling my eyes, I lean against the door frame, tracking his movements.

"It's not that serious."

"The last time you went down there—without me, mind you—you had an episode. Why would I willingly put you in that position again?"

"You're not putting me in that position. I am. At what point did you assume you would be making decisions for me?"

"When you decided your life doesn't matter!"

He wheezes, planting his hands on his hips and ducking his chin to his chest. I don't know how he came to the conclusion I'm risking my life by seeing someone who is literally chained to a chair, but I doubt I'll be able to convince him otherwise. I wait for him to lift his head, to say something else, but he's frozen, locked in whatever horrible outcome that's playing in his head.

"I won't put myself in danger, Mason. You need to realize I'm capable of taking care of myself."

"Everyone in my life is capable, Lacey. Doesn't mean they always do," he says, exhaustion lacing his tone.

"This doesn't have anything to do with me, does it?"

His head whips up, alarm resting in his eyes. "I don't know what you're talking about. Of course this is about you."

He pushes past me to the bedroom and perches on the end of the bed. Resting his elbows on his knees, he runs his hands down his face, as if he can scrub away all the anxiety riding him. I lean against the door frame, crossing my arms.

"Is it Sam or Colin?" I whisper.

Covering his head, he groans. "I wasn't there. If I would have—"

"Would have what? Not gotten shot? Not gone to the meeting? If what, Mason? Because from where I'm standing, there's nothing more you could have done. You saved her when it mattered. And if you were around, then she wouldn't be with people who love her. She'd still be hiding behind a mask."

"And Colin? Are you going to tell me that wasn't my fault, either?"

I wave away his words, not that he sees me. "Of course it wasn't. Colin made his own decisions. He put everyone in an impossible situation with his choices. The fault lies with him."

The silence stretches, and I wonder if that's all I'll be able to pull from him. I get the feeling this is the first time he's talked about what happened. Colin bringing in the Guild, trying to force Mason's hand to expand their territory when it wasn't what anyone wanted, set into motion so much heartache, but it healed old wounds no one could remember as well. I can't say I understand what it was like for him to have to shoot Colin to save his sister. In fact, I doubt there's anything I can say that he'll believe.

"I'm the one who brought him in," he mumbles.

"Duh," I say, rolling my eyes and his head tips up. "He was your best friend. You grew up together, and it stands to reason that you wouldn't be able to see the change in him because you were too close. You were used to him being on your side and having your back. No one could have anticipated he was conspiring against you. And to him, he wasn't. Still doesn't make it your fault."

He holds his hand out, and I settle next to him, his arm tucked around my waist. I don't know what else to say to make him understand. No one blames him for the Guild coming in. At least I don't think they do. They haven't exactly been understanding of what he's going through.

"Is it hard?" I murmur, resting my head on his shoulder.

"Not exactly the time to try to seduce me, but I won't complain." He snorts as I smack him in the chest, and he laces our fingers together.

"When I first came—"

"You mean when you stalked me," he chuckles.

I clench my jaw even as my stomach tightens. This is the most honest conversation we've had and we're treading toward dangerous territory.

"Did you keep me here because you were lonely?" I hold my breath, hoping he doesn't blow up and run away like every other time we've tiptoed toward the edge of this conversation.

Instead, he sighs, pressing a kiss to my hair. "I don't know. Probably. I liked having you here, knowing I was coming home to someone, but I didn't realize it until you left. Or I didn't admit it until you were gone. Even after you were taken and Moss was convinced you were in league with them, I couldn't believe it. There was something about you that answered a question I didn't know I was asking."

"What do we do now?" I whisper.

"I don't know."

He shakes his head, dropping his arms from me, leaving me bereft and cold. I crave his touch the more time that passes. One day, I'm afraid he'll walk away forever, leaving me with nothing more than the memory of his warmth. I wonder if it wouldn't have mattered who came into his life—if anyone could have filled the hole within him. I'm not ready for that answer. We're not ready for that conversation. We have other things to deal with. Even as we sit here, there's more pressing issues to address that have nothing to do with our relationship.

"What are you going to do about Roman? We can't keep him locked up in the basement forever," I say, pushing to my feet.

Pulling my phone from my pocket, I tap the screen, not really doing anything other than keeping my hands busy.

"Why do you do that?" he snarls, ripping my phone from my hand and tossing it on the bed.

"What the hell, Mason. I don't even know what you're talking about?" I could guess, but I'd probably be wrong.

He bursts from the bed, crowding into my space until my back presses against the wall. "You keep saying 'you' when it should be 'we.' What are *we* going to do? But you keep separating yourself, as if you don't have a stake in this. As if you won't be around long enough to see shit through. Or you'll skip town without a fucking word and leave me behind to wonder where the hell you are."

"I wouldn't do that," I whisper.

He snorts, planting his hands on the wall, boxing me in. He glares at me, clearly looking for more, but I don't want to admit to him how hard it is to feel like I'm a part of this world when most of the others just want me to disappear.

Biting my lip, I glance away from his probing eyes. His hand wraps around my throat, guiding my chin back with his thumbs until my gaze clashes with his.

"I don't care what they say. You know that, right?"

He doesn't give me a chance to answer before his lips descend on mine. Tension eases from my muscles as he kisses me, all the problems we're facing receding into the shadows of my mind. Here, they don't matter. In his arms, nothing else but the press of his body against mine, his hands skimming over me, his lips devouring me, matters.

He pulls back, resting his forehead on mine as he sighs. We're locked in a moment I'm afraid to disrupt, as if popping the bubble around us will have devastating effects. His eyes find mine and I lean into him, pressing my lips against his to capture the feelings. I'll bottle them up and store them close to my heart.

His phone blares, cutting through the protective space we've found. He growls against my lips before shoving off the wall and answering. Tracking his movements across the room, he becomes more agitated with each step.

"What the hell do you mean, the river's on fire?" Mason barks.

I gasp, taking off for the bedroom door. Mason yells my name, but I don't slow. I practically slam into TJ as I skid around the corner. My office isn't that far from Mason's bedroom. For some fucking reason, it seems to take forever to get there.

My trembling fingers falter three times before I put the code in correctly and the keypad glows green. My screens sit dormant, filling the space with a persistent hum. It's almost peaceful except for my wheezing breath. Slamming into my chair, I wake them up, my leg jumping a million miles a minute as I whisper to them to go faster.

"Talk to me, Lacey," Mason says from behind me.

"Seeing as how I got here five fucking seconds before you did, I don't fucking know yet," I snap, eyes darting over the screens. "Who called you?"

"Sam. Said her contact in the Barrens, Mack, called her." He leans over my shoulder, and I contemplate elbowing him to get him to back off.

"The guy she saved from his guts being used as sidewalk chalk?"

He snorts, turning his head toward mine. "If that's the way you want to describe it."

"Are you smelling my hair?" I ask, jerking away. He grins and I shake my head, scowling. "Let me fucking work."

There aren't any cameras in the Barrens, or if there are, they haven't worked for a long time. Glancing at Mason, who's buried in his phone, I wonder if I should reveal this piece of information I have. It's a risk, since I'm pretty sure Nicki would skin me alive if she ever found out I told him. I grab my phone, spinning until I'm facing Mason.

"Who are you texting?"

"A client."

"Care to share which one?" he asks, raising an eyebrow.

I smile as I hit send. "Nope."

Tapping my nail against the case, I wait for her reply, which comes an agonizing thirty seconds later. I sigh, spinning back to the screens and pulling up the two cameras Nicki had me install two years ago on either side of the river. The Egg is awash in flames, though the longer I look, the more I can make out. If the Egg goes, so does most of the business within the Barrens. They have their own little market set behind the tall gates to keep anyone who doesn't belong on their respective sides of the river. It sits smack dab in the middle of Synd, situated on a low cobblestone bridge that's a lot wider than normal.

"How the hell did you get cameras in the Egg?" Mason growls.

"Nicki." I don't elaborate as I watch people run back and forth across the bridge. The gates are thrown wide, allowing people to get their things to safety.

"We need to get men down there now," he murmurs, leaning over me again.

"Nicki said no. She just wants the fire put out."

He grumbles something about stubborn women, and I give him a hard side-eye.

"Don't give me that look. Did she tell you what happened?"

"Oracle. Apparently, someone had the brilliant idea to take it and convert the powder form to liquid. I don't know the whole story, but some shit went down when Nicki found out. They must have added an accelerant," I say, snatching up my phone as it buzzes.

"Why an accelerant?" Mason asks, watching the chaos on the screen.

"Because it wouldn't have set the fucking river on fire otherwise. Mason, there's nothing we can do but let it burn out. Unless we throw that foam shit on it for chemical fires. I don't even know if Nicki would let the fire department in."

Mason runs his hand through his hair. "She won't. She locked shit down, which is probably why they went after the Egg in the first place."

"Well, then we'll just have to wait, I suppose."

I sit back, leaning my head against Mason's stomach and his fingers thread through my hair as we focus on the world burning through the lens of a camera.

Forty-Nine

Mason

"Come here, Lacey," I say, staring at the computer screen.

She's loitering by the office door, glancing down the hall. She sighs finally stepping inside, then closing the door behind her. The last twenty-four hours have been a whirlwind since the shitstorm at the Egg, and exhaustion is etched in every line of her face.

"What are you working on?" she whispers.

"Here, Lacey. Not over there," I say, pointing at my lap.

She shuffles around the desk, easing down on me. Her body relaxes as she leans her back against my chest. Wrapping my free arm around her waist, I press a kiss to her head. Even with Drake being locked up, we're still putting out fires everywhere. I keep expecting shit to settle down the longer he's down there. Shane called earlier, complaining as if it was my fault, like I let Drake out for unsupervised yard time.

"You could reroute them through Reaper territory," she mumbles, eyes tracking across the screen.

Most of my contacts have pulled out, refusing to deal with us now that the city is so volatile. It's honestly worse than when the Guild was fucking with us. Whatever Drake did, he did it well enough to decimate our shipments. I'm almost to the point of begging some of them to stick with us. I have a feeling I'm going to have to take drastic measures with Drake to make him tell us where to find his accomplice.

"Even letting Helms do it, they're still being seized outside the city limits. The only way is if we go get them ourselves, but we don't have enough men to deal with the shit going on here and send teams out the retrieve product."

I pull up another screen, checking the cameras around the house. It became routine long before I found Lacey in the woods. Even though I know it was her tripping the sensors, I still do a sweep every night. It settles my nerves, reassuring me that no one is lurking in the shadows ready to grab her.

"Nicki said the fire burned out finally. She thinks it was a rogue group of others from the Barrens who were upset with her for locking shit down. She's pissed at me, so I doubt she'll give me more info."

"What'd you do to piss her off?" I chuckle. Nicki essentially runs the Barrens now, yet she still acts as if she's not on the same level as us.

"I told her unless she lets the Kings in, there's nothing we can do to help set the Egg back up. I'm worried people won't get enough food down there." She squirms, wiggling her ass into my crotch, and I dig my fingers into her side.

"Keep that up and I'll be bending you over my desk before you can moan my name." I press a kiss behind her ear, and she shivers.

"You say that like it's a warning."

She squeals when I tickle her side, and I abandon what I was doing. Turning her head, I capture her mouth with mine, sweeping my tongue in as she slides her hand up my chest. My phone buzzes, and she pulls away, leaping up from my lap before I can stop her.

Scowling, I grab my phone as my eyes track her meandering around my office. I need to deal with the warehouse that was set on fire, and the lower gang that defected, not to mention the businesses along the edge of the Barrens that were robbed two nights ago. Except all I can think about is spending time with Lacey, whether I'm worshiping her body or watching her work, it doesn't matter.

I don't want to answer, but as Hawk's name flashes across the screen, I realize I don't have a choice.

"Hawk."

"Byrns. Willow would like to talk to Drake. What are you going to do about that?" he snaps.

"Well, hello to you too, Hawk. Was Willow unable to call me herself?" I ask, and Lacey glares over her shoulder.

"I'm arranging this whole escapade. What's your plan?"

Leaning back in the chair, I drop my chin to my chest, pinching the bridge of my nose.

"I get the feeling that you want me to tell her no," I mumble, trying to keep my voice down. Willow is one of the few people who doesn't hold a grudge against Lacey. Plus, I don't know if Willow is listening in on the other side.

"Not my call. In fact, I'd rather not talk to you at all right now."

"Blame me all you want, but Willow got out of that relatively unscathed. After all the shit that woman's been through, she held her fucking own," I growl.

Hawk is silent so long I glance at the screen to see if he's hung up. He finally clears his throat, and a door clicks behind him, confirming my suspicions that Willow was with him.

"What'd she do?" he mutters.

"What she had to do," I say. If Willow hasn't told him the full story, then I won't betray her trust, no matter how much I'd like Hawk to get over this shit.

"I can't handle her seeing him alone."

"It's not your choice, Hawk. She has to do shit on her own, and I won't stop her."

He scoffs and the line goes dead. Glancing at Lacey, I toss my phone on my desk, dropping my head in my hands.

"That didn't seem to go very well," she says as she shuffles through the paperwork on the side table.

I haven't looked at the research in a couple weeks now. For months I was dedicated to ferreting out the secrets hiding in our pasts, but once Lacey stepped into my life and shit started going sideways, it fell to the side. Before Lacey, it was the only thing that kept me going. And yet I haven't even given them a second thought since she showed up.

I clear my throat, trying to remember what she said. "He's not exactly happy with me, but that's nothing new."

Pushing to my feet, I come up behind her, wrapping my arms around her and rest my chin on her shoulder. She flips the piece of paper over. It's a copy of an article, the one that mentions the Drakes in the same paragraph as the Byrns and Kings. Helms's dad never attended this bougie shit, opting to stick to his territory, so of course he isn't mentioned. She pulls out another one, scanning the clipping.

"What was the point of looking all this up? Most of these things have nothing to do with Roman."

I sigh, dropping my arms and going to the window. "Helms was trying to pull me out of whatever the hell was wrong with me and gave me a project."

Tucking my hands in my pocket, I scan the tree line for anything out of place. Since Lacey was taken, there hasn't been much activity around here. Drake's men have concentrated on the lower gangs and sowing general discord throughout Synd. I feel like I've been on high alert for months, waiting for the next crisis.

"Did it work?" she asks, shuffling through the stack and picking up a book.

I snort, shaking my head. "Lacey, I realize we didn't have the best start, but you saw how I was. It hasn't been the smooth road to recovery the doc promised."

"Hmm," she says, and I raise an eyebrow at her, but she's scanning the book of records I barely even cracked open.

"We don't exactly have the time to be distracted by the past."

I'm pretty sure she didn't hear me. She's still flipping through the book, not even flinching when I approach her, sliding my hand along her hip.

"Did you know your family founded Synd?"

"We've been ruling this city for quite a while, but I don't know about actually starting the damn thing."

"This is a record from the first city census almost a hundred and fifty years ago. Obviously, it wasn't as big as it is now, but there's quite a few names on here that are still around."

She pulls away from my touch to round my desk, plopping down in my chair to pour over the book. This isn't exactly how I thought the night would go, but I'm finding once Lacey fixates on something, she goes in with full force and not much can distract her.

I grab her wrist, tugging her up and she grumbles, leaning over the desk with her eyes still glued to the book. I collapse into my chair and yank her onto my lap, running my hands under her shirt. Tipping my head back, I sigh, the tension easing from my muscles the longer she's in my arms.

My phone buzzes again and I groan, digging my fingers into her flesh. Lacey grabs it, holding it over her shoulder. I think about chucking it against the wall, but I've found it's pretty indestructible.

"Take it, Mason. It's your sister."

I answer it, resuming my trek across her skin and goosebumps scatter across her stomach.

"What is it, Sam?"

"Uh, can we talk? I got a thing," she mumbles. It sounds like she's running, and I straighten.

"What's wrong?"

Lacey tries to stand, but I hold her tight against me. If there's any time I need her close, it's now.

"Nothing. I mean, everything is fine. I just have a thing I have to talk to you about. And I realize it's a little weird timing, but I'm freaking out just a little," she says breathlessly.

"Just spit it out, Sam, because in a minute I'm going to start freaking out too."

"So, the guys just gave me—"

"Wait, is this a conversation for me or for Mac? Because I don't know if I can handle—"

"Shut the fuck up and listen. It's hard enough to talk about without you interrupting." She takes a deep breath, letting it out in a whoosh. "Okay, so the guys had a deed drawn up."

Silence descends and I drop my chin to my chest, resting my forehead against Lacey's back. I have no idea what the hell she's talking about, but she sounds like she did when we were younger—unsure and out of her depth.

"Did they buy you a house or something?"

"Or something. They want to put me on the deed for the house. Like their house."

"Oh, uh, okay." I have no idea why she's calling me about this. "And this is a bad thing?"

"You don't care?" she cries and Lacey glances over her shoulder, wide eyes meeting mine.

I shrug, shaking my head. Her guess is as good as mine as to why I'm having this conversation, but I suppose this is my life now.

"Of course I care. I just don't know why—" I stutter to a stop as Lacey glares at me. "Uh, what I mean to say is, seems like a good thing to me, Sam."

"Duh," she snorts. I can practically hear her rolling her eyes. "But like, that means I can't come back."

Realization dawns on me and I squeeze Lacey's side. She stands and I pace back to the window.

"Sammy, you never were coming back. And that's okay. You're where you belong. Sign the deed," I murmur.

"But what if..."

After ten seconds of silence, I chuckle. "Can't come up with anything, can you? Sam, are you going to stay with them?"

"Yes," she whispers, tears in her voice.

"Do you love them?"

"Yes." She sniffles. "I really fucking do."

"Do they love you?"

"They say they do," she says ruefully, vulnerability lacing her tone.

"Sammy," I warn.

"Okay, yes. They do. Even when they're being assholes, they do."

"Then let them do this for you."

"Okay," she whispers. "Does she help? With the loneliness?"

I glance behind me to Lacey, still leaning over the desk, pouring over old records as if the people will leap off the page and tell her their life story. She brushes her black hair over her shoulder, narrowing her eyes at the text.

"Yeah, she does. Better than anything else so far."

Lacey's eyes meet mine and she gives me a small smile before looking down again, and my stomach flips. She's exactly what I needed to pull me from the black hole I was hurtling toward. If someone tries to take her, I'll tear the world apart to get her back.

"Then don't let her go, Mason."

"I don't plan on it," I say. "Love you, Sammy."

"Love you too, Mase. Glad to see you're as fucked as the rest of us. Now stop being an asshole and figure your shit out."

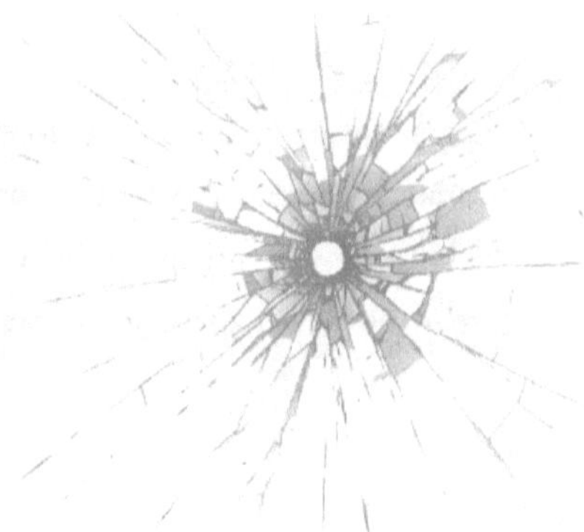

Fifty

Lacey

I turn when a knock echoes through the room and scowl. Ever since the day the river was set on fire, there's rarely a time Mason and I aren't interrupted by more shit hitting the fan. Even over the last few days, when we clearly had things we needed to work through, someone would knock or call or text. It's infuriating. I don't blame Mason. He has a territory and obvious shit to deal with. Still doesn't make it any easier.

Ripping open the door, I jolt back. "Sam?"

She spins to face me, her face the careful mask I've seen on countless screens. Between watching her on the cameras and seeing her in the tabloids, I've learned she hides most of her emotions from the outside world. I don't blame her. Even if she wasn't the Wraith, playing the part of a socialite affords her protection she normally wouldn't have. I'm sure it comes at a cost, but at least the people of Synd never see her cry.

"Didn't mean to interrupt, but we need to talk," she says, leaning to glance around me.

Easing back, I sweep out a hand, waiting for her to step in. I catch TJ's eye and he hides what I'm sure is a grin behind his hand.

Sam brushes past me and I swing the door closed, cutting off his smug expression. I realize my mistake when she purses her lips. I don't want to open the door again, so I make my way over to the panel, intent on escaping through the tunnels. The keypad beeps after I put in the code.

"Going somewhere?" Mason calls, stepping from the closet.

"Why don't you stop sulking and figure it out," I snap, and Sam swings wide eyes to me.

Shrugging, I slip into the darkness before he can respond. My head throbs and I stumble, barely catching myself from tumbling down the rest of the stairs. Plopping down on the last step, I half expect Alex to materialize from the shadows with a briefcase tucked under his arm. When I'm sure he's not lurking in the darkness, I push to my feet, sighing.

"Hey," Sam murmurs from behind me, and I jump.

Her hand grabs my arm, stopping me from falling down the next staircase, sending my heart thundering in my chest.

"Holy shit, what the hell was that?" I rip my arm from her grasp, twisting to face her.

"Whoa. Didn't think you'd be so jumpy. I *did* say we needed to talk."

"Make a fucking noise every once in a while and maybe I wouldn't freak the hell out. Fuck," I wheeze, pressing my fist to my chest, and bending over.

"You're being dramatic, but whatever. What's his problem?" she asks, throwing a thumb over her shoulder.

The door hangs open, no sign of Mason. I'm not about to air all his issues to his sister. Not only would that be weird, but she'll probably tell the Kings. Mason would not be okay with that, and I'm not about to cause more of a divide between them. He's going to need them sooner rather than later. I might not be very happy with him, but he needs someone on his side for now.

The latest argument is merely an extension of the last one, anyway. Mason keeps making subtle comments about me talking to Roman. Every time he brings it up, it's just another indication that he thinks I can't take care of myself. I can't tell Sam any of that, though.

"Why don't you go and ask him? I'm sure that would be a lot more productive than standing in a darkened stairwell with me."

"Okay, so you're pissed off. Got it. Not that I blame you. Things have been kind of shit lately." She tips her head back, holding her hand up when I open my mouth. "I understand I'm part of the problem."

"Oh, like how you acted like you wanted to be my friend and then suddenly I was to blame for every little thing that's happened?"

She purses her lips, glancing back again. "Yeah, that's definitely part of it. Listen, I've been a bitch, but I need your help. We can hash out all the bullshit after we take care of the problem."

I almost refuse outright. The only reason she's coming to me is because she thinks her brother will deny her. Sam thinks she can push me around. Then again, this is my job. Being petty isn't going to help any of us. I can set aside my hurt feelings and work with them. At least I'm pretty sure I can.

"Fine. I'll need my computer," I mutter, clomping down the stairs.

Sam skips past me, intent on leading the way. "Not that kind of help."

Sighing, I follow her through the twists and turns, not really sure where we're headed. When we pass the panel leading to the kitchen, I freeze. These stairs only lead to one place—the dungeon. I'm not exactly keen on going another round with Roman Drake at the moment. And Sam wanting me there doesn't make any sense.

She spins, planting her hands on her hips. "Don't tell me you're going to bail on me now."

"You haven't given me a reason not to." I mirror her stance, raising an eyebrow.

Rolling her eyes, she peers over her shoulder, tapping her foot. Sam could make me if she wanted, at least physically. She could probably torture me into talking, too. I'm not delusional. I'd never hold up under her scrutiny. The only reason I made it as long as I did with Razor was because they asked me barely any questions. They also didn't physically hurt me until the end.

"Okay, I'm not going to tell you to not tell Mason, but maybe say I forced you. We need to see Drake, and you're our ticket in.

Plus, I figured it might be something you'd like to be involved with."

"You don't need me to get in there. The code is your birthday."

I drop my arms, wrapping them around my stomach. It would have been nice to be included for nothing more than being me. Having my suspicions confirmed, that they're only involving me because I can get them in, is a hard pill to swallow. I shouldn't be surprised.

"Uh, no, that's not the code. But that's besides the point. We think you'll be able to get him talking. Alex said Drake knows your last name, which apparently means something."

"He also knows I'm Nemesis, so there's that. I'm sure he just wants to use me if he can ever get out of here."

She tucks her hand in her front pocket, pulling out a bag of Clementine slices. Her nose crinkles before she shoves one in her mouth. Her phone buzzes, but she doesn't move to answer it. Gesturing with her food, she gives me an expectant look.

"Who's we?"

"Mac and Willow. We had to sneak away, but we don't have a lot of time before the guys figure out our ruse. I get it. You don't trust us. Yada, yada, yada, but we need to do this together."

"Because he'll only talk to me," I say with zero expression.

"I mean, it's not like we're going to release him and let him go all murdery on you in a locked room. That would definitely push Mason over the edge. He's been teetering on it for a while," she says, finally pulling her phone from her pocket.

"Great to know Mason is the only reason you won't let Roman kill me."

She waves away my sarcasm. "Already told you that, but whatever. There are reasons for the other shit, as I'm sure you've figured out, but we don't really have time to talk it all out. So, how about this? You go with me right now, we figure this shit out, and then we'll go out to eat. We've got this breakfast place…" Her words trail off as realization floods her face. "Wait."

"Thought we didn't have time to go into this?" I mumble, glancing away.

"You have got to be fucking kidding me," she cries. "Wait, wait, wait. The hospital? Seriously? And the coffee shop. Fucking-A, everywhere. How the hell—"

"I'm pretty good at being invisible in plain sight."

"Does Mason know?" she asks, wide eyes finding mine.

I shrug, not willing to admit I have no idea. Obviously, he knows I was at the coffee shop, but I'm pretty sure Sam is talking about when I worked as a barista there. The various stints of employment I've picked up over the years often crossed paths with the mafia families. At first, it wasn't intentional. I just happened to get a job and one of them would come in, but the more my obsession grew, the more I sought out the places they went. Honestly, I'm surprised they didn't notice sooner.

"Would you two hurry up?" Mac hisses from the dark.

"Shit. Dammit. Why can't surprises come when we're not on a time crunch? I'm actually impressed, and now I have to deal with this bullshit. Come on. We're *definitely* going to the Flaming Skillet after this."

She lopes off toward the whispering voices and I follow. Do I think she's going to leave me in a room with Roman alone? No, probably not. No matter what I told Mason, I am afraid I might lose it again in that space. It hit me with little warning before. I have no desire to go through an episode again, especially in front of these women. When we step into the damp hallway housing Roman's prison, my body tenses. Mac and Willow turn to face us, and Sam skips over, throwing the last orange slice in her mouth.

"Vouch for me I ate the whole thing," Sam says to Mac.

"To who exactly?" Mac asks as Willow gives me a small wave.

"Shane. He was getting on me about not eating enough fruit. Thinks I'm going to get sick if I 'keep going like this.' Then Alex said something about scurvy." She rolls her eyes as she tucks the bag back in her pocket.

"He wouldn't believe me. Can't ask Willow either. She can't lie to save her life. Which is exactly why she shouldn't come in with us, no matter what the hell she says."

"Perfectly capable of lying. Just not to Shane fucking King. That dude is scary." Willow shivers, twisting her fingers together.

"But you wouldn't be lying. You just saw me eat it," Sam cries.

"Actually, we only saw you eat one. For all I know, you dropped the rest in the tunnels, hoping no one would notice." Mac says, smirking.

Sam huffs, spinning to me. "You're not scared of Shane, are you?"

"Nope. He's an asshole, but what's he going to do to me? Besides, if any of you fuck me over, I have protocols set in place to deal with you."

They gape at me, and Mac sputters, failing to find the words as I smirk. Did they really think I'd work with a bunch of mafia members—essentially criminal overlords—and not have a safeguard in place? From their faces, apparently that's exactly what they imagined. Sam's face morphs, a glint entering her brown eyes. I don't need their approval, but satisfaction still flows through me.

"Well, I'll be," Willow mumbles. "So, we ready to get this shitshow going? Personally, I'd really like to know what the hell Mr. Sexy Pants is all about."

"Mr. Sexy Pants? You can't be talking about Roman Drake," Mac says.

"Lacey can attest to that man being fine as hell. Right?"

"Uh, I mean, he was covered in soot and dirt when I saw him, but I guess I could see the appeal," I mutter.

Mac scoffs as Sam waves me forward, presenting the keypad to me. "Open it."

"I don't know the code."

"Well, it's not my birthday anymore, so it must be yours." She says it so matter-of-factly, I almost believe her myself.

"Except Mason doesn't know my birthday. There's no reason he would pick that. I'm only here for—"

"For what, Lacey?" Mac sneers, eyeing me up and down.

Sam grinds her heel into Mac's foot. A heated conversation starts so quietly I can't overhear. I don't care. Our conversation in the Barrens wasn't exactly a productive one. I get why she's pissed, even if I was only doing what was right. I doubt her feelings toward me will change, no matter how many discussions we have over a plate of hash browns. With what I did, she's decided I'm not to be trusted. Maybe I'm not. Maybe I am the bad guy to her. I don't have the space in my brain to decipher their feelings and make them feel better, even if there was a way to fix shit.

"Just try something, because I'm out of options at this point," Sam hisses before pulling Mac further away.

"Why don't you try some dates that are significant to you two? He seems sentimental like that," Willow whispers, sidling next to me.

"I don't know where to start," I confess as my finger hovers over the keypad.

"When in doubt, start at the beginning."

My head pulses, the beginning of a headache starting in my temples. My mind blanks as I try to remember dates of literally anything.

"You said he was nice to you?" I murmur, trying to take my mind off the pressure of Mac's eyes boring into my back.

"I wouldn't call it nice, but he certainly wasn't like what you experienced. Are you sure he's the one who kidnapped you? Or I mean, his men?"

"Anyone else wouldn't really make sense. He's made it pretty clear he's behind all this, and I don't have any enemies that I know of."

She nods before wandering off to lean against the wall, watching as Sam and Mac bicker. Sucking in a deep breath, I put in the date Mason and I ran into each other at the coffee shop and it flashes red. Disappointment crashes through me. Trying to convince myself he'd pick a date that had nothing to do with me didn't work. Hope still bloomed in my chest, even though I knew I was setting myself up for heartache.

Glancing at Willow, she tilts her chin, urging me to try again. I go through every date I can think of with no success.

"Sam," I call, and she peers over her shoulder at me. "When did you go to that gala? The one you met the Kings at for the first time?"

"Um, September eighth," she says, and Mac gives her a strange look. "I only remember because Alex says it's the hippo's birthday. Why?"

"Because that's the first time I ran into Mason. I was a cocktail waitress that night."

Inputting the date, I hold my breath as I press enter. It glows green and the door unlocks. The others hurry over, but Sam grips my wrist, pulling my hand away from the handle. She steps back, pulling Mac with her while pushing Willow toward the door.

"You two go in first. We'll wait fifteen minutes and then come in. I don't think he'll talk with us there. We're too abrasive."

Willow nods, shoving the door open before I can respond. Roman Drake looks more than a little worse for wear, but at least he's not tied to the chair anymore. The silence is pierced by a chain being dragged across the stone floor. When he reaches the end of his tether, he pivots, resuming his pacing. He barely glances at us as we move closer.

"Well, fancy meeting you two here. Care for a drink?" He gestures to the dried puddles of blood surrounding him. "Perhaps not."

Bruises pepper his face and bleed into the ink along his neck. Red welts lash his wrists, marring the tattoos along his arms. The reasons Willow dubbed him Mr. Sexy Pants are still visible, though. A couple showers and he'd look like he stepped off a porn set. With his shirt torn in strips, his abs poke through, and I catch Willow's eye. She tries to hide her smile, most likely thinking of her nickname for him too.

"Mr.—" She coughs to hide the giggle. "Drake. I'm sure I don't need to introduce myself."

"You certainly don't, Ms. St. James. Or is it Mrs. Shea now? I don't know how a joining works within an MC," he drawls.

A flush creeps up her cheeks, staining them pink. "Willow is fine. This is Lacey, though I'm sure you already know that. It seems like you know quite a bit about all of us."

He grins, an edge of revenge in his blue eyes. "Tell me, Willow, did the judge beg as you ended him?"

She tilts her head and I'm afraid she'll fold. When she came to Synd, I dug into her past, trying to figure out who could be stalking her. She was timid and unsure, the ideal stepdaughter to a corrupt judge. She's come leaps and bounds into her own in the last few months, but being openly taunted with a death she facilitated might be what pushes her over the edge.

"Unfortunately not. He was sneering until the bitter end. Although, he did make a little gurgling noise when I slit his throat," she says as if we're talking about the weather.

Choking, I bury my face in my arm. I didn't see that coming. I didn't think she'd break down crying, but I also didn't think she'd fuck with him. Roman tips his head back, a deep chuckle bursting from him.

"I always knew he'd meet a humiliating end. And I knew you'd be the one to do it. There's a darkness within you I don't think they saw," he says.

"Are you from Rima, then?"

"Oh, I see what this is. Send in the two lambs to loosen me up before the wolves descend upon my softened body to rip me to shreds. Why don't you invite Samantha and MacKenzie in as well? Might as well get it over with."

"No." I say and his eyes whip to me, narrowing.

Willow shifts, drawing his attention back to her. She plasters on a simpering smile. I'm sure it's the same one she wore all the years her stepfather paraded her around at parties—the perfect stepdaughter on display for all to see.

Roman doesn't seem to know which of us to focus on. As his eyes bounce back and forth, I fold my arms, leaning against the metal table bolted to the wall. There's nothing on it now, probably so whoever they keep down here doesn't have access to weapons. It's smart but gives the space an abandoned feeling.

Although, that could be on purpose. Leave someone down here long enough and they'll lose their mind thinking they've been abandoned, too.

"Interesting. With all the secrets you're keeping, I'd think you'd be more willing to accommodate my requests. Wouldn't want some of them to slip now, would we, Miss Webb?"

"You keep throwing my last name in my face as if that's supposed to mean something."

"Oh, the implications of your last name run far and wide, as I'm sure you know." He cocks his head, studying me. "Or perhaps you don't."

I latch on to Willow's elbow and pull her toward the door. She never takes her eyes off Roman, who tracks our every move. Part of me wants to escape this place—yank her out the door and leave him to rot. A voice in my head, though, is whispering to read between the lines.

Leaning in, I pitch my voice low enough so he won't over-hear. "I don't know what he's talking about, but I think he has more dirt on all of us. I've seen the way people like him operate. Threads weave through every aspect, his plan meticulously set, and if you pull one string, the rest tighten, choking off any hope of unraveling the mess he's made."

"Well, if that's the case, how do we get him to reveal all his secrets?"

"We don't." Biting my lip, I close my eyes as a plan forms in my mind. "Follow my lead."

Sauntering back, I resume leaning against the table. Silence descends, smothering the small space, highlighting every shift and sigh.

From the corner of my eye, I notice Willow's eyes on me, but I keep mine on Roman. I count in my head as the minutes slowly spin away. Just when I'm about to give up, he opens his mouth before snapping it shut again. I raise an eyebrow, daring him to continue, and he scowls.

"Is this your new strategy? Wait me out? It's a poor plan, if that's the case," he says, but frustration bleeds into his tone.

Willow sighs before making her way to me. Brushing off the table, she jumps onto it and leans against the wall. It's hard to watch her while keeping my focus on Roman, especially when he skips between us once again. Willow waves her hand at him to continue, as if she's a very bored queen presiding over her subjects, and I almost lose it.

"Tell me, Willow, did you ever find out what actually happened to your mother?"

She flips him off, eyes still closed. The change in her from when she first came to Synd is startling. I underestimated what a change freedom and love can have on a person.

"Do you ever think of him, Lacey?"

I raise an eyebrow. He could be referencing so many people, none of whom I particularly think about if I can help it. Razor's face flashes in my mind, and I barely suppress a shudder. Neutrality is the only way he'll finally break.

"Is it possible you don't even remember your own brother?" He laughs and my chest seizes.

"Clearly, you've received poor intel. I don't have a brother. I'll even throw you a bone. I don't have any siblings. Or parents. Just little ole me in this world."

The predatory grin stretching across his face has my heart skipping a beat. Honestly, I have no idea whether my parents are still alive. They've been dead to me since I left a decade ago. As soon as I could, I severed every tie I had to them. I have no desire to seek them out and reconnect. They can rot for all I care. Whether they're still out there, living their miserable little lives, or buried deep in the ground, I don't care. With Roman's reaction, I assume he found them alive and well. I wonder what lies they fed him. Or perhaps they skipped town again, like we did so many times while I was growing up.

"Oh, little Lacey. Gaining the knowledge of the existence of a twin—your other half—only for me to cruelly rip it away by informing you he's long since dead."

"I think it's entirely possible you couldn't find anything other than my last name, so now you're making shit up. That seems much more plausible than I have a long-lost twin I never knew about," I say, unable to keep quiet any longer.

He snorts, rattling the chain a little. "Believe what you want. It's no consequence to me."

"Then why bring it up?"

"I thought we could commiserate."

I have no idea what he's talking about, unless he's lost someone. Maybe he's projecting his own pain onto me, but unless he assumes Mason is responsible, I don't understand why he would care.

"Why are you so set on the destruction of Synd?" Willow murmurs.

"Not the destruction of Synd, just the men running things. Unfortunately, you two were caught in the crossfire."

"Seems like a shitty plan," I mumble.

"Destruction should be met with ruination. I don't expect you to understand," he sneers.

"Are you just a prick? Or is there a point to all this?" Willow asks lazily.

The blue of his eyes dims, taking on a faraway look. Whatever memories he's immersed in have his jaw clenching and a tremble taking over his hands. His head tips to the side as his eyes fall closed, and I wonder if he'll even answer. Finally, he shakes his head, then stares at the wall, as if it holds the past within its cracks.

"The sins of the father are often dealt with by the sons. Not that it matters, as I'm down here and they're still free to rule without consequence. Now if you'll excuse me, I'm late for my appointment with my own self-loathing."

Fifty-One

Mason

The pounding on my bedroom door is nothing new, but the yelling certainly is. Sam and Lacey disappeared almost thirty minutes ago, so I'm sure it's the Kings on the other side. I take my time, splashing water on my face and slowly drying off before making my way through my bedroom. I don't live by their schedules. They forget that I may be one person, but I hold just as much power as they do. I wait until they've finished their latest attack before gently opening the door.

"Ah, Shane. What can I do for you?" I ask, almost dropping the mask I've plastered on when I spot the lot of them crowded in the corridor. I expected the Kings, but Hawk and Helms being here is a surprise.

TJ catches my eye, silently asking if he should step in, and I shake my head. Shane cranes his neck to peer behind me. My bedroom is empty, of course.

"Where are they?"

"If you're asking about Sam, then I'm not entirely sure. Why don't we take this conversation to the conference room?"

No one moves. There are more than a few hostile faces here. I'm not about to invite them into my bedroom for a meeting.

Hawk pushes Alex to the side, causing him to stumble into the wall.

"Do not fucking relegate me to a fucking conference room. Tell me where the fuck she is. Now," he snarls, crowding into my space.

"Why the hell do you care where my sister is?" I'm not even pissed. The bafflement must be clear on my face since Helms tugs Hawk back with no resistance.

"Everyone is gone. They left notes but didn't say where they were going. We tracked them here," Helms says, stopping Alex's pacing with a hand. "We're assuming they're with Sam."

"They left through the tunnels," I say, gesturing behind me at the panel still hanging open.

Hawk tries to barrel his way through again, but Helms stops him. "I thought you said it was only Sam?"

"Fuck off. You realize there's another person who's staying here, right? Lacey went through the tunnels and Sam followed."

The fact they forgot Lacey tells me all I need to know about how they will continue to treat her. I can't let this continue unless I'm ready to cut myself off from them like we were before, living our lives with little interference from the others. Maybe it's time we got back to that, or at least time for me to get back to that if I want to keep Lacey. My gut turns at the thought.

"Why don't we all calm down? We know they're here. Unless they all turned off their phones and slipped off the property…" Alex says, his voice faltering by the end.

"They didn't. I'm pretty sure they're in the basement. Talking to Roman Drake," Ren murmurs, taking TJ's vacated chair.

Everyone starts yelling at once, their voice melding into a mind-numbing roar. Sighing, I step back, intent on slamming the door in their faces, but Helms's hand shoots out. Glancing back at the others, he steps into the room and closes the door.

"I'm not taking you down there," I say, making my way to my closet and pulling out a hoodie.

"Didn't ask you to. Kenzie is quite capable of taking care of herself." He collapses in a chair, pulling his phone from his pocket.

"Not concerned about Willow?"

"She'll be fine. She's with the others. Hawk still spirals when she's not in his back pocket. Not surprising with the shit that's gone down with her."

He opens his mouth but is cut off by more pounding on the door. Heaving to his feet, he saunters over and opens it. When Hawk tries to push his way inside, Helms shoves him back, closing it again.

"Want to tell me what you've got planned?" I ask, leaning against the wall and nodding to where the others are yelling again.

"They need to calm the fuck down. I'm not going to deal with their childish shit. Our women are fine. Better me doing this now, rather than the girls when they get back."

A scuffle has me turning toward the panel and I raise an eyebrow as Willow steps through. Her eyes widen before finding mine. She presses a finger to her lips, fading back into the shadows. I turn away, waiting for Helms to face me.

"If our women do get back before they've calmed down, they probably shouldn't slip out without a word. That would probably piss some people off," he calls, raising his voice.

Grinning, I drop my chin to my chest. "I'm sure they wouldn't want anyone to worry."

Helms rolls his eyes. "While we're waiting, you want to fill me in on why you flipped?"

I debate not going into it. When we left the meeting, I was dead set on Lacey staying as far away as possible from Roman Drake. After she slipped off, I calmed down enough to realize she can take care of herself. If she has another episode, Sam will be there to help her. Add that to the fact they're all treating Lacey like she's an interloper, and I was done with their bullshit.

After all our families have been through the last year, I doubt Sam will be able to get any info from Drake. He's clearly done his own research on us and will only reveal whatever he thinks will get a reaction from us. The fact he knows Lacey's last name and alias shows he's dug deep into our pasts, ferreting out any hidden secrets.

"Like you said, they're capable of taking care of themselves. Which Lacey kindly reminded me of when we got home."

Helms bursts out laughing, tipping his head back. The voices behind the wood cut off. I wouldn't be surprised if they had their ears pressed to the door. The image of Alex finding a glass to hear better has me chuckling.

"Are we interrupting something?" Sam asks, leaning against the wall next to the panel as the others file into my bedroom.

I catch Lacey's eye, and she widens them before glancing at Helms. Someone knocks on the bedroom door, but it's calm this time around. Willow sighs, shaking her head.

"You might as well let them in. Or better yet, we could go to the conference room. You have one of those here too, right?" Willow says, eyeing the door as she gestures back to the tunnels.

"Yes, but I doubt they'll meet you there. They're not exactly happy you slipped off without a word," I say.

"Don't start, Kenzie," Helms cuts off whatever Mac is about to say. She rolls her eyes as she crosses her arms. "Leaving a note saying 'be back later—don't freak out' doesn't count."

Lacey slides next to me, slipping her hand in mine. With everything going on lately, we've barely scratched the surface of shit we need to hash out, and it's tearing me up inside. I'm not used to talking with someone about my decisions, but I need to start. If I want Lacey to stay when all this is over, I need to start acting like it.

Another knock comes. "Open up, Princess. I can hear you in there. You can't hide forever."

Sam sighs, unraveling her arms, before stomping over and ripping open the door. Shane's face softens as he scans her, probably checking for injuries. It's the same thing I did when Lacey appeared. I turn away, not wanting to notice the similarities between our relationships.

"Did you get anything?" I murmur, dipping my head to Lacey's.

She subtly nods, tilting her head, and I press a kiss to her temple. A shiver runs through her, and I wish I could throw everyone else out. The need to be deep inside her overrides my common sense. We don't have time for me to bend her over and fuck her. Dealing with Roman Drake should be at the top of my list. As I squeeze her hip, though, the only thing I want is to remind myself she's here and safe.

"Let's get this over with. The sooner we talk, the sooner I'm back in that sweet little pussy of yours," I whisper in her ear.

Her hand shoots out, smacking me in the chest. Grinning, I pull her from the room, following the others. I'd rather not have another long, drawn-out meeting with them, but I can't keep pushing them away. This clearly affects all of Synd in one way or another.

Settling Lacey at the head of the long conference table, I wait until the rest are seated before taking my own. I didn't care about never meeting here before when I was wallowing in my own misery. Now it grates on my nerves as I see the dust gathered on the tabletop.

"Well, Sam? Start talking," Shane commands, brows pulled low.

She holds up her hands. "I get that you're all pissy because we went off without you, but slow your roll. You think you're the queen bee or something, presiding over us all. Check yourself, because your attitude is pissing everyone off. Besides, I didn't even go in the room."

Willow raises her hand, like we're back in school. "Um, Lacey and I went in. We thought that would be less intimidating."

I lean in, whispering in Lacey's ear, "You going to tell them about your special daggers?"

"They're not special and absolutely not," she hisses through clenched teeth. "I didn't tell you about them so you could bring them up to mock me."

Willow clears her throat, pursing her lips when my eyes meet hers.

"Anyways, Drake—are we calling him Drake or Roman? It's confusing with two first names," Willow says, glancing around.

Lacey's hand hits the table. "That's what I said!"

Willow grins. "Well, we'll call him Roman for now. He seems to be set on the destruction of the families who run Synd. He knows quite a bit about us, probably our pasts as well. However, he said something about the sins of the father. I believe this is a vendetta he's carrying out in his dad's name."

"What did he reveal about our pasts?" Alex asks, eyes narrowed as his hands curl into fists.

Willow's face blanks before glancing at Lacey, shaking her head. Whatever happened in the basement had a much deeper effect on her than she's willing to discuss with so many people around. Hawk's fingers lace together with hers, and she pulls in a calming breath.

"He knows about Willow's stepfather and her mother. Taunted her with them," Sam murmurs, eyes fixed on Willow.

Lacey clears her throat. "Obviously, he knows I'm the hacker, Nemesis. Somehow, he found my last name. Could be another Webb since I dropped it a long time ago. I'll dig around, try to figure out how he found me. I think he has some bad intel, though."

"Why do you think that?" Ren asks.

"He said I have a long-lost twin brother who died. Except I'm an only child."

"Could you ask your parents?" Alex asks.

"No. I'm pretty sure they're dead."

"Pretty sure doesn't really count here, Lacey," Ren mutters.

"I haven't spoken to my parents in over a decade. And they've been dead to me long before that. There is nothing to tie them to me. Not that I would ask them even if that weren't the case. If I had a twin, he would have died long before I could remember, which defeats the purpose of Drake taunting me with his memory."

I reach out, lacing our fingers together. She tips her chin up, challenging anyone to refute what she's saying. She's stayed hidden for so long, I'm sure revealing anything about her past is difficult. I've never pried. I didn't have the opportunity in the beginning, and I didn't want to after that. Whatever she wanted to tell me was fine. Prying information out of her would only hurt her, and I can't handle that. I've seen her suffer enough.

"What if he's not taunting?"

Lacey scrunches her nose. "Seemed like taunting to me."

"Listen, I don't think it matters how much he knows. It seemed like he was throwing my mother's death in my face, but he actually just asked me if I knew what happened. What if, when he was talking about your name, he was referencing Nemesis, not Webb? And your supposed twin brother? He said he brought it up to commiserate. Something doesn't add up with him. But he almost seemed happy when I told him Joseph was dead." Willow says. Hawk's face morphs, but she rubs his arm.

"What else, Willow?" Helms asks gruffly.

"He talked about the sins of the father and how he wanted to bring down the men running Synd. The thing is, he's not going to the media. He's focused on destroying your base. If he can chip away at that, then using us against you is the logical next step, but it's almost as if his heart isn't in it. Where does he go next if he's not attacking the shipments?"

"He's going after the money, the shipments, fucking with our ability to keep our people safe. That will destroy the confidence of the men under us, as well as the community," Helms says.

"A solid plan, but he fucked up when he told me where you were, Willow," I interject. For a mastermind who's been terrorizing us for weeks, he's not very good at his job.

Alex's head whips up, glancing around as if he's just noticed where he is. Shane opens his mouth, but Sam clamps her hand on his arm, eyes fixed on Alex. Soon, we're all staring at him, waiting for him to reveal whatever he just figured out. His tongue darts out and his gaze skips around before settling on Ren, of all people. Ren nods before burying his head in his tablet, fingers flying over the screen.

"I don't think Drake was the one who texted you." Alex says, licking his lips. "I think it was Victor. And I think he's been trying to piece together what's been going on. Victor's been trying to save us."

Fifty-Two

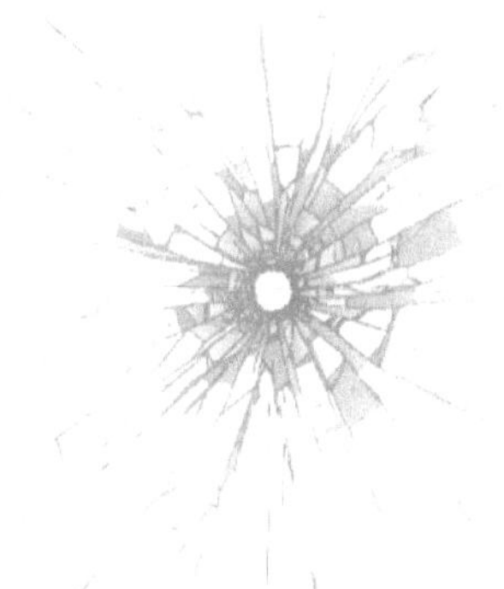

Lacey

"Sam, we really shouldn't be down here again," I whisper, my stomach plummeting when I miss the last step and I catch myself. "Especially in the middle of the night."

The darkness pressing down on me makes me think I'm about to run into something. Sam refused to let me bring my phone, and I'm regretting it now.

"Shit is still happening. The guys seem to think everything will calm down since we have Drake locked up, but he either has a partner in crime or there's someone else. He's the only one who can give us any insight into who blew the warehouse he took Willow to. And who is still fucking with us."

"He lured Mason there using Willow as bait, and then the charges went off too early. It's the most plausible explanation," I say.

"Unless Alex is right," she mutters.

I can't tell where Sam is, and her silence makes my movements feel like an explosion in this dead space. I wish I could be as quiet as she is. There's no one down here to overhear us, but the darkness is deceiving.

"But if my uncle was the one who warned Mason, then Roman wasn't expecting him. Which means he had other plans and then was surprised by my brother's appearance. He wouldn't blow the place with himself in it. That defeats the purpose of doing all this."

We stop in front of the heavy metal door. Sam thinks she can get answers from him, and I have no doubt that she can. I just don't know if I can stomach watching her. I wasn't exactly tortured, but the scar on my face says otherwise. Sam in Wraith mode would decimate anyone who tried to torture her. Personally, the thought makes my stomach fold in on itself.

"Here's the plan. You're going to go in there and ask him the questions and if he doesn't answer, I'll give him a little incentive to talk." She pats her pocket, or maybe it's her thigh, I don't know.

"I don't know if I can handle watching you…"

I swallow hard, fighting against the bile traveling its way up my throat. I can't even finish the sentence, knowing firsthand what it feels like for a blade to break skin, how easily it slices through.

I spin, leaning a hand against the wall while I gag. Nothing comes up, but a sour taste invades my mouth. Sam rubs my back, and I can't tell whether it's helping or making things worse. I wave her off when I'm pretty sure I'm done, although all it'll take is her pulling out a dagger for me to spiral again.

"There's other ways of getting someone to talk. No knives." She pulls a gun from her back, and I shudder. "Seriously? What the hell did they do to you?"

"I'm fine, just don't make me use that thing and I'll be okay. Let's get this over with."

I'm still not sure what questions she wants me to ask. I guess I'll just wing it and hope for the best. The keypad rings through the silence and the lock thuds open. She shoos me away when I try to step through first, sliding into the narrow gap, and I follow.

I expected it to be dark, but bright light floods the room. I'm sure it's some sort of sleep deprivation thing. Roman is propped against the far wall, shackle still in place, fast asleep. Sam pulls a baggie from her pocket and chucks it at him, hitting him square in the face. He scowls, blue eyes opening into slits.

"There are other ways of waking a person, Ms. Byrns." His voice is guttural, much deeper than before. It's been nearly two weeks since we caught him, and apparently the only people he's talked to are Willow, Alex, and me.

"Yeah, but that's a brownie. Homemade. Don't worry, there's no weed in it. Or poison."

She pulls out another baggie, offering me a dessert, but I shake my head. I'd rather not puke. That would ruin chocolate for a while, and I'm rather fond of it. She shrugs, shoving half in her mouth before sweeping out her hand and bowing for me to take the lead.

"Come for another little chat, Ms. Webb?"

Glancing around the room, I search for something to say. I'm supposed to ask questions, but my mind blanks. Sighing, I lean against the table. Sam bounds over, leaping up to settle on top of the metal, resting against the wall to finish her snack.

"Why do you keep using our last names?" I ask, scrunching my nose up. It's the only question that pops in my head.

He tilts his head, breaking off a piece of the brownie and tasting it. "Perhaps it's a tactic to disarm you. Or maybe I respect you enough to be polite."

"Or it could be a force of habit," I murmur.

My hand flies to my pocket for my phone, but I huff when there's nothing there. Fucking Sam, making me leave it behind. I'm sure she thinks it'll take longer for Mason to find us then, but I left a note. The last thing I want to do is make him think I was kidnapped again. Neither of us needs that type of panic in our lives.

"Someone's wheels are turning," he chirps, completely at odds with his rugged exterior. He takes another bite of the brownie before shoving the entire thing in his mouth.

"Oh shit. You're him. No, not him. Someone else. Wait, why would you tell us your name then? That doesn't make sense."

"What the fuck are you talking about Lacey," Sam hisses, but I wave her away.

I'm mostly talking to myself, staring at a spot on the far wall. There's only so much information I can hold in my head at once and dredging up something I looked into months ago isn't easy.

"Marcus Erickson. Roman Drake. Oh, that's clever."

"Uh, you want to share with the rest of the class?" Sam says around a mouthful of what looks to be a lemon bar.

"Marcus Antonius was a famous Roman. Leif Erickson was a famous Norseman. Drake is old Norse. He buried the money he stole from Mason under the name Marcus Erickson. Not only that, but Mr. Drake here used to live in Synd. Didn't you?"

I knew Roman was behind Mason's missing money, but I couldn't find the link. He didn't make it very hard to recover, though. It took me all of an hour once I finally sat down to do it. He's able to dig into my very well hidden past and yet not hide money? Something isn't adding up.

"Look at you, figuring out all of my secrets. Although, I didn't hide those things. Not really if you knew where to look. The question is, can you find the others?"

"What I don't get is why blow the warehouse? You never intended to kill Willow unless it was necessary. Plus, why would you kill yourself? Your mission wasn't complete, even if Mason was dead."

"How do you know that wasn't the end goal?" he asks, raising an eyebrow.

I pace, trying to fit the rest of the pieces into a puzzle I don't have a picture for. Roman wouldn't have been very old when he left Synd, if he's related to the Drakes I found in the article.

While it may seem like his moves were erratic, when I pull back and look at everything he's done, I realize the unpredictability *was* the plan all along. And it was executed perfectly. Subtle moves we barely saw, chipping away at the base, but everyone was blinded by the missing shipments and the hits on the safe houses. The explosions and car bombs covered the meetings with people like the mayor and police chief.

"Sins of the father. You're carrying out your father's vendetta against the families. It was never about Mason or the others. It was always the families. But why tell Mason you had Willow?" I ask, and he scowls.

"Unless it wasn't him," Sam mumbles.

"Clever, but you still haven't ferreted out the rest. And if you brought that thing along to motivate me, you'll be surprised to learn I'd rather die than reveal anything," he says, pointing at Sam.

"Hey, this thing has a name. And why would you be scared of little ole me?" She bats her lashes at him.

"Would you prefer me to call you the Wraith?"

I expect her to throw a knife at him, shoot him, maybe attack him, but instead she smirks. He narrows his eyes, expression turning sour. Apparently, he had the same thoughts I did. Either she doesn't think he's getting out of here alive, or she thinks her non-reaction will have a greater effect on him.

"You can call me whatever you want, sweet cheeks. Personally, I think you fucked up and you're attempting to save your pride. But that could just be me." She gives him a simpering smile, pulling out her knife and using it to pick at her nails.

I turn away, suppressing a shudder. Roman gazes at me, tilting his head. His eyes focus on the scar on my face, and I swear it burns. I don't owe him an explanation. I refuse to be ashamed of something I had no control over. No matter how much I've felt otherwise, I couldn't have saved myself.

"I didn't set the bombs. I'm many things, but I'm not ignorant. Now that I'm stuck in here, my operation has ground to a halt, and I'm sure I won't accomplish anything I set out to do. I'm sure your men will recover just fine." Bitterness laces his tone.

I refuse to glance away from him, no matter how much I want to see what Sam is thinking. Her face is probably firmly behind a mask, anyway. She's much better at this than I am. While I hide behind a screen, she hides her emotions, using the shadows to shape what others want to see.

"Any idea who tried to blow your ass up? I'd like to thank them for their effort." Sam smirks, pulling out another baggie full of brownies and tosses him one.

He catches it with one hand, studying her the entire time. We're not very subtle and he's not stupid. We all know we're fishing for information, but I'm banking on him wanting to figure out who took out the building as much as we do. Sam bribing him with desserts instead of torturing him isn't how I saw this going. I snort, tucking my chin to my chest.

"Depends on what was used."

"Oh, a little homemade concoction of C-4 and dynamite. It was hard to decipher anything beyond that."

"Pretty standard shit. It's not enough to go on, which you're well aware of. So, why ask me? Wanting to connect with my enemies? Sorry to break your heart, but the only villains in my story are the men whose beds you occupy every night," he sneers.

Silence descends as Sam munches away, seeming to not have a care in the world. Drake's eyes are fixed on me. No, not me—on my scar. Most people's eyes skip over it, probably so I'm not as self-conscious about it. In reality, I think about it less and less these days, unless I'm in the throes of an episode.

"Something you needed?" I snap when I can't take it anymore.

"You never answered my question."

"You're going to have to be a little more specific if you want answers. And be prepared to give us something in exchange," I say, crossing my arms. Sam's eyes bounce between us, her dessert frozen halfway to her mouth.

He tips his chin at me. "How did you acquire that scar? It wasn't there a few months ago."

"The real question is, why are you pretending you don't already know?"

Doubt clouds my mind, seeping into my memories of my time in captivity. I could have sworn someone mentioned the name Drake. Although I was half-delirious for a lot of it, wishing for the nightmare to end. Those men usually referred to him as boss, but once or twice they let his name slip. I'd put money on it. Willow's words float through my mind, making me question everything.

"I am many things—a manipulator, a villain, and a monster, just to name a few—but I am not a liar. So, when I say I have no idea how your pretty little face was carved up, trust those words to be truthful."

He looks so earnest, listing his faults in the same breath as his virtues. Sam tilts her head, narrowing her eyes at him, before turning to me. She's probably better at deciphering lies. I'm sure she can spot them from a mile away within her line of work. She blinks once, as if I'm supposed to know what that means. She scowls, then nods her head, as if she believes him.

"I'll humor you then. Some men kidnapped me, threw me in a hole, then moved me to an old office building, all while starving me. Their leader, Razor—" I swallow hard as Roman snorts at the name. "Decided I needed some extra motivation to talk."

His brows pull low, and I swear he's biting the inside of his cheek. "Motivation to talk about what?"

"Mason, of course. I thought that was obvious. And I'm pretty sure they mentioned *you* by name."

His eyebrows pop up at that revelation. He shakes his head before running a hand through his already mussed hair.

"I can't claim to know everyone I was leading, but I certainly did not have a Razor in my crew, Ms. Webb."

"I don't believe you," I hiss, stepping forward, and Sam's hand shoots out.

I wasn't going to get near enough for him to hurt me. I may not be good at interrogating someone, but I'm smart enough to not put myself in the line of fire. Roman didn't even notice. He's dropped his chin to his chest, muttering to himself. When his fingers push through the blond strands again, I realize his hand is trembling.

"Are you sure you didn't put anything in the brownies?" I mutter from the corner of my mouth.

"Definitely not. Ren made them—figured since my handing out sweets in the Barrens works so well for them to open up that it might work on him. He knows I wouldn't be able to resist eating some. He would have given me a heads up," Sam mutters. "It looks like he's having a breakdown, but we haven't even done anything to him yet."

Roman clears his throat, but his voice is still shaky when he speaks. "These men—are they dead?"

"Of course they are," Sam snaps, as if it'd be a personal insult if her brother hadn't shot them all.

"Good. That's good."

"Why is that good?" I ask, scrunching my nose.

I understand why it's good for me—for us—but for Roman? It doesn't make sense. Wouldn't he want them to hurt me? To kill me? It would have been a surefire way to hurt the mafia families, even with the stilted relationship Mason and I had then.

"I believe this was a coincidence," he finally says, clearing his throat again. "I had nothing to do with your kidnapping. So perhaps Byrns has more enemies than just me. A lower gang or some such thing."

He pulls out a bottle of water, practically chugging the entire thing in one go. It's strange to see this man who seems so in control of his emotions dissolve before our eyes.

"I don't believe in coincidences," Sam says.

"Well, you'd better hope it is because the alternative will make you wish I was still the one terrorizing you."

Fifty-Three

Mason

"You've got to be fucking kidding me. You went alone? Who the hell does that?" I yell, pacing across my bedroom floor.

It's the middle of the night, yet every light blazes in the room. With the encroaching problems we've had, I upped the protocols of lock down to a level three, to no avail. Usually, they wouldn't include lighting up the night like we're on the freaking sun.

When the threats started pouring in this afternoon, I wasn't about to risk anyone's safety, especially Lacey's. She keeps insisting she's fine and I don't have to watch her, but as soon as I leave her alone, she pulls some bullshit. At least she wasn't taken again.

"I wasn't alone. I was with Sam, which I *thought* you'd be happy about." She glares at me from where she's posted up against my headboard.

"Happy? For fuck's sake, Lacey. Just yesterday you were saying you had too much shit piled on top of you, and then you take it upon yourself to pull info from a man who tried to blow me up," I bellow. She grimaces, then bites her lip. "What's that look for?"

"Uh, Sam and I don't think he set the bombs."

"Because of course he wouldn't lie," I grumble.

"When Sam described them, he said he was the only villain in this story. He's been pretty clear he works alone and that everything should have ground to a halt now that he's locked up."

I throw my hands up, pacing away from her. Why they keep insisting there's someone else at fault is beyond me. I slam the closet door behind me and brace my hands on the dresser. Lacey going with the others to see Drake was one thing. Even if I wasn't explicitly told that's where they were going, I figured it out. This feels like she deliberately kept it from me, waiting until I was out of the house to sneak away.

"Are you pissed I went down there or that I didn't clear it with you first?"

I didn't hear her come in, and I refuse to turn around. I'm not ready for her to explain her reasons. The more I'm around her, the further I fall. All she has to do is pin me with her green eyes and I forget everything I was angry about. Whatever spell she's put me under, I've gone in to willingly. Finding the balance between giving into her and worrying about her is as elusive as the enemies still plaguing us.

"Does that even matter to you? Or would you do whatever you want, regardless of how I feel about it?"

"This is ridiculous. I keep telling you I'm perfectly capable of taking care of myself," she huffs, and I spin around. "And don't say I couldn't before. I never once asked you to save me. You made those choices on your own. You never once asked me what I wanted. You ran roughshod over me every time I brought up something you didn't agree with."

I open my mouth, then snap it shut when nothing comes out. She might be right, but I'm not going to tell her that. She crosses her arms, raising an eyebrow and daring me to dispute her claims.

"And what would have happened had I not? You'd probably be dead."

She jerks back as if I've slapped her. We've never talked about how she acted after I pulled her from the office building. Her hallucinations might have tapered off, but she still wakes up almost every night, fighting some invisible force that has a grip on her mind. I hold her through it, never saying a word. I bring her to the shower, letting the water wash away what my words never could. I coax her body into a frenzy, using pleasure to erase whatever lives under her skin.

To throw the words at her feet, expecting her to gather them up on her own, isn't fair. Reaching for her, I drop my hand as she turns to the door. Our inability to connect grates on my nerves. After we've dealt with everything, convincing her to stay will be hard. If I let her walk out of here, she'll vanish into her office, ignoring everyone around her, including me.

"What did you find?" I ask before she disappears.

I don't care, but it's the only thing I can think of to get her to stay. She's more important than my pride, and fighting against it will only push her away. We can't keep doing this or we'll never make it.

She swings around, leaning against the closed door. "Are you going to go nuclear again?"

Prowling closer, I press my body into hers, leaning an arm over her head. Her breath hitches as she drops her arms to her sides.

"That, Kitten, was not nuclear. That wasn't even close."

"Seemed pretty close to me," she mutters, glancing away.

I guide her eyes back to mine. "I know you can take care of shit, but my world isn't run from behind a screen. It's hands-on and dangerous. I don't want you suffering because I fucked up."

"Have you ever gone over the edge?" she whispers.

"If someone tries to take you from me, hurt you," I murmur, tracing her scar before tipping her chin up, "you'll get a front-row seat to the detonation."

Capturing her mouth with mine, I wrap my hand around her neck, holding her in place for me to devour. Her fingers creep under the hem of my shirt, nails digging into my skin. I drink her in, her essence filling my pores and dousing my senses.

I rip my mouth from hers, whipping her shirt over her head, and mine follows. I unhook her bra and her tit falls into my waiting hand. Swooping down, I suck her nipple into my mouth, and her fingers dig into my scalp. I switch to the other, giving it the attention it deserves, and her head thumps back against the door as she moans.

Our pants land on top of the rest of our clothes. I grab her hips, lifting her up and her legs wind around my waist as I slam into her. I groan, digging my fingers into her ass. She sighs, and something in me slots into place. I only feel whole when I'm inside her. She heals something within me. I don't want to examine it too closely, afraid it will slip away.

"Fucking mine," I grunt, thrusting into her. "So fucking wet for me."

"Harder," she moans.

Pressing my body into hers, I pound into her as her pussy clenches around me. She digs her nails into my skin, dragging them down before pinching my nipple. I jerk back and snarl, even as her teeth sink into my neck. I swear she's breaking skin, but it only spurs me on. When her hand sneaks between our bodies, I almost lose it as she circles her clit.

Her pussy spasms around my cock, and she shudders, a low moan leaving her. Slowing, I draw out her orgasm as long as possible until she becomes pliant in my arms and her legs drop from my waist.

"Oh, Kitten. You didn't think we were done, did you?"

She smirks, pushing against my chest, and I slip from her, gasping as her pussy clings to my cock. My heart stutters along with my breath when she sinks to her knees, licking her lips. When her hand wraps around my base, I slap my hand against the wall, burying the other in her hair.

"Be a good girl and clean off my cock."

She glances up, raising an eyebrow as she squeezes.

"Be a good boy and let me take care of you," she purrs.

My reply is lost in the wake of her lips closing over the tip. She hums, and I'm close to coming down her throat. Gritting my teeth, I throw my head back. Her mouth is sweet torture as her tongue licks up my cock. It takes everything in me not to twist my hand in her locks and fuck her mouth.

When she grazes her teeth along my length, my eyes fly open. I almost come, intoxicated by the sight of her on her knees. She gazes up at me, sucking hard, and I groan long and low. My hips move of their own accord, and I push forward, my cock hitting the back of her throat. I don't slow, even when she gags.

"Fuck, Kitten. I'm going to come down your throat, and you'll swallow every last drop." I'm lost in the sensations, until her head jerks back and my cock slips from her lips.

Lacey hangs her head, panting, and I stroke her cheek, waiting for her to recover. Slowly, she lifts her head to meet my eyes, and she smirks. I thought I hurt her, but desire swims in her eyes. The need for control rushes through me. Gripping my cock, I stroke it once to ease the tension, intent on her finishing what she started.

Tilting my head, I track her movements as she pushes to her feet. She slips out the door before I realize what she's doing, and I rush after her. Whipping a blanket off the bed, she giggles as she races for the bathroom and slams the door behind her, taking any hope of my own orgasm with her.

"What the hell crawled up your ass and died?" Shane mutters.

"Maybe the fact that my territory is going to shit, I'm constantly terrified Lacey's going to go missing again, or the fact that we're standing in front of this fucking door ready to ask our enemy for help. Couldn't be any of those options, could it?" I sneer, but he's already shaking his head.

"Pretty sure he's not getting laid," Helms says, leaning against the wall behind me.

"Mind your own fucking business, Helms."

Shane chuckles, leaning next to Helms and crossing his arms. "You gonna put in the code, or are you trying to seduce it open?"

"If this is how he woos Lacey, no wonder she's shooting him down." Helms snorts.

"For fuck's sake," I mutter, jabbing at the keypad.

I'm glad I pulled the guard from down here. There's no way Drake can escape anyway, so the extra protection isn't needed. I have no doubt Sam could have removed anyone I put down here, but at least I didn't have to deal with someone complaining.

The keypad beeps, the thud of the lock echoing off the stones. Glancing back at the others, Shane nods and I pull open the heavy door. I jerk back, almost plowing into Helms. I expected light, but it's pitch black inside the room. The click of a hammer rings out and Shane steps up next to me, gun in hand. Reaching around the door frame, I hit the switch, flooding the space with light.

Blinking back the spots in my vision, I find Roman Drake sitting against the far wall, still tethered to the chain. I wasn't about to leave him tied to a chair. The cleanup from something like that isn't a pleasant task, but I wouldn't trust one of my men to deal with his body if it came to that. The fewer people outside our circle who know he's down here, the better.

"Finally. What'll it be, boys? Questions or torture first? Ooh, or are we doing a two-for-one deal?" Drake asks, rubbing his hands together.

Shane and Helms file in behind me, fanning out as much as we can in the narrow room. I tip my chin to Shane, and he scowls as he puts his gun away. Helms is already buried in his phone, but his nostrils flair before he stuffs it in his pocket. I forgot to tell him there's no service in this concrete block.

"We have some questions you'll be answering for us," I say, tucking my hands in my pockets.

"Is that so? Perhaps you could soften me up first. Samantha was nice enough to bring me brownies. Do you have any offerings?" He raises an eyebrow, smirking.

Shane tenses, a rumble in his chest. We can't afford him flying off the handle and shooting Drake. There's too much information he holds. With the supply lines decimated and Drake's underlings still running amok, we need some insight on how to stop them. They're scattered around the city, and we have no way of tracking them all down.

"Who are you working with?" Helms asks.

Drake chuckles, rolling his head to the side. "As if I would leave this in someone else's hands."

"A regular one-man show. How unfortunate for you," Helms growls.

"Hardly. I merely know what bringing others in on secrets does. Look at you three. Once divided, living and dying separately. Now, you're all one big, happy family, who weakened their positions in the process."

I snort. "How do you figure?"

I could spout quotes at him, citing books and leaders who expound on allies and combining forces, but I'm not here to convince him he fucked up by not having anyone with him. In fact, he's probably lying, which is much more likely. I wouldn't give up who I was working with, either. If it comes out he's aligned with Victor, though, I don't know whether I'll laugh or tip over the edge.

"The moment you all fell in love, you weakened yourselves. King knows. It eats away at him, wondering when Samantha will be used against him. Helms realizes it too. Eventually, they'll be taken with only one purpose in mind. Your enemies won't care about them. Their goal will be to hit you where it hurts, taking the one thing you can't live without."

"Is that why you took Willow?" Helms asks, before I can interject.

Drake waves away Helms's question. "A means to an end. I suppose that was part of it, but she holds knowledge I required."

"And Lacey? Why'd you kidnap her?" I hold my breath, trying to tap down on the rage swirling within me.

He scowls, nostrils flaring. "As I informed Ms. Webb, I have nothing to do with her being taken. I am many things, but I draw the line at intentionally harming women."

"Except you hurt Willow," Helms says.

"Did I? Or did I merely take her for a short drive? She would have been returned whole and virtually unscathed when I was done speaking with her. It wasn't until Byrns showed up that she was harmed, and even then, she walked away with very few injuries from what I saw."

"What I can't understand is how you went so fucking soft in the span of, what, a couple weeks?" Shane sneers and Drake swings his eyes to the mafia leader. "Carve Lacey up, but leave Willow untouched? Weak."

"I didn't carve her up," he growls, heaving to his feet. "Besides, if I had Nemesis in my clutches, wouldn't it stand to reason that I would use her hacking skills to further my plot? I also had the opportunity to snatch her multiple times, yet never did. So perhaps before you start throwing around accusations, you should dedicate some of your brain power to thinking logically. I didn't fucking take her."

It takes everything in me not to react. My mind blanks, at a loss for where to go from here. I need to steer the conversation back on track, but I'm frozen, wanting to race back to make sure she's safe. Shane shifts and I whip my head to him. He subtly shakes his head, eyes fixed on Drake, and I roll my neck, trying to ease the tension.

"We seem to have hit a nerve," Helms says.

Drake drops down, leaning against the wall again. "I don't take kindly to being accused of hurting women."

Shane clears his throat. "Let's pretend we believe that you're working alone. Why blow up the warehouse while you were in it? Unless that was a mistake you're not willing to admit."

"Interesting you don't believe your woman. I've already had this conversation. I fail to see how having it again will change anything. Now, if you'll excuse me, I have some wallowing to do." His eyes fall closed as he crosses his arms over his chest.

Shane turns to leave, but I hold up my hand, glancing at Helms. He tucks his chin to his chest, sighing. Torturing Drake will get us nowhere. I'm sure we all realize that.

If their training was anywhere close to mine, they'd never break under pressure. Being taught when to use those methods to get someone talking was just as important as withstanding the pain. Drake seems like one of us, never giving in or handing over more than he intends. Although, apparently pushing him cracks his resolve. Or maybe it's only the accusation of harming a woman.

"What's the alternative?" I tilt my head as his eyes fly open.

"You're going to have to be a little more specific," he drawls.

"Cut the bullshit, Drake. If you're not responsible for the warehouse blowing up, then someone is trying to take over your operation. Shouldn't that piss you off? If you're so intent on our deaths, then why check out now?"

I can practically see the gears in his head turning as he eyes me. He opens his mouth, then snaps it shut. Helms pushes off the table and moves past me. Drake tracks his movements, narrowing his eyes. Helms didn't want to come in the first place, saying it was a waste of time. The only reason he did was to show a unified front.

"There are only two people I personally know who would like to see you three in the ground."

"Clearly, you're one. Who's the other?" Shane asks.

"My father," Drake says, tipping his chin up. "But he's dead."

Helms mumbles something to Shane, but I'm focused on Drake. He raises an eyebrow, challenging me to figure it out. Unless he's taunting me, which is much more plausible.

"Why did you tell Willow your name? There was no reason. You could have kept it to yourself."

Drake presses his lips into a thin line, and I wait, but he doesn't answer.

"You were going to set her free, and you knew she'd tell the rest of us. You weren't ready to reveal who you were, but then I showed up. You weren't expecting me, were you?"

"You definitely weren't a welcome addition to the party," he sneers, but his heart isn't in it.

"You weren't ready for us to know who you are," I murmur. "Unless you're protecting someone?"

What little color there is drains from Drake's face and then his blue eyes find mine. I glance at Helms and Shane, confusion mirrored on their faces.

"I have no one left to protect," he replies bitterly.

"Then this is all for what? To teach us a lesson? To take over Synd?" Helms asks.

Drake shakes his head, and I wonder what memories are floating through his mind. Whatever he's ultimately after, he won't be accomplishing it from my dungeon. Usually, I'd assume he was lying, covering his own ass in hopes he'll eventually escape. Instead, Drake seems resigned to his fate, as if his heart was never really in it.

"What else did you have planned? After decimating us financially and fucking with our territories, what then?"

Drake tilts his head, brows pulling low as he eyes me.

"Interesting," he murmurs.

Shane steps forward, blocking my view of the battered man. "Give me a name and we'll make it a quick death."

Drake's sharp laugh rings throughout the space, and Shane's shoulders stiffen.

"There are no names. No more grand plans. No more disasters hiding in wait. Whoever blew the warehouse effectively cut off my balls and landed me here. You're better off searching for them rather than picking my brain for information that doesn't exist."

"You're hiding something, and we're going to figure out what it is sooner or later," Shane threatens.

"There are a great many things I'm hiding, King. But none of them will help you find out who else is out there. But I can assure you, their timeline is not nearly as long as mine was."

Throwing up my hands, I make my way to the door. All this man does is speak in riddles. I wouldn't even be surprised if he was merely the scapegoat for someone else. We might have thought we caught the culprit, only to be blindsided when the real villain reveals themselves. Either way, Drake knows something, but I doubt we'll get any more information from him.

Fifty-Four

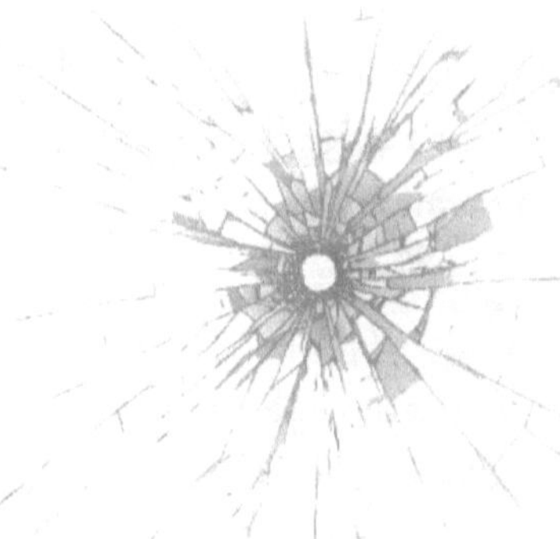

"Is it weird being here when you used to work here?" Willow asks softly.

I'm stuffed in the corner of a booth at the Flaming Skillet, tracking Mia's movements. We used to work together and then I disappeared. I don't know how she'll react to seeing me again. We weren't close, but then again, I never formed friendships at the random jobs I've picked up over the years. Some places made it easier than others to slip away, but this one was the hardest.

"I don't know. I don't normally come back. Mia might be pissed I skipped out on her."

"She's a good egg. I'm sure it'll be fine." She pats my arm, glancing around the space.

"So, let's put it all out there," Sam says, sliding next to Mac. "No one is pissed at you."

"I am," Mac mumbles, glancing out the window.

Sam sighs, shaking her head. "Okay, Mac is upset, for obvious reasons. But it's not your fault that Willow was kidnapped."

I bite my tongue, wanting to blast them. None of this is my fault, but if they need someone to blame, then I'd rather it be me than Mason. He's been the bad guy in their eyes long enough. I'm sure these women don't care either way, but they'll back their men. Mason might not say anything, but I can tell it bothers him. Every time someone comments on him not doing enough, his face tightens and he checks out.

"She didn't exactly help the situation," Mac mutters.

"We've been through this, Mac. You need to look at the big picture," Willow says. Mac sighs, her face falling the slightest bit.

"You know it's not your fault either, right?" I mumble, then clamp my lips together. I didn't mean for them to come out, but of course I couldn't keep my mouth shut.

I've never been in this position before. When I was growing up, we moved too often for me to become a part of a group. Then I fell into hacking and kept myself on the outside to protect my identity. I don't know how to have these conversations, especially with women who are so close. They understand how to have these kinds of relationships, and I am woefully unprepared.

Mac scowls, crossing her arms and sliding down in the seat. "You helped him."

I should have seen this confrontation coming. I knew it was unlikely Mac would forget our altercation in the alley. She had the brilliant idea that I could help her find her missing brother. Her face was so hopeful, I couldn't lie to her.

"Your brother texted me before he left Synd. I only helped Dante because he came when Helms called. I didn't ask what he was going to do with an alias."

Her body shoots upright, leaning across the table to hiss, "You could have fucking told me. After, when you knew I was searching for him, you could have said you helped him. Or tracked him down."

"He doesn't want to be found, Mac," I whisper, glancing around the thankfully empty restaurant. "Besides, I didn't know he was missing until Willow came to town."

She scoffs, leaning back again, and Sam glares at her.

"I realize you're upset, but I did for him what I would do for any of you. I protected him as best I could."

"So, where is he, then?" she snarls.

"I don't know. He told me not to search for him. He said to wait for his call. I have some alerts set up in Rima, just in case. I have my suspicions, but so do you."

Her face falls, tears filling her eyes before she swipes them away. It takes a couple minutes for her to pull herself together and I glance out the window. No one wants an audience while they're losing it. I know that all too well.

"Sorry I was a bitch. With Dante missing and you refusing to help, only to find out you knew, I lost my head. Then everyone was saying you're like some miracle worker and yet you couldn't find Willow's stalker, and then you ghosted everyone."

"To be fair, I didn't ghost anyone. I was being held hostage by *her* brother." I point at Sam, whose wide eyes find me.

Everyone busts out laughing as Mia approaches the table. I duck my head, sneaking glances at the server who grins. Willow starts pointing at the menu, asking questions she probably already knows the answers to. I'm sure she's trying to make this as painless as possible, but I don't think it'll work. Mia's eyes keep darting to me and then away.

"Hey there, Ingrid. Long time, no see," Mia says, and I wince.

I forgot I told her to call me Ingrid. What a terrible name to give to someone. It's a perfectly fine name, but it doesn't exactly scream anonymity. I should have told her it was Jessica or Jane—something that would blend in. I ran out of names, unfortunately.

"Mia, little thing, her name is Lacey. We're not going to talk about why it's not Ingrid," Mac says, raising an eyebrow, and Mia nods. I wonder how much she understands about the underbelly of Synd. Clearly enough to be okay with my sudden name change.

"Lacey, you want the usual, then?" Mia asks, and I nod, still wondering what the hell I'm doing here.

She struts away, glaring at a teenager who removes his hand from the back of a girl's chair. She clips the back of his head, and he snarls at her while the girl giggles. I smother a grin behind my hand.

"What's that about?" Willow whispers, leaning in.

"That's Mia's little brother. He's still in high school. She's trying to keep him in line."

"Are we all good now? Please tell me we don't have to get all deep and spill our secrets and braid each other's hair." Sam turns to me with pleading eyes.

"Uh, sure?" I mutter.

"You don't sound convinced. It was us mostly, not you. Everyone is a little on edge. But we talked and decided to just blame the guys. So much easier that way. We fucked up, but I'm not great at groveling."

"Well, I'd rather we didn't blame Mason, but you can do whatever you want."

Willow giggles, burying her face in her arm, her entire body shaking. Sam smiles, glancing away as Mac starts chuckling. I have no idea what's happening, but it only makes me feel like I'm on the outside looking in yet again. While Mason may be fighting for me to be by his side, I doubt the others will ever fully accept me.

"Anything else we need to discuss, or can I go?" I ask, not really expecting an answer. Every time they peek at each other, they dissolve into another fit of laughter.

Willow holds her hand out to me. "I'm sorry, Lacey. We're not laughing at you. It's just that…"

Sam wheezes as Willow giggles again. "It's just that you're totally fucked."

I rear back as they burst out laughing again. Willow gives me a look of pity and my stomach drops. Jealousy floods my chest, making it hard to breathe.

"We've all been there." Willow says, face flushed. "Comes with the territory of falling in love, I suppose."

"I'm not in love with Mason," I blurt out as butterflies erupt in my stomach.

Mac sobers, wide eyes fixed on me, and then she gasps, "You might want to work on that delivery."

Huffing, I cross my arms and peer out the window. Mia drops pie in front of us, swiping up a book Willow brought before retreating. Willow's words loop in my head, over and over.

I don't think I'm that deep yet. Sure, I care about him. Clearly, I'm attracted to him. I've been low-key obsessed with them, especially Mason, for a while now. He's always seemed like a mystery, one I thought I could solve. The more time I spend with him, the deeper I fall. I'm not naive, thinking I'll get out of this unscathed. I'll cart my broken heart behind me if I'm forced out of Synd. He's the closest I'll ever get to feeling loved.

"It doesn't matter," I mutter, mostly to myself.

"What's that?" Sam asks before she stuffs another bite of pie in her mouth.

"Nothing."

"Oh no. We don't do that here. Tell us how your mind is fucking with you," Mac chimes in.

"This is weird doing this in front of Sam, but I have a feeling you all are convinced Mason and I are in love and will live happily ever after. I hate to break it to you, but that's not in the cards for us."

Sam clears her throat, ducking her head. With one statement I've sucked all the mirth from the air, shattering whatever fairy tales they had dancing in their heads. I can admit it was one I entertained for a long time.

Mason has never talked about me staying after the threats we're facing end. Sure, he throws out that I'm his, getting all fucking possessive, but only when we're fucking, and everyone knows that doesn't always translate. Other conversations we've had dance through my head, telling me to read between the lines, but he hasn't said anything except he wants me safe. But I can be safe at home, or far away from Synd.

When his territory is stable, I'll go back to my house, fading into the shadows of their lives. The pain will be too much. I'll leave, if only to make the transition easier on him. Ren is capable of taking over most of the things I do. Leaving would be the only thing that would heal the wounds Mason will inflict upon my heart.

"This seems like a morose party." Mason's voice floats over me, a dagger cracking open the gap forming in my chest.

Channeling Sam, I plaster on a mask before I face him. Regardless of how much it will hurt, I'll steal whatever time with him I can. I'll keep aiding them—helping him until I'm wrung dry. Giving everything I have left in me to him will be my final act before I disappear from his life—an afterthought in the grand scheme of everything we are.

"We've got news, so if you're finished, let's go," he says when no one responds.

The others slide from the booth, and I watch them rush to the men who apparently followed Mason here. Mac stops, glancing back. I hold my breath when she leans down.

"If you hear anything, you'll tell me?" Her voice holds a hint of vulnerability. I nod, and she smiles sadly. I let out the breath in a whoosh, tracking her as she makes her way out the door.

I'm surprised when Sam jumps into Shane's arms, wrapping her legs around his waist. His face lights up in a way I've never seen before. He swings her around before they disappear into the back of a car.

The rest follow them out of the parking lot, leaving only Mason's car parked next to a beat up two-door that probably belongs to Mia's brother. When I can't take the silence anymore, I turn back, but Mason is propped against the counter, chatting with Mia.

The dagger twists, spilling acidic heartbreak into my lungs, drowning me in despair. Swallowing hard, I force the nausea down. He's not doing anything wrong, but after the conversation, my thoughts are spiraling out of control. I can't help but see everything through a layer of jealousy. Shaking my head, I try to rid my mind of the thoughts plaguing me.

When he glances back, he raises an eyebrow, and I slide from the booth. Whatever happens, I need to get my shit together. Walking around like a kicked puppy won't get me anywhere.

Disgusted with myself, I tuck my hands in the front pocket of the hoodie I'm wearing. I stutter to a stop, looking down at the hoodie I snatched off his closet floor. The soft fabric envelops me, and I suck in a deep breath, Mason's scent filling me up. When I lift my head, I catch his soft brown eyes following me. Numbness seeps into my limbs and an ache blooms in my chest, tumbling into my stomach where it sits like a lead weight.

"Holy fuck," I breathe, and he tilts his head.

Panic slices through me as he makes his way over. I scramble for the mask I dropped somewhere between sliding from the booth and where I'm frozen now. Hopefully, he can't read the emotions I'm desperately trying to hide. Telling him won't change his stance on what we are. I have no doubt he cares for me, though I'm sure those feelings are still rooted in guilt. I knew getting involved was a bad idea, but I pushed all the doubts aside, if only for a taste of what love is. Guess I got my wish.

Mason leans down, whispering in my ear, "What's wrong?"

"Nothing."

"Bullshit. Tell me what happened." He loops his arm around my waist, pulling me close.

The words stick in my throat and my mouth goes dry. I try to step back, but his arm cages me in, refusing to let me run. Excuses of why we shouldn't have *any* conversations, much less this one, in the middle of a fucking diner ping-pong around my brain, but he won't let me go until I've confessed. It's his nature to prod until he gets answers so he can fix whatever the problem is. Pulling in a deep breath, I glance up at him.

"I don't think the others will ever be okay knowing who I am. It was just a very awkward meeting."

He nods before pulling me along out the door, and my heart twinges. Not so long ago, I never would have gotten away with lying to him. He would have noticed whatever tell I apparently have that alerts him. I didn't lie, exactly. It was an awkward meeting, but I think that was mostly me.

As I slide into the backseat of his car, I glance back as he settles next to me. I can never reveal how far I've fallen. Mason Byrns can never know I'm in love with him.

Fifty-Five

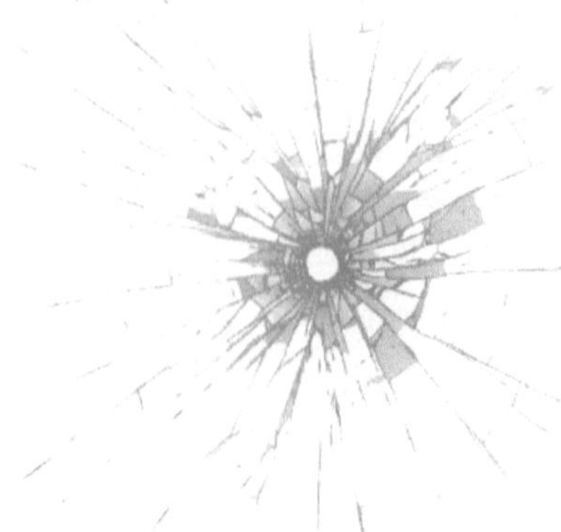

Victor could have been doing a lot of things in the front room he took over. My mind ran wild with the possibilities, including stockpiling bodies of his personal enemies that would eventually start stinking up the entire house. A full-on murder wall was not on the list, though. All he's missing is a red string to tie it all together.

I should have broken the door down a long time ago. The plan was to have Sam do it, but with all the other shit going on, I forgot. Gazing at the unhinged chaos surrounding me, I realize I should have pushed it more.

Turning slowly, I try to decipher the physical representation of the inner workings of my uncle's mind. He's done more in the last few months than I have since Helms planted the seeds of our history in my mind almost a year ago.

Notes and maps cover the walls, stacks of books are everywhere, and I even spot a whiteboard leaning against the fireplace. Picking up the nearest book, I realize they're not blank like they once were, but filled with handwritten notes. They're barely legible, which shows just how much he's deteriorated in the last year.

Stepping further into the room, I scan the mess, wondering where to start. Now I'm wishing he would have actually used a red thread to point me in the right direction. There's too much here to even start in the middle and follow it back. The whiteboard is a mess of scribbles with arrows pointing in several directions. As I pace around the room, one name repeats over and over, highlighted and circled—Drake.

I stop in front of an old newspaper clipping pinned to the wall. Scanning it, I realize it's an article from over twenty years ago, talking about some gala the bigwigs within Synd attended. The Byrns and the Kings are mentioned briefly. Apparently, they were heading up an initiative to fund a new wing of the hospital. It's the same one I stayed in while in a coma. The rest is a mess of people probably long-since dead or moved on. I don't recognize any of them until the second-to-last paragraph.

Anders Drake arrived late, displaying his usual disdain for such events. When questioned whether he was involved in the funding of the new hospital wing, he said, "Our families have long since strived for peace and cooperation. The advancement of our community is unprecedented, driven by families such as the Drakes and we'll continue to achieve great heights for those within Synd." He declined to comment further on the matter.

"Who the fuck is Anders Drake?" I mutter.

He's clearly related to Roman, but I didn't realize how prominent their family was. I search the other articles more closely, trying to piece together a past I barely remember. I was a kid when most of these events took place. There are precious few moments I retain from my childhood. Mostly I remember blood and pain, coupled with harsh lines in the sand. And always Samantha—protecting and shielding her from the atrocities I was forced to witness. I've blocked out most of it, only recalling moments in the dead of night or the most desperate of times.

When I was shot, images of Sam flashed behind my lids before everything went black. When I took out Colin, snapshots of us growing up played through my head like a fucked-up slide show. When my car blew up mere weeks ago, the memory of my little sister crawling into the back of a car on her way to training for the first time as she glared at me rose to the forefront. Now, my mind feeds me pictures of when I was young—dark haired boys scowling at each other, another boy with sparkling green eyes playing pranks on everyone. And there, tucked away behind the adults, is a boy, smaller than the rest, with slicked-back ice blond hair.

"Holy shit."

Memories come flooding back, mostly of the various functions we all were forced to attend when our fathers met. It wasn't as rare as I thought, but the older I got, the more tension laced the air. Then it all stopped. No one spoke of why we never went over to the Kings, and soon my young mind was overrun with other seemingly more important things.

Most of what I recall was my father ranting and raving about the Reapers fucking with the north and the Kings encroaching on our territory. The older I got, the less I thought of his hatred for them. My father never explained. And then he was dead.

By that point, everyone kept to their own areas, so I never questioned what the issues were back then.

Whipping around, I stalk from the room. There are only two people who can answer the questions swirling through my mind. Since Victor went to ground, I can't exactly ask him. I can't help but think he wanted me to find his obsession. I'm sure he knew Alex was tailing him. The enforcer thinks Victor is on our side, but with the state of his makeshift office, I'm inclined to believe he's been conspiring with Roman for much longer than I imagined.

Victor may be a misogynistic asshole, but there was a time he was good at what he did for my father. Those aren't skills one loses over the course of time. They're instilled in our bones so deeply there's no chance of digging them out. It's the only reason we haven't been able to find him, unless others are hiding him.

I hesitate when I reach the kitchen as the darkness seeps into the room from the stairway leading down. This isn't the mad dash I was in a year ago, muddled and confused. Victor was the one who pointed me toward the basement. A random notepad left on my bedside table in the hospital with a note telling me to go home was the only reason I found Sam. As hard as it was to shoot Colin, at least I spared her the nightmares that plague me.

Descending into the shadows, I slough off the recollections with every step, replacing them with the mask my father passed to me. A clanking through the pipes lining the wall echoes past me as I approach the door. I shouldn't be here. Finding Victor in his current state would be the more sensible thing to do, but I have easier access to Roman.

Punching in the code, I swing the door open. Bright light floods the hallway as I step inside. It doesn't look like Roman has moved an inch in the last two days, though that's impossible. The guard I had stationed down here before is tasked with keeping him fed, and the remnants of his duties are spread around the man propped against the wall.

"We need to talk," I say, stopping next to the chair bolted to the floor.

He doesn't even bother opening his eyes. "Tell me, Byrns, what am I still doing alive?"

"I'm not in the business of throwing away assets, Drake. How old were you when you left Synd?"

He raises an eyebrow, slitted eyes finding mine. "Left isn't exactly an appropriate word for the situation, but I was nine. Why?"

"How involved was your family in the running of Synd?"

He sits up, scrubbing his hand over his beard. It was short cropped before and well maintained. During his stay, it's become unruly, still streaked with black from the explosion. Even now, Willow's nickname of Mr. Sexy Pants seems to fit in a rugged way, I suppose. I'm sure they didn't think I overheard them giggling about it. If we don't kill him, we'll have to give him access to a shower, which will only make them titter more.

"Why do you ask?"

"Your family left—"

"We were exiled," he snarls, leaping to his feet. Only the shackle on his ankle stops him from reaching me.

I nod in acceptance to calm him down. The answers I need won't be gained if he's worked up. He'll get to the point where he'll refuse to speak, and I'll be right back where I started—putting together a puzzle I don't have all the pieces to. Unraveling Victor's research will take too long. At least I can fall back on finding my uncle if Roman decides he's done cooperating.

"My father exiled your family?" I ask when the flush recedes from his face.

He settles back against the wall. "He was but one of many."

I nod again, staring over his shoulder at nothing. If the elite of Synd pushed his family out, it would explain why Roman is seeking vengeance.

"Why now? Why not ten years ago? You had the perfect opportunity to swoop in when we were at our weakest. Finishing the job the lower gangs started would have been easy. Shane, Ryker, and I were untried and inexperienced. Getting our own men to follow us was a feat I never thought we'd accomplish. You could have exterminated us and taken Synd with minimal casualties."

He chuckles, long and low, before a smirk appears. "Is that the line you were fed? That it was the lower gangs that rose up to decimate your rule?"

"I didn't need anyone to tell me. I watched the destruction sweep across Synd in a tidal wave, taking out almost all those at the top one by one, leaving us behind to salvage our city." Bitterness seeps into my tone.

Roman wipes his hand down his face, trying to erase his grin.

"For someone who wasn't even there, you seem pretty confident you know what happened," I growl.

His face drops, blue eyes piercing into me. "I may not have been there, but I know who was leading them. My father came back to punish those who stole our rightful place. And your father killed him. I'll take whatever joy I can from watching you crumble into nothing."

"Except you fucked up. Once we find your men, and we will, your plans will vanish. Nothing more than a minor blip on our radar. We've dealt with enough over the past year that your little stunts barely even register. You're an annoying gnat compared to the Guild."

He scowls, but I don't know if it's because he knows I'm right or if he abhors the Guild as much as we do. They'll be back to finish what they started, but not today. We'll have to deal with them, eventually. I hope that we have time to fix the issues Drake has stirred up before they come calling again, demanding their pound of flesh for the blow we dealt them.

"Whatever issues you're currently having are not a result of my doing. Without me giving them orders, they're to hold all positions."

"Well, aren't we a little controlling," I murmur.

He snorts, shaking his head. "You're one to talk. Between Shane King and you, the way you control every aspect of this city is obnoxious. Throw in the Reapers and one would think you're all afraid of giving up any power."

This conversation isn't getting me anywhere. I don't even know why I came down here in the first place. I thought if I could talk to him, get him to reveal the reasonings behind why he's set on dethroning us, the answers would magically appear. Instead, I'm left with more questions. Ones Roman Drake can't answer.

I turn, intent on the door. There's no reason for me to stay. He'll only keep talking in circles. As my hand grips the cold metal handle, I suck in a breath, resigning myself to one last attempt.

"You say your father is dead, but he's not, is he?"

"A few strokes of a brush do not wash away the certainty I have that my father died ten years ago at the hands of your father, Mason Byrns. No cunning schemes on your part will erase that fact," he snarls.

Glancing over my shoulder, I eye him. "I remember your father. Bits and pieces of him. And if he was anything like mine, he wasn't a good one. So why fight his battles? Why come here for a revenge that isn't yours?"

"You're right. He was an asshole, as most men in our position are. Unfortunately for you, your family didn't just kill my father. You stole my little sister's life as well. And that is a sin I'll never forgive."

"I didn't know you had a younger sister."

His nostrils flare, as if my ignorance of her existence is a personal affront to him. If she came to any of the gatherings we were forced to attend, she must have stuck to her father. I barely remember Roman being there. At my mere ten years old, she wouldn't have registered to me, anyway. The only reason I have memories of Sam is because she was a pain in my ass. Every time she would slip off into the tunnels, I would get blamed and beaten.

"She followed him here. Slipping out her bedroom window and—" He swallows hard, his throat bobbing. "Called a car to take her all the way to Synd."

I lean against the door, sucked into his story once again. If he's lying, then he's very good at it. Most people assume they just need to make the words convincing when it's the emotions swimming in their eyes that give them away.

"Then how do you know she's dead?" I ask.

He explodes again, leaping to his feet and rushing me. The chain stops him, and he stumbles, catching himself on the wall. Pulling in a deep breath, he straightens before brushing his hands down his tattered clothes, as if he's swathed in an expensive suit.

"I understand you had to kill your best friend in this very room. Your sister, clearly someone dear to you, was injured, bleeding. I wonder how you would have fared had she called you while she was being beaten. Would you have wept as her screams echoed in your ear, knowing you'd hear them in the deepest parts of the night? What punishment would be suitable for the crime of torturing her as she sobbed your name until her voice gave out and the line went dead, just like her?"

His words cut deep, splaying open the memories of Sam with Colin on his knees before her, holding a piece of glass to my best friend's throat. I don't have an answer for him, so I slip from the room, turning off the light as I go. It's the only compassion I have to offer.

Fifty-Six

Lacey

I swear my eyes are crossing, but I can't stop staring at the screen in front of me. I've been poring over the histories that Victor dredged up for hours now. Flinching, my eyes dart to the door when the click of a lock rolls over me. It doesn't move, though, and a chill snakes up my spine.

Spinning around in my chair, I find the panel to the tunnels sitting wide open. I scan the room as my breath hitches in my throat, threatening to suffocate me. It wasn't open before. I know because I check it every time I come in here. The thought of someone sneaking up behind me and wrapping a wire around my neck to strangle me to death may be irrational, but it's ever-present in my mind.

"Ms. Nemesis, I'm in need of your assistance," a wheezing voice rings out of the darkness.

I jerk back as Victor materializes from the dark, stepping into the room. I almost blurt out how terrible he looks but bite my tongue. His suit hangs from his frame, even more so since the last time I glimpsed him weeks ago. Bald patches peek out between the thin gray hair covering his head. He swallows, and the move accentuates his sunken cheeks.

"Quite a few people are looking for you," I murmur, pushing back in my chair.

My phone is behind me, but I don't want to turn my back on him. As if he can read my thoughts, he sighs, pulling a gun from his back. It hangs by his hip, the weight dragging his body to the side.

"I'd rather not have to hurt you, but you must listen. Things are not as they seem." The gun trembles in his hand and his entire body shakes.

"What do you expect *me* to do about it? I'm just a hacker. You're better off going to Mason or hell, even Sam."

Waving the gun to the side, he scoffs. "They'd shoot me on sight. I haven't survived this long by ignoring the signs of someone's imminent demise. Besides, you're more than a hacker. You're intertwined with Mason. He most likely loves you, therefore he'll listen when you speak."

I don't bother refuting his claims. Everyone seems to see something I'm missing. Or perhaps they're the ones ignoring the obvious. Mason's attachment to me is merely a coping mechanism—his way of quieting the guilt deep inside him at my kidnapping. Even if that has eased, he's never said anything about the future.

A bolt of pain shoots through me at the thought. I've buried the knowledge under layers of what-ifs and justifications. None of them will truly hide the truth, though. At least if Victor thinks Mason will listen to me, he's less likely to kill me. I still don't want to know what it's like to get shot.

"Fine. Say your piece and then slither back into the shadows," I say, gesturing to the dark staircase.

He narrows his eyes, some shred of the man Mason has talked about coming through. No matter what the others think, I never saw Victor as a threat. Now I'm wondering if I've miscalculated. When he took over after Mason was shot, every move felt like it was riddled with mistakes. At every turn, I would run into another mess he left behind. I tried to clean them up, but there was only so much I could do.

"My dear, I would remind you of whom you're speaking to, but we don't have the time. I see you've gathered some of my research. There are a great many things no one seems to remember but me. Again, we don't have time to peruse it all. Your issue is you're seeing it through the eyes of an outsider. You'll never understand the full history."

His words shouldn't hurt, but they do. The longer I stay in this house—with Mason—the more I feel like I'll never belong. The fact I kept my true identity from them for so long isn't something they'll just get over, no matter how they're trying to include me lately.

A thin barrier stands between us. Mason might be different, but when it comes down to it, he'll choose his family over me, and I wouldn't even blame him. Their relationship is more important than anything that could grow between us, even if he is in love with me.

"If I'm just an outsider who can never understand, why come to me? I won't be able to properly explain to Mason what you want, anyways."

When he steps toward me, I tense, waiting for the sharp report of the gun, but he doesn't lift it. He stops a good ten feet from me, fire burning in his watery eyes.

"I assumed you were smarter than Samantha, but perhaps you're another useless ornament hanging on the arm of a powerful man," he sneers, and I bristle.

"Spit it out or fuck off. I have work to do, and you're distracting me from getting my job done."

Is it smart to mouth off to a man with a gun? No, but I still don't view him as a threat, which is ridiculous. If I can live through someone using me as a carving block, I can deal with an old man who doesn't know when he's outlived his usefulness.

He sniffs, crinkling his nose in distaste. "Very well. I'll spit it out, as you so eloquently put it. Anders walks among the living, bloodthirsty for the lives of those who justifiably wronged him."

"What the fuck is that supposed to mean?"

"Perhaps Mason should visit Mr. Drake. Although he might have insights he refuses to reveal to anyone but you. Beware, my dear. Oftentimes the truth cuts deeper than any knife ever could."

He steps back toward the stairs, turning at the last second to disappear into the darkness. I'm frozen for several minutes, waiting for him to come back, but nothing happens.

Rushing to the panel, I push it shut. I shove a dresser in front of the hidden door, wishing I could block the entrance more permanently. The only extra security I've seen is on the panel into Mason's room. Having a keypad set outside them would draw attention, though, defeating the purpose of keeping them secret.

Collapsing in my chair, I wonder if Victor actually wanted me to tell Mason. If Victor thinks Roman won't say anything in front of him, then telling him about his uncle's visit won't help. He would insist on coming with me, thinking he was protecting me. I also don't know how much I want Mason to overhear of my past. If Roman dug into my history and found something, he didn't come across a happy childhood filled with love and support. Victor was probably trying to goad me into going alone, which means I shouldn't.

Shaking my head, I shove from my chair and start for the panel. I hesitate, realizing I could be walking into a trap. Victor could be waiting down there for me to take the bait. Why he'd want to take me out doesn't make sense. Unless he was trying to get to Mason through me. I pivot, marching for the door.

Inching it open, I spot TJ in his usual place, eyes closed. I peek my head out before tiptoeing past him to Sam's old bedroom. Slipping into the tunnels, I trip down the stairs, hoping I can stumble upon the right hallway. After twenty minutes, I'm ready to give up, when I notice the air infused with a familiar musty scent.

The door to the dungeon looms ahead of me, and I suck in a deep breath, hoping it steadies my racing heart. It doesn't, but I pretend my hands aren't trembling as I punch in the code. The beep vibrates in my bones, and I hesitate before pushing the handle down and stepping into the dark.

"Hello?" I call, then curse myself as I flip on the light.

Roman sighs, rolling his head to me. "Seriously? You people need to get your shit together. This new tactic you've come up with might be annoying, but it won't get me to reveal all my nefarious plans."

"Have you spoken to Victor?" I probably shouldn't have asked that.

"Victor Smith? No, although he's been a pain in my ass and a thorn in my side for quite some time now," he says, scowling.

"Who's Anders to you?"

He blinks and I realize he's about to lie to me. He'll say he doesn't know who I'm talking about. But I've already found the evidence I need. The level of involvement the Drake family had before the falling out twenty years ago was more than anyone other than Victor knows.

"No need to answer. I already know he's your father. I know your family was another pillar of Synd, perhaps even tracing back to the founding. All signs point to the fact that the Drakes were another mafia family, running the south side. But none of this really matters if he's dead, does it?"

"If you know all of this, then why come talk to me?"

"I want to know what you know about me," I breathe, trying to school my face. He chuckles, the wariness leaving his eyes.

"You won't like it," he warns.

"There aren't many things from my childhood I liked, so I'm sure it'll be fine."

Roman may have found some things in my past, but I'm sure he didn't get the full picture of what it was like growing up for me. My parents didn't seem to even want kids. They wanted a son and got me instead. They never let me forget what a failure I was for not having a penis. Why it was so important to them was never explained to me. Absentee is a nice way of describing them.

"What do you remember from Kyol?"

"I don't know what that is," I say, frustration welling up inside me. I don't want to go round and round with him, pulling out possible truths one question at a time.

He nods, rubbing his beard. "You lived there when you were young, until you were three or four. Your parents were clearly into some shit I never figured out, but they ran. They left your twin brother's body behind in a grave they didn't even put a marker on. Changing their names and yours, they reinvented themselves. They're supposedly dead, if you were wondering. Though they've done that before."

"How?" I whisper, my unfocused eyes staring over his shoulder.

"House was blown up. Cops blamed it on gang activity. No bodies recovered."

"My parents weren't in a gang. We were middle class at best. My father was a fucking accountant."

"Didn't say they were, but they were clearly mixed up with some shit before they left Kyol. And your brother paid the ultimate price."

Nausea bubbles in my stomach. While they weren't the best parents, I assumed they were just people who shouldn't have had kids. None of this makes sense, until I remember us moving from city to city, never staying in one place for too long.

They explained it away, saying we had to for my father's job, but looking back now, that excuse doesn't hold any weight. My mother would get paranoid, corner me to see who I was talking to at school, which teachers seemed interested in me, and what I was telling them about our family. I thought it was controlling, but if it was because they were running from something, or someone, I never took the time to find out. I didn't care. I don't know if I care even now.

"Are you sure Anders is dead?" I whisper when I'm sure I won't puke.

"You wanting a body? Unfortunately, Byrns fucking floated him. But he's dead."

"Here's hoping you're right, because if he's not, then we might have a scarier enemy than you could ever be."

He scowls. "Let me out of here and we can test that theory."

"Nice try. Thanks for the info."

I slip out the door again, hoping Roman Drake never makes it out of this forgotten space. One Drake running around is bad enough. With their history, two of them teaming up could very well be our demise. If he makes it out, I'm pretty sure we're all fucked.

Fifty-Seven

Mason

"It's too quiet," Helms mutters, crouching behind a low concrete wall next to me.

"It's the Barrens. It's always too quiet down here," I whisper, peeking over the top of the barrier into the rapidly forming shadows.

"You know what I mean. It's been, what, a month of shit blowing up or a gun battle of some kind? Now, three days of nothing. Feels like the calm before the storm."

"Don't say shit like that," I snarl, my eyes snagging on a darker shadow tucked away in the alley.

Scowling, I glare at it, convinced the shadow is Sam. For some reason, she's taken to following me around like a bodyguard. I'd rather she wasn't here tonight, though. Helms's presence is an unfortunate accident, as he was there when I received the tip about squatters being in the Barrens. Usually, I wouldn't care, but Nicki herself was the one to inform me, claiming they were a part of Drake's group.

We move without speaking, weaving further into the Barrens, and desolate buildings pop up out of nowhere. Here in the south there's even less light than normal, which disorients me. The further we travel, the more signs of others moving back in creep into existence. Helms points at the side of an old warehouse, and I squint.

"Dagger and dragon. Same symbol that was painted on the road leading into Reaper territory from the Barrens," he murmurs, as if I don't have eyes.

"I'm sure it's just another group trying to establish their territory down here."

"Except we found it on the lawn of the house burned down in Reaper territory. King said it was crudely painted on the last three box trucks that were supposed to hold shipments but were empty. Not to mention the bridge they blew up near club row. This isn't some ragtag group trying to hold a few blocks in the Barrens. We sure Drake doesn't have an accomplice?"

"No, we're not. Lacey hasn't found any evidence. Drake is adamant his people won't continue without him and that he's working alone."

"Why is he talking? Doesn't make sense. Someone is fucking with us, and I'd put money on it being him."

We creep around another corner. I don't bother answering, mostly because I don't have anything to refute his claims. None of it makes sense, much like every other battle we've faced over the past year. Drake has obviously been planning this for ten years, maybe longer. His father probably filled his head with all sorts of wild accusations about the people running Synd, corrupting him.

"Where'd she say to go?"

"Close to the river. Said we'd know it when we saw it, whatever that means," I mutter, rolling my eyes.

The low vibration of his phone is amplified by the surrounding silence. He glances around before ducking into the mouth of a dead-end alley to pull it out. His low curse comes seconds later.

Leaning across from him, I pull out my own phone, sending a text to Lacey. I showed her the room Victor took over, never revealing I talked to Drake. Guilt eats away at me, but she has enough on her plate trying to chase down all our enemies. Most nights, I have to drag her away from her office. When she doesn't come willingly, I'm forced to throw her over my shoulder. The only way to calm her down is to sink into her pussy, fucking the brattiness out of her.

"We've got a problem."

"Of course we do," I grumble.

He sighs, swiping at the screen, and Shane's muffled yelling fills the line. Raising an eyebrow at the biker, Helms clears his throat.

"Helms, Mac is freaking out. You need to get back here. Something about Doc being in trouble."

"Put her on the phone," he barks.

I glare at him. We might be several blocks away from our destination, but that doesn't mean others aren't creeping around here. Muffled noise comes over the speaker and then Alex's frazzled voice rings out.

"Shane, you can't go over there alone. I'm coming with you."

"Fuck off, Alex. I'm capable of taking care of shit by myself. Concentrate on putting out the fires here. And someone get a hold of Titus to check on Emma."

The voices fade until Mac's voice comes through. It's clear she's been crying. "Ryker?"

"Tell me what happened, baby."

I walk far enough away that their conversation is muffled. Toying with my phone, I contemplate calling Lacey, but there's no reason Helms and I should both be distracted.

I try to find Sam in the shadows, but nothing seems out of place. Most of the time, she flits in and out, making sure I'm not making a mistake. I told her she didn't need to protect me, but she just smiled and waved as she walked away.

"Byrns, I gotta go. Kenzie isn't okay. Call one of your guys to come down. The rest are tied up with all the other shit hitting the fan."

"I'll be fine," I grunt, dismissing him before he's even gone.

"Don't do this shit on your own, Byrns. That's just asking to get shot. Again."

Gritting my teeth, I keep walking. As if I need a reminder not to step in front of a bullet. His footsteps fade away and I'm left alone.

This isn't the first time I've been down here by myself, but my feet drag the closer I get to what I'm assuming is a warehouse. Instead, it's an old brick storefront staring back at me.

No one loiters out front, though there's concrete barriers that someone dragged in front of the boarded-up windows. Backtracking down the alleyway, I loop around to check out the other side. Nothing stirs until a gust of wind blasts between the buildings. Thunder rolls in the distance, like an omen of impending darkness descending upon Synd.

The back is as desolate as the rest of the area. Splashed across the door and every window I've passed is the emblem I've been trying to dismiss. When I asked Nicki about it, she said no one had claimed it. No new groups have popped up in the Egg using it. The more I notice it, the more I'm convinced it's tied to Drake, no matter what I told Helms.

My phone vibrates and I glance at the screen, stepping further into the shadows to read Sam's message.

Get home now

Shooting off a reply, I tap the device against my leg, eyeing the building as I wait.

Your home dipshit. We need to meet

As I squint at the screen, a chill runs up my spine. Why wouldn't she just reveal herself? She's been following me the entire night. Unless she wasn't the dark shadow I saw before. Glancing around the dead space, another bout of thunder rolls through the sky.

As it tapers off, a single muffled gunshot rings out. Whipping my head around, I try to pinpoint the source. Lightning crackles, electrifying the air and a metallic taste sits in the back of my throat. Another gunshot echoes into the alley, followed by a soft thud. Cursing, I step closer to the building, convinced the noise is coming from inside.

Another pop, followed by the rolling thunder as if they're competing for my attention. Slipping my gun from my back, I sidle up to the corner next to the rear window. Minding the jagged edges of glass left behind, I peek through the part that isn't covered with plywood. A small glow flickers further inside, but the light doesn't reach me.

Three more pops and my hand wraps around the metal door handle before I realize I've moved. Helms's warning runs through my head when another flash of lightning cracks the sky in two. A grunt from inside has me turning the knob, and it gives readily.

Easing it open, I crouch before peering around the corner. The room beyond is cluttered with old paint cans and other refuse, which isn't unusual for this area. Skirting around the frame, I inch the metal closed in case someone happens to walk by. A door practically hangs off its hinges, the glass from the small window busted out.

This must have been a stockroom for a long-abandoned paint store. I can't even begin to imagine how long these cans have been sitting here. Yellow solvent sits in jugs, precariously balanced on broken shelving. This is an explosion waiting to happen. My skin crawls as I creep across the tile floor.

"You all have a choice, of course. However, I can't guarantee you'll live to see another sunrise if you refuse my offer," a low voice rumbles from the front of the store.

"Offer? Not much of a fuckin' offer," someone answers.

"Is that so?" the first man says.

Pulling my phone from my pocket, I turn it off. I'd rather not get caught because I wasn't smart enough to silence my electronics. My missteps are already piling up, starting with continuing on when Helms left and ending with me coming in here out of some morbid fucked-up curiosity.

I flinch when another gunshot rings out, louder now that I'm inside. Stepping gingerly over the remnants of a table, I almost stumble. If I'm not careful, my own clumsiness is going to get me caught. The silence following the sharp report is deafening, seeping into my pores.

"Anyone else have an issue with my offer?"

Men's voices rumble out, though whether in assent or displeasure I can't tell. Clearly, whoever this man is doesn't care about taking people out. I might have blundered into some Barrens meeting of new recruits. Here, they run things based on their own set of rules. Everyone operates on the assumption that we don't fuck with each other, and life goes on. I have contacts within their ranks, plus Sam's if need be. If I interfere, I'll be breaking the unwritten rules between us, which will put me more in the shit.

"Now that you're all up to speed, we can get on with blowing the bridges," he says.

I jerk back, catching myself against the wall before I trip over the door.

"Which ones?" a man asks, but his voice sounds young.

"Why all of them, son." I can practically hear the grin in his tone.

"There's a shit ton of bridges in Synd. You can't blow them all."

There's a shuffling and then a thud. "What's your name?"

"Rooster…sir."

Peering around the door frame beyond the hallway, I make out a dozen men, most of them young, scattered around the abandoned showroom. They're crowded to one side, no weapons in sight except the one an older man holds. He's dressed like Victor usually is, expensive tailored suit that's thirty years out of fashion. A soft glow spreads from several kerosene lanterns sitting on a mishmash of tables. Several bodies litter the space, as if they were executed.

The older man has his gun pressed to the forehead of a biker with a ruddy complexion, who clearly let himself go over the years. He's on his knees, hands shaking at his sides. I don't know him, but I assume he's part of the Reapers. I reach for my phone before shaking my head and abandoning it. Texting Helms in the middle of this situation would be another mistake.

"You seem like a smart man, Rooster, though your name leaves something to be desired. Perhaps you could tell me exactly why I shouldn't shoot you."

"Because I can get you in with the Reapers. I know shit." Rooster's throat bobs. Even from here, it's obvious he's practically shitting his pants.

"Oh, you know shit, do you?" The older man straightens, gesturing with his gun and several men flinch. "Anyone else here *know shit* about the biker gang in the north?"

Several men shake their heads, never taking their eyes from the weapon. As much as it pisses me off there are people defecting to this asshole, I can't help but agree with the biker. Taking out all the bridges in Synd would be a horrendous undertaking. They'd never accomplish their task before they were caught, unless they somehow staged them all to blow at once. Even that plan would be ludicrous. Getting past the people in the Barrens alone would be a feat.

"I suppose you've found your in then, haven't you, Rooster?"

Rooster stumbles back to the wall, glaring when the man in the outdated suit turns. Scanning the space, my eyes catch on a pile of weapons in the middle of the room. At least I know why no one is fighting back. None of the faces are familiar, but they're all wearing various insignia from a multitude of lower gangs. Working together to bring him down would be hard enough. Not knowing if they can trust the person standing next to them makes it worse.

Horror sweeps through me as I gaze around the room at the open alcohol containers sitting next to paint thinner and rags. The rest of the tables are filled with the makings of Molotov cocktails in various stages of assemblage. What the fuck are they even thinking? This is a dumb way to die.

"If you"—his lip curls as he gazes at a disheveled man no older than twenty—"gentlemen can prove your worth, you'll be rewarded within my organization."

One of them raises his hand, and I roll my eyes. "Uh, sir, what's the end goal?"

"Why to take Synd, of course. My son was kind enough to start the job, but I'll be the one to finish it. Now, if you'll excuse me, I have other places to be." He points his gun at a slender man who looks to be the same age as the older man. "Higgins will assign you roles. Assume he's an extension of my authority."

I tense as his words filter through the ringing in my ears. His son—Roman Drake might have thought his father was dead, but if the older man is telling the truth, then Anders Drake is very much alive—and planning to finish what he started ten years ago.

Anders walks out the front door, the tinkling of the bell overhead a stark contrast to what I've witnessed. Higgins is already barking orders to several of them to remove the bodies. I should leave, but my feet won't move.

Following Anders and taking him out would be smart, but he'd be long gone, eaten up by the ever-present shadows of the Barrens before I'd make it to the back door. I may not be able to finish him off yet, but I can stop the production in front of me.

I grin, tucking my gun in its holster as the nerves in my stomach settling into a low buzz of energy. Crouching, I slide into the room. The others scramble around, not paying attention to the back of the space. My back ends up pressed against a table, and I reach up to grab a Molotov.

Pulling a lighter from my pocket, I peer around the edge. Rooster bellows at a group of men, trying to take over. Higgins palms a gun, a smirk blooming on his face.

I light the fabric stuffed in the neck of the bottle, waiting until it catches before I shoot upright. Aiming for the kerosene lamp next to the biker, I throw it as hard as I can. I'm already reaching for another one when the glass shatters, knocking the lantern to the floor. Oil spreads, but doesn't catch fire. Rooster tumbles back as the fumes explode in the air in front of him.

Lighting another bottle, I smash it against the ground at Higgins's feet as he raises his gun toward me, his eyes meeting mine. His shot goes wide, and I dash for the stockroom.

As I reach the back door, a high-pitched whine reaches my ears, followed by a series of pops, drowning out the screams of the men inside. Crashing out the back door, I run for the alley, looping around to the front.

Coming around the corner, I skid to a stop just as the front door pops open, revealing a man engulfed in flames. Rooster falls to his knees, his screams echoing through the night. Satisfaction rolls through me as he writhes on the ground, desperately trying to douse the fire consuming him. Another man skirts around him, tripping on the concrete barriers in his haste to get away from the storefront.

Raising my gun, I stumble back as the entire store blows, blasting out the plywood covering the front windows. I duck back around the corner, heart racing. No need to pick them off. I'm almost certain the blast took out the rest of them.

The sky opens up as I run across the mouth of an alley, lungs burning. The sweet release of rain washes away any guilt I had at killing the men who willingly aligned against us.

Fifty-Eight

Lacey

"Sorry, Lacey. I don't know what to tell you," Willow yells, clearly out of breath. "We're dealing with the fire at Trigger's bar. I have to go."

I scowl at the screen as it goes black before slipping my phone in my pocket. Willow was my last chance at figuring out where Mason is. He was supposed to be in the Barrens with Helms, checking on a tip from Nicki, but when I called Mac, Helms was with her. Apparently, Mason was supposed to come home an hour ago.

Pacing across my makeshift office, I stop by the window. Rain comes down in sheets, obliterating the view. I can't even make out the trees lining the property. A deep chill runs down my spine, and I shiver, wrapping my arms around my middle. Something in the air is wrong, though I can't put my finger on what it is. Sam said to wait at home for Mason to show up, but the more time passes, the deeper my unease becomes. I haven't heard from her since.

The panel next to me clicks, then pops open silently and I stumble back. Hope blooms in my chest, then dies as Alex steps through. Blond hair plastered to his head, he scans me up and down before settling his green eyes on mine. Sam said he was dealing with Victor.

"Where is he, Nemesis?" Alex growls.

He steps toward me, and I instinctively move back. Raising his arm, he gestures me away from the window with the gun I didn't notice until now.

"I don't know where Mason is. What's going on?"

Even with the way he's acting, I can't imagine Alex would hurt me. He's one of the few who accepted me—took who I was in stride. Hell, he's helped me more than a few times over the last several weeks. Maybe he's just stressed from everything going down.

"Not talking about Byrns." He stalks to me, crowding me against the wall as he presses the gun to my temple.

Every muscle in my body seizes as my breath stalls in my lungs. I don't even think my heart beats for the ten seconds he digs the barrel into my skin. He eases back, rage burning in his eyes, and the air whooshes from me. My entire body trembles from the effort to stay upright as darkness licks at the edges of my vision.

He points the weapon at my knee. "Start talking or I start taking body parts."

"I don't know what you're talking about," I wheeze, blinking to rid the red mist seeping through the closed windows.

My stomach rolls when he pulls back the hammer, lifting an eyebrow. There's nothing I can say that will make him believe me. He's convinced I'm hiding someone, but I can't fathom who. The only person I've seen today, other than Mason, is…

"Are you talking about Victor?" I whisper, then swallow hard when he slowly releases the hammer.

"Tell me where she is, and I'll let you walk away with your life."

Tears fill my eyes, spilling down my cheeks. "Alex, just tell me what you want. Sam? Is that who you're looking for?"

He nods, narrowing his eyes.

"I haven't heard from her. Willow said she was dealing with the police chief, but that's all I know. Please."

The familiar scent of copper fills my nostrils. Next will come the blood, running in rivulets down the walls, but I refuse to take my eyes from Alex's face to check. I can't afford to lose it when his gun is still trained on me. He won't be as forgiving as Mason was when I passed out. Alex will assume I'm faking, probably shoot me to get me talking.

"She wasn't. She was tracking Victor, who you met with earlier, didn't you? Was that before or after you let Drake go?"

Ice floods my veins, and my body goes numb. Shaking my head, I reach for my phone, but freeze when his gun rests on my forehead, pushing me back until my head hits the wall. I blink and Alex's face morphs into Razor's.

Closing my eyes, I choke back the sobs crawling up my throat. When I sway the cool metal leaves my skin, but I can't look. The more I try to fight the panic threatening to drag me down into the icy void of nothingness, the harder it is to control my body.

"Give me your phone," he barks, and I jolt, smacking my head against the wall.

I paw at my pocket, and he bats my hands away. Raising them to my head, I dig my knuckles into my temples. When he pulls it out, my legs give out and I collapse in a heap on the floor. Liquid washes over my arms and I peek through narrow slits, shuddering when I find blood coating my skin.

A shrill ringing echoes through the air, until I realize it's coming from me, and I clamp my lips together. Alex shoves my phone under my nose.

"Unlock it."

With trembling fingers, I bypass the securities I've put on the device, leaving streaks of crimson behind. I shudder when he rips it from my hands, blood smearing across his skin. Breathing through my mouth, I try to center myself in reality, but the tainted air suffocates me. Familiar dark spots dance in front of my vision.

Alex's hands grip my arms, hauling me to my feet, and I gag. His curse is soft, but I don't know if it's because he whispered it or if my ears are plugged. The entire room spins, sending waves of crimson sloshing over the furniture. I've never lasted this long before passing out. I'm not exactly holding it together, but at least I'm not drowning yet.

"Sam said she was coming for you. Where is she, Nemesis?"

Doubling over, I moan, "I don't know."

"What the fuck?" A shrill voice lashes against my skin, but I can't tell who it belongs to.

Alex argues with them, but their voices warp into an unintelligible roar. Small hands press against my skin, burning my flesh where they grip me. Slamming my eyes closed, I can feel the darkness crashing over me until a familiar scent infiltrates my nose.

An image of Mason smiling over his shoulder at me flashes behind my lids. His lips ghosting across my skin settles the rolling in my stomach. His autumn scent fills my pores as the feeling returns to my fingers. Clutching the sweatshirt that's been shoved into my hands, I bury my nose in the soft fabric.

"You're okay. I walloped him, so he won't be an asshole anymore." Sam's voice washes over me as the blood slowly recedes, disappearing into the fissures that have opened in the hardwood.

Finding Sam's eyes, I realize they're the same brown as Mason's, though the shape is different. They're calming nonetheless. It hits me she could be here to finish me off. Scrambling back, I hit the wall again. Sam raises her hands, then glances over her shoulder at Alex, who shuffles further away.

Facing me, her brows dip. "Are you okay?"

"Back up, Sam," Alex growls, still gripping his gun.

She launches to her feet, advancing on him and poking him in the chest. "You asshat. I can't believe you came in here threatening her. What the fuck is wrong with you?"

"You said you were coming for her," he cries, throwing up his hands.

"Yeah, so no one would fucking kill her. For fuck's sake, Alex. When are you going to learn I can handle my own shit? You've got to stop trying to save me."

His face falls and she sighs. I pull the hoodie over my head, letting the fabric envelop me. Heaviness seeps into my limbs, and I slide down the wall, wrapping my arms around my knees.

"I'll stop when you figure out I can't live without you, Bug. Stop thinking you have to do this alone."

I turn my face away now that I'm out of immediate danger. This conversation seems too personal, and honestly, it hurts my heart. Mason's face swims behind my lids. Our lives are intertwined more every day, but with everything else, we haven't talked about the future. I doubt his feelings of guilt have diminished. Guilt doesn't morph into love.

"We'll fight about this later," Sam murmurs.

Meeting her eyes when she crouches in front of me, I bite my lip before whispering, "Sorry."

"We don't have long. Did Victor talk to you?" she asks, and I nod. "Did you talk to Roman?"

"I think I was the distraction. He just talked about my family. Sam, I'm pretty sure Anders Drake is alive."

"I know. We'll deal with it. You just keep your phone on." She pushes to her feet. "Let's go, Alex. We need to find Victor and Roman before they meet up with Anders."

Alex's eyes fix on me, shame pulling his brows low. I give him a soft smile, hopefully conveying that I'm not going to hold it against him. He was doing what he had to, to find someone he loved. I wouldn't be able to do the same, but I'd like to think I'd try. I'd be shit at threatening someone, even to save Mason. It'd be hard since my choice of weapons has diminished even more now. I'd have to find another way, like using a cast iron pan or a hammer to defend him.

Alex sets my phone on my desk, giving me one last look before he shakes his head and follows Sam to the tunnels. The panel snicks shut behind them, leaving a heavy silence in its wake.

Pushing from the floor, my muscles scream in protest. I wish I could crawl into Mason's bed and sleep for days, but there's more than a few fires we need to put out. The bar in Reaper territory was hit. Shane is apparently dealing with a set of safe houses that were set on fire.

Another message from Ren is waiting for me when I get to my computer. Several shipments were waylaid, bodies scattered around them. Another warehouse went up in flames on the east side, and the Barrens is in full lock down. I doubt Roman had time to execute everything that's happening within Synd unless Victor has been running things since we locked Roman up. I don't understand how Anders plays into all of this, unless Roman is a very good liar, which is entirely possible.

Roman working with Anders is the only plausible explanation. Pulling up the program, I systematically go through the cameras again. It's what I was doing before Alex ambushed me. There are a million other things I could be doing to help the others, but the pit in my stomach says something isn't right.

My phone vibrates, and I snatch it up, expecting it to be Sam or Mason. Horror sweeps through me, and it slips from my fingers, tumbling across the hardwood. The glow from the screen mocks me as it rests at my feet. With trembling hands, I scoop it up, reading the message again.

So unfortunate my nephew was caught in the rain. Thankfully I recovered him. Please collect him before something catastrophic were to befall him.

An address appears as I stare at the screen. Doubling over, I dig my fist into the ache in my chest. I gasp, trying to ease the pain consuming me. I crash to my knees, shoving my fist in my mouth and screaming out my rage.

Chaotic thoughts rule my mind and I stumble to the hidden panel, stealing into the dark. I send one last message to Sam, but the other one is still unread. I don't have time to wait for her to respond. Victor's finally tipped over the edge, and I don't have the luxury of allowing someone else to help me.

Mason saved me when I thought no one was coming. Our demons may await me in the shadows, baying for our blood, but I can't leave him to the same fate.

Fifty-Nine

Mason

The one night I could really do with a clear sky and it's a torrential downpour instead. At least the rain will stop the fire I started from spreading throughout the Barrens. Anders's trail has gone cold, but he was headed north. Looping through the mishmash of buildings and long-abandoned alleys, I come to another dead end. I curse as I wipe my face on my soaked sleeve, as if that'll do anything.

Ducking under an overhang, I pull out my phone before remembering I turned it off. It was almost dead when I went to the Barrens, and I don't want to use it unless I need to. I told Lacey it would be hours before I was home. She's probably down some rabbit hole, trying to unravel Victor's pet project. She said she can take care of herself, so I need to trust that she will, even if the ache in my chest is back.

I still don't know where my uncle fits into the grand scheme of things. I don't know if Roman is in league with his father. I don't know what the hell the others are doing. All of it is wearing on my nerves.

I dash from the relative safety of the doorway toward the edge of the Barrens. Anders is probably scuttling around, making connections near the river, but I doubt he'll have much luck. They aren't exactly welcoming, especially when someone tries to tell them how to do things.

A bolt of anxiety hits me, wondering if Anders will convince any of my men in the lower gangs to turn on us. I only have myself to blame. I'm paying for my hubris, assuming they'd stick around while I got my shit together.

A looming figure steps out of the shadows, blocking my way, and I freeze. Hanging my hands by my sides, I wait for him. My authority doesn't extend here, so I won't shoot him unless I have to. He steps back into the light from a streetlamp as the rain eases just enough for me to make out a bushy, red beard covering most of his face. His massive frame towers over me, even from ten feet away.

"Byrns," he grunts, crossing his arms.

"Mack." I don't have much interaction with him, but Sam knows him well. "How's your guts?"

He tilts his head as his lip twitches the slightest bit, and some of the tension leaves me.

"Thanks to the girly, they're inside my body still."

"You repay the one who cut you?"

He shakes his head, glancing off to the side before swinging his gaze back to me. "Not yet. Not really. Kid who did it was following orders."

"Who's his boss?" My stomach dips when he drops his chin. Mack might pass info to Sam, but we've never been on that level. I have my own informants in the Barrens.

"You gonna deal with the bastard?"

"Depends on who it is," I say.

The rain tapers off, leaving massive puddles and streams of water behind. Mack shakes his head violently, droplets scattering around him. Forcing a name from him won't do any good. Not only could he pop my head from my body with minimal effort, but risking the fallout would be foolish. Even with Mack being a recluse within the Barrens, others still listen to him.

"Older dickhead. Gray hair and fancy-ass suit. Drives a shiny. Shitty name."

I school my face into my familiar mask of indifference, though my emotions are running rampant.

"Anders Drake?" He nods and I grit my teeth. "I'll take care of it."

"Was gonna tell the girly but haven't seen her since the exile. Bastard's holed up in C-block," he grumbles, glancing off into the dark.

"Noted. Do I need to run the gamut?"

He shakes his head before rumbling away. I countdown a full minute before I move. I don't want him to think I'm following him and give him an excuse to take me out. Another bout of thunder rolls across the sky as more streetlamps light the way the further I travel from the Barrens.

The warehouse Mack referenced is at least half a mile from where I am. I don't want to walk all that way, but I left my car deep in the south of the city.

My chest tightens as I make my way down the empty streets. Anders taking over one of our warehouses, abandoned or not, pisses me off. The building was one of the first ones hit when Drake came to town. We moved everyone closer to the Depot, our home base, a couple months ago.

The one-story building appears from the dark, the pock-marked concrete a harsh contrast to the other buildings sur-rounding it. It may sit on the outskirts of the Barrens, but com-mercial businesses flank each side, though they've long-since closed. It looks abandoned with one window boarded up. Skirt-ing around the side, a beam of light flashes across the window, and I duck behind a bush. I let out a sigh of relief when the beacon extinguishes.

I don't spend much time down here, leaving it to my men to deal with the lower gangs. Thankfully, I know my way around this particular building. We used it as a warehouse until a couple of months ago when we abandoned it. There wasn't enough time or resources to reinforce it at the time.

Slipping around the back, I find the door set into the ground and covered by a false air conditioning unit. The keypad glows but stays silent when I put in the code. Lifting the door, I clamber onto the built-in ladder before struggling to pull the heavy metal closed.

It thumps into place, and I hold my breath, straining to hear if someone will investigate. After a minute, when it appears no one is coming, I slowly descend into the shadows. A narrow hallway juts off under the floorboards above my head and I follow it to the small concrete room. Several boxes line the walls with guns in various states of assembly, along with several cans of rations.

I only have one pistol and two magazines, hardly enough to take out a whole crew if anyone is upstairs with him. A snort leaves me when the image of throwing cans of beans at Anders flashes through my mind since I can't use any of the weapons. I wish I would have listened to Sam when she told me to carry a knife as well.

Creeping up the rickety stairs, I sit just under the trap door for five minutes, trying to track where he is. It isn't until a thud echoes through the space from the back of the warehouse that I push open the wood and peek out. Muted light greets me, but no sign of Anders.

Not much has changed since I was here last. When the fridge tucked against the wall of the small kitchenette starts up, I ease from my hiding spot, gently setting the wood back into place. Sliding between the counter and the round table that takes up most of the space, I pull out my gun as my stomach tightens.

I hate walking into something I can't control. No brilliant plans flash through my mind, and at some point, my luck is going to run out. Tamping down the unease bubbling in my gut, I can only hope it lasts long enough for me to take out Anders. Then I can deal with Roman and Victor, and we can clean up the riffraff who chose the wrong side.

Edging around the door frame toward the back of the room, I grip my gun tighter. An electric lantern lights the space, casting shadows along the white walls. Devoid of windows, the room's only decorations are a chair bolted to the concrete and a drain set in the middle of the floor.

We didn't use this space often, mostly to house guns I already had moved. Empty shelves line one wall now, but detailed maps of Synd, red lines slashed across the paper, plaster the back wall on either side of the only other exit. I'm surprised he hasn't brought in his men to take over the space.

Shuffling forward, I whip my head back and forth, searching for Anders. The thud I heard earlier came from back here, so he can't have gone far. The back door has a keypad, but I doubt he'd know the code. The closet to my right has a small attic access leading to the rafters of the structure, but he wouldn't be able to reach it unless he pulled a ladder in there. Judging by the lack of furniture, I doubt he brought one.

Just as I turn away, the closet door pops open, and I press myself against the wall as the wood swings toward me. Feet scuffle mere inches from me, but I wait for him to come into view. I doubt I'll get a second chance to take him out, so I need to make my one shot count. My muscles strain as I lift my gun.

Then the door smashes into me, crushing me between the wood and wall. Grunting, I shove at it, but I get nowhere. He won't be able to kill me this way, which is a small mercy.

I press my arm into the door, and it gives the slightest amount. I twist before ramming my shoulder into the wood. The older man grunts and then I'm hit again. Dropping my gun, I let out a string of curses through gritted teeth. He bashes into me once more and my foot connects with my weapon, sending it skittering across the concrete.

Grappling with the handle, I use my body to shove it back toward him. We're stuck in a reverse tug-of-war, each trying to overpower the other and getting nowhere. With one final push, he stumbles back and my feet stutter as I attempt to stop myself from crashing to the ground.

Anders snarls, pulling a pistol from his back and pointing it at me. I throw myself toward my weapon as a bullet embeds itself into the floor inches from my feet. Abandoning it, I launch myself toward him, tackling him to the ground and knocking the breath from his lungs. He smashes the gun into my temple. I roll off his body to all fours, stars exploding in my vision. Bracing myself for the searing pain I know all too well, I'm not ready for his foot to connect with my stomach.

Groaning, I fall to my side as his chuckle echoes around me. When I finally feel like I'm not going to puke, I peel my eyes open. Anders trains both guns on me, and I close my eyes again, Lacey's face swimming up from the depths of my mind. I should have done more for her. I should have kept her safe. I should have told her everything. Instead, I let what I thought was important get in the way, waiting for when all this was over.

"Oh, little Byrns, don't hide from me. I'd like to savor this and I can't if you're cowering." Anders's voice swirls around me as my head pounds and a trickle of blood runs down my cheek.

Glaring at him, I struggle to my feet. If I can delay him long enough, I might find an opening to take him down. I almost wish I had grabbed a can of beans to beat him with. The satisfaction of bashing his head in with something as innocuous as a canned vegetable would be amazing.

I swipe the back of my hand across my mouth, red shimmering along my skin. "Thought you were dead."

"I'm sure my *dear* son told you that. As far as he's concerned, I still am, unless you've informed him otherwise," he says, gesturing me to the chair with the barrel.

I keep him in my sight line as I step over to it, waiting until he cocks the hammer before sinking onto the metal.

"If you're not working with him, then you're clearly alone. How the hell do you expect to take over Synd? Even if you kill me, there are others who are just waiting for a shot at you."

"I'll just start with you. The others will fall eventually. Now, secure your feet to the chair." He smirks, but I don't move. "Unless you'd like to lose the use of your legs first."

Leaning down, I slowly close the cuffs around my ankles. They snap shut and I can barely move my feet. Sliding my hand to my pocket, I track his movements as he sets my gun on a shelf. Through the fabric, I press what I hope is the power button. Lacey put in emergency measures, but the phone has to be on for it to work. I wish I would have texted her when I had the chance.

"Your arm next, little Byrns. And you can stop trying to contact your little girlfriend. I'm sure she's tied up at the moment."

I secure one arm, letting my hand fall back to my pocket, squeezing it in my hand. Anders looms next to me, not close enough for me to grab. Pressing the gun to my temple, he raises an eyebrow and I place my other arm into the cuff. Once I'm strapped in, he steps back, setting his gun beside my own.

"What did you do to Lacey?" I growl.

"Me? Nothing at all. I may have planted the seed of doubt amongst the others, which I'm sure they'll act on."

"Let me guess, you'll take out the Kings next, and then dismantle the Reapers before finally ruling Synd all on your own, ushering in a golden age of whatever-the-fuck-you-want, right?"

Anders isn't the first man I've met with intentions of bringing us down, imagining a transgression we've wrought upon him and his own. Vitriol runs rampant, spilling into our lives, and then we're forced to deal with it. The Drake family might have more of a claim on Synd than the others, though. Victor's research never explained why they left in the first place, but I'm sure my father had something to do with it.

"I don't owe you an explanation. Suffice it to say, your death will be the ending of an era that should have died twenty years ago. Destruction should be met with ruination. I intend to finish what I started. I'm sure you can understand the need to avenge wrongs. You're well-versed in such things."

"Your issue lies with my father, who is long dead. Why come back now?"

Picking up a knife from the shelf I failed to see before, he sneers at me. "Sins of the father, my dear little Byrns. When all else fails, kill them all."

Sixty

Lacey

My body started trembling when I crossed the invisible line into the Barrens. The closer I come to the address Victor sent, the harder I shake. Even before the building appears, I know where I'm headed. Skipping around a large puddle, I stuff my hands in Mason's black hoodie. I shouldn't have rushed off, letting panic rule my actions, but I can't go back now.

Studying the building, I realize it's an old doctor's office, long abandoned. Low concrete barriers surround the front, blocking my path unless I'm going to climb over them. I should have grabbed a weapon, but even the thought of trying to shoot someone has my stomach rolling, especially after the incident with Alex.

The quiet of the night presses down on me as I stumble to the side of the building. Unfortunately, the door doesn't open. Neither does the one in the back and I huff in frustration. No lights shine through, but that's not surprising. They kept this place dark when I was there, preferring to use lanterns.

In fact, I'm sure this area doesn't have electricity. It's spotty in the Barrens, anyway. Mason tried to get the people here to let contractors in a couple years ago to fix things enough to at least have consistent power, but they refused.

I don't have the skills to take Victor and Roman down. I'm not Sam, flitting through the dark with a knife, or Mac, whose presence alone seems to make men cower. I don't have a way to protect myself or Mason. My only hope is to trade my life for his. With the skills I possess, I'll be forced to help them take down Synd. Tricking them into thinking I'm helping shouldn't be that hard. It's not a great plan, but it's the only one I have with everyone else going dark.

"Lacey, why don't you stop skulking around and just come in here?" Victor calls from inside the building.

I can't make him out, but the hair on the back of my neck stands up, and I raise my hands.

A soft snort echoes through the night. "You can put your hands down, Ms. Webb. We have no cause to shoot you." Roman's chuckle follows his words, weaving through the shadows as if his voice were crafted from them.

A chill snakes down my spine as I lower my hands. My feet crunch on the glass scattered across the concrete, and I step gingerly through the broken windows. Dark puddles grace the space and I shudder, remembering the bodies soaked in the blood.

Mason tried to turn me away from the carnage his men caused, but I caught glimpses before he buried my face in his chest. Dizziness invades my head, and I sway before pulling my eyes away. I doubt I'll get out of this building without falling headlong into another hallucination.

I spot Roman first, leaning against the far wall and smirking at me. His beard is still out of control, but it seems like he cleaned up a little.

"I see you found some clothes." I gesture to the dark jeans and hoodie he's wearing. I'm pretty sure they're Mason's. "Too bad you couldn't find a razor."

Victor emerges from the dark hallway, gun hanging at his side. "If we're done commenting on his appearance, perhaps we could discuss the issues at hand."

"Where's Mason?" I mean for it to come out decisive and demanding, but even I can hear the note of vulnerability lacing my words.

"I apologize, Lacey. I realize this space must hold terrible memories for you. Unfortunately, it was the only space we were sure not to be discovered," Victor says, tucking his gun away.

"Where's Mason." It's a demand now, not a question.

"Told you, Vic," Roman murmurs before stuffing what looks like a whole granola bar in his mouth.

Victor shushes him, stepping closer to me. I jerk back, almost tripping through the open windowsill. Righting myself, I catch Victor lowering his hand, as if he was going to catch me.

"We have things to discuss." Victor glances at Roman before finding my eyes.

"The only thing I'm here to discuss is what you've done with Mason. Anything else and you can fuck right off."

He sighs, running a hand through his thinning gray hair. My eyes keep dancing to Roman, waiting for him to make his move. Eventually, he'll pull a gun or knife and threaten me. If I can see it coming, I can...do absolutely nothing. Diving out of the way will only delay the inevitable.

Victor opens his mouth, then snaps his mouth shut, scowling.

"I'm prepared to trade my services for him. Allow him to go free and I'll work for you." I pin Roman with a glare as he snorts again. "I realize you may not know how lucrative the deal I'm offering is."

I wait for the startled looks, the incessant questions, hell, even laughter. Instead, I'm met with stony expressions until Roman bursts out laughing. I scowl, even if I expected his reaction.

"You probably don't understand what that means—"

He waves away my words as he doubles over, gasping. "That's your big trade-off? Fuck, I needed that."

"Excuse me?"

He grins. "Regardless of your skills, there's not much you can do that I can't, I'm pretty sure. Inflating your hacking abilities isn't going to do shit."

I roll my eyes, realizing he has no idea what my actual job is. Most people don't, but now it might affect what happens to Mason. A shiver runs down my spine at the thought.

"Roman, please." Victor scolds him. "There will be no trading of people, especially not for my nephew. Besides, he's not here. We don't need your skills, although he might."

Confusion sweeps through me. "What are you talking about?"

"Why don't you let me handle this?" Roman saunters closer and I tense. "Ms. Webb, Vicky here tells me that perhaps my plan to avenge my father, making those that killed him pay for their crimes, is a moot point, since apparently he's alive and well. Therefore, the enemy of my enemy and all that applies, I'd say."

He runs his knuckle along my scar, leaving ice in his wake. I still don't know if the man who gave it to me was working for Roman. Rage sweeps through me, tightening my chest. When he steps back, I narrow my eyes.

"Why the hell should I help you?"

For all my thoughts of turning myself over to them, I refuse to be forced into working *with* them. If Mason isn't here, then maybe I can get away. The extra information I bleed from them in the process can't hurt.

"Other than the fact that we could just make you?" He raises an eyebrow, turning to Victor.

"Because Mr. Drake here is not the one who hurt you. He can help to bring down Anders."

"First of all, he was leading those who hurt me. Second, I doubt he'll be able to help me with anything," I scoff, crossing my arms and kick out my hip.

I want to appear confident and blasé, but in all actuality, I'm hiding the trembling in my hands. Roman won't be able to help me, although Victor was probably talking about the others. I assume Roman hired someone to dig up dirt on us all. Unless he has hacking skills I couldn't find. It's not much of a stretch since I couldn't find anything about him when I searched. He's wiped himself from existence as thoroughly as I have.

Roman scowls, resuming his nonchalant stance against the wall. "Your kidnapping was not my doing, as I've told both you and Byrns. I realize I've done nothing to garner your trust, but under no circumstances would I have harmed you as they did."

"Give me one fucking reason I should believe you," I snap.

His chin drops to his chest. "Because I know what it's like to deal with the aftermath—to live side-by-side with the horrors others inflicted upon those I loved. I would never willingly put someone else in that position. Even Mason Byrns."

"If you weren't leading them, then who was it?"

"I'd assume it was my father. It's definitely something he would do. The man faked his own death, but even when I was growing up, he was a sadistic bastard," he says bitterly.

"Doesn't tell me why you'd be able to help us bring him down."

"And I'd argue I'm the most qualified to confront my father since he's the one who made me who I am."

I wrinkle my nose, and he rolls his eyes. Now that he's not locked up anymore, he's less intimidating. It's weird, since having him tethered to a wall should have made me feel safer. As his mannerisms come out, the rolling in my gut eases, leaving me fumbling with how to react.

"Let's get back on track. There was an explosion within the Barrens roughly an hour ago. I believe Anders is behind it," Victor says, setting the gun on the front counter, and I nod as if I know what he's talking about. "He's escalating within the other territories as well, as I'm sure you've seen."

"Seems like you don't really need me then, hmm. In that case, I have other things to do," I murmur, unwinding my arms and twisting my body so I can make a quick escape out the window.

"Like finding Mason?" Roman asks, and I whip back around.

"If you know where he is, then perhaps you'd like to tell me? Sharing is caring, after all."

He shrugs as he pulls out another granola bar. I don't think he was starving like I was when I was in the hole, but he's snacking as if his life depends on it. I have the irrational urge to march over and rip it from his hands. This entire trip was a waste. I thought I was doing the right thing—ready to trade my life for Mason's. Now all I've done is waste precious time when I could have been helping the others and figuring out where Mason disappeared to.

Victor sighs, shaking his head. "We're not entirely sure, but you *can* help us locate Anders."

Victor slides a tablet from next to his gun and I tense, waiting for him to grab the weapon and force me. Instead, he shuffles forward, extending the device to me. I take it, if only so he'll give me some space. Having him close enough to touch is giving me the heebie-jeebies.

"What am I supposed to do with this?"

"Anders must be operating from somewhere. He's not as adept at these types of things as you are. Therefore, you should be able to locate him."

"And then what?"

"What do you mean?" Roman growls.

"What do we get out of this?"

Roman narrows his eyes, opening his mouth, probably to spout some bullshit when Victor cuts him off.

"You're failing to see that we're on the same side, my dear. Also, I'm sure you'd like for his hold over the city to be broken."

A headache is starting to form behind my eyes, and I pinch the bridge of my nose to ease the ache.

"I can *maybe* see how you're on our side, Victor, but him?" I gesture toward Roman, who smirks. "And Anders doesn't have a hold over Synd. Sure, he's being a little dickhead–ish, but it's nothing we can't handle."

"Except he's preparing to blow the bridges over the river. He also has the police chief, the mayor, the commissioner, and some of the lower gangs in his back pocket. He's been fucking with the supply lines for months. He's behind a fuck ton more than I am. Everything that's occurred since I was taken is tied to him. He's much more powerful than you think," Roman snarls.

"Except he's been dead for like a decade."

I roll my eyes before glancing at the tablet. It's nothing special, just standard issue. Anything I do on this thing could be traced and our location pinged. I can cover my tracks, but the lack of security makes my palms itch. Accessing the mainframe for the cameras is easy, but I'll only have a few minutes before someone catches on if they're monitoring things. And if Jason Grayson is involved, he'll definitely have someone keeping an eye on the program and who's watching.

"While I understand your hesitancy at doing anything for me, Ms. Webb, and I can't guarantee I won't try to take out your lover, I can promise I won't do it tonight."

"Excuse me if your word doesn't hold much weight with me, Mr. Drake."

"Would it help if I gave you the gun, my dear?" Victor asks, advancing on me with his weapon in hand.

I recoil, smashing into the window frame. Suddenly, Roman slides in front of me and grabs my arm to steady me. Victor freezes, and I catch the snarl on Roman's face before he turns to the older man.

His fingers flex before he drops his hand, blocking my view. I'm caught between terror at Victor shoving a gun in my face and uneasiness at Roman's defense. There's no reason he should care. In fact, he should be basking in my fear. Instead, he's shielding me from something he knows I can't handle.

"She doesn't like guns and for good reason. Back the fuck off."

Victor stumbles back, watery eyes wide as he sets the gun back on the counter and steps away from it. The tension eases from my muscles as Roman advances on the older man.

"Why don't I like them?" I whisper before he can rip into Victor. At least that's what I assume he's about to do.

Roman glances over his shoulder, pinning me in place with the intensity of his gaze. "That's how your brother died."

It's not an answer. Not really. This is the second time he's brought up a long-lost brother. I dismissed his claims before. None of it made sense, but as the weight of my trauma threatens to suffocate me, I'm questioning why Roman would lie. In the grand scheme of things, none of this matters, but I desperately want to know what knowledge he holds. Who wouldn't if they found out they had a long twin who died, especially one they couldn't remember? If there's even a sliver of possibility that he's telling the truth, I can't let this opportunity slip by.

He could still be lying, playing with my emotions just enough to get me to trust him and then pull the rug out from under me. Still doesn't make sense in my brain. These aren't the type of things I decipher. I deal with codes and documents. I find the patterns within the numbers. Then I hand the problem off to someone smarter than me to analyze them. I get people into places so they can handle the mess other people have created. I washed my hands of trying to decipher the motives of other people when I left my parents.

Glancing down, I get to work, unwilling to explore the emotions bubbling up inside me. The sooner I can get this done, the sooner I can get back to finding Mason. If Victor and Roman find Anders and take him out, then maybe I'll actually have a future filled with something other than heartache.

My fingers freeze, the screen blurring as the thought of a future with Mason. Not running from him or retiring on some beach far from here. A future filled with love and bickering and sneaking statues of hippos into Reaper territory. A dream of living by his side instead of merely existing while nursing a broken heart.

Mason wouldn't care that I work strange hours. He wouldn't care that I lose track of time. He wouldn't care about any of my quirks as long as I came home to him.

I shake away the illusion, and their muffled voices break through, flowing over me. As my fingers fly over the screen, an alert pops up and I swipe it away without even thinking, then freeze again. Pulling it up again, I read it twice before I search the cameras once more. The timer in the corner blinks, reminding me I'm almost out of time.

There's one building that went offline months ago, right before Mason caught me sneaking through the woods. I asked him about it after I told him I was Nemesis, but he decided it wasn't important. They'd abandoned the building and shut off the cameras, so he told me not to worry about it. I went against my better judgment and pushed it to the bottom of the list. Now I wish I would have paid attention.

I pull up the feed and the camera flicks on. A familiar smirk, one I've witnessed a thousand times, graces his face as blood trickles down his cheek. Brown eyes find mine, piercing even through the screen, and he raises an eyebrow, challenging me. An older man's face blocks my view, a sinister grin on his lips. The image goes black.

The tablet crashes to the ground, screen shattering as it slides to rest at Roman's feet. He grabs my arms, squeezing until my eyes meet his. His mouth moves, but the ringing in my ears drowns out whatever he's saying.

Victor's hand falls on Roman's shoulder, shaking him. Or maybe I'm shaking. His nails dig into my skin before he releases me, rounding on Victor. I climb out the window, shins scrapping on the broken glass, and then I stumble into the shadows. My mind empties of all but one thought—

Save Mason.

Sixty-One

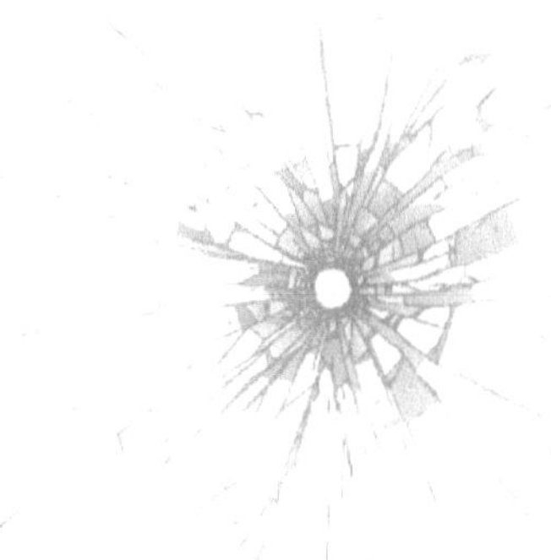

Mason

Flames lick at my face, engulfing my senses, as Anders runs the tip of the knife down my cheek. Gritting my teeth, I hold back the yell gathering in my throat. Apparently smarting off to the older man is not the way to deal with the anxiety rolling through me. Time warps the longer I'm strapped to this chair, the metal cuffs chafing against my skin.

Digging my wrists into the metal restraints, I use the bite of pain to distract me from the knife tearing up my face. If this is what Lacey experienced, I'm even more in awe of her. I'm barely holding back my anguish. And she wasn't tied down like I am. She stayed still while Razor tortured her. If I get out of this, I'll kiss the ground she walks on, promising whatever deity willing to listen that I'll spend the rest of my days worshiping her.

"I'm impressed, Byrns. I didn't take you for someone able to withstand this type of torture. I'd assume you'd become complacent and weak."

"I wouldn't call what you've done so far torture."

Anders's hand whips out, punching me in the jaw, and my head snaps back. An ache rattles across my face and my ear rings from the force.

"Your father wailed while I filleted him like a fish," he snarls.

Turning to the side, I spit blood at his feet. "If you're trying to piss me off, you'll have to use something other than my bastard of a father to do it."

His grin sends a chill down my spine. "Oh, like your dear sister Samantha? Perhaps Lacey, or should I call her Nemesis?"

My chest tightens as I school my face. "Threaten Sam all you want. She's a lot better with knives than you are. As for Lacey, she's an easy distraction, but you understand how that works. I'm sure she took off as soon as she figured out you were alive."

Leaning into the public persona of who I am is harder than I thought. Anders doesn't look convinced as he scoffs and adjusts his knife. I keep expecting him to stab me, but the worst he's done is hit me a few times and cut my face.

Lights flash across the front of the building, barely reaching us in the back, but they disappear along with my hope. I glance at the camera tucked in the corner of the room. It's dangling by a thread now—useless. I tried to keep my eyes from it, but a stirring in my chest had me focusing on the lens. When the tiny red light blinked on, I couldn't hold back my grin, knowing she had found me. Anders noticed, and he bashed it with the butt of his gun and then started in on my face with the knife.

"You're cocky, much like your father. I wonder if you'll last longer than he did. Although we might not have much time if your girlfriend was watching."

He slams his hand into my chin, and my teeth clack together, forcing my head back again. Groaning, I roll my neck before I swallow down the bile. He drives his fist into my stomach, and I struggle to pull air into my lungs. I'm pretty sure he clipped a rib, though I doubt it's broken.

Anders fingers wrap around my throat, squeezing, and I shake my head violently to ease his grip. He snarls, pushing my head back, restricting my airflow even more. Waving the gun in front of my face, he presses the barrel against my lips. I clamp them together, shaking my head again, but his hold is too tight.

He eases off my throat and instinctively I gasp, only to have the gun shoved into my mouth, metal scraping against my teeth. I gag, tears filling my eyes of their own accord. There's no way I'll survive if he pulls the trigger. The pressure on my throat returns as my eyes fall closed.

Images scroll past my lids—Lacey scowling, poking me in the chest. Lacey's sleepy smile greeting me in the morning, Lacey pacing back and forth, eyes bright with excitement as she explained some new piece of tech. She stole my heart, wholly and completely. I can't think of a better way to die than with the vision of her seared in my mind.

Just when the tension eases from my muscles and I've accepted my fate, the pressure eases and the barrel is ripped from my mouth, tearing the corner of my lips. Coughing, I tuck my chin to my chest, tears streaming down my face. My cheek is numb and blood drips from my chin onto my dark shirt.

The lights wink out, darkness descending in the blink of an eye. Shuffling feet off to my right are the only indication of where the older man is. My entire body aches and my head lolls. Anders's punches were weak but strategic, aimed at incapacitating me until the fight drained out of me. I didn't notice before, I was so distracted with trying to find a way out of this.

His fingers dig into my hair, forcing my head up, and he presses the barrel to my temple. I don't have the energy to fend him off. A soft beep echoes around the room, and I realize that must have tipped him off to someone coming. Hope blooms in my chest, then crashes into a deep pit of despair as the lights flare to life.

Lacey frames the doorway, hair a riot around her head, and eyes trained on me. I narrow my own, willing her to run. As much as I wanted her to find me, I wanted her to send someone else, anyone else. She's not trained for this type of thing. Her skills lie behind a screen.

"Ah, *Nemesis*. How lovely it is for you to join us," Anders sneers. "Unfortunately, I only have the one chair, but it will be unoccupied soon."

She blinks, tilting her head, and I shudder. We've spent enough time together for me to know what's coming. She'll mouth off and get herself killed. And it'll be my fault.

"I believe you have something of mine," she murmurs, hands tucked behind her back, and she rocks on her heels.

Anders snorts, the most normal sound I've heard from him so far. "Yours? Hardly. Why just a few minutes ago he was spouting off about your temporary status. I believe you've backed the wrong horse, little Lacey."

The corner of her lip pulls up, more of a curling of her lip than a smirk. "Wrong answer."

Pulling her arm from behind her back, she hurls something at him. She may not be able to shoot a gun, but she certainly has good aim as it smacks him in the face. His roar is more annoyance than pain, but his fingers release my hair as a can of baked beans rolls past my feet. Lacey throws herself to the side, probably expecting him to shoot her. He stalks around me, scooping up the can as he goes. As he advances on her, she scrambles into the corner, terror etched in her eyes.

Fighting against my bonds, I bellow her name, wishing I would have fought harder—that she never would have come here at all. I scream at Anders, tearing the skin from my wrists and blood drips to the floor, puddling at my feet. I almost choke when Victor slips through the door, making his way silently to me. When Roman follows, I know we're fucked.

Victor slashes his hand through the air, but whatever he's trying to convey is lost when Anders spins around, dropping the can. I scream at him, hoping to distract him long enough for Lacey to run. A manic grin crosses Anders's face as he points the gun at his son, who freezes.

His arm wavers as he swings it toward me. My eyes lock on Lacey's green ones, urging her to look away, but she holds my stare. Time slows as the sharp report of the gun rings out and I brace for the searing pain I've felt once before. I wait for the blackness to overwhelm me. A body diving in front of me cuts off my view of her, his frame jerking ever so slightly before time speeds up, and my uncle's body crashes to the ground.

Anders curses as Roman rushes him, but my eyes fix on Victor, dead at my feet. Gasping breaths fill my ears. It's not until Lacey's fingers start digging at the cuffs, I realize they're my own. Her tear-filled eyes find mine.

"Mason, how do I get these off?" she whispers, whipping her head around when Roman smashes his father into one of the shelves.

"Pick the lock," I say, tracking the grappling men's movements.

"I just threw a can of beans at him. What makes you think I can pick a goddamn lock?"

I can't help the grin from spreading across my face. I sober when Anders throws Roman into the wall and he crashes to the ground, head bouncing off the concrete.

"Lacey, run."

"No, I'm not leaving you here," she sobs, tugging at the metal.

"Lacey," I murmur, lifting my hand as much as my bonds will allow to brush my fingers against hers. "I love you."

"Abso-fucking-lutely not," she snarls through gritted teeth. "You don't get to fucking do that."

Anders prowls toward her, tangling his fingers into her hair and dragging her back. Her hands fly to her head, feet sliding as she tries to gain purchase. He tosses her against the shelf, and she moans, curling in on herself.

"Get the fuck away from her," I roar, renewing my efforts to free myself, though I know it's no use.

He must have lost his gun in the struggle with his son, because he grabs mine off the shelf and points it at her.

"Who shall I shoot first, hmm? Your little hacker?" He swings the barrel to my chest. "Or you?"

"Let her go. She doesn't have anything to do with this," I growl.

He twists to Roman, still passed out on the floor. "I could start with my own flesh and blood, I suppose. Though, I think it would be more appropriate to incapacitate her and then let her watch you die as she bleeds out. Then I can take care of the rest."

Roman groans, struggling to his hands and knees before lifting his head. Bruises pepper his face and blood trickles into his beard from a cut below his eye. He sways, leaning against the wall as he gains his feet. Anders smiles, blue eyes identical to Roman's crinkling around the edges.

"Ah, Roman. How you've grown. So unfortunate we weren't able to have more time together."

"Father." He swipes the back of his hand across his mouth. "Whose fault is that?"

Glancing at Lacey, I track her as she scoots toward me. Frustration bleeds through my body, and I bare my teeth at her. She should be running for the door, not willingly putting herself in more danger.

"You've done a magnificent job so far. I'll take over from here. As I've told you a thousand times, I always finish what I start."

"You did live by those words. I also seem to remember you promising to protect Aelia," he spits out.

Lacey heaves to her feet, staying crouched as her eyes track Anders. She glances at me and I shake my head. Reading the decision in her eyes, I silently plead with her to abandon her plan. Anders pulls my attention away from her when he chuckles.

"Your sister was a necessary pawn in a larger picture you couldn't possibly grasp at seventeen. I'm sure living with two lies was hard, but you won't have to suffer for long." Shock flits across Roman's face then morphs, his pain almost palpable as it radiates from his body. "Don't worry, she served her purpose, just as you did."

I'm so focused on their exchange, I jerk back when Anders doubles over, clutching his head. Lacey stands behind him, blood smeared across the can in her hand. She skips around, bashing him again, and he whips his arm out, catching her in the stomach. She stumbles back, fear flashing in her eyes when Anders aims the barrel at her chest.

"No," Roman bellows.

He rushes Lacey, shoving her to the side as a gunshot reverberates around the space and Roman falls to his knees. Lacey dashes in, sobbing as she hits Anders in the head again. My stomach rolls as he turns to her, but Roman launches at his legs, tackling him to the ground. Blood trails in their wake and the weapon tumbles from his hand, resting at Lacey's feet.

Her eyes find mine and it looks like she's about to puke. Anguish fills me, wishing I could be the one to save her from this fate. She'll live with it the rest of her life, relive killing him in her nightmares. I can only hope she'll let me hold her through them.

Anders kicks at his son's leg, forcing a yell laced with pain from Roman. Lacey lifts the weapon, her hands trembling as she trains it on Anders, who's scrambling for the back door. Keeping my eyes on her, I suck in a breath as tears stream down her face.

A soft crackling noise fills the space, then a hissing overpowers it. Craning my head around, I spot Anders grinning as he tosses a smoke bomb toward my chair.

"I'll give the Guild your regards," he declares before the smoke envelops him.

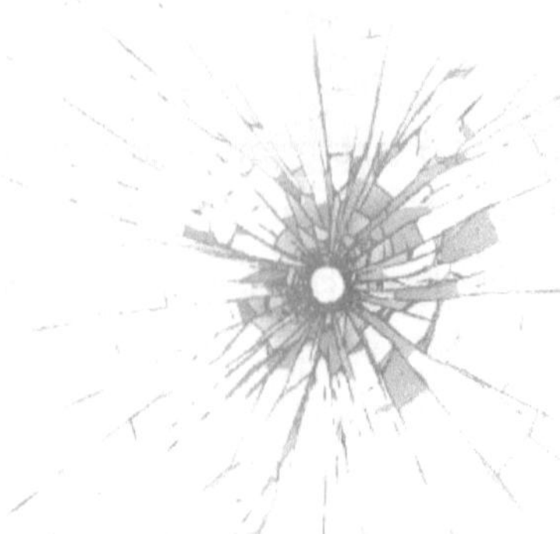

Sixty-Two

Lacey

Terror cascades down my body, every muscle locked as the cold metal of the gun bites into my palms. My vision tunnels until only the barrel remains, wavering in and out of focus. Rapid thudding drums in my ears, and I realize it's my heartbeat, thrashing through me like a wild beast begging to be set free. My knuckle pops as I wrap my finger around the trigger, but I can't bring myself to do anything more than that.

"Lacey!" Mason's voice pierces the bubble I'm in.

The gun is pried from my hands and my limbs drop, fingers tingling as the numbness slowly seeps away. The rest of the room comes into focus, though I can't make out more than a hazy film over the space. Smoke fills the room, rapidly obscuring Anders's grinning face.

I jolt when a gunshot rings out, and Roman's body tumbles to the ground. When I was holding the weapon, the bubble wrapped around me felt like a vise, slowly closing in on me. Now that the immediate threat is gone, the space around my body is safety come to life. If I step over the invisible line, I'll shatter, bits of myself scattering across the concrete, forever lost in the shadows rippling through the still air.

A hand brushes my arm, featherlight but burning nonetheless, and I stumble away from the flames licking up my skin. The illusion of invisible protection is broken as my chest heaves and the world around me comes into focus.

Clamping my lips together, I cut off the whimpers that were escaping without my permission. My gaze bounces from one body to the next—Victor's lifeless eyes staring up at the ceiling, Roman writhing and clutching his leg, and Mason's mouth a slash across his face as he stares at me.

Sam's face swims in front of me, blocking my view, and her brows dip low over her brown eyes. She tugs the hood from her head, brushing the hair from her face as she glances over her shoulder and then back at me.

"You okay?" she asks, concern etched across her face.

I nod, afraid I'll puke on her if I open my mouth. She doesn't look convinced, but moves to Mason, kicking Victor's arm out of her way as she passes.

"Seriously? You had a whole-ass battle and didn't even call me? How rude," she says, planting her hands on her hips.

"I was a little tied up," Mason says, pursing his lips.

Pressing my fist into my mouth, I bite down, hoping to stop the tears from falling. Mason is a mess of dark slashes and smudged bruises. Blood covers the right side of his face. He grimaces before rolling his neck. I have no idea how long he was here before I saw him on the camera. How many other wounds cover his body?

"At least you're still conscious," Sam says. "I'm guessing I have to save your sorry ass from this chair, then? I told you it was a bad idea to weld the cuffs to it."

"Seemed like a good idea at the time," he mutters, wincing when Sam pulls at the restraints.

"Lacey, you got a bobby pin?" she calls, looking back at me. I drop my hand before shaking my head.

Stumbling closer, I skirt around Roman, still clutching his leg, averting my eyes from Victor's lifeless body. I don't want to crowd her as she works, but I can't keep losing it next to the door. She sighs, pulling out a knife from fuck knows where before pushing the tip into a small slit on the side.

"Do not fucking cut me," Mason growls, eyes fixed on what she's doing.

"If my dagger breaks, you're buying me a new one." She wiggles it back and forth, cursing, and then it pops open.

Her cry of triumph startles me. I jerk back, almost stumbling over the can of beans smeared with blood and lying innocently on the floor. It rolls away before resting against the wall.

"Don't lose that, Lacey. It's dinner," Mason says, his tone lined with laughter, and I glance up.

Sam frees his other wrist, and he groans, tipping his head back as he tucks his arms to his chest. The outlines of the cuffs are etched into his skin, angry crimson marks painted along his flesh. Gingerly, he touches his cheek, flinching. Sam tosses a black bandanna on his lap, then gets to work on his legs. I sink to my knees next to him, hands fluttering by my sides, unsure how to comfort him. Sam crows again in triumph as the cuffs around his ankles release. I stumble upright, swaying as the adrenaline ebbs away with the smoke that lingers in the air.

As he presses the fabric to his face, I blanch, my own cheek screaming an echo of pain. My scar pulses as I slam my eyes shut to keep the images of my time in captivity at bay. Mason wraps his arms around me, cradling my head against his chest. The pounding of his heart resonating in my ear grounds me in the present.

"How are you still standing?" I whisper, trying to push him away, but his arms tense, holding me close.

"Not the first time I've been in this position. I'll be okay." He pushes back, gripping my arms lightly and glaring. "What the hell were you thinking?"

"Hardly the time, Mase. What are we going to do with this asshole?" Sam calls, digging her toe into Roman's ribs. The man groans, rolling to the side before pushing up.

"Leave him be, Sam."

She rolls her eyes, stepping back and crossing her arms. Roman glances toward me, scanning me up and down.

"Are you okay?" Roman asks, harsh breaths leaving him as he presses a hand to his leg.

"I'm fine," I whisper.

Sam's head swivels between us, pursing her lips. "So, are we killing him or…?"

"Don't," I cry, tearing myself from Mason's grasp, ready to throw myself between Roman and Sam.

Mason grunts as he wraps an arm around my waist, tugging me against him. Sam holds up her hands, stepping back. Mason murmurs into my hair, but I'm fixated on Roman. For all his asshole comments, he's saved me twice. I won't be able to convince them to let him go, no matter what he did for me. He terrorized Synd, blew up buildings, fucked with Mason's money, and yet I still can't bring myself to think of him as the villain.

"We're not going to kill him, Kitten. I'll take care of it," he murmurs.

Tugging from his grasp, I spin on him, poking him in the chest. "Don't fucking start with me. You always say that and then what? How are you going to fix this, Mason? Because from where I'm standing, all you've done is shoulder everything yourself. Look where it got you."

Roman clears his throat and I spin around. "Hate to interrupt, but someone should go after my father."

"He's long gone. Probably slipped off into the Barrens," Sam says, giving him a wide berth as she walks to the back door. "Was he shot?"

Mason staggers toward her, almost falling to his knees, before slowly lowering himself to the ground and cradling his head in his hands.

"Roman shot through the smoke at him. Sam, we need help."

She crouches, pulling out another bandanna from her pocket before swiping the fabric across the floor. Glancing up, she meets my eyes as she lifts the cloth now smeared with blood.

"He was definitely hit. I'm not one to assume, but maybe he'll die a slow death from sepsis. I've heard that's painful."

"Sam, we have to go. Call the doctor or someone. We have to get them home before they pass out," I say, settling next to Mason. He leans on me, his breath rattling in his chest.

"Here we go," Roman mutters and I turn.

Alex fills the doorway, grinning as he takes in the carnage around us.

"What the hell are you doing here, Alex? You were supposed to be tracking Grayson." Sam scowls, dropping the fabric on the puddle of blood before standing.

"Just searched where the best place to eat out was and it brought me here," he says, smirking at her.

She sighs, and Mason lets out a noise in the back of his throat. There's a beat of silence and then Roman chuckles, clutching his side and groaning.

Alex claps his hands. "Welp, this was fun. How about we skedaddle before someone bleeds out, yeah?"

Padding down the dark hallway, I glance behind me. Moonlight glitters across the hardwood floors, lighting my way. I keep expecting someone to jump out, demanding to know why I left Mason alone. This is the first time I've left his side in four days. Even being down the hall from him is making my skin itch.

He was sound asleep when I left, snoring softly as I slipped from under his arm. Normally, I wouldn't be up at three in the morning on my way to a secret rendezvous, but when Samantha Byrns requests my presence, I understand I don't really have an option.

The heavy door to her old bedroom swings open silently, spilling darkness from the room into the hall. I hesitate, bracing myself before I step inside.

"Why are we sneaking?" Sam's whispered voice floats past me, and I spin around.

Pressing my hand to my chest, I scowl. "What the hell is wrong with you?"

"Sorry, forgot how jumpy you are."

She skips across the room and a lamp flares to life, banishing the darkness to the far corners of the massive bedroom. Settling against the headboard, she pats the space beside her and pulls out a plastic container.

I sit next to her, stretching out my legs out on the black comforter. "Why do you have celery?"

She rips a piece off the stalk with her teeth before munching away, grimacing the entire time.

"Shane keeps telling me I need to snack on healthy shit, too. You remember the oranges." Her voice drops, imitating the mafia leader. "'All in moderation, Princess.'"

I smile, waving her away when she tries to hand me one. "I thought celery didn't have any nutritional value."

"That's what I said," she cries, waving the stick around. "Wouldn't listen to me until *Alex* said something. As if he's all-knowing about random shit. I mean, he is, but still. I know shit too."

"Did you want to meet so you could grumble? Because if so, that's fine, but could we maybe not do it in the middle of the night?" I suppress a yawn as my eyelids droop.

"Not getting much sleep?" She makes a face at the celery before shoving the cover back on. "Probably a stupid question. Mason was always shit at being laid up for whatever reason. One time, he got the flu and thought he could still do a run. Ended up puking on a box of guns. TJ was *not* happy."

"He's fine. I mean, not fine, but he's healing."

We sit in silence, and I pick at the hem of Mason's shirt, twisting the fabric around my fingers.

"You can't let him slip, Lacey. Before—" She pulls in a shaky breath. "It was bad. If you don't yank him back from the edge, we'll lose him forever."

"That won't happen. It's not like before."

She doesn't look convinced. She drops something between us, nudging it toward me.

"What's this?" I ask.

"It's a Taser. Figured you could use that since you're not really up for the other options I would typically suggest."

"I don't know how to use this." Even as I say the words, I grip the small device, turning it over in my hands.

"Uh, you're a freaking hacker. I'm pretty sure you can figure it out." Rolling her head to me, she pins me in place. "What'd we find out about Roman?"

"The Drake family apparently helped form Synd, or at the very least, were here for quite a while. Twenty years ago, there was a falling out. The papers said it was over a woman, but who knows how accurate that is. Apparently, the other families drove the Drakes out, burned down their house, and wiped them from existence. The Drakes disappeared until Anders came back eight years later for his revenge. He succeeded, sort of, but it wasn't enough."

"So Anders wanted to take over, hmm?" Sam says, tapping a finger against her lips.

I shake my head. "He didn't just want them destroyed. He wanted Synd to fall. When the Guild came, it seemed like the perfect opportunity. You saw how that worked for them. I'm sure he'll be back, but he'll need to regroup. He didn't have enough support this time. I'm sure he'll plead with the Guild for help."

"Well, that fucking sucks," Sam sighs, her head thumping against the wood.

"I'm sure you'll figure it out," I say, patting her knee.

"Me? Uh, fuck that. I ain't doing this shit alone."

"You know, the founding families were crazy close to each other. They had this dream of forming a town that wouldn't be overrun by stagecoach bandits or something. They settled here, the Byrns, the Kings, and the Drakes. Once it became big enough, they had one of the Drakes build the mansions, complete with secret tunnels." I grin as her mouth drops open.

"I mean, it makes sense, but why?"

"Because they were so close. Then if something happened, they could run to the nearest house and know exactly where they were going to keep themselves safe. It was their final defense."

"Please tell me they didn't inter-marry or something like that," she says, shuddering.

I chuckle, shaking my head. "They didn't mingle their blood-lines. I found an old diary that talked about how they were worried about concentrating too much power in one family in case there was a bad egg. Oh, and they were raised like siblings, so they'd most likely get icked out by that."

She nods, leaping off the bed before poking through the dresser. I track her as she moves to the desk, rummaging through the drawers.

"Are you looking for something in particular?"

She sighs. "Yeah, I used to have this necklace Mason got me for Christmas one year. I hid it so Dad wouldn't find it, but now I can't remember where I put it. I had a dream about it and can't get it out of my head."

"You should have Emma try to find it." Pushing up, I shuffle toward the door, yawning.

"Emma?"

"She's a fourteen-year-old girl. You think she's not hiding shit in her room? Because she totally is. She'd find your hiding spot in an hour."

Sam nods, narrowing her eyes. "You just might be right."

She saunters to the window, pushing the sill up before throwing a leg over.

"Don't fall to your death," I call, and she ducks her head back in.

"Don't worry. I'm pretty sure I'd bounce anyways." Her laughter trails off into the night as she vanishes.

Sixty-Three

Mason

Peeling my eyes open is harder than I expect. Five days is apparently not enough time to heal from getting my ass handed to me. I keep waiting for someone to call me on it, how I fucked up going after Anders alone, but I've barely seen anyone other than Lacey and the doctor.

"Psst. Byrnsie, you awake?"

I groan, slamming my eyes closed again. "What the fuck do you want, Alex?"

"It's my turn to make sure you haven't plummeted into nothingness. Not gonna lie, thought you'd be awake since it's the middle of the day, but I guess getting your shit beat down really does a number on ya, huh?" He picks up the can of beans I grabbed on our way out of the warehouse, raising an eyebrow at me and I shrug.

I scowl as he pulls a chair closer, swinging it around and straddling it. "I'm fine. Anything else you needed?"

"Oh, don't be like that. Where's Lacey?" He glances around the room, as if she'll pop out of the fireplace.

"She's working—something about trying to find where Anders slithered off to."

"So, she's sticking around then? Or are we going to do a stake out her house again?" He almost looks excited for another recon mission.

"Of course she is. Synd is her home."

He rolls his eyes. "You know staying in Synd and staying with your sorry ass isn't the same thing. Hell, I was terrified when Sam was here after, well, you know. Ren kept saying to trust her, but that was never the problem."

"It's trusting everything around you," I murmur, and he nods.

He clears his throat, dropping his head. "Is she mad at me?"

"No. She understands, but if you ever pull that shit again, I'll bury your ass."

"Noted. In fact, I'll help you. You know I called this."

"Called what? Me gallivanting off after a rogue former mafia head of Synd intent on our destruction?"

He grins. "Nope. Remember when Lacey took off when we were staking out her house?"

"We weren't staking out her house," I growl.

He waves away my words, face softening ever so slightly. "I told her I thought you were falling for her."

An ache forms in my chest. "How'd she respond?"

Sighing, his head dips. "She asked how someone like you could ever fall for someone like her."

I scowl, wishing I could storm off and shake her for thinking that shit. "Fucking hell."

"You tell her?" he demands, pinning me with a glare, and I shake my head.

I tried to tell her when I was bolted to a chair, but she stopped me. My only thought was I couldn't die without her knowing how I felt. Afterward, I was too strung out on pain meds to even broach the subject. The panel behind him pops open, revealing Lacey. She freezes, glancing between Alex and me.

"Maybe you should," he says.

I meet her gaze as she steps back and shake my head.

"She's the moon peeking through the clouds on a summer night, the soft breeze rustling through the trees in spring, the sun setting over the river on a brisk autumn evening. She's everywhere and everything—seeping into my life and filling the gaps within my soul, making me whole. She's the best and the worst and everything in between, and my life would be nothing without her. It would *mean* nothing…without her."

Alex opens his mouth, then snaps it shut when a choked sob leaves Lacey. Leaping from the chair, he salutes me before marching past her, patting her on the shoulder as he leaves. The panel thuds shut behind him. I hold out my hand and she stumbles toward me, tears streaming down her face.

Grinning, I grab her hand and pull her next to me. She curls into my body, resting a trembling hand on my chest, and I lace our fingers together. Sighing, I kiss the top of her head, breathing in her scent.

"I should have told you earlier," I murmur.

"I wouldn't have believed you."

"I thought it was pretty obvious how I felt. Even before, I couldn't stay away. You became essential to me."

"So leaving Synd is off the table?" She chuckles and then presses her lips to my neck.

"You go, I go, Kitten. If you leave, you take my heart with you, and I would die without my heart."

She lets out a strangled cry, burying her face in my chest. I hold her as she soaks my shirt. As her tears slow, she shudders.

"I love you too, Mason." Lifting her head, she knocks into my chin. My teeth clack together and I groan. "Shit, sorry."

Her hands run over my face, careful to avoid the still healing wound on my cheek. It wasn't as deep as I thought, though it bled like it was down to the bone. When the doctor told me it might not even scar, I was more in awe of Lacey and the way she held her shit together.

"Does it hurt?" she asks, eyes fixed on the wound.

I shake my head, pulling her mouth to mine and brush my lips over hers. She sighs, easing away, and I cling to her.

"Mason, you should rest."

"Except I've been resting nonstop for four days and I miss this," I growl, cupping her pussy.

She shudders before glaring at me. "The doctor said—"

"Fuck the doctor."

"No, thanks. I'd rather fuck you," she says, smirking.

Thumping my head against the wood, I laugh, the ache in my chest easing. I've carried it so long, I didn't realize how heavy it was until I let go, clinging to what I have in front of me rather than what could have been. I held on to the guilt for so long,

I didn't know how to function without it. Lacey's bright eyes meet mine, a grin playing on her lips.

"Okay, but seriously, we shouldn't glaze the donut."

"What the fuck is 'glaze the donut'?"

She giggles, running her fingers through her hair. "Willow said it, and I thought it was funny."

Gripping her waist, I haul her over me so she's straddling my hips. "I never want to hear that come from your mouth again."

Her giggle turns into gasps when I drag her over my hardening cock. Her hands fall to my chest, nails digging through the fabric of my shirt and into my skin.

"Mason," she moans, throwing her head back.

"Hmm?" Skimming my hands up her sides, I groan when I realize she's not wearing a bra. "If you're trying to get me to wait, maybe you shouldn't have all this skin available to my wandering hands."

Gathering the hem of her shirt, I whip it over her head and toss it to the side. I cup her tits, brushing my fingers over her nipples, catching the piercing with my nail and flicking it. Her back arches, jutting her chest out, and I wrap my lips around her nipple, toying with the bar with my fingers on the other as I do. A whimper escapes her as I swirl my tongue around the bud.

When her fingers dig into my hair, holding me in place, I know I've won her over. She pushes me back and my head smacks against the wood. She rests her forehead on mine as she catches her breath and huffs as my hands continue to explore her skin.

"Something you wanted to say, Kitten?"

"Rules," she gasps when I pinch her nipples, rolling them between my fingers.

Her hips rock against mine, creating the friction her body is begging for.

"Which rules do you have in mind?" I murmur against her skin.

She quivers as I swipe my tongue against her flesh and then nibble on her neck. Latching onto her hips, I dig my fingers in, stopping her movements. My cock swells the more she rubs against me. It's been too long since I've been inside her, and I'm already close to losing it. I could flip her over and thrust into her wetness, but she's right. I'm not fully healed and then I'd have to wait even longer to fuck her again.

"You have to take it easy," she says, trying to sound firm, but the breathlessness in her voice gives away how riled up she is.

"Oh, don't worry, Kitten. You'll be doing all the work," I murmur.

I hook my thumbs in the waistband of her leggings and tug them down her hips along with her thong. She stands, feet planted on either side of me, and I tug them down until she steps out of them. Before she can sink down again, I wrap my hands around the back of her thighs and yank her toward me, burying my face into her pussy.

She squeaks, hands slapping against the wall to hold herself up, and I grin. Peeking at her, our eyes meet, a warning in hers. They roll back when I lick through her wetness and swirl my tongue around her clit. Head thumping against the wall, her legs quiver as I repeat the move, basking in her taste as it explodes in my mouth.

Her harsh breaths fill the room, swirling around me and egging me on. Sliding one hand to her ass, I knead the flesh as my tongue continues to savor her essence. When I push a finger inside her dripping pussy, I suck her clit into my mouth, and she crumples, knees colliding with my shoulders. I add another finger, and her pussy spasms as I curl them inside her.

Flicking my tongue against her clit, she detonates, moaning low and long as she rocks her hips in time with my fingers, still deep inside her. When her breathing slows, I pull them from her and lick them clean, eyes fixed on her as she gazes down at me.

Lifting my hips, I shove my sweatpants down and free my cock, stroking myself as she watches. Desire drips from her and I run my gaze down her body. Her pussy glistens and I lean forward, licking the inside of her thigh, straight to her core.

"What the hell was that?" she squawks, body shivering.

"Just cleaning you up, Kitten. Now get down here and ride my cock."

I don't wait for her to respond, grabbing her hips and yanking. Her squeal turns into a whimper as I guide my cock into her. Thrusting up, I groan when I'm fully inside, her heat enveloping me. Sliding my hands up her sides, I cup her face, bringing her mouth to mine. She moans when I lick her lips and sweep my tongue into her mouth. She pulls away when I rock my hips against hers.

"Like how you taste?" I ask with a smirk.

"Oh god," she moans.

Wrapping my hand around her throat, I squeeze. "The only name you should be moaning is mine, Kitten."

Easing her back, her hands hit the comforter, my cock swelling at the new angle. I grip her hips, surging into her, eyes fixed on her tits as they bounce with each thrust. Her voice is needy as my name falls from her lips, over and over. When her pussy clenches around me, I stop. Her cry of frustration echoes around me as I grin.

"Mason," she whines.

Hooking an arm around her back, I tug her close, melding our bodies together. I kiss her slowly, sliding my fingers into her hair and tugging her head back. Kissing down her throat, she hums, the sound reverberating through me. While I'd love to make her come, I want to make this last.

"So fucking beautiful," I murmur, nipping at her piercing, and she quivers around me.

"Please," she begs, arching her back.

"You can do better than that."

"Mason, please. I need it harder—deeper," she whimpers, rocking her hips.

Growling, I lift her off me, and she cries out.

"Turn around."

She scrambles to obey me, and I squeeze my cock to relieve the pressure building within me. As she drops to her hands and knees, I groan, stroking myself. I slap her ass, and her head dips as I eye the blush developing on her skin. Usually, I would love her in this position, ready and waiting to take me as deep as her pussy can, but not today. I caress the mark I've made and then tug her back, easing her onto her knees.

Slipping inside her once more, she lets out a soft "oh" as her pussy pulses around me. I reach around to cup her tits, massaging them as she starts to move.

"Faster, Lacey. Use my cock to make yourself come."

Her chest heaves under my hands as she slams down, her pace becoming erratic. Dropping a hand to her clit, I circle the bud, keeping time with her. I've barely worked her up when she shatters, falling forward as her pussy clings to me.

When she catches her breath, I ease her off me once more and she whimpers, falling to the side. Rolling her over, I cover her body with my own, slipping into her warmth again. Nuzzling her neck, I thrust into her steadily, stoking the flame inside us both. I want to bask in her body, savoring each breath falling from her lips. Gazing into her bright green eyes, I'm caught, wholly and completely—entranced as our bodies meld together.

She wraps her legs around me, running her hands across my back. Bracing on my forearms, I bury my cock into her, grunting with every thrust. I dip down, covering her mouth with my own, drinking in her whimpers. When her nails dig into my skin, I grunt, and she thrashes under me. Her legs fall to the side, and I rip my mouth away and sit up. Latching onto her hips, I surge into her over and over.

"Play with your clit, Lacey. Make me come for you," I growl.

Her hand slides down her body while her other lifts over her head and grips the edge of the mattress. Fixing my eyes on her touching herself, I almost tip over the edge. Desperate noises fall from her lips as she arches her back, and I slide my hand under her, holding her up. She shudders, sailing into oblivion. I let go, a weightlessness overwhelming me as she spasms around me.

I drop to my forearms, peppering her skin with kisses as she moans my name. Nipping and sucking at her flesh, I roll my hips, prolonging her pleasure. I turn us to the side, cradling her body to mine. She sighs, laying her head on my arm as I brush my fingers across her damp skin.

"We should get up. Go do…something," she mumbles.

"We should stay just like this, me deep inside you, until I'm ready to make love to you again."

"Make love, hmm?" She giggles, peering up at me.

"Fuck, Lacey," I groan, tipping my head back. "You're never going to let me live that down, are you?"

She kisses my throat before scraping her teeth across my skin. Sliding my hand up, I grip her hair, tugging her head away before devouring her mouth, sweeping my tongue along hers. She squirms and my cock twitches inside her. When she wiggles again, I roll on top of her, holding her in place for me to dominate her body, her pleasure. A noise from the back of her throat urges me on. I pull out of her slowly before slamming into her again. Tearing my mouth away, I rest my forehead against hers, panting while desire swims in her eyes.

"What do you need, Lacey?"

"You," she breathes, moving her hips in time with my thrusts.

"You have me." I kiss her softly, surging into her, and she cascades into ecstasy, humming as she comes.

She gazes up at me and my heart clenches at the vulnerability in her bright green eyes.

"Do I?"

"All of me—forever."

Epilogue

Lacey

Yawning, I trip over the rug lying innocently on the floor and I wonder what the hell I'm doing. Two nights in a row of waking up at three in the morning is not something I particularly wanted to do. Pulling myself away from Mason and his ridiculously comfortable bed was harder tonight than it was last night when I met with Sam.

Another yawn escapes me, and I lean my hand against the wall as I squeeze my eyes shut. It isn't a long walk from Mason's bedroom to where they set Roman up, but it feels like a trek up the tallest mountain. He's been recovering and, according to Sam, biding his time. She's convinced he'll kill us in our sleep, even though he can't walk without crutches. I told her we'd have plenty of time to hear him coming for us, but she didn't think that was very funny.

I nod to the guard leaning against the opposite wall before I knock softly on the door, half of me hoping he isn't awake.

A grunt for me to enter dashes those hopes, and I sigh before stepping inside. I swing the door mostly closed, leaving a sliver of moonlight slashing across the hardwoods. Asking Mason not to kill him didn't erase the wariness turning in my gut. What to do with Roman has been crouching in the back of my mind, cropping up at the most random times. We have a meeting tomorrow, so we need to deal with shit now.

Leaning against the wall, I cross my arms, more to chase off the chill that's snuck up on me. I expected him to be propped up in bed, but when the lamp flares to life, I find him lounging in a comfy chair, leg elevated on the desk. He sets his phone down next to a book that looks suspiciously like one of Willow's and folds his hands over his stomach.

It's strange to see him dressed down in sweatpants and a t-shirt. Hell, it's strange to see him not covered in dirt and blood, to be honest. Willow's nickname of Mr. Sexy Pants really does apply now.

"Evening, Lacey."

"Oh, so it's Lacey now? Not Ms. Webb or Nemesis?" I ask bitterly. I didn't realize how much resentment I had built up against him.

He sighs, dropping his chin to his chest. "You know, in another life, I believe we would have got on quite well. Unfortunate that we met the way we did."

My mouth drops open. "Are you hitting on me?"

Roman chuckles, a smirk overtaking his face as he lifts his head. "Absolutely not. I like my head attached to my body, thank you very much. But also, you're not really my type."

His eyes skip past me, unfocused, as if he's locked in another world. He shakes his head, clearing his throat, and fixes his gaze on me again.

"What can I do for you?"

"I have questions."

He gestures for me to continue. Or maybe he's offering me the other chair in the room. I'm not quite sure. While it might not be the best decision, I definitely can't remain standing for this conversation.

"I'm assuming you want to know more about your family?" he asks when I settle in the chair I dragged closer to the door.

"Among other things, but we can start there."

"What would you like to know?"

He tilts his head, looking at me expectantly, but I don't know what to ask. I open my mouth, hoping something will magically fall out. It doesn't. There's no good place to start. Without all the information, or hell, even a smidgen, I don't know what I want to know.

He nods, and I'm pretty sure he's biting the inside of his cheek. "Why don't I just tell you what I know, hmm?"

"How do I know you'll tell me the truth?"

"I have evidence, if that's what you're asking. I'll gladly hand it over."

My finger traces my scar as I stare at his feet. "Why?"

"Why would I hand it over? Because it's not my history. It's yours. You deserve to know."

I huff, glancing around the room. "You're fucking confusing."

"I'm well aware. I understand why you're all leery of me. I would be as well. Clearly, I haven't done anything to endear me to you."

"You stopped Victor from handing me that gun," I whisper, but he waves away my words. "And you saved me from Anders. He would have killed me."

"He would have killed us all. How do you know I didn't do it to bamboozle you into thinking I was trustworthy? You brought me into your home, fixed me up, and are giving me the perfect opportunity to destroy you from the inside."

I smirk, tucking my hands into the front of my hoodie. It's actually Mason's, but I've worn it enough that it's mine now. I toy with my phone, wondering how much I should reveal. While Mason has been laid up recovering, I've been digging.

"You forget I'm a hacker, Mr. Drake. And you're not the only one who can uncover secrets," I murmur.

He scowls before leaning over and grabbing a blanket off the end of the bed. He tosses it to me, and I catch it instinctively. When I raise an eyebrow, he flushes.

"You're clearly chilled. Now would be the time you say thank you," he mutters, crossing his arms again.

"My, my, aren't we grumpy? Why don't you tell me about what you know and then I'll ask my questions."

"The questions you already seemingly know the answers to," he says, narrowing his eyes.

I grin, spreading the blanket over my legs. I didn't even realize how cold I was in just my leggings.

"Exactly. Proceed."

"Erasing your existence was done quite well, I must say. However, I had a—" He clears his throat. "Contact who helped me uncover some of your past. Your parents, June and Harry, as you knew them, fell in with a group."

"What group?"

"I never found out. I'd say the Guild, but that might be projecting my own issues. Once your mother became pregnant with your brother and you, I believe they felt they were in over their heads and ran. That strategy worked for several years, but when you were about four, the group caught up with them. There was some sort of firefight, and your brother was either killed in the crossfire or on purpose by the group. I'm not entirely sure which without knowing who the group was. You were by his side when he was shot. You held him while he died. There's a video, but I advise against watching it. The images are unsettling, to say the least."

He picks up his phone, fiddling with it for a minute, and then my own buzzes. I don't bother to take it out, as I'm sure he just sent me all his supposed evidence. I'll comb through it later, when Mason has recovered more. Or when we've dealt with putting our city back together. Or when I have literally nothing else going on. Right now, I doubt I'm ready. Maybe I'll have Mason watch through it first. He'll be able to figure out what I can handle and what needs to wait.

"What else?" I whisper.

"Your parents moved quite a bit after that, as I'm sure you know. Unfortunately, they blamed you for their downfall and your brother's death, I believe. After you left, they disappeared."

"Did you try to find them?"

He nods, sighing. "At first I thought they were dead, since there were death certificates. However, I believe the organization either finally caught them, or they've left the country. Either is plausible."

Tipping my head back, I suck in a deep breath. My parents were assholes, but at least they didn't leave me on the side of the road like they threatened so many times. I doubt I would have learned how to hack if that had happened. I feel…absolutely nothing. Which only makes guilt swirl through me. I should feel *something*, shouldn't I? Shaking my head, I push the thoughts away.

"And you?" I ask, fixing my gaze on Roman. "What's your story? All we've received are bits and pieces and cryptic riddles from you."

"Bear in mind, I was very young when I left Synd, almost ten, I believe. All my knowledge comes from my father, whom I'm sure you realize was not a particularly good one or a reliable source." He gestures to his leg, as if I can see the white bandages wrapped around his wound.

He grunts when he lifts himself from the chair, resettling with his feet on the floor. His face flushes, and he presses his hand to his chest as he struggles to breathe. I almost ask him if he's okay, but then he rubs his hand over his beard and his muscles tense.

"He took my sister and I to Westmont. Said it was far enough away that no one would follow us, but close enough we could exact our revenge when the time was right. I was raised on hatred and revenge. He spent years raging against the Byrns and the Kings in particular."

"Not the Reapers?" I ask.

He waves away my words. "To him, they were a minor inconvenience. He was more upset with the fact the MC was allowed to come into Synd in the first place. Said they were interlopers, even though they'd been there for forty years before my father was even born. Anders Drake is an elitist, expounding on heritage and bloodlines as if they mattered. If someone wasn't a part of the founding of Synd, they weren't worthy of holding power. It was a strange concept, but he was fucking obsessed with it almost as much as taking back his rightful place within Synd."

"So, if the Drakes helped form Synd, why were you pushed out? I wasn't here when the fathers were in charge, but it seems like they weren't very different than yours."

He chuckles, though there's nothing funny about what I said. "They weren't. In fact, there were a great many years that they worked together. Aelia and I used to play with the others, though I doubt they remember."

"Mason does. At least a little. How old was Aelia?"

His face shutters, wiped of any emotion. When his throat bobs as he swallows, I doubt he'll even answer me. Roman Drake is much more affected by his sister's death than I am about my supposed brother's. I wonder if that makes me an asshole.

"She was eight when we moved," he murmurs, fingers flexing in his lap. "Sixteen when she died."

"What happened?"

"I'd rather not relive those memories, Ms. Webb. They plague me enough when I manage to fall asleep. Suffice it to say, I was under the impression she made a stupid mistake and paid the ultimate price. I'm not surprised it was my father who killed her, though. She was never anything more than a pawn to him. I protected her as much as I could, all while following in his footsteps, allowing him to corrupt my mind. Perhaps he's not the only one at fault for her death." Bitterness rolls through his voice, spreading across his face as his dull eyes fixate on his fingers.

"Why come here after Anders faked his death? Why did you care so much if he was an asshole father?" I tuck my leg under the other, trying to find a comfortable position.

"I didn't. I still don't. Actually, I couldn't care less whether they rule Synd."

"My, your feelings certainly changed quickly," I murmur, raising an eyebrow, and he scowls.

"When I was seventeen, I was biding my time until Aelia was old enough to leave. When she was killed, I became obsessed with making someone pay. The logical choice was to exact revenge upon everyone here."

"But you can't make people pay when they're already dead," I say, shaking my head.

He leans forward, wincing slightly as he rests his elbows on his knees. "Ah, but you forget we live in a world where the sins of the father are transferrable. It's the way we were raised, to never allow someone to take what's yours. In our world, it isn't an eye for an eye. It's your life *and* everyone you've ever loved in exchange for the taking of that eye. They insult you and you bury them. Our justice is swift and cruel, never giving any quarter."

"Except that's not how Shane or Mason run things," I say, as a flush travels up my neck. Roman sits back, the corner of his mouth lifting.

"Which I didn't realize until they captured me instead of torturing me. I'm sure they still engage in other activities, but they weren't as cruel as they could have been." He gestures around us. "Hell, they put me in here afterward merely because you asked. I've never experienced that before."

"What? Kindness?"

"Are you looking for a reason to kill me, Lacey? Or to redeem me?" He tilts his head, more curiosity than anything in his blue eyes.

I don't know how to answer, since I don't know myself. I came here for answers and to see if he would lie to me. All the research Victor did points to Anders being the villain of this story. Mason's uncle seemed to have absolved Roman of a great many things, dismissing his role because of the corruption of his father. Personally, I don't agree, but I wonder if Mason will see it that way.

I pull out my phone, ignoring the notification for the file on my past. Tapping on the screen, the list I prepared appears, and I send it to him. I'm surprised Mason even allowed me to set up a device for Roman in the first place, but at least it's secure. He won't be able to call anyone, and from the tracking on it, he hasn't done anything more than look at the weather.

"Ah, a list of all my misdeeds," he says, perusing the list.

"Are they?"

His head whips up, blue eyes searing into mine before they drop to the screen again.

"Some, but not all. Are you asking which of these I'm responsible for?" He purses his lips, still scanning it.

I tap my own screen again and it rearranges on his device, separating into two neat bullet point lists. His eyebrows creep up his forehead, disappearing under a flop of white-blond hair.

"I didn't blow up the car," he mutters. "Nor the bridge. In fact, I never blew up anything other than safe houses I knew were empty. What does this mean? River on fire?"

"Uh, part of the river was set on fire. Probably an internal issue within the Barrens, which is why it's not assigned to Anders or you. I'm confused, though. If that was all you did, then it doesn't really seem like your heart was in it. You had the opportunity to shoot Mason and yet you didn't. You could have left us when we went to save Mason, but you didn't. Hell, you could have joined forces with your father and you didn't. So, why would you do it at all?" I ask, glancing up as he explodes from his chair.

Terror floods me and I jerk back, scrambling from the chair, but Roman spins, teetering on his uninjured leg. His fingers dig into his hair, and he doubles over. I expect him to scream, but silence descends, smothering the room while he loses himself. Cowering behind the chair, I slide my hand in the pocket of my hoodie, gripping the Taser Sam slipped me last night. Roman rolls his shoulders, straightening even as he sways. I'm sure the move didn't do his injury any favors.

"I'm sorry," he whispers harshly. I wait for him to go on, but he's frozen in his own mind.

There's a knock on the door and I tug it open, but no one is there. The sound comes again and I realize it's coming from a hidden panel. Mason locked it on both ends, reinforcing it before they moved Roman in here. I keep one eye on Roman while I make my way over, sliding the bolt, and it pops open, revealing Ren's stoic face.

"Lacey. Am I interrupting?" He steps inside, closing the panel behind him, and I make my way back to the chair.

Most people would assume he's accusing me of something, but he really is asking if he's bothering us. If I were to say yes, he would turn around and leave.

"Roman and I were just talking about some of the decisions he's made recently."

Roman turns slowly, sinking into his chair again and propping his leg on the desk. I'm sure the angle isn't comfortable, and I wonder if he's been using the chair I'm sitting in. Ren takes his place next to me, tucking his hands in his pockets as he gazes at Roman impassively.

"I may have heard her last question. And your subsequent reaction. Perhaps you took all of your grief at the loss of your sister and funneled it into a revenge plot that was never your own. You threw yourself into the only avenue left, the only thing that would assuage your guilt at the loss of your sister, regardless of whether or not you were to blame. It's quite common, actually, though usually with less hazardous results for those around you," Ren says as Roman gapes at him.

Roman snaps his mouth shut, scowling. "I'd rather not discuss this."

Ren nods, gazing around the room. "Perhaps later then. I think I speak for most, if not all, of us when I say that we'd prefer you to channel your rage and grief into something a little more productive for Synd. Unless you have plans to return to Westmont. I've heard you have quite the setup there."

"What exactly did you have in mind?" Roman says, eyes darting to me, then back to Ren.

The corner of Ren's mouth twitches. "I'm sure something will come along. The recovery efforts would be a good start."

"Fix what my family broke?" he snarls, but it's a weak attempt.

"If that's the way you'd like to look at it."

Ren turns to me, nodding toward the door, and sighs. There's not much more I'd ask Roman, anyway. Other than the story of my early childhood, there wasn't much he revealed I didn't already know. Ultimately, I came for the why and to see if he would try to lie to me. He may have been a cryptic asshole while he was being held, but surprisingly, he always told the truth.

Standing, I move the chair closer to him, and he transfers his leg to it. I gather up the blanket, handing it to him as well. I jolt as the bedroom door shuts, but it's just Ren. He pulls open the panel, waiting for me. I meet Roman's gaze and his face softens.

"Lacey, I apologize for what my father did to you." His gaze traces the scar on my face, but it doesn't burn this time. "I would have…"

"Would have what?"

"I would not have allowed it. My father has many sins to pay for, but I'll add your injury to the list."

I nod, not sure how to respond. In fact, I'm not entirely sure how to feel about him at all. At this point, he seems like a very lost man whose world has been uprooted yet again.

"Well, that was interesting," Ren mutters as I slip into the dark tunnels.

"You have no idea." I whisper. "We definitely need to talk to the others about Roman Drake."

"I believe we're on the same page. The problem will be convincing the others that he isn't the enemy we all thought he was."

* * *

Mason

"Why are we having the meeting here?" I grumble, tugging on my shoe.

"Because it's been less than a week since you were strapped to a chair and you still fall asleep after, well, everything," Lacey says, giving me a side-eye before she pulls my hoodie over her head.

My chest tightens as I scan her body. I wish we could stay in bed, watching a show or cuddling, but she'd never let me. Ever since Alex came to check on me two days ago, I've been putting this meeting off. I doubt there's anything new to discuss. Anders has vanished, evaporating like a mist in the face of dawn.

"Still don't think there's anything pressing enough to drag my ass out of bed for," I mumble, pulling on my other shoe. "Besides, I have plans."

"Plans?" she asks, narrowing her eyes.

I grin as I lace up my shoe. "Did you think I wouldn't find out?"

She gives me a puzzled look. I wish I could drag this out, or even make it a surprise, but I didn't have much time to put everything together.

"After this meeting we're going to have a little date," I murmur.

"Date? What are you talking about?" Her eyes widen, hands fluttering at her sides.

Catching her wrist as she passes, I tug, wrapping my arms around her as she tumbles on top of me. She shrieks, trying to scramble away, but I roll on top of her, pinning her in place. A gasp leaves her when I grind my cock into her.

"No one should ignore their birthday, Kitten."

She rolls her eyes. "Please tell me you didn't."

"Oh, I most certainly did. If you don't want to wait, we could just ignore the meeting. I could give you your first gift of making you come over and over until you're a puddle underneath me," I growl, nuzzling her neck and then sucking her earlobe into my mouth.

"Sam said it was an emergency," Lacey says, even as she wraps her legs around my waist.

Dropping my forehead to her chest, I sigh. I heave off her, pulling her to her feet.

"Well, that was a quick turnaround," she says, straightening her clothes.

"You mentioned my sister. Surest way to get me to stop," I grunt, tugging her to the door.

Raised voices reach us when we turn down the hallway leading to the conference room. I raise an eyebrow at Lacey, and she shrugs. When I push open the double doors, no one notices. Half of them are standing, yelling at each other, and I tug Lacey to a stop. Everyone is here and my stomach tightens, wondering if they're going to blame me or Lacey or both of us. Again.

Clearing my throat does nothing, so I pull her along to the head of the table. Ren catches my eye and then tips his head toward Roman, tucked away in the corner with his leg propped up on a chair. The bullet went clean through, so he'll heal faster than I did when I was shot.

With so many people yelling at once, I can't make out what they're fighting about. Lacey drops into a chair, waving to Willow, who gives her a concerned look, but doesn't return the greeting.

I wait, but no one seems to care that we've walked into a shitshow. Slamming my hand on the table, I hold back a wince. My muscles still ache from everything Anders put my body through, not to mention fucking Lacey as much as she lets me. She kept telling me we should take it easy, but once I was inside her, I was addicted all over again.

The voices die down, heads swiveling to me, and I'm met with identical glares on all their faces. Devices and glasses cover the conference table, as if they've been here awhile discussing shit without us.

"Someone want to explain what's going on?" I ask calmly.

Everyone shouts at once, and I sigh, easing down in my chair to wait. Alex finally shushes the others, and they fall into their own seats. Sam tucks her legs underneath her, crossing her arms and glaring at the table. She looks exactly like she did ten years ago, and I duck my head as a grin blooms across my face.

"Probably not the right time to be smiling," Lacey whispers, and I wipe it away.

"We have a problem," Helms says, holding up his hand when Shane tries to cut him off. "We're divided on how to deal with it. That leaves the decision up to you."

"Is it Anders?" I ask before pouring a glass of whiskey. Lacey grabs a bottle of water when I try to hand it to her.

"Not exactly. Kenz?"

Skipping my gaze to Mac, I finally notice the tears streaking her face. My stomach flips, knowing whatever she's about to say is going to turn our world upside down.

"I got a call from my brother, Dante, an hour ago," she whispers, and Sam reaches out, gripping her hand. "He said he's been in deep with the Guild."

Shane grunts, crossing his arms, and Sam glares at him. "Knock it off, Shane. He helped us with them before. He's not with them."

"Never said he was, Princess. But who the hell is going to stay behind?"

"Wait. Stay behind? What the fuck are you talking about?" I bellow as they start bickering again.

Mac pulls in a shuddering breath before laying her phone on the table and swiping her finger across the surface. A low pulse of music filters through the speaker, and then a man's low voice takes over.

"MacKenzie, I'm sorry. I don't have time, and I hate to ask, but I need you. Call everyone. I'm in with the Guild in Rima. I think I can—" A crash echoes out, cutting off his words. "Back the fuck off. She's mine." Dante's voice is muffled. Then another man's voice mumbles something. "Touch her and I'll cut your fucking dick off and shove it down your throat and make you thank me for the service." He grunts into the phone. "Mac? Just get here. I can't bring them down alone." The line cuts off, leaving a heavy silence in its wake.

"Call him back," I demand.

More tears stream down her face as she cradles the only evidence she has left of her brother being alive. A broken sob leaves her, and Helms wraps an arm around her shoulders, tucking her head into his neck.

"We tried," Hawk answers, concerned gaze fixed on Mac. "It's out of service now. Best we can figure is he wiped it after he made the call. Ren tried to track it, but that was a dead end."

Lacey's eyes are fixed on the phone as her hands flex again and again. She'll have to convince Mac to hand over the device if she wants a crack at the information on it.

"So, what's the plan?" I glance at each of them.

"That's what you need to decide," Shane says dejectedly, waving his glass at me.

"We either stay here and hope he makes it out, but that leaves Rima to fall to the Guild. We could divide and conquer, some of us staying here to run Synd while the others go to help, but we all know what we're up against once we get there. Or we all go, leaving Synd to…someone," Helms says as Mac sits up, glaring at him. "I didn't say you had to stay here, Kenz, but someone needs to lead."

"Plus, they've had a lot longer to dig their claws into Rima compared to here. They don't have the infrastructure in place like we do to fight them off. Which also means we'll need more people to infiltrate their ranks and take control of the city. It won't be easy with only the remnants of the Vipers left," Ren says, scowling down at his screen.

"Maddox is gone," Mac whispers. "Escaped or something. Blaze called and told me last night."

"And Anders all but confirmed he was scuttling back to them, so if we want to kill him, we'll have to go to Rima to do it. Unless everyone is cool being fucking ambushed—again." Helms runs his hand through his hair.

"So let me get this straight. Dante is embedded with the Guild in Rima. Anders has slunk back to them, probably telling them where to hit us to do the most damage. Your deranged half-brother who sold you to a goddamn rival MC has escaped, probably running to them as well. *And* we're considering all of us going and leaving our women behind to lead in our stead?" I'm bellowing by the time I'm done.

"Geez, Mase, didn't peg you for someone thinking a woman couldn't run shit," Sam mutters, rolling her eyes.

"I don't give a fuck if a woman leads. For fuck's sake Sam, you were my choice to take shit over if something happened to me after Colin died, but that doesn't mean the others will follow you. And how well do you think the rest of us will fare, constantly worrying about you being left here?"

"Then us girls will go, and you guys can stay here." She smirks, tilting her head, challenging me to refute her.

I smirk right back at her, counting silently in my head to three, and the room explodes. Sitting back, I tuck my hands behind my head and keep my eyes on my younger sister until she's pulled into a yelling match with Alex.

There's no easy solution here. I wish we could divide and conquer. Honestly, I would take Sam with me if I thought the Kings would agree to it. We've all been separated enough from those we love. We shouldn't be forced to do it again.

"Is this usually how you guys decide things?" Lacey murmurs, glancing around at the chaos.

I smirk, rolling my head toward her. "Kitten, you've been to most of the meetings lately. Have you seen anything to suggest otherwise?"

"You know we have to go, right?"

"I don't know about that. Obviously, Helms and Mac will go. Hawk could take care of Reaper territory. Either we go or the Kings do. I doubt they'll split up. You can work from here, so we can hold down Synd."

"Uh, no I can't. Not something like this. I've been trying to crack their system for months now and I'm no closer than I was when I started. If you want my help, I'm going to need to tap directly into their operation."

"What the fuck does that mean?" I yell, adding to the chaos of voices filling the room.

"If I can link directly to their system, I can corrupt it from the inside out. Hacking into their system from here just isn't possible. We have to go."

I scowl, taking another drink, knowing I don't have an argument. Lacey's skills aren't something we can find just anywhere and hiring someone else would be a disaster waiting to happen. The Guild would buy them off or already be in with them, and then we'd be fucked.

Lacey huffs, crossing her arms, muttering, "I could just go with the Kings."

"The hell you are," I snap. "You think for one fucking second I'm going to let you fuck off to Rima by yourself and leave my ass behind, then I wasn't very clear about how much I fucking love you."

Silence greets my outburst. I'm sure they're all staring at us, but I refuse to take my eyes off Lacey. Her mouth drops open, trying to find the words, but there's none she could say that would change my mind. If she goes, I go. I told her that before and I fucking meant it.

I've spent enough of my life alone, hoping I'd find someone I loved and could fit into my world. Like hell will I let her gallivant off to another city, putting herself in danger without being two steps behind her to watch her back.

"That was never…that's not what I meant, Mason," she hisses, glancing around before settling her eyes on me.

"You go, I go. End of discussion." I turn to the others, who quickly look anywhere but at me. "Anyone else got a problem with that?"

"Can't do it alone, Byrns," Ren says.

"I'll have Helms and Mac." I wave my hand at the two, though Mac looks like she's going to break down again.

"Still not enough. The Guild is fucking huge. We're going to have to tap into resources here, call in all the favors piled up. Hell, we might even have to use the police." Alex shivers, as if the thought of dealing with the cops is the worst part of this whole mission. "Who's going to stay behind?"

Hawk glances at Willow, who twists her fingers together and purses her lips. Hawk presses her glass into her hand, urging her to drink.

"We'll stay, take care of shit up north," Hawk murmurs, gripping Willow's hands while Helms glares at him. "Willow can't go back, not with the investigation still open with her stepfather. I've been gone so long, I doubt I'd be much help."

"So, who stays?" Alex asks.

No one volunteers, instead avoiding eye contact. A frustrated noise comes from Sam, but even she doesn't say anything.

"I'll stay."

Every head swivels to Roman. He shrugs, leaning against the wall. The bruises have faded from his face, but his beard is still out of control. Propped beside him are the crutches he refused to use until he crashed to the ground last week. This is the quietest I've seen him. Mostly he's been yelling about having to go find his father. The fact Anders got away, leaving more questions than answers in his wake, actively eats away at Roman's sanity.

"Why the hell would we put you in charge?" Shane sneers.

"Because you all need to go after the Guild, and I am un-equipped at the moment to do such a thing. I would request if you capture my father, bring him back so I can make him pay for killing my sister. I'd appreciate it." Bitterness colors his tone and twists his face.

"Are you capable of running all of Synd? That's a lot of territory to deal with," Ren says, eyes fixed on his screen, completely missing Shane scowling at him.

"He already is," Sam says, locking eyes with Lacey.

"Oh, um, yeah. He totally is." Lacey grimaces as Sam rolls her eyes. "He was running Westmont before he, uh, came here."

"Came here to destroy Synd and take us all out. You missed that part," Alex chimes in.

The conversation devolves again, and I stare at Drake. He might not be the perfect choice, but he might be all we have. Helms and Mac will go to Rima whether or not any of us follow. The rest of us can't leave them to do it alone.

I slam my hand on the table again. "Shut the fuck up. Even if one of us stays here, we're going to need to make plans before we do. Grayson took off, probably with Anders. The mayor quit—"

Sam snorts, mouthing "quit" before giggling, and I groan.

"Did you fucking kill the mayor?" She shrugs, a smile playing on her lips. "Fucking hell, Sam. Stop offing everyone who pisses you off. We're going to run out of people who want the job."

"He told me good riddance when I asked him where Ren was."

"And why would he know where Ren was at the time?"

"Ren met with him right beforehand, duh. It's not like I shot him. I stabbed him like a decent person. I *told* him not to take the blade out, but he didn't listen. Honestly, it's his fault he's dead. That's beside the point. I think we need to start putting our own people in there. TJ would be great as the police chief."

"Great. You can convince him to take the job," I say, smirking.

"We need to go now," Mac whispers harshly, eyes still fixed on her phone.

Helms leans in, murmuring in her ear. Tears cascade down her face, even as she nods.

"One month. We've got one month before we go to Rima and take on the Guild." I stand, lifting my glass in a mock salute. "Here's to all of us making it out alive."

Thank you so much for reading Mason and Lacey's story!
Ready for the next adventure?
Dive into the spin-off duology Ruins of Rima by pre-ordering
Dante's story.
Out August 25, 2023.

If you'd like to hear about the other stories that have been living
in my head, sign up for my
newsletter (including extra scenes & novella), visit my
website, or follow me on social media visit:
emiliaabraham.com

Special Thanks:
K.B. Barrett Designs–Cover Artist and Formatter
Emily Michel–Editor
Emily Renee–Beta Reader
Sapphire and Krysten–Omega Readers
Hillary Raymer–Sanity Saver

Also by the Author

Also by E. Abraham:
Shadows of Synd:
Under the Shadows - Book 1
Running From Shadows – Book 2
Becoming Shadows – Book 3
Shadows Within Us – Book 4

Ruins of Rima: *Spin-off Series*
Chasing Darkness (August 25, 2023)
Charmed by Darkness (October 2023)

Available on Newsletter:
Extra Scenes
Epilogues
Holiday Novella

Also by Emilia Abraham:
Stuck at Sundown

Emilia Abraham

After many years of dreaming of becoming a full-time writer, Emilia Abraham took the leap, bringing her words to print. From sweet contemporary romance to spicy why choose and everything in between, she focuses on the happily ever after.

Emilia lives in the Upper Midwest with her husband (who's probably sick of listening to her expound on fictional men) and three kids (who try to steal her post-it notes). When she's not writing, she enjoys reading, playing video games, and consuming copious amounts of energy drinks.